I0702476

Cover design by Alexis Ovitt

Loring Lane Press

ISBN 979-8-9881067-0-8
First edition
10 9 8 7 6 5 4 3 2 1

THE
KIEV
CONFESSION

KATHLEEN HART

LORING LANE PRESS

Also by Kathleen Hart

Eating in the Dark: America's Experiment with Genetically Engineered Food, Random House.

For Craig

THE KIEV CONFESSION

1

KIEV, MAY 1986

Vasyl and Larysa Marchenko sang along with "A Hard Day's Night" as they dressed for the May Day parade. Vasyl put on the brown suit he wore every year, then hurried to the hallway mirror to adjust his necktie. Larysa scooted in front of him to weave a rose-flowered headband into her straight, blond hair. While Vasyl ducked out on the balcony to look at his tomato plants, she tied a scarlet ribbon around their seven-year-old daughter's ponytail. Meanwhile, Dmitry, who was itching to march with his friends, knotted a red neckerchief over the shirt of his Young Pioneer uniform and paced by the door.

"Do you think Katya will need a sweater?" Larysa called to her husband. "She's wearing a short-sleeved dress."

"Hardly! It's hot enough for the beach," Vasyl boomed, striding into the kitchen. "Now, who wants a balloon?" He encircled his daughter's small hand in stout fingers stained with red ink from yesterday's printing job.

"I do," shrieked Katya.

Dmitry yanked the hallway door open and raced down the stairwell ahead of his father and little sister. Larysa turned off the record player and followed them down the stairs. All four had reached the second-floor landing and were out of earshot when the phone rang. The bell pealed through their kitchen, where the dishes from breakfast sat in the sink, and the living room, where crooked French doors hung open to a balcony crammed with potted plants.

The Marchenkos exited their block and joined the crush of celebrants pouring down Marshal Tymoshenko, a wide boulevard eight miles north of the heart of the city. Men wore suit jackets studded with red stars. More than a few women showed off costumes unpacked once a year, embroidered blouses with puffy sleeves and flowers woven into braided hairdos. At Minska Station the family boarded a crowded car for the metro ride to Khreshchatyk, Kiev's central street. After disembarking, the four jostled through throngs lining the street. Musical instruments appeared everywhere, with silver flutes and trumpets glinting in the morning sunlight.

On the corner where Dmitry's Pioneer group was gathering, Ilya, a skinny boy with dark curls fringing his face, waved a red banner. Dmitry charged off to meet his friend. While Vasyl fetched a balloon from a man surrounded by children dressed in their holiday best, Ilya's mother beckoned to Larysa. After years of attending pageants and their sons' sporting events together, Larysa, who worked as a translator, and Maria, a teacher, had grown close.

Larysa approached her friend with a smile. As they leaned forward to kiss each other's cheeks, however, she saw furrows creasing Maria's forehead. "Is something wrong?" she asked.

"I'm worried about my sister. Iryna and my niece were evacuated from Pripyat. They're staying with me." Maria's answer came in a rush. "Iryna's husband works at Chernobyl, you know, at Reactor Three, not the one damaged by the fire."

"When were they evacuated?" Larysa had never seen Maria this rattled. "Were they in danger?"

"The authorities insisted it's only a precaution. They put out the fire. They said the reactor was fine, but they herded everyone into a thousand buses Sunday afternoon. No pets allowed. Only one suitcase each."

Maria's words struck Larysa like a blow to her solar plexus. She had heard about the Chernobyl accident on television Monday night, of course, and like everyone else she suspected the accident might be more serious than the terse announcement suggested. After all, Moscow never acknowledged failings unless the outside world forced its hand. But then yesterday, Larysa's neighbor had told her that Western newspapers were reporting two thousand corpses stacked on Kiev's streets, which anyone could see was preposterous. Chernobyl was some sixty miles north of the city, and Larysa had no family near the nuclear plant. Until now she hadn't given the accident much thought.

"My sister's out of her wits. They put her husband up with workers ordered to stay at the station. My niece cries for their dog. You cannot blame her. Who will feed the poor thing?"

"Did they tell your sister when she can return home?" asked

Vasyl, who had caught much of the conversation. He inched closer to his wife and Maria.

"Three days, the authorities claimed. My sister refuses to go outside. Saturday was so hot in Pripyat she brought her nursery school class outdoors for an hour. Natasha, my niece, went with her friends to a rooftop to watch the glowing reactor. All the kids wanted to get a good look. Now, Iryna fears they're both contaminated—"

Maria stopped talking and stiffened. A man behind them was telling his companions something about October Revolution Hospital clearing wards for Chernobyl patients. Maria, Vasyl, and Larysa strained to make out the man's words over a cacophony of music and voices.

Whispers about the nuclear plant rippled through the crowd. No one knew what to believe. Everyone, it seemed, knew someone from the Chernobyl area or had caught unjammed Voice of America broadcasts warning of radiation spewing from the reactor. Yet Kiev was awash in pageantry as always on May Day. Crimson banners flapped under a clear blue sky, and stirring songs filled the air. Waves of children marched past Party officials in the reviewing stand. There was nothing about the celebration to arouse suspicion, nothing unusual about the holiday—except the weather. It was not just hot. It was beastly.

Maria turned her pinched gray eyes on Vasyl. "What are they saying at your shop about the accident?"

"Nothing beyond what we heard on TV. You know, we only print posters and honor certificates." Vasyl paused, giving Maria a thoughtful look. "I'm no scientist, to be sure. Still, I think radiation in Pripyat must be serious for authorities to take such an overt action as evacuating an entire city of forty-five thousand people."

"That is what I believe." Maria nodded, her lips forming a taut line. Raising her arm, she used her sleeve to wipe beads of sweat off her forehead. "They would tell us if there's any danger here, would they not?"

Larysa's startled look betrayed her doubt. Kiev was the Soviet Union's third largest city, with two and a half million people, tens of thousands of whom were filling Khreshchatyk Street. "How could they not?" she murmured, more to herself than her friend. She reached down to untangle the string of Katya's pink balloon from the ribbon on her ponytail.

Vasyl said nothing. He was lost in thought, his eyes scanning the hot blue sky, the square crowded with children, and the chestnut trees thrashing in a stiff breeze from the north.

2

WASHINGTON, APRIL 1990

Vickie cut a swift path through Lafayette Square, scarcely noticing the wind dusting her gray suit with cherry blossom petals. A flush of pride filled her chest when she caught sight of the White House. Three months ago, she'd been waiting tables in a Hoosier backwater, but whether by dumb luck or divine providence, here she was in the nation's capital. Even more miraculous, she'd finally found a purpose. From the time she was eight, Vickie had been dogged by the idea that she was meant to do something important. Why else had her life been spared, and her little brother's life taken? Exactly what she was supposed to do, however, had always eluded her until she landed this reporting job. Exposing corrupt corporations harming the Earth and its innocent creatures struck her as a worthy mission—and one she'd embraced with her entire being. But despite throwing herself into reporting, she had yet to publish a single byline story. Nor had she cracked the code for acquiring what she perceived to be the most critical asset of every bona fide Washington journalist: a reliable source.

She pictured her editor, Thane, hunkered down with his honey-tongued White House source. Thane had boasted during the morning editorial meeting that his source was about to spill why the Hubble Telescope was beaming back blurry pictures. The mystery behind that billion-dollar glitch would make the front page of all the Newhart chain's newspapers. Meanwhile, she was headed to a nuclear utility meeting no one else had wanted to cover. The Nuclear Regulatory Council's vote on whether to allow a downed power plant near New York City to restart would be lucky to rate two inches on the back pages, and she needed a big story to save her job.

Vickie's fleeting euphoria evaporated, replaced by the cold dread that seeped into her gut whenever she thought about her looming three-month review. Somehow, she would have to find an important story. Fighting back a wave of despair, she exited the park, crossed H Street, and entered the historic Hay-Adams Hotel. Midway down a chandeliered corridor, she spotted a room where three dozen electric utility executives sat around tables adorned with orchids. A scrawny-necked official in a plaid bow tie stopped her at the door. Glancing at her press pass, he pointed to a long table bookended by two lone reporters. She scanned the room for TV cameras and saw none. Not a story the networks planned to cover, she thought, taking a seat and pulling her tape recorder from her shoulder bag. She popped in a fresh cassette as a few onlookers straggled into chairs for the public beside the press table.

NRC Chairman Patton advanced to the podium, and Vickie pushed the record button. She harbored a sliver of hope he might veer off script and "commit news," as her colleagues dubbed those rare occasions when a spontaneous nugget of truth escaped the practiced mouths of bureaucrats. No such luck. He droned on about nuclear plant "assessment methodologies." Meticulously attired executives stifled yawns and peeked at their Rolexes. To her right, she noticed Mitch Sanders from *The Times* doing a crossword puzzle. To her left, Joe Polk of United Press studied the sports page. After forty mind-numbing minutes Patton finally concluded: "We have unanimously approved restart of the Hardwick Nuclear Power Station." A handful of CEOs started to clap, but a booming voice drowned out their applause.

"The people vote no!" shouted a baritone with a black braid snaking down his back. His voice clattered off the walls like thunder in a canyon. Bolting up from a chair four feet from Vickie, the man thrust out his right arm. Her heart leapt into her throat as something bright flashed in his hand. She flinched, anticipating an explosion, but almost simultaneously she saw the flash was simply the corner of a shiny yellow banner. Emblazoned on the unfurling satin fabric were three red triangles in a circle and the words, "Stop Chernobyl Here!"

"The public portion of this meeting is over. We are going into closed session now," the bow-tied official intoned, appearing at the podium. "Members of the public and press are asked at this time to exit the room."

Vickie picked up her tape recorder and notebook. She eyed the protester, wary of what he might do next, but he offered no resistance to the official who materialized by his side. Waving his banner like a Cub Scout in a Fourth of July parade, he filed out with the other onlookers. The utility executives chatted as if nothing noteworthy had happened. Mitch and Joe chuckled as they collected their newspapers. Judging by everyone's reaction, she got the idea that this protester was no stranger to NRC meetings. She hurried to a pay phone in the lobby and dialed Sean on the news desk to give him the unanimous Hardwick plant restart vote.

"No surprise there," Sean responded in his good-natured drawl. He begged off for an incoming call before Vickie could tell him she planned to go schmooze with staffers on the Hill.

Heading to the hotel door, Vickie replayed in her mind the moment the protester shouted and jumped up from his chair. She hoped no one had noticed her flinch. One thing DC reporters never did was betray their emotions, especially fear. Pulling her shoulders back with resolve, she stepped outside determined to find a story lead.

She was about to hail a cab for Capitol Hill when she spotted the protester. His glossy braid swung over his blue Oxford shirt as he knelt on the grass in front of St. John's Church, rolling up his banner. He didn't strike her as the least bit intimidating kneeling there. In fact, he looked more thoughtful than many of the activists she had observed marching on Constitution Avenue chanting slogans for one cause or another. She wanted to ask him why he believed the Hardwick plant was like Chernobyl, but she was reluctant to waste more time on this assignment. She was still weighing whether to approach him when Mitch and Joe sauntered past without a second glance. Not surprising, she thought. No doubt her editor also would shun this guy as an anti-nuke flake.

Yet something in the determined cast of his face drew her interest. She decided there was no harm in taking five minutes to ask him a few questions.

"Victoria Evans with Newhart News. Could you tell me why you were protesting in the meeting?" she asked, walking up to him. "What do you mean by stop Chernobyl here?"

"Before Chernobyl blew four years ago, Soviet scientists claimed their reactors were as safe as samovars. Tea pots! So harmless you could plop one down in Red Square. Scientists here are every bit as cocky. That Hardwick nuke's a fire hazard, and their evacuation plan's a farce. Can you imagine if it blows, twenty miles from the Big Apple?" He stood up, towering over Vickie. "There's fifteen million people in Metro New York. The feds should give them all KI."

"What do you mean, KI?" Vickie thrust her tape recorder closer to his face.

"Potassium iodide. In nuke explosions radioactive iodine is released, which causes thyroid cancer, especially in children. If kids are given KI pills right after a nuke blows, their thyroids fill up with good KI and don't absorb the bad radioactive iodine. I know of a doctor who's finding kids in Poland given KI right after Chernobyl exploded aren't getting thyroid cancer like kids in the Soviet Union, who didn't get KI. I can fax you some info on this."

"I'd appreciate that." Vickie paused, impressed. "I didn't catch your name."

"Gareth Will."

"Are you with an organization, Gareth?"

"CANWAP, Coalition against Nuclear Weapons and Power—two sides of the same coin. Remember that. Hey, can we get something to eat? I'll fill you in."

Vickie hesitated, leery of getting mired in a lunch that would probably yield nothing. Three months here had taught her that Washington runs on status. Credentials, job title, and pedigree mean everything. A long-haired, no-name environmental activist would warrant little more than a colorful quote to spice up a bland story. Still, Gareth did seem to know about nuclear power plants, and she didn't have anything else. Roaming the corridors of the Senate and House buildings chatting up interns had failed to land her anything newsworthy yet. A cup of coffee would not take long, she calculated, then she would head to the Hill.

"Sure, we can grab a bite at Park Café." Vickie pointed west on H Street.

3

KIEV, MAY 1986

Vasyl carried his watering can to the kitchen, where Larysa was preparing *varenyky* for supper. At one end of the kitchen table, Katya was helping her to spoon mashed potato onto circles of dough for the dumplings. At the other end, Dmitry bent over a worn algebra book. Katya's puckered balloon, which somehow survived the trip home from the parade, dragged on the red tile floor.

"The heat wilted my seedlings. I'll have to stake them after supper." Vasyl moved cooking utensils from the sink to make room for his tin can. He waited patiently for it to fill.

"I hope the yield will be like last year, Vasya." Larysa glanced at her husband. When he'd proposed growing vegetables on their concrete balcony, she had viewed the idea as just another of her husband's curiosities. Vasyl was a tinkerer by nature, always planning designs and building furniture or toys from scraps of wood. He had used his talents to support her puppetry passion by making an ingenious puppet stage. After Katya outgrew her crib, he had turned their flat's two bedrooms into three by constructing a divider through one. Dmitry had claimed the large, windowless side, leaving Katya a tiny, bright space big enough for a bed and shelf. For his garden, Vasyl had arrayed containers across their balcony, leaving a path for Larysa to hang laundry. In August, when tomatoes as big as oranges glistened in the sun, she had grasped the value in his scheme.

"Who would believe such a small space could yield so much food?" Larysa marveled to her husband, whose hazel eyes lit up with her praise.

Vasyl carried his watering can to the balcony and drained it on his parched seedlings. After supper, he returned to the balcony to tie the limp tomato plants to tall dowels. He worked methodically, finishing the job as a single purple cloud feathered the horizon. He stood up slowly, his back stiff from stooping. He was about to go inside when the door opened to the balcony downstairs. Cigarette smoke wafted up with the voices of two men.

"Exactly what did he say?" asked a man with a sharp, nasal voice.

"That the wind carried a radioactive cloud here," came a deep, husky response.

"What cloud? The sky was clear all day. Do you believe everything he says?"

"Why wouldn't I? He's a scientist," the second man answered. Their voices carried clearly in the still evening air. Vasyl lingered, hanging on their words.

"So, is this an invisible mushroom cloud?" the first man pressed. "The peaceful atom makes electricity—"

"I can't explain the difference between a bomb and a power station, if that's what you expect. We're taking our baby to my cousin's place in Moscow tomorrow. Do as you like."

The door slammed shut leaving the evening quiet again. Shaken, Vasyl rubbed the goose bumps rising on his arms. Later that night, after the children fell asleep, Vasyl told Larysa what he'd overheard of the smokers' conversation.

"I think you should take the kids away. I wasn't sure what to believe before, but that conversation added substance to the rumors we heard all day," he said as they lay in the dark, their bodies touching.

"How? I can't leave my job," Larysa protested. "Where would I take them? If we're really in danger, we should all leave, together."

"Mikhail would never go for that. Besides, I'm a bear! I can survive anything."

"Others are talking about leaving, Vasya. You heard it on the balcony. Maria wants to leave. You saw it written on her face." Larysa sat up and switched on the bedside lamp. "If what you heard about a cloud of radiation is a senseless rumor and we flee, we risk losing everything for no reason. On the other hand, if the danger is real, we have no choice but to leave."

"There it is, then." Vasyl leaned on his elbow. "That's why everywhere people whisper about leaving yet stay. We lack information. You know, Larya, there is one person who may be able to advise us." He gazed into his wife's wide-set blue eyes.

"Anatoly," she whispered, understanding at once. Her uncle

directed a nuclear research laboratory. He also was a stalwart member of the Communist Party—and the black sheep of her family. Anatoly had done nothing to help his older brother, Larysa's father, in 1969 when Alexei was accused of founding an underground journal. For his role in circulating Western poetry espousing "flagrant anti-Soviet propaganda," her father had paid the ultimate price. Alexei Kulyk was stripped of his faculty position at the Foreign Languages Institute and sentenced to seven years of hard labor in the mines. He died of pneumonia before the second year was out.

To the end of Alexei's life, Anatoly had remained loyal to the Party, shunning his brother. Larysa's grandmother, Tatiana, never forgave her younger son. She went to her grave in 1983 without speaking to Anatoly. Ever since Tatiana's death, however, Anatoly had been taking steps to build a bridge back to the family. He had procured a land line for Larysa and Vasyl. He heaped praise on Dmitry for his quick grasp of mathematics. The last time she brought the children to visit, he had effused over Katya's singing and promised to arrange private voice lessons for her one day.

Larysa remained wary of her uncle. She knew her children could benefit from his connections. Anatoly would be able to nurture Katya's musical talent and help Dmitry secure a university spot. But to confide to him her concerns about the Chernobyl accident would mean crossing a sensitive line. How could she tell her uncle that she didn't trust the authorities? No, she was unwilling to seek his counsel on such a political matter.

"You know I can't trust him, Vasya. He's a lonely, vain man. Why wouldn't he want our children in his life? Dmitry and Katya are his only link to the future. Maybe he has regrets. But I can never forget he is a Party zealot, and they murdered my father."

Vasyl pulled Larysa to his chest and wrapped his arm around her.

"My head is swimming. We need to learn if there is anything to what you heard on the balcony," Larysa whispered, settling into the firm mounds of Vasyl's arms and chest, the fortress where she felt safest in life.

"Yes, we can talk more in the morning." Vasyl reached over Larysa to switch off the lamp. He ran his hand down her neck and let his fingertips trace a circle around the hollow in her throat. She raised her face to his and they kissed deeply, kindling the desire for each other that mysteriously renewed itself each night, undiminished after sixteen years together.

∽

Larysa stepped onto the balcony and scanned the morning sky. She half expected to see something ominous—a hazy scrim hanging on the horizon—but the sky sparkled clear and blue. Not a single cumulus cloud or cirrus spray marred its shimmering brilliance.

Outside, pedestrians headed to work and school. The day was warm, and a pleasant breeze ruffled the white ribbon on Katya's ponytail as they walked four blocks to her school. Clusters of children congregated, briefcases dangling by their sides. The scene could have passed for an ordinary school day save for one peculiar sight that caused Larysa's heart to skip a beat. A girl Katya's age walking with her father up the sidewalk was draped in an ankle-length gray raincoat and wide-brimmed cap. A few yards from the school door, the man whisked the coat and hat off the child and stuffed them into a rucksack. He slung the satchel over his shoulder and kissed his daughter's cheek. She waved to him and entered the doorway, looking like the other girls in her knee-length dress and ruffle-trimmed apron.

Throughout the metro ride to work, the image of the girl cloaked against an invisible rain troubled Larysa. However, when she entered the Institute library, a towering stack of journals on her desk diverted her attention. Settling into her chair, she noticed Dr. Mazur hovering by the rack of new periodicals. A shy immunologist who never made unreasonable demands, he bobbled toward her carrying a sack in front of his shabby twill suit jacket.

"I don't know how to ask for such a favor," the scientist mumbled, his face reddening, "but I must have this article translated." Setting his bag down beside Larysa's chair, he thrust a photocopied French article into her hands. "Would you be able to translate this today?"

She thumbed through seven pages of text, charts, and graphs. Larysa had inherited her father's knack for languages. When she was a child, he used to engage in a nightly labor of love, translating contemporary works of English, French, and German poets into Russian. Sitting by his side at their kitchen table, she had begged him to teach her English words. She could pick her way through his volume of *The Adventures of Huckleberry Finn* by the age of twelve. At fifteen, she was able to translate Beatles songs at parties where she and her friends excitedly listened to forbidden tape recordings of the beloved group. She graduated from university proficient in English and French, as well as Russian and her native Ukrainian. Unlike her romantic father, however, whose devotion to Western writers incurred the wrath of the State, she took a sensible path, using her linguistic abilities to translate non-ideological scientific articles. Still, in her fantasies, she often pictured herself in the United States, conversing with Americans and riding a riverboat down the Mississippi River.

"I should be able to translate this today, Dr. Mazur."

"I will be forever in your debt. My wife baked you a *paskha*." He pointed to the sack by her chair.

Peeking inside the sack, Larysa was delighted to see a tall, cylindrical loaf of bread iced with frosting. This gesture made her feel safe enough to seek his opinion on the reactor accident.

"If I might ask you a question," she began, looking around to be certain no one was nearby. "There are rumors of a cloud of radiation from Chernobyl extending to Kiev. Do you think we have reason for concern?"

"I've heard rumors but nothing official." He shrugged. "My colleagues are not worried."

A weight slid off Larysa's shoulders. If scientists were not afraid, this talk of a radiation cloud was probably nonsense—as silly as wrapping a child in a raincoat on a sunny day.

"Thank your wife for the *paskha*," Larysa whispered. The scientist nodded and scuttled to the door. She dove into the French article on the body's inflammation response to allergens.

It was after lunch when the director made his appearance in the library. He rushed to the conference room trailed by two assistants. Their grim faces told Larysa this would be an inauspicious time to request a meeting. She decided to wait until later to ask for leave.

On her way home, Larysa shopped for milk and an ingredient she had been unable to find for her Easter egg dyes. Like most members of their generation, she and Vasyl considered themselves atheists. Still, both sets of their grandparents had been Orthodox Christians. While they had not baptized Dmitry and Katya, they did keep alive the Easter tradition of eating *paskha* and coloring eggs. Last week she had bought beets for dyeing eggs pink and a head of red cabbage, which by some mysterious alchemy turned eggshells blue, but she had been unable to find turmeric. She took it as a good omen when she found a packet.

⁓

"Did the director grant you leave?" Vasyl asked when Larysa walked through their door.

"I never met with him. It wasn't a good time. Perhaps next week will be better." She unpacked her sack on the kitchen table. "I don't think we have to worry, in any case, Vasya. I asked Dr. Mazur—he's an immunologist—if he thinks there is any danger from radiation here. He's not concerned. His colleagues are not worried either. See what his wife baked for us!"

Vasyl put his nose to the loaf of bread, inhaling its sugary yeast aroma. "I didn't know you were friends with Dr. Mazur and his wife."

"We are now, it seems." Larysa laughed. "He wanted to jump his translation to the head of the queue and enlisted his wife's help."

Katya skipped into the kitchen singing an anti-nuclear song she'd learned at school, "Peaceful skies for all of us."

"Would you like to color Easter eggs?" Larysa asked her, arranging twenty eggs and two bowls of dye on the sideboard.

Katya hopped to her mother's side. "What color will we

make the eggs, Mama?"

"We'll make pink eggs from the beet dye. Watch this, now." Larysa opened the packet of turmeric and let Katya empty it into a bowl of water, which instantly turned yellow.

Katya was spooning an egg into one of the bowls when Dmitry returned home from changing-of-the-guard duty at the War Memorial. Anatoly had secured him a position as a Pioneer in the solemn ceremony.

"What are you doing?" Dmitry's stormy eyes pierced his mother with scorn. He was starting to fear his parents would keep him from achieving his goals. He wanted to join Komsomol in the fall. He also dreamed of following in his granduncle's footsteps as an important physicist one day.

"Coloring eggs." Larysa did her best to ignore her son's petulant tone. "You can join us."

"Why? Religion is forbidden."

"We color eggs every year, Mitya! You never objected before." Larysa was growing tired of her son's zealous embrace of Party dogma, which went against everything her father had believed, but she also knew it was best that Dmitry fit in. The last thing she wanted was for him to fall on the wrong side of the authorities.

"I didn't know any better then," Dmitry shot back. He wished his parents would be more serious and spend less time listening to the Beatles album they'd bought a few months ago. He admired his granduncle's behavior and attitudes. His grandfather's brother listened to opera and had a car and a dacha in Odessa. He also had kept himself out of prison. Even at fourteen, Dmitry had decided there was no glamour in a life of poverty or a death in the gulag like his legendary grandfather's.

"This is our tradition, Mitya! It's not as if we're decorating *pysanky*," Larysa snapped. The Soviet Union had banned the ancient Ukrainian art, but babushkas in villages around Kiev caried on the practice in secret. They used a stylus filled with melted beeswax to draw on eggshells, then dipped them into layer upon layer of dyes—yellow, red, blue, green—creating intricate geometric designs.

"Even so, what's the harm?" Larysa continued. "My grandmother believed people gave each other *pysanky* to bring good luck."

"I'll be turned down for Komsomol. You're ruining my future."

"The Russians banned *pysanky* because they were jealous of Ukrainian artistry, just as they have tried to wipe out our mother tongue," Vasyl interjected. "But you see, Mitya? We speak Russian, yet we have not forgotten the language of our ancestors, and we still color eggs at Easter. As for Komsomol, you don't have to worry about being rejected. They take everyone."

"That's not true. Viktor Karpenko was denied. Everyone was talking about it at the meeting. They said it was because his family is religious."

"Ah, the Karpenkos—they're a special case. Viktor's father proselytizes a Protestant sect of Christianity," Vasyl answered. "What we do here is to honor the beliefs of our ancestors. And no one needs to know what we do in our home, my son."

Dmitry glared at his father but held his tongue. Turning on his heels, he retreated to his dark room.

"Papa, look!" Katya used a long wooden spoon to lift a pink egg from a mug of dye. Larysa and Katya were spooning pastel eggs onto a plate when a terrifying scream erupted in the hallway, followed by banging on their door.

Vasyl opened the door to find their neighbor, Nina, with her three-year-old daughter in her arms. Tears streamed down the child's face.

"What have I done?" Nina sobbed. The girl coughed. "Have I poisoned my Olena?"

"Poisoned? What do you mean?" asked Larysa, her eyes darting from Nina to the distraught child's blotchy face.

"Iodine," Nina managed between pants.

Larysa and Vasyl exchanged puzzled looks.

"What about iodine?" Vasyl prodded Nina.

"They said Polish children are getting iodine tablets."

"Who said this?" Vasyl pressed.

"Radio Free Europe. Poles are giving kids iodine tablets. Radiation from Chernobyl is falling over Poland. The newsman said children in Kiev and Minsk should take iodine tablets too." Nina cradled the small girl against her apron. "I went to the medicine chest to look for iodine. I found a bottle and poured it down Olena's throat. She started choking and crying. Then I remember the newsman said tablets. What have I done to my baby?"

"The child must have medical attention," said Vasyl, springing into action. Larysa and Vasyl didn't have a car, but Nina's husband, who was deployed to Afghanistan, did.

"Bring me your car key!" Vasyl commanded, taking the child from Nina's arms. "The key, Nina, quickly!"

4

WASHINGTON, APRIL 1990

Gareth opened the Park Café door for Vickie and snagged a free window table.

"If Americans knew about the radiation being released every day from the hundred nuke plants in this country, they'd demand every one of them be shuttered. I can fax you studies on leaks." Gareth tucked his banner against the window. "I'll have ham on rye, mustard, Swiss cheese, no lettuce or tomato, and a large Coke," he said, shifting his attention momentarily from Vickie to the waitress who appeared beside their table.

Vickie ordered a muffin and coffee.

"See, the government can never admit these plants have been leaking radiation or they'd be liable for all the deaths of Americans from cancer—"

"What's your background, Gareth?" Vickie interrupted him,

annoyed by his over-the-top claim about radiation from nuclear plants causing cancer. She could ill afford to waste time with someone who lacked credibility.

"I got my degree in physics from Cal Tech."

"Was that a bachelor's degree?" she asked, relieved that he had attended a reputable university.

"No, Ph.D. I did my undergrad in geology at Berkeley." Gareth cocked his head and studied Vickie's face. "Hey, I know all the DC reporters covering nukes, not that many do. The press mostly give nukes a pass. You must be new."

Vickie nodded. "I joined Newhart News at the beginning of February." She rifled through her bag for business cards and handed him one.

"You work with Gabe Green?" He pocketed her card. "Green's top notch—doesn't touch nukes, though."

The waitress set their order on the table, and Gareth drained half of his Coke. "Thane Bailey's in your outfit too, right?"

At the mention of Thane's name, Vickie felt her stomach clench. She squinted, eyeing Gareth with suspicion. "How do you know so many reporters?"

"Oh, we have our ways. One of my jobs is keeping tabs on the Washington press corps." Gareth winked as if he were letting her in on a conspiracy.

Vickie smiled, relaxing a bit. Gareth stopped talking and attacked his food with singular focus. She broke the top off her blueberry muffin and took a bite. Staring out the window, her mind returned to her upcoming job review with the bureau chief, Alan Graves. Given her meager work experience, she knew Alan had taken a chance on her. She also suspected he hired her because

Professor Blake, her journalism mentor, had given her a stellar recommendation.

"Blake and I go way back—to our days at Columbia," Alan had reminisced when he welcomed her on board. "I'll be expecting lots of enterprise reporting from you."

His glowing words echoed in her head now, taunting her. Vickie felt sick, wondering how it was possible she'd been in Newhart's Washington bureau for nearly three months without producing a single byline story. But she knew the reason: Yale-bred, Pulitzer-nominated Thane Bailey. Alan had hired Vickie as the new energy reporter with the idea that she would split her time between generating her own stories and helping Thane and the science reporter on the environment beat.

Alan's brainchild sounded great in theory—a crack, three-person "E-team" covering all the hot environmental, energy, and science news of the day. In reality, as the E-team leader, Thane had been doing his utmost to reduce her to his assistant. He shot down every story idea she pitched and kept her busy doing research for his multi-part series. Not that Vickie minded writing sidebars for his articles in the "Earth Matters" section, which the bureau launched on April 22nd to commemorate the twentieth anniversary of the first Earth Day. She was willing to write sidebars for Thane and do whatever needed doing for the E-team. It was about paying her dues. She got that. The problem was Thane condensed every story he assigned her into an anonymous paragraph for the Federal News Briefs.

Several times, she'd been on the verge of marching into Alan's office to lay out the situation, but she always stopped short of his door. There was no percentage in complaining about

Thane. He was one of the bureau's shining stars. Who was she? A thirty-something single mom who'd spent the past three years waiting tables to finish her degree one course at a time. No, what she needed to do was find a major story, one too big for Thane to spike or reduce to a brief. Only problem was, Thane and Jeff Hodges, the science reporter, grabbed all the sexy stories, like the Exxon-Valdez spill cleanup. Last month, the bureau had sent Thane to Alaska to interview volunteers flocking to the state to scrub viscous oil off the feathers of petrified ducks. Right now, he was covering the Hubble telescope's problem. Jeff, meanwhile, was reporting on precious endangered species. While they winged across the continent or zipped to flashy news conferences, she'd been hoofing it to long-winded hearings on Capitol Hill and nerdy industry meetings like the one today at the Hay-Adams.

The waitress cleared Gareth's plate and refilled Vickie's coffee mug. Gareth took the opportunity to order lemon meringue pie.

"I wonder what brought all these head honchos to DC. It's hard to believe they flew in to hear that little speech Patton gave," Vickie mused, probing Gareth for his thoughts. The meeting had been billed as an industry meet-and-greet, with remarks by the NRC chairman open to the press and public. After calling everyone she could think of, she'd only been able to learn what Chairman Patton had been expected to say during the public portion of the meeting. If anyone knew what was on the executives' agenda for the closed session, they weren't telling her.

"I know exactly why they're here." Gareth flashed a smile at their waitress, who set a pie wedge on the table. "They're trying to figure out what to do about the cracks two utilities found in the reactor vessel heads of their nukes. They need to hatch a plan to placate the NRC."

Vickie's eyes widened. "How do you know that? Who told you?"

Gareth glanced from side to side then leaned over the table, his brown eyes dancing maniacally. "If I told you, I'd have to kill you," he whispered.

Between bites of pie, he explained that three weeks ago, operators had found a hairline crack in the Keats nuke plant near Rockford, Illinois. Barely a week later, Jersey Electric discovered a crack in the same component of the Willow Creek plant, sending the entire cadre of nuclear utility executives into panic mode.

"As they say in this biz, a problem at one nuke is a problem at every nuke." Gareth licked meringue off his fork tines.

"How so?"

"Because deep down, every person on this planet with a pulse is terrified of radiation. It's primal. So, the one thing that could force a halt to nuclear power everywhere is a serious accident and radiation leak. No matter where that accident happens, all hundred nukes around this country will come under pressure from the public to close." Gareth leaned back, a picture of bliss. "You really should order a piece of that pie. It's out of this world."

Vickie shook her head. She never let herself eat dessert at lunch—if half a muffin counted as lunch. "How serious are these cracks?" Intuitively, the idea of cracks in structures meant to keep radiation from leaking into the environment struck her as troubling.

"Fifty bucks says they'll turn out to be a major headache."

"What do you think the NRC will do?"

"Hell if I know." Gareth rolled his eyes. "They don't exactly fill me in on the workings of their inner sanctum. Hey, don't quote me on that inner sanctum shit!"

"I won't," Vickie promised, turning off her tape recorder. Their interview over, she stashed her recorder and notebook into her shoulder bag and picked up the check.

Thanking her for lunch, Gareth uncurled his six-foot-six frame from the chair and retrieved his banner. He left the restaurant, walking in the direction of Connecticut Avenue.

Newhart News owned eight far-flung newspapers, including the *Newark Post* in New Jersey and the *Rockford Times* in Illinois. If Gareth's tip about these cracks proved true, this could be an important story for both papers, Vickie figured. She decided to bag the Hill and return to the Hay-Adams to see if she could corner one of the CEOs and get him to talk. It was a long shot, but she didn't have anything else.

Entering the hotel lobby, Vickie glanced at her watch. Half past eleven. With luck, the executives would break for lunch around noon. She settled into a chintz chair with a line of sight down the corridor. She took a newspaper from an end table and leafed through the pages. She didn't have to wait long. At quarter past twelve, she saw two men engaged in lively conversation emerge from the meeting room. She watched the pair pass by, knowing the odds of getting them to talk to her were next to zero. She might be able to catch one person off guard, but two people would be impossible, as neither would want to say anything in front of the other. Three men emerged next. She watched the door, letting another pair pass by her chair. Finally, a single, middle-aged man with graying hair stepped into the lobby. She approached him quickly.

"Victoria Evans, Newhart News. Could you tell me what you've been discussing?" she asked, walking along beside him.

"This is a closed session." He brushed her off.

Vickie returned to her chair. More men walked past in twos and threes. The next lone official she cornered also declined comment. Nearly everyone had left the room, and she was despairing of getting someone to talk. When a bald, fiftyish man drifted toward the lobby, she decided to change tactics and bluff. She would act as if she already knew they were discussing reactor cracks and grill him about the danger to residents living near his plant. Public safety was a sensitive subject for every nuclear plant executive. She felt confident he would not want to appear to be dodging a question about his plant endangering the public. Of course, if Gareth was wrong, and they were talking about something else, she'd feel like an insane fool.

"I'm wondering if the cracks found in the reactor vessel head are dangerous. Do you think they're a cause for concern?" she asked the pudgy man in her sweetest demeanor. "I'm Victoria Evans with Newhart News," she added.

"You shouldn't refer to them as cracks. They are cracking indications. And the hairline crack, cracking indication, that is, in our plant poses no danger to the public," he answered.

Vickie felt a surge of adrenaline. He had confirmed Gareth's information. She walked close by his side. She recalled seeing a business story about the CEO of Jersey Electric and an accompanying photo of a slim man with dark hair. That meant this bald man must be the CEO of Illinois Energy. She had to know for certain but didn't want to break the flow by asking him to identify himself. She figured she only had another second or two before it dawned on him that he should not be talking to a reporter.

"I'm sure the people in Rockford living near your plant would be relieved to know there's no problem." Vickie bluffed again. If he ran another utility, he would correct her.

"It would be premature—" he began.

"So you don't think the crack poses a threat to people in Rockford near the Keats plant?" she interrupted.

"That's right. There's no danger to anyone from our Keats plant. Now, if you'll excuse me." He broke away and dashed to the door.

Vickie returned to her chair and scribbled down what he had said. Closing her notebook, she could barely believe her good fortune. He had confirmed Gareth's tip about a hairline crack at the Keats plant. The fact that Gareth had been right about the Illinois plant meant he was probably right about the New Jersey plant, but she would have to confirm that.

Walking back through Lafayette Square, Vickie's face broke into an irrepressible smile. Washington shimmered before her like an Impressionist painting. Scarlet tulips tossed in the breeze near her feet, and cherry blossom petals flitted above her head. As she rounded the statue of Andrew Jackson flying on his bronze steed, her stride felt sure, stronger than ever before in her life, each step connected to the current of history. *This is where I belong. This is what I was meant to do,* she thought, as the outline of her first big story took shape in her mind. She would lead with the NRC's decision on the Hardwick restart, then go into the closed, high-level discussion about newly discovered cracks. She debated whether to include Gareth Will's protest at the end of Patton's speech. She decided that giving it a quick mention would allow her to pull in a couple quotes from Gareth on both the Hardwick plant restart vote and the reactor cracks.

Thane wasn't in the newsroom when Vickie returned, so she told Sean on the news desk that she planned to file a story on cracks discovered at two U.S. nuclear plants. She called Jersey Electric's spokesman and got him to confirm that his boss was attending the Washington meeting to discuss a newly discovered "cracking indication" in their plant's reactor vessel head. She phoned the NRC public affairs office, which had no comment. However, she did get the agency's spokesman to put her through to an engineer who explained what the reactor vessel head is in a nuclear plant. Next, she called the *Rockford Times* and had the editorial assistant fax a clip with a photo of the CEO of Illinois Energy. Vickie knew she was on solid ground when a page showing his unmistakable round face and shiny pate rolled out of the fax machine.

Vickie was so engrossed in writing she didn't notice until five o'clock that Thane had returned to the office. She printed a copy of her story and brought it to Thane, then returned to her desk to change from her pumps into sneakers. She was anxious to get to her daughter's baseball game. It was the team's first away game of the season, and Molly was pitching. Vickie was stashing her pumps in the bottom drawer of her desk when Thane appeared in front of her computer.

"Maybe some anti-nuke kook waving a banner about a hairline crack would be big news in southern Indiana, but you're not writing for the *Bloomington Times* now." Thane's voice, unusually high for so large a man, rose to a shrill pitch. "What we do here in the Washington bureau is cover national news for eight newspapers with more than half a million readers in five states."

Keys stopped clacking, and the newsroom fell silent. Vickie sensed everyone's eyes on her and felt her cheeks burning.

"The protester had credibility, and I checked out the Rockford—" Vickie began, her voice trembling.

Thane cut her off. "These plants have been pumping out electricity for fifteen years. If one of them develops a real crack that poses an actual problem, we'll hear about it, and the NRC will make the utility shut the plant down and fix it. I sent you to get the vote on the Hardwick restart because it matters to our Jersey readers, and even then, it's only worth a graph."

Hooking his thumbs under his red suspenders, Thane swaggered back to his desk. Vickie slinked out of the newsroom feeling humiliated and wronged. She knew in her bones there was a good case to be made for writing about the cracks—and that she hadn't given Gareth Will too much ink.

Vickie hailed a cab to the Solomon School, hoping to catch the last few innings of Molly's game. Rush-hour traffic was backed up on Wisconsin Avenue, and the cab barely moved. She kept looking at her watch, willing the minute hand to stand still. Too late, she realized that she should have taken the metro to Cleveland Park and grabbed a cab from there. By the time she reached the field, the game had ended. She felt miserable when she saw Molly and two other children lingering by home plate, waiting for their parents. As she approached the diamond, however, she could hear them excitedly reliving high points of the game.

In January, when she was offered this job, Vickie had worried that Molly would miss her Indiana classmates. Yet despite the abruptness of their move midway through the school year, her eleven-year-old daughter was flourishing. She had a new best friend, and they lived close enough to her school that Molly could walk home alone on days when she worked late—a godsend. Watching Molly, a smile flickered over Vickie's face, chased by a pang of dread as Thane's rebuke replayed in her mind. She'd been so certain this would be her first byline story, the one that would save her job. Why didn't Thane think it was important? Did he want to fire her and hire someone else? No, she couldn't entertain that possibility. She had to succeed at this job. She couldn't bear to uproot Molly again.

"We won, Mom!" Molly shouted, spotting her. She tossed her glove in the air, caught it, and ran to meet Vickie. "We were behind in the seventh inning, and I hit a triple! Charlie hit a single, and I scored. Then Julia hit a double, and he scored." She spoke fast, her green eyes sparkling behind red glasses frames that gave her an adorable, studious look.

"A triple? That's super! Way to go, Pumpkin!" She hugged Molly, and they high-fived. Her daughter's joy was contagious, lifting Vickie's spirits. They stopped at Sam's Shack to celebrate Easton's win over Solomon with cheeseburgers and chocolate shakes.

"Did you see anyone famous today?" Molly asked on their walk home.

"No, but something kind of exciting happened."

"What?" Molly was always eager to hear her mother's work stories. "Tell me."

Vickie told her about Gareth Will, and how he had shouted and leapt up at the meeting. "Something flashed in his hand. For a second, I was afraid it was a spark, but the flash turned out to be the corner of a yellow satin banner he unfurled that had the words, 'Stop Chernobyl Here,' printed in red."

"Wow!" Molly looked up at her mother in awe. "What's Chernobyl?"

KIEV, APRIL 1986

Squinting at his watch, Anatoly Kulyk stumbled to the phone.

"Tolya?" a quavering voice asked. Hearing his friend's voice, Anatoly felt a rush of relief followed quickly by alarm.

"What's—?"

"There's been an accident at Chernobyl," his friend Vladimir interrupted.

"What kind of accident?" Anatoly asked. He and Vladimir had worked their way up through the austere ranks of Soviet nuclear physicists over the decades. Their true bond, however, was forged in a shared love of chess and the trust that comes with knowing someone from childhood.

"I only know it's Reactor Four. Workers are suffering acute radiation sickness. There's a meeting at six. I was hoping you could tell me more," Vladimir whispered.

"I was asleep when you called. I haven't heard a thing."

Naturally, the Minister would call him, Anatoly thought, hanging up the phone. Vladimir Boyko served as a deputy in the Atomic Energy Sector for Ukraine. The Chernobyl station's four reactors produced fully fifteen percent of the Soviet Union's electricity, and Gorbachev had demanded an increase in nuclear energy. He would not want to be in Vladimir's shoes right now.

Anatoly inhabited a more theoretical realm, supervising a research laboratory, but his head was not in the clouds. He had spent four years advising construction of the South Ukraine nuclear plant. Vladimir's mention of acute radiation sickness troubled him. Workers would have to be exposed to high levels of radiation to develop the nausea, vomiting, and disorientation that characterize radiation sickness. Too jangled to go back to bed, Anatoly slipped into his robe and pattered to the kitchen. He was tamping coffee into his pot when the phone rang again. He could not recall getting one call this early before—never two.

This time it was Pavlo Popovych, deputy to the Kiev Regional Committee Second Party Secretary. After repeating news of an accident at Chernobyl, he asked Anatoly to join him at the emergency committee meeting.

"Moscow's commission will arrive this afternoon," Pavlo said. Unspoken was his fear that Moscow would blame bureaucrats in Kiev for whatever had led to the accident. "Nuclear energy is out of my field of expertise, but I'm fortunate to have such a brilliant comrade as you in my circle."

The corners of Anatoly's lips pulled back in a satisfied smile, despite the apparent gravity of the situation. It would be hard for anyone who knew Popovych to name a field of study he did excel in, beyond the art of ingratiation.

Anatoly felt relieved to be tapped for inclusion. Ukraine's top officials would be at this meeting. Proving himself valuable could advance his prospects, he reasoned. He ate breakfast quickly, then dressed carefully. When Pavlo's driver rang at Chekhovsky Lane, Anatoly surveyed his reflection in the gold-leaf framed mirror on his foyer wall. White flecks glittered in his wavy black hair, but he felt certain his taut profile gave the appearance of a man much younger than his fifty years. He hurried downstairs, followed the driver to a black Volga, and climbed in back beside Pavlo.

Reaching into his trousers, Pavlo fished out a handkerchief and mopped his forehead. "We need to stay ahead of Moscow. I will see to it you are made a technical advisor. It won't take any convincing," Pavlo said, tacitly acknowledging that Anatoly no longer depended on him to maintain his position and perks. Theirs was a lopsided bond, however, based on a debt Anatoly could never repay. Pavlo had stood by him in 1969 when questions were raised about his loyalty. Anatoly could have been tainted by his brother Alexei's anti-Soviet propaganda and agitation. He could have lost his security clearance and access to nuclear secrets, which would have doomed him. Instead, Anatoly's appointment in Pavlo's division had sailed forward smoothly. Of course, Popovych had not been acting from altruism. He had a vendetta against the other candidate for the post, who had justly accused him of filching certain luxury items.

Anatoly and his superior fell into a tense silence as the car whipped through the misty first light shrouding the city streets. Anatoly had thought the meeting would take place at the regional committee offices on Radyanska Square. Instead, the driver turned onto Kirov Street and stopped at the Council of Ministers building. The two men stepped out of the car and passed under the building's towering Ionic columns, Anatoly marking long strides as his stout companion scrambled to keep pace. A guard ushered them to a room furnished with a large mahogany table facing a wall of windows.

Pavlo squeezed into a chair at the table while Anatoly sat behind him with a bevy of advisers and assistants. General Kushnir, Chairman of the Political Department of the Kiev Ministry of Internal Affairs, entered within minutes. A spindly man with white hair sprouting from a mottled scalp, the general rambled for fifteen minutes, revealing only that there had been a fire at the reactor and police had erected roadblocks to close off Pripyat. Built in the 1970s, Pripyat was a model city, filled with coveted amenities for families of the engineers who worked at the Chernobyl nuclear plant.

Anatoly was growing impatient to learn details about the accident when a secretary entered the room with a message from the Chernobyl manager. Kushnir read it aloud: "Graphite in the core is burning, and the reactor is releasing massive amounts of radioactivity."

Several conversations broke out at once. Anatoly's pulse quickened as he tried to imagine the scene unfolding at the plant. He wanted to speak to the operator. How had an accident of such proportions taken place? His mind raced through scenarios. He wondered how he would gain access to information with police blocking roads into Pripyat. He leaned forward and tapped Pavlo's shoulder.

"I must learn details of the accident and collect data on radiation releases," he told Pavlo.

"I recommend that Anatoly Kulyk, whose laboratory you all know, be put in charge of collecting radiation data." Pavlo's announcement was met initially by an awkward silence. Finally, Kushnir signaled his approval with a vague nod. After several moments more of disordered discussion, the General ended the meeting.

Turning to leave, Anatoly caught the reflection of his deep-set eyes and square jawline superimposed like a double exposure over the rising sun. The dazzling image on the glass, in which he fleetingly saw a heroic scientist called upon to tame the blazing atom, flooded him with an unaccountable rush of euphoria.

After a quick evening meal, Anatoly went to his bedroom and removed the quilt covering a trunk in the back of his closet. Opening the lid, he lifted a wood tray crammed with medals and certificates, revealing a collection of leather-bound diaries. The handsome journals dated back to 1956. The sole gap in his otherwise thorough journal record had come during the tumultuous period from 1958 to 1960, when his fiancée, Anya, had left him no time for reflection. She heaped scorn on diarists, calling them "dreary accountants of life." That was how she judged Anatoly, ultimately, before jilting him for a flamboyant cellist.

Shaking off unbidden memories of that disastrous relationship, Anatoly ran his index finger slowly over the rich leather spines of his journals. He picked up a fresh one and carried it to his drawing room. As a bachelor, Anatoly had little occasion to entertain. His sole guests of late had been his niece Larysa's little girl and adolescent son. Yet his flat gave the appearance of a salon where Kiev's intelligentsia might gather to discuss art, literature, and history. Prints of Renaissance masters he'd acquired in Odessa intermingled on his walls with contemporary Soviet paintings. Tiffany lamps sat on carved end tables flanking a plush velvet sofa. He put on his recording of *La Bohème*, poured a glass of Moldavian red wine, and sank into his wing-backed armchair.

On his way home, Anatoly had been struck by the historic significance of events unfolding at Chernobyl. Never before had scientists witnessed this kind of nuclear disaster. The Three Mile Island Station in America had come within half an hour of total meltdown, from what he had learned, but the radiation remained largely contained. What would happen at Chernobyl, and with what consequences for the surrounding area? How far would its deadly plume of radiation spread? No simulation existed for such an accident. The image that popped into his mind was that of a pine-tree shaped plume of pumice and dust shooting into the sky, as it had in ancient times from the Mt. Vesuvius volcano. Uncapping his pen, Anatoly determined to follow in the footsteps of Pliny the Younger, a historic figure he had long admired. The Roman naturalist had done humanity the inestimable service of recording for posterity details of his uncle's death in the devastating eruption of Mt. Vesuvius in 79 A.D.

Cracking open his journal, Anatoly entered the date: *26 April 1986.*

"Based on such facts as I have been able to ascertain, during the afternoon of 25 April, operators at Chernobyl Atomic Energy Station reduced power output of reactor 4 to prepare for a safety test," he

began in a precise script. *"As part of preparations, they disconnected the reactor's emergency cooling system. By 1:23 a.m., 26 April, reactor 4 had become unstable. Power output suddenly spiked. Operators heard a blast, which they speculated to have been a steam explosion. Fires broke out across the station, and fire brigades were called to extinguish the flames."* Words flowed quickly as Anatoly recalled his conversation with a Chernobyl operator.

"Several firefighters developed symptoms of acute radiation sickness. Radiometers could not be located. Available monitoring equipment registered 3.6 roentgens per hour, the maximum level the equipment was capable of measuring. A civil defense worker from Pripyat arrived at the station at 3:40 a.m., 26 April, to measure radiation. He recorded 250 roentgens per hour, the maximum his dosimeter could register. The station director doubted the accuracy of that measurement. Note: Exposure to 500 roentgens over 5 hours is fatal to humans."

Anatoly paused to sip his wine and listen to the sublime duet of Rodolfo and Mimi ending the first act of *Bohème*. After savoring Puccini's music, he returned pen to paper. *"At 9:00 a.m., 26 April, the deputy chief engineer climbed to block 4 to survey damage. He reported that the reactor was 'completely destroyed.' Moscow placed Valeri Legasov, First Deputy Director of the Kurchatov Institute of Atomic Energy, in charge of investigating the accident."*

Summarizing the conversation with his colleague, Leonid V., at Minsk Nuclear Institute, Anatoly recorded that the wind was blowing to the north, sending the plume of radiation toward Minsk. When Leonid arrived at work in the morning, dosimeters at his Institute were going crazy. At first, Leonid worried they had a leak, but the radioactive cloud turned out to be everywhere—over the city, too. Next, Leonid had contacted the Ignalina plant, and their readings were also off the scale. By early afternoon, everyone knew the radiation was coming from Chernobyl. *The reactor was running for 2 years, making 2 billion curies of radionuclides in the core,* Anatoly wrote. *If the total inventory were to melt down, emissions could be equivalent to 350 to 400 Hiroshima bombs.*

Anatoly capped his pen, feeling eerily sober. He had always loved the purity of physics and its power to explain the universe. When chaos reigned over his personal life, he had been able to draw comfort from his chosen discipline. He could count on the immutable laws of physics to carry on, untouched by human foibles, betrayals, or death. Now, inexplicably, bunglers had turned the peaceful atom into hundreds of bombs. Returning the journal to his trunk, he vowed to learn how.

Anatoly would be history's scribe.

WASHINGTON, MAY 1990

After the morning editorial meeting, Thane asked Vickie to look into the national landfill crisis for the upcoming "Earth Matters." She picked up a pen and began taking notes.

"I want you to spend the next couple days researching landfill legislation and recycling rules that may be coming down the pike. Interstate trash wars are heating up." Pivoting, Thane trained a puckered smile on Cynthia Ames, who was powering across the newsroom.

"Very impressive!" Thane raised his arm to slap Cynthia on the back but abandoned the gesture midway, leaving his plump hand suspended in midair.

Cynthia, the bureau's other female reporter, covered education and a constellation of domestic topics for the lifestyle pages.

A slight, brittle woman with a closet full of designer shoes, she was tottering on four-inch spikes that gave her much needed height but forced her to take quick, short steps. Her sharp nose jutted ahead of the rest of her body, giving her the appearance of a ruffled bird ready to attack an intruder to her nest. Ordinarily, the guys didn't pay attention to her family-oriented features. This week, however, they were fawning over Cynthia because of her coverage of protests at Wellesley College. Her story about the iconic college inviting maternal Barbara Bush rather than an outspoken feminist as commencement speaker had attracted national attention. This morning the White House had invited a handful of reporters to hear the First Lady's side of the story. Cynthia was one of them.

"On your way to chat with FLOTUS?" Thane fawned. He used his floating hand to pantomime bringing a teacup to his lips, his chubby pinky outstretched like a raw breakfast sausage. Cynthia was having none of it. She minced past him, leaving a trail of French perfume in her wake.

"Start this morning with House staffers. Find out what bills they're considering," Thane continued, sneering at Cynthia's rear end. "Tomorrow, find out if the EPA has any landfill or recycling regulations in the works. Then talk with Senate staffers to see what they're planning."

As usual, Thane's commands were loud enough for half the newsroom to hear, making Vickie feel more like his lackey than a reporter in her own right. As she stuffed her tape recorder into her bag, Gabe Green stopped by her desk. Not only was Gabe a big-name political reporter, he was also a real looker. She guessed he was about her age. He had broad shoulders, kinky black hair, bushy sideburns, and full, sensual lips. What she found most extraordinary about him were his intense violet-blue eyes. They drew her in yet made her uncomfortable at the same time.

Vickie had noticed him glancing her way a few times, but he'd never started a conversation with her. Surprised by his sudden approach, she lifted her eyebrows high and gave him a toothy smile. She blushed, fearing she must appear gawky and unsophisticated. Without taking his eyes off her, Gabe cracked a half-grin that put her at ease.

"I'm heading to the Hill if you want to share a ride," he offered breezily.

Nodding, she picked up her bag and followed Gabe to the elevator. They rode in an awkward silence to the lobby, where he hurried ahead of her down a half-flight of stairs. Outside on F Street, he hailed a cab as she caught up to him.

"Rayburn Building," Gabe directed the driver.

Vickie climbed in back beside him. "Your legs look pretty cramped. How tall are you?" she asked, reaching to tuck a loose strand of hair into the black ribbon at the nape of her neck.

"Six-three, I'm used to it." Gabe looked pointedly at Vickie's slim legs. His eyes traveled deliberately from the hem of her snug skirt to the full bodice of her fitted blue suit jacket before stopping at her face. "You wear contacts or are your eyes really that green?"

"It's my natural color. I'm used to being asked that," Vickie parried.

"Sorry we haven't caught up yet. The past few months have been nuts." Gabe glanced at his watch. "And let's be frank. Re-porters come and go. Where'd you come here from?"

Vickie turned away and looked out the window. She hated that question. She generally tried to avoid bringing up Troy, New

York, where she was born, or her move to Indiana when she was eight, after her father died. She dreaded the look of concern that invariably froze people's expressions whenever she answered straightforward questions about her childhood. Their sympathy, while well-intentioned, inevitably created an unbridgeable moat between her and people who grew up in normal families—with parents. Now, even the part of her life she had been responsible for seemed pathetic. She felt foolish about her decision to drop out of Indiana University her junior year to marry a philosophy lecturer named Jake Evans. The last thing she wanted to do was recount the futile years she'd spent wandering from St. Louis to Ames, Iowa, to Oklahoma City and Murfreesboro, Tennessee, then back to Bloomington as Jake's career and their marriage wobbled in tandem into a death spiral. Who wanted to hear such a pedestrian tale of woe? She decided to go with an abridged version.

"Indiana. I moved here three months ago."

"No, I mean where were you working?"

"Oh, that! I was freelancing," Vickie fudged. This was how she described her scanty work experience on her resume: freelance writer, *Bloomington Times*. Clips attached. She omitted mentioning that the three articles attached, which appeared in the fall of 1989, were the only ones she had published, outside of her college newspaper.

Gabe did a doubletake. "So you were unemployed?"

Vickie forced a laugh. She thought about telling Gabe that her journalism professor had roomed with Alan Graves in college, but she didn't want that detail getting around the newsroom. "How about you? Where did you work before?" she asked, changing the subject from her background to his.

Gabe was happy to oblige. "I was at United Press for a few years, then Knight-Ridder for nine. Three years ago, Alan made me an offer I couldn't refuse," he answered, apparently feeling the need to explain why he had left a prestigious newspaper group for the upstart Newhart News. "The money's good. If old man Newhart thinks he can build a news empire by scooping up bankrupt papers and shoveling his fortune into the DC bureau, who am I to argue?"

Vickie wanted to tell Gabe how terrified she was of being fired at her review but decided she didn't know him well enough to confide in him. "I'm excited about being part of the E-team," she said, instead. "Energy's really heating up with Congress getting into global warming—pun intended."

"I wouldn't cream my jeans. You're our fourth energy reporter in under a year."

"What?" It was Vickie's turn to do a double take. She wondered why no one had shared this crucial piece of information with her. Maybe everyone was waiting for her to get canned, she thought. Truthfully, Vickie had to admit that she hadn't tried to get close to any of her colleagues. She came in at nine most mornings, buried herself in work, and tried to leave the office by six to make it to Molly's after-school program before closing time. Rushing off at six most days ruled out joining other reporters for drinks after work—not that anyone had invited her. She had thought about asking Cynthia to lunch, but she always seemed to be rushing around surrounded by an impenetrable cloud of purpose.

"You can't be serious. What happened to the other three?"

"There was Leon Cohen. He lasted on energy three months

before moving to the courts beat. Real mensch. You've met Leon, right?" Vickie nodded. "The guy before him, from the *Santa Barbara Journal*, crawled back to California on his knees begging for his old job back after a month here on energy. Then there was Ellie McBurnie, a real sharp lady. She snagged a job with *The Herald* after five months. And you."

"Let's hope I break the streak," Vickie managed, her voice husky.

"Hey, keep the faith, baby." Gabe punched her arm with a soft fist.

The cabbie pulled in front of Rayburn. "I'm stopping in at Longworth to see someone before I go to Glenn's office," Gabe said after paying the driver. "See you back at the shop."

"Thanks, Gabe. It was nice talking with you." Vickie didn't even try to fake a smile.

Gabe paused to flip his press pass in front of his tie. After buttoning his sports jacket, he turned serious. "You want my advice? Get off the E-team first chance you get. Who wants to cover dumps and power plants? Or read about them, for that matter. And Victoria, about yesterday, pardon my French, but Thane's an arrogant prick."

"*Merci*," Vickie murmured. She reached inside her suit jacket and rubbed her press badge like a rabbit's foot. Then she dashed up the Rayburn Building stairs, praying for a good lead.

~

After spending three hours trying to pry information about land-fill legislation from House staffers, Vickie headed back to the Press Building empty-handed. When she stepped off the elevator on the sixth floor, she collided with Thane, waiting to go down.

"Watch it, will you?" Thane adjusted his bow tie and stepped around her into the elevator. "I'll be at the World Bank all afternoon. You'd better get into the fax room and clean up that mess."

"What do you mean?"

"That anti-nuke luna—" The elevator door swiped across Thane's fleshy face and snapped shut before she could hear him finish the sentence.

The fax machine occupied a windowless room that once had done duty as a mop closet. Day and night, it churned out a continuous sheet of paper with dashed lines demarcating breaks between pages. Everyone kept hinting that Alan should hire someone to cut and distribute faxes. That was the last thing he wanted to spend resources on, which left reporters haphazardly doing the job. Opening the door, Vickie was met by billowing waves of paper writhing on the floor. Crouching down, she spotted her name here and there on the paper curling around her heels. True to his word, Gareth Will had faxed her scads of government documents and journal articles on radiation and nuclear power. She was embarrassed about clogging up the fax machine but impressed by the high-level nature of the papers Gareth was sending her.

Scissors in hand she squatted, searching for the start of each new fax, cutting along the dashes, and stapling the pages together. She was sifting through loops of paper when the words *hot snow* grabbed her attention. The oddly juxtaposed words jumped out from a hand-written note from Gareth giving her a heads-up about a team of University of New Hampshire scientists who had found radiation in snow at the South Pole. The lead researcher, Jack Dibb, in a letter to the journal *Nature*, speculated that the radiation was from Chernobyl. Skimming the single-page letter, she was surprised to see that the radioactive snow had fallen on the South Pole 20 months after Chernobyl exploded. The research piqued her interest.

"Thank you, Gareth," she whispered under her breath, ready to take possession of the story. Her enthusiasm faded abruptly, however, as her mind replayed Thane's blistering words from yesterday. What if Thane returned to the office in time to spike her story? She couldn't endure another public humiliation. The safest course of action, she told herself, was to hand the page over to Jeff, since science was his beat, and get back to clipping faxes. Yet this hot snow tugged at her like a puppy with a ball, keen to play fetch. She wanted to ask the researchers how they found the radiation. Did they expect to find it, or did their discovery take them by surprise? Had scientists ever seen radiation in snow from Antarctica before? How had radiation from Chernobyl traveled so far? And why had it taken so long to get there?

Vickie stood frozen by the fax machine, hesitant to take on the story, but equally loath to give it up. What tipped the scale for her was realizing how jealous she would be if she read an article about this Chernobyl snow by a reporter from a rival newspaper. She could not allow that to happen. She cut Gareth's cover sheet from the fax and walked to Jeff's desk.

"I just got this fax." She showed Jeff the page. "It's new, and it looks interesting. I thought I'd check it out."

"Sure, why don't you." Jeff glanced at the page through thick aviator glasses. "There's a flap over NASA's budget I'm waiting for calls on."

Vickie was relieved at how easy it had been to get Jeff's okay.

She called the lead researcher and left him a detailed message. Then she put down the receiver, praying he would call right back. If he returned her call by two o'clock, she calculated, she would be able to interview him and write her story by six.

Thirty minutes ticked by, and she began to sweat. What if he didn't return her call? He could be anywhere, attending a conference or traipsing around some frozen spot on the planet. Three o'clock came and went with no call. At five past three, Vickie started to panic. What would she write about if the scientist didn't get back to her? She dreaded having to tell Jeff she couldn't follow through on the story after she had proposed covering it. He would see her as a failure. She couldn't afford to fail, not this time, not with her job review looming.

At quarter past three, her phone rang. Vickie pounced on the second ring. Fortunately, it was the lead researcher, and he was happy to talk to her. He began by explaining that as snow forms, it crystallizes around particles of dust, pollen, and volcanic ash in the atmosphere. The trapped particles fall to the ground in the snow. During the South Pole's summer months, the snow forms a layer that has a different chemical composition and texture than snow falling in the winter months. Because the snow freezes in discernible layers, scientists get a glimpse of the atmosphere at the time each layer formed.

The UNH team found radioactive isotopes in snow corresponding to bomb fallout from atmospheric tests conducted in the Northern Hemisphere from the 1950s to the mid-1970s. While the researchers had expected this, it came as a surprise to Vickie. She had assumed that fallout was a localized phenomenon. She had no idea that radiation from America's nuclear bomb tests had made its way to Antarctica.

What did surprise the research team was a spike in radioactive cesium-137 in snow desposited in the summer of 1987 to 1988. The South Pole summer extends from October through March. Cesium-137 is not found in nature. The researchers speculated that the radiation, which was more than twenty times higher than background levels, had come from the Chernobyl reactor accident in April 1986.

After finishing the interview, Vickie wanted to get more background on the spread of radiation from nuclear bomb tests in the 1950s. She called Ian Hoffman, the Newhart News correspondent in Berlin. Ian covered international politics, including nuclear treaties, so she hoped he could refer her to an expert. It was after eight o'clock in the evening there, but she lucked out, catching Ian as he was about to leave for a dinner date.

"The person who knows more about nuclear weapons testing than anyone on the planet is Darren Cunningham. He got his start as an arms negotiator in the Reagan administration. Now, he's on Bush's negotiating team at State. You can give him my name. Oh, on another note," Ian added, "I'm coming to the States next month for a week. We'll have a chance to meet face-to-face."

Vickie thanked Ian for the contact and called Darren Cunningham. Getting his voicemail, she left a detailed message. Next, she called Gareth Will to see if he knew an expert on weapons testing. He referred her to Dr. Gilmore Harris at the Association of Radiation Health Scientists. Gareth also named Darren Cunningham as a leading expert on Cold War weapons testing. She reached Dr. Harris on her first try. He gave her a succinct summary of nuclear weapons testing from 1945 through 1974.

At ten past four, Vickie threw herself into writing the story. She finished at ten to six, read it over, and looked around for Thane. She was relieved to see he had not yet returned to the newsroom, but as she was about to send her story to Sean on the news desk, Thane made his entrance. He stopped in front of her computer.

"Did you get anything on landfill legislation?" Thane asked.

"A few things may be in the works, but nothing concrete," she answered. "I talked to House Energy and Commerce staffers who may be drafting a bill. No one's ready to talk about introducing anything, but I'll keep checking in with them. Tomorrow, I'll talk to Senate staffers."

Thane nodded. Vickie knew she would have to hand her story over to Thane. He was her editor and head of the E-team. There was no way around it.

"I'm about to send you a story I did on a team of scientists who found radiation from Chernobyl in snow at the South Pole. I told Jeff about it, but he was busy, so he had me look into it." Vickie prayed Thane wouldn't ask who gave her the tip. What would she tell him? He had made it clear he thought Gareth Will was a kook.

Fortunately, Thane didn't ask. "Send it to me."

Vickie spent the ride to Cleveland Park worrying that Thane would spike her story. Or worse, condense it to a brief. Her one hope was that Jeff would intervene on her behalf. She felt sure it was a good story, certainly interesting enough that some editors in the Newhart News chain would want to run it—if Thane didn't cut it to shreds. The headline alone, "'Hot Snow' Found at South Pole," was bound to grab attention. She had devoted several paragraphs to the history of above-ground nuclear testing in the U.S. The idea of radioactive isotopes from bombs detonated in Nevada in the 1950s frozen for all time in snow in the coldest place on Earth disturbed her. There was another dimension to this story floating on the periphery of her consciousness that had eluded her all afternoon—one of those maddening associations that dissolved as she was about to bring it into focus. She was still trying to catch it when the train pulled into her station.

Vickie climbed two flights to the street and hurried south past Cleveland Park's mom-and-pop shops. She stopped at the wine store to buy a bottle of chilled Chardonnay, then crossed Connecticut and headed up Macomb Street, leaving traffic noise behind. Towering oak and sycamore trees shaded the porches, porticos, and cupolas of the magnificent houses lining both sides of the road. The neighborhood got its name from President Grover Cleveland, who bought a summer home here after he was elected in 1884. More than a century later, it was still easy to envision this part of the city as a serene retreat from the heat and mosquitoes that had plagued residences near the White House. She was renting the first floor of a Queen Anne, which the owner had converted into two apartments. Her dream was to buy one of these gorgeous houses and put down roots for her and Molly—if she could keep her job.

She planned to offer Sandy Carlson a glass of wine before she headed off for her date. So far, her relationship with Sandy had been purely practical, caring for one another's daughters, who had become inseparable. Vickie realized that being single moms might turn out to be the only thing they had in common. Sandy, whose successful real estate business had enabled her to buy a home nearby on Newark Street, struck Vickie as outgoing and urbane. Sandy's colorful wardrobe was certainly more vibrant than her own subdued palette of gray, blue, and cream. But whatever their personality differences, Sandy was dependable. Vickie could trust her to take good care of Molly when the girls were at her house. That was comfort enough.

Vickie quickly tidied the living room. As she arranged the pillows on her sofa, her attention wandered to the top shelf of the bookcase, where a snow globe sat nestled between a pair of crystal candlestick holders. Of course! That's what had been circling in the periphery of her mind on the way home. She walked over to the bookcase and picked up the memento from her childhood. She often pictured the Earth as a snow globe, its thin layer of atmosphere acting like glass to trap in particles. She turned the globe gently and smiled as sparkling snow settled over two familiar figures under the glass dome.

The bell rang, interrupting Vickie's reverie. She set the snow globe back on the shelf as Molly rushed to the door to welcome Julia and her mother. Sandy, who dressed more like a Parisian than a Washingtonian, was wearing a low-cut, crimson cocktail dress and strappy red heels. Her stylish black hair was cropped at the neck, slanting at an angle toward her chin.

"You look beautiful, Miss Carlson! I love your dress," Molly said. Then she and Julia skipped to Molly's bedroom.

"Your place is gorgeous—so spacious, and stained-glass windows," Sandy enthused, taking in the high-ceilinged living room. "These don't come on the market often."

"We're renting, but I do love it. Can I offer you a glass of wine? Do you like Chardonnay? If you have time, that is."

"I'd love to, but I'm running late. I should be back before ten," Sandy apologized. "We want to have Molly over to our place real soon. Do you have any plans coming up?"

"Well, I was thinking about maybe buying a ticket to a concert next Saturday night."

"Buy that ticket. It's a date," Sandy interjected, happy to even the score.

Lying in bed that night, Vickie's thoughts drifted back to the schoolyard where she met her own best friend, whom she hadn't seen in a few years. The February day was windy and cold. Thirty years later, Vickie could still picture the nickel sky and feel the frigid air nipping her nose. Midway through recess, huge snowflakes the size of quarters began swirling around her. She extended her hands palm up and tentatively licked a snowflake off her mitten. A girl wearing pink earmuffs appeared out of nowhere, thrusting her hands out beside Vickie's and licking the snow off her mittens. "I'm Colleen," she announced, and soon they were giggling and clapping their mittens together. Colleen leaned her head back and stuck out her tongue. Vickie mimicked her, and they twirled until they were dizzy, capturing snowflakes on their tongues.

Picturing snowflakes on the schoolyard brought back the day Vickie's aunt gave her the snow globe. Her mother had gone into a hospital after her father died, and Aunt Lydia had driven Vickie from Troy, New York, to her house in the woods of Santa Claus, Indiana. During her first few days in Indiana, she'd repeatedly asked Aunt Lydia when her mother was coming back from the hospital to get her.

"We don't know when she'll regain her health, dear," Aunt Lydia had answered, clasping her hands over her arms as if she were trying to get warm. After a week passed, Vickie stopped asking. Her aunt's vagueness confirmed what Vickie had known in her gut: she would never be returning to her old house in Troy. Then, on the day before Christmas, a driver dropped her mother at Aunt Lydia's door. She handed Vickie a green, knitted scarf and Lydia a blue one. Both woolen scarves were short and lumpy, with holes from dropped stitches—totally unwearable—but Vickie didn't mind.

"I didn't have any wrapping paper," her mother apologized.

"That's okay, Mommy." All Vickie wanted was to snuggle on her mother's lap and feel her arms around her. But when she leaned against her, her mother's slack arms remained crossed in her lap.

"Not now. I'm tired, Vickie," she said, her blank eyes seeking something in the distance.

"Your Mama's tired, dear," Aunt Lydia repeated, gesturing for Vickie to come to the rocking chair where she was seated beside the Christmas tree. "Open this, dear. It's from me." She reached under the tree for a package wrapped in gold foil.

Blinking back hot tears, Vickie turned toward Aunt Lydia and stumbled across the living room. Her aunt placed the gift in her hands. Under the gold foil, a thick layer of tissue paper cushioned something round. It must be delicate, Vickie thought. She peeled away layers of tissue with care, revealing the most beautiful object she had ever seen. A smooth glass globe was mounted on a base the color of cream. Under the glass, an angel in a blue robe knelt beside a fawn that looked like Bambi. She fell in love with both figures at once.

"Shake it," Aunt Lydia urged.

Vickie shook the globe, and a dazzling blizzard swirled around the angel and fawn. When the snow settled to the ground, she shook it again. She held the globe throughout the day. She placed it beside her plate during dinner and cradled it against her chest when the driver picked up her mother, who left without kissing her goodbye.

Vickie wondered if the angel was the Little Lost Angel from the book Aunt Lydia read with her at bedtime. Sometimes she felt like that lost angel patting the timid fawn. At other times she felt like the motherless fawn, looking to the angel to comfort her. Vickie took the globe to bed with her that night and watched the snowflakes glitter in the blue moonlight streaming through the window.

Until she met Colleen, that snow globe angel was her best friend in the world.

Vickie's mind returned to the professor this afternoon telling her that snow falling on the South Pole contained radioactive particles. The idea of fallout from nuclear bombs and power plant explosions rising to the clouds, blowing across the globe, and falling back to Earth in snow upset her. Snow was supposed to be pure. Children slid on it and built igloos and snowmen from it. Little girls flopped down in it and waved their arms and legs back and forth to make angel wings and robes. The crystalline snowflakes falling from the sky that tickled your eyelashes and melted on your tongue were not supposed to contain invisible radiation. Snow should not be hot, she thought, drifting off to sleep.

7

KIEV, MAY 1986

Vasyl was running a sheet through the letterpress at the front of the shop when Mikhail Kovalenko's daughter opened the door and guided her pram through the vestibule. Her face damp from pushing the carriage in the afternoon sun, she hurried past Vasyl's press to the table where her father sat drinking tea.

"Papa, they've banned the sale of milk at the market." Her voice verged on hysteria. "What will happen to Petro? Where will I get him milk?"

"Sit, Anna," Mikhail said over the rhythmic wheezing of Vasyl's press. Mikhail had taken Vasyl on as an apprentice fresh out of technical school. After working side-by-side for over a dozen years, they had gained a rare reputation for craftsmanship and punctual delivery of decorative posters, certificates, and handbills.

Kiev's cultural groups sought them out for official business. The men also had seen each other through family crises and had come to trust one another.

Mikhail called for Vasyl to join them. Vasyl pulled a print of a heroic-style worker gazing rapturously at a chunky, green transmission tower from the letterpress and walked to the table.

"What's this about banned milk?" Mikhail patted Anna's hand.

"Inspectors at the market found radiation in the milk. They made farmers dump it. Moscow was supposed to send clean milk, but people have been waiting since early morning and no milk arrives." Anna's attention roamed from the men's faces to the pram. "The authorities told us to drink only bottled water and canned or powdered milk."

At the sound of fussing, Anna flew to the carriage. Bouncing the boy on her hip, she paced by stacks of trays filled with metal type. A large press pounded and whooshed in the back of the workshop.

"How is there radiation in the milk?" she asked, looking from her father to Vasyl.

"Radiation must have fallen on fields around the Chernobyl plant. When cows grazed on the grass, their milk must have become radioactive," Vasyl said, the significance of this ban draining the blood from his face. He pictured Dmitry and Katya at the kitchen table this morning spooning radioactive milk from their cereal bowls, Katya last night, swallowing a glass of milk, and yesterday, the whole family slurping potato soup made with milk. Questions raced through his mind. How much radiation have the children ingested? How far around Chernobyl has the contamination spread? Why would radiation fall only on the grass where cows graze? What of the strawberries and mushrooms? Would they not also be contaminated? How much radiation had settled on Kiev? How much was falling on them still?

"They knew that reactor's been belching radiation and didn't tell us? Bastards." Mikhail glanced over his shoulder, but the large press was making too much noise for workers to hear him. "The Chernobyl fire was more than a week ago, was it not?"

Mikhail counted the days aloud, ticking them off on his fingers. "This makes eight days since the accident." He stood up, jaw muscles twitching. "We're going to find milk. Clean the letterpress when you finish this run, Vasyl. Then you can go home for the day."

After Mikhail and Anna left, Vasyl went to the phone and dialed the Polytechnic Institute.

Larysa was translating a *New England Journal of Medicine* article on coagulation disorders when she got the call. Her throat tightened. Vasyl never phoned her at work short of an emergency.

"We have to get the kids out of here," he said, his voice hushed.

Larysa's breath caught in her throat. "What is it?"

"They've forbidden farmers from selling their fresh milk in the market. They say that the radiation is too high."

"No!" Her hand flew to her mouth. All the misgivings she had pushed out of her mind returned. "Where did you hear this?"

"Mikhail's daughter came here from the market. Officials are telling everyone to drink only powdered or canned milk and bottled water."

"Where should we send them?" Larysa asked, already weighing the options. Her mother lived half a world away in Magadan, on the Sea of Okhotsk. She had traveled there to be near Alexei after he was sentenced to hard labor in the Kolyma mines. A talented singer, she had found work in Magadan's theater. After Alexei died, she had fallen in love with an actor and stayed there. Larysa had no doubt her mother would take Katya in, but Magadan was eight time zones away. She couldn't imagine sending Katya on such a long journey without her brother to watch over her. Dmitry would be going to the Artek camp in Crimea at the start of June and wouldn't be able to accompany his sister.

"Do you think they can stay with Eva?" Larysa asked, deciding that would be the best option. Vasyl's sister and brother-in-law were teachers in Saratov, a day's train ride southeast of Moscow. However, their apartment was cramped. Between their three children and Vasyl's mother, who lived with them, Larysa wondered whether there would be a corner where Dmitry and Katya could sleep.

"Yes, I'm sure of it. I'll call her when I get home."

"I hope Dmitry and Katya have not—" Larysa's voice trailed off. What came next was too terrifying to say out loud. What if the milk they have been drinking for the past week has poisoned them? She wondered whether radioactive milk could cause cancer in children.

Larysa told the director's assistant that she had to leave early. She brought *The New England Journal of Medicine* to the circulation desk.

"I need to check this out," she told the librarian, who stood at the counter absently fingering a strand of smoky glass beads on her flat chest.

"I don't know what to make of this." The librarian shook her head and frowned at Larysa.

"What?" Larysa asked, desperate to leave. "I need this now."

The librarian located her logbook. "I heard the radio is instructing everyone to wipe our shoes with a wet cloth before we enter our flats." Clutching her necklace, she looked blankly at Larysa. "Then we're to dispose of the water."

Radioactive particles must be covering the streets, like snowdrifts we cannot see, Larysa thought, stunned by the librarian's revelation.

"I haven't heard that." Larysa was curt, avoiding a drawn-out conversation. While the librarian jotted down the journal title, she pictured radioactive particles blowing through the windows of their flat. A cold terror crept into her stomach as she hurried to the metro.

The station seemed more crowded than usual for this time of day. When the train pulled up to the platform, people boarded quickly, as if they had heard a siren and were rushing to the nearest air raid shelter before the bombs fell. Only no warning siren had sounded, and there would be no blast. The calamity raining down on Kiev was as silent as it was invisible and more frightening than bombs because there was nowhere to hide.

Walking through Minska Station, Larysa passed several people draped in hats and long coats, now a commonplace sight. Reflexively touching the top of her head, she shuddered, picturing radioactive particles dusting her hair and penetrating her scalp. She hurried to a milk shop west of Tymoshenko. At the entrance, she encountered a man, woman, and three young children huddled close together, their clothes wrapped in plastic and their faces obscured by kerchiefs. The store had neither condensed milk nor bottled milk. Panic had set in across the city, and the store shelves were denuded of canned goods. She tried a milk shop two blocks north of Katya's school, but the shelves there were bare as well. Fleeing the empty shop, she rushed home.

Climbing the stairs, Larysa tried to think of something she could cook that would be safe for her children to eat. She reached the third-floor landing breathless. A pan of water sat beside Nina's door, and three pairs of shoes stood against the wall. Larysa slipped out of her pumps and entered their flat. Dmitry and Katya were already home. Instead of poring over his textbooks, his usual habit after school, Dmitry was chasing Katya.

"The monster will get you!" He growled, spreading his fingers like claws and lunging after Katya. His little sister was the one person who could still be counted on to stir the child in Dmitry. She ran from him, shrieking, then erupting in giggles. The scowl painted on his face since their argument over Easter eggs had vanished, and his eyes betrayed an innocence Larysa hadn't seen in months.

"We don't have to go to school anymore!" he crowed.

"Who told you?"

"Our teachers. They're letting school out and opening summer camps. Do you think I'll be able to get a place at Artek early?"

Most Soviet children attended Pioneer camps, beginning in June, when school ordinarily let out. The Artek camp in Crimea was the most prestigious in the USSR, with three swimming pools, a film studio, and a stadium that seated 7,000 people.

"I don't know." Larysa knelt on the kitchen floor in front of the sink and retrieved a chipped porcelain basin from the cupboard. "Could you step into the hall and take off your shoes, Mitya? You too, Katyenka." She filled the basin with water. "We're supposed to wipe our shoes with a wet rag before coming inside."

The children followed Larysa into the hall.

"Why do we have to wash our shoes?" Dmitry asked.

"Same reason they're letting school out early, I suppose. Particles of radiation must be drifting here from Chernobyl, collecting on the streets. Go back inside. I'll take care of your shoes."

Larysa wiped Katya's buckle shoes, wringing the rag out frequently in the bowl, then swabbed down Dmitry's loafers and her pumps. Once the shoes were clean, she lifted the basin slowly, as if it contained nitroglycerin. Terrified of spilling the radioactive water, she carried the basin to the sink and slowly poured it down the drain. She dropped the wet rag into a paper bag and deposited it in the trash, though she couldn't imagine how any of this would protect her family. She worried about radiation clinging to her hands. And what about their clothes? Should she have the children put on clean clothes? She poured fresh water into the basin, carried it to the hallway, then dashed back to the sink and scrubbed her hands with soap until her skin smarted.

As she was drying her hands, the phone rang. She picked up and was greeted by Maria.

"You don't know how good it is to hear your voice, Maria." In a matter of hours, Larysa had seen her familiar world transformed into a nightmarish landscape where the lives of the people she loved were threatened in ways she couldn't grasp.

Larysa and Maria exchanged notes on the milk ban and the planned evacuation of Kiev's children.

"Ministry of Health officials have decided to evacuate nearly all the city's children. They're stepping up preparations at the camps to receive kids two weeks early. Students who are taking their eighth-year test will have to stay for that, they're saying. I think they're planning to evacuate pregnant women and mothers with children seven and younger."

"Katya turns eight in August. Do you think we'll be sent somewhere?"

"I don't know. They're emptying sanatoria and taking over hotels to make room. You've heard we're not supposed to hang laundry on the balcony?"

"No, I hadn't heard that. I suppose radioactive particles must be falling everywhere. I want to get Katya and Dmitry out of this city. How I regret not acting sooner. Is Ilya leaving school right away?"

"Yes, I have a cousin on a farm east of Moscow. He's offered to take Ilya and my sister and Natasha. Iryna got train tickets. They're leaving tomorrow morning. I would go with them, but I have to teach until school officially closes. What do you plan to do?"

"Vasyl's going to call his sister in Saratov. Her place is cramped, but they'll find room for Dmitry and Katya. My mother is in Magadan, but I'm reluctant to send Katya that far—although maybe it's the best idea, to get as far away as possible."

"Siberia may finally be good for something." Maria started laughing. Larysa joined in, laughing until tears streamed down her cheeks. Their laughter died suddenly, as unexpectedly as it had begun.

"It will be good for my niece to get away and take her mind off her dog. She refuses to go to school here, you know." Maria lowered her voice. "A boy called her radioactive and told her not to sit near him."

"How cruel."

"It's not possible for a child to take in radiation and contaminate others, is it?"

"No, I don't think so." Larysa tried to reassure Maria, but she had no confidence that she understood anything about this radiation from Chernobyl and what it might do to people.

An hour later, Vasyl entered the flat in his stocking feet carrying two bottles of water. He went to the phone to call his sister. Eva offered to take Dmitry until the start of his Pioneer camp and Katya for as long as needed.

"I can't thank you enough, Eva. I'll buy tickets first thing in the morning and call you with their arrival time," Vasyl told his sister.

The idea of traveling on their own to Saratov put Dmitry and Katya in high spirits. The journey took more than a day and night, with a change of trains in Moscow, and they wouldn't have to go to school the next morning. While they chattered about their cousins and the train trip, Vasyl hauled two suitcases from the closet and worked to make them functional. He cleaned a large suitcase for Dmitry and jiggered for an hour with the lock mechanism. Unable to make the lock of the smaller suitcase stay closed, he found a cord to loop through the handles.

Long after everyone went to bed, Larysa stood in the kitchen folding garments to carry Dmitry and Katya for several weeks. When she finished packing them in the suitcases with books and toys, she poured a glass of wine and sat on the sofa. Staring out the French doors into the blackness, it occurred to her that she and Vasyl had been too busy making arrangements for Dmitry and Katya to talk about when they could take leave from work.

It was past midnight when Larysa crawled into bed. She shut her eyes, but sleep would not come. Thinking about the shoes outside their door, she wondered how many radioactive particles the four of them had already tracked across their flat. How many particles had lodged in their lungs? She got up to check their bedroom window. Vasyl had cracked it an inch to allow in a breeze. She shut it tight. She returned to bed but couldn't get comfortable. She felt distant from herself, as though a sheer curtain had dropped between the life she used to know and this foreign world where an enemy she could not see imperiled everyone she held dear.

When she closed her eyes, Larysa saw the haunted faces of families encased in plastic and children in dark coats scurrying like shadows under white pear blossoms luminous in the sun. Vasyl mumbled in his sleep and flipped over on his side. She pulled the cover up to her chin and turned on her side, spooning her husband to still her shivering. Overcome by exhaustion, she fell into a shallow sleep.

❧

Vasyl slipped out of bed and dressed quietly. Forgoing his usual glass of tea, he stepped into the hall. While he was putting on his shoes, Nina emerged from her flat wearing a stylish summer dress and heels.

"We're on our way to Danya's mother's, outside Piter," Nina said as her husband pushed a suitcase into the hall. "Thank you again for your help with Olena. The doctor believes she should recover with no lasting effects."

"That's wonderful!" Vasyl waved to his neighbors and hurried down the stairs. Outside the air was warm, and the streets were congested. He boarded the train at Minska and changed at October Revolution Square for the line to Vokzalna Station.

Getting off the metro, he joined a river of people streaming into the railway station. His heart sank as he squeezed into the lobby and surveyed the crush of humanity pressing toward the ticket windows. Children wedged against parents holding crying babies. The air smelled of cigarettes, sweat, and sour milk. Scuffles erupted, as people tried to get close to the windows. Shoving proved futile, however, as no one was moving. Word made it back to Vasyl's position that no tickets were to be had leaving Kiev to anywhere. He stood amongst the crowd, hoping the information was wrong, waiting for a miracle.

"There's not a seat on a train to Moscow until mid-June," a despondent man called to a thin woman surrounded by children.

"What about planes?" the woman asked when the man reached her side. He picked up one of their children, who had started crying, and tapped the child's back.

"Same. Flights out of Kiev are booked."

"There are three people wanting tickets for every train seat leaving Kiev," an elderly woman standing near Vasyl muttered, addressing no one in particular.

Vasyl grew agitated as the reality of his situation sank in. His wife and children, the loves of his life, were trapped in this city inhaling radioactive fumes, drinking contaminated milk and water. He recalled with regret the conversation he'd overheard on the balcony on May Day. He remembered how the hairs had stood up on his arms at the mention of a radioactive cloud blowing over Kiev. But later he had questioned the idea that an invisible cloud from the nuclear plant could pose a deadly threat to people here.

Like everyone in the Soviet Union, certainly everyone in his generation, born after the Great Patriotic War, he knew about fallout from nuclear weapons. He had viewed photographs of the horrors wrought by the atom bombs America had dropped on Hiroshima and Nagasaki. Like his classmates, Vasyl had come of age fearing a nuclear holocaust and hoping that the leaders of his country and America would avoid an exchange of nuclear weapons. During bomb drills in the 1950s, he used to file downstairs with the other pupils to a stocked air raid shelter under his school.

But no one had ever warned him about radiation dangers from the peaceful atom, as nuclear power was called. He had never heard of a mishap at a Soviet nuclear power station. Still, why hadn't he followed his instincts when he heard that conversation on the balcony? He should have called his sister the next morning. He would have been able to procure tickets then, ahead of the masses trying to get to Moscow and points beyond now.

His mind raced for options. If he had a car, he could drive his family hundreds of miles east and sleep under the stars in the forest, but he had not been able to buy one. His name had been on the trade union list for years, and Mikhail assured him this year would be his time for a car. Little good that promise did now, he thought, anger roiling in his chest like hot lava.

Looking around at the anxious families, he could see that he was not the only person who had waited too long to act, but this gave him no comfort. After spending half an hour in the melee, Vasyl threaded his way back to the metro. He decided to call Larysa from the print shop. They had one remaining avenue that might offer a chance to get their children out of Kiev, he realized, and that was her uncle. Given Anatoly Kulyk's rank as a leading scientist and his stature in the Party, Vasyl held out hope that he would be able to obtain tickets to Saratov for his niece's children. Surely, the authorities must have kept seats available for top officials who needed to travel from Kiev to Moscow.

Vasyl got off the metro at October Revolution Square, figuring it would take twenty minutes to walk from there to work. He hurried along the sidewalk and dashed across intersections. However, three blocks from the print shop, pedestrians were stopped by a truck stationed in the road. Hoses from the truck were shooting arcs of water to the top stories of the buildings. Sudsy scum gushed down the brick and stone facades, collecting in puddles and running along the curbstone.

"Now they're washing radiation off buildings," a man in front of Vasyl muttered to his companion. "How do you wash this shit out of your lungs?"

"For that, you need vodka," the man answered.

Once the trucks rumbled on, the crowd lunged forward. Vasyl sprinted the rest of the way to work and called Larysa to tell her the trains were full. She responded as he knew she would.

Larysa dialed her uncle's laboratory. His secretary answered after several rings.

"May I speak to Dr. Kulyk please? This is his niece, Larysa."

"He is in a meeting. I will give him the message that you called when he returns. What is your number?" The woman exuded efficiency but no warmth.

"Please tell him it's urgent," Larysa said after reciting her phone number.

Leaden minutes passed with no call from her uncle. She made breakfast for Dmitry and Katya, who milled about the kitchen looking glum. They were crushed that their father could not buy train tickets for them. Dmitry asked if he could go visit Ilya.

"No, he's on the train with his aunt and Natasha. They have relatives on a farm east of Moscow."

"Ilya's aunt got train tickets, and Papa can't? Why not?" Dmitry glowered. Larysa had no answer. How could she tell him the truth: that she and Vasyl had waited too long while other parents had been wiser and acted quickly?

Katya wanted to play with her tilting dolls, but they were packed. She pleaded with her mother to open the suitcase, but Larysa had spent considerable time getting it shut tight and was in no mood to fiddle with the knot. Both children said they would rather be at school than stay home with nothing to do, but she didn't want them to go outside.

Larysa opened *The New England Journal of Medicine*. She tried to pick up the translation where she'd left off but found herself reading the same paragraph over and over without comprehension. Closing the journal, she went to the kitchen to make soup from bottled water, potatoes, and green onions. The children ate sullenly.

She persevered until mid-afternoon. Unable to bear the tension any longer, Larysa placed a second call to her uncle.

"This is Larysa Marchenko, Anatoly Kulyk's niece. I called this morning and left a message, but he has not returned my call."

"He has not returned. I can assure you he will receive both your first message and this one when he returns," the secretary stated.

"This is an emergency." Larysa fought back tears.

"Could you leave a more specific message?" the woman asked, her tone harsh.

Larysa hesitated. She wanted to talk to her uncle privately. She didn't want this cold woman to know that she was seeking a personal favor, yet she was desperate to get Katya and Dmitry out of Kiev. She had no choice but to state her request.

"Please tell him his niece needs two train tickets to Saratov. They are for my children. He will understand. I will give you my number again."

The secretary interrupted her. "Comrade Kulyk will receive your messages. There is no need to repeat your number."

"Do you know when he'll return?"

"I cannot give you that information." The secretary hung up.

Larysa pressed the phone to her ear long after the line went dead.

8
WASHINGTON, MAY 1990

Vickie stepped into the brass elevator in the Press Building lobby and rode to the sixth floor. The eleven-story building provided office space for correspondents covering Congress and the White House for their hometown newspapers or newspaper chains. Some of these Washington bureaus consisted of a sole reporter working in a tiny, windowless room. Other bureaus bulged with dozens of correspondents. Newhart fell somewhere in the middle. Opening the frosted glass door stenciled with Newhart News in black letters, she looked across the room filled with men hunched over computers. The air smelled of stale coffee and after shave cologne and was charged with the hum of low-register voices and banging teletype machines—a sensory jumble she found inexplicably soothing.

She glanced at the newspapers fanned across the reception

counter. The headline above the fold of the *Newark Post*, the chain's highest circulation paper, trumpeted Gabe Green's story: "US Hostages Released in Lebanon." She was tempted to thumb through the neat display of newspapers to look for her story but resisted. Sean always heaped a pile of papers for the reporters on a table by the wall where he hung long strips of wire copy. She headed straight for that table without stopping at her desk to change out of her sneakers.

The *Long Beach Tribune* and *Santa Barbara Journal*, the second-highest and third-highest circulation papers Newhart owned, sat atop the piles. She picked up the *Santa Barbara Journal* and began flipping through it. The front page had Gabe's hostage release story and Cynthia's feature on the First Lady. Page three carried a big splash on a California water project. When she turned to page five, her heart stopped. The headline popped off the page: "'Hot Snow' Found at South Pole," by Victoria Evans. Her story had been cut by nearly half, but it was there, in print. The *Long Beach Tribune* ran her story on page seven. The *Syracuse Post-Dispatch*, Newhart's only New York newspaper, and the *Rockford Times*, the sole Illinois paper, featured it on page six. Her story appeared near the back of both New Jersey newspapers, the *Newark Post* and *Seaside Press-Mail*. The *Harrisburg Star-Ledger* in Pennsylvania gave it top billing on page three. *That makes seven for eight,* she mused, rifling through the pile for a copy of the *Allentown Courier*, the company's lowest circulation paper, also in Pennsylvania. She didn't see the story inside, but when she refolded the paper, it leapt out at her from below the fold on the front page.

"Slow news day, huh?" Gabe snickered, peeking over Vickie's shoulder.

Vickie looked at him confused, then laughed as she got his joke. He picked up the *Santa Barbara Journal* and strolled back to his desk. If she were at home, she would jump up and down with her daughter. They'd high-five and shout, "Yes!" Her celebration with Molly would come later, but here in the newsroom she acted as understated as Gabe. She brought a copy of the *Long Beach Tribune* to her desk and read through the story in print. Thane had cut most of the material on the history of above-ground nuclear testing, but she had a byline story.

Putting the paper down, she noticed the message light on her phone glowing red. She punched in her extension, and a reedy voice came on. "Hi, Victoria. This is Darren Cunningham at State returning your call. Sorry to be so late getting back to you. I was tied up in a meeting. I'd be happy to talk to you about nuclear weapons testing. Give me a call, and let's see if we can find a time for lunch. Oh, and please say hello to Ian for me. Bye for now."

Yesterday, Vickie had been anxious for the State Department official to return her call, but she hadn't given him another thought after she'd filed her story. Had he not left such a sincere message, she might have forgotten about him altogether. His voice sounded so inviting, she replayed the message, pleased that an important government official had offered to meet her for lunch. Who knew what juicy stories she might be able to coax from him?

Moments later, Alan Graves rang saying he wanted to see her. Vickie stood up and fastened her suit jacket buttons. She walked to the back of the newsroom, passing Gabe, who was engrossed in a call. Taking a deep breath to calm her nerves, she rapped on Alan's door. His steady voice invited her in. He peered at her above oval wire rims, gesturing to the chair facing his desk. A soft-spoken man with silver hair brushing his temples, he was wearing a navy vest and red-print tie over a starched white shirt. Unlike Thane, Alan never barked out imperious orders. Reporters worked their hearts out to please him out of respect.

Easing into the chair, she noticed the *Newark Post* on his desk, opened to her story—a good sign, she thought. Sunlight streamed through a window to her right. Framed architectural prints of New York City's Chrysler Building and Flat Iron hung on the wall beside his desk. His office felt serene, an oasis from the chaotic activity unfolding in the shadows racing across his frosted glass door.

Thinking back to her first day of work, Vickie recalled Alan sending her to the Dirksen Building to get her congressional press credentials, which she needed to cover a Senate vote. "I'm afraid it will be baptism by fire for you," he had apologized, promising to give her proper introductions the following day. Of course, news was breaking on the Hill the next morning, and the morning after that. By the end of the week, she had settled into her desk beside Jeff Hodges and found the supply closet on her own.

"It looks like the E-team is starting to take shape," he began. "It's taking time, but energy and environment are complicated beats." He formed a steeple with his fingers in front of his face and leaned his lips into them. "I want to see you develop the energy beat. You should be trying to take a source to lunch once or twice a week."

Vickie nodded. She had been joining low-level EPA and Energy Department staffers for lunch religiously although none of them had tossed any real news her way. They mostly pitched her fluff about minor achievements at their agencies. She'd also had lunch with two congressional staffers in the Longworth cafeteria. They did a lot of name-dropping but gave her nothing of substance.

"The Earth Matters sections you've been helping Thane and Jeff put together are selling newspapers like funnel cakes at a county fair," he continued.

"That's good to hear." Vickie smiled. Warmed by a rush of nostalgia, she remembered crunching the sweet fried dough while visiting livestock stalls with Molly at the Monroe County fair. Most of the reporters she'd met in Washington seemed to be from the Northeast. She wondered if Alan might be a Midwesterner.

"I haven't seen enough of these from you, though." He lifted the newspaper and snapped two fingers against her hot snow story with a crack that made her jump.

Her smile faded. She met his gaze, dreading the worst. He was going to fire her.

"The reason for our three-month probation is so we can get a sense of how a candidate who looks good on paper will work out—and you get to see if the job suits you." Alan leaned back in his chair.

Vickie's mouth went dry, and her lip started to quiver. She knew he was going to let her go. At this point, all she could do was concentrate on not crying.

"I know it's challenging starting out here with no contacts," he continued. "I've decided to give you another six months of probation. I want you to work on cultivating sources. I expect you to generate more of your own stories, but don't let up on your work for Thane."

A cavernous silence filled the room.

"Do you have any questions?" His brisk tone signaled an end to their meeting.

Vickie didn't know what to say. She felt sick about failing to make the grade but relieved that Alan wasn't firing her. He was giving her a second chance. He relished the idea that his E-team seemed to be functioning smoothly, so bashing Thane would be idiotic. Whether she liked him or not, he was editor of the special reports that were making the chain money.

"I'm really eager to develop the energy beat." She swallowed hard. Standing to leave his office, she dedicated herself to meeting Alan's expectations.

"So?" Gabe glanced up as Vickie passed in front of his desk.

"I'm hanging on. He's giving me six months to write more stories."

"Got any lunch plans?"

"I'm heading to the Senate. I'm tied up all day."

"A drink after work, then?"

She immediately declined. Molly was old enough to walk home by herself, and they lived only five minutes from the school. Still, Vickie wouldn't feel right socializing downtown with Gabe after work while her daughter sat home alone. She returned to her desk to call Darren Cunningham. She was desperate to cultivate sources, and he might prove useful. Maybe she could get him to tip her off to an international treaty on nuclear waste or wildlife issues. Or he might have an Energy Department colleague he could refer her to for a story. As she was about to pick up the phone, Thane appeared in front of her desk.

"Do you have anything more on recycling and landfill legislation?" Thane asked. He didn't mention her hot snow story.

"I'm getting ready to head to the Hill." Vickie reached for her bag. "I'm talking to a Senate Environment Committee staffer today. Then I'll stop by the EPA."

"Don't forget the EPA Science Advisory Board meeting from two to five. If they say anything worth dropping into the briefs, call me.

Vickie could see her day filling up without a story. Somehow, she would have to find her own leads and keep Thane from monopolizing her time. On her way down to the lobby, she realized that she had forgotten to pack her tape recorder and a copy of the *Newark Post* to show Molly. She rode back up to the sixth floor. As she was stashing her cassette recorder in her bag, she noticed the red light on her phone. She picked up and heard a second message from Darren Cunningham, again offering a lunchtime interview. She called him back, but he didn't answer.

"It's Victoria Evans at Newhart News returning your call. You're it," she told his message machine. What a crazy game of telephone tag with a government official she'd never seen, Vickie mused, as she ducked into the elevator. Still, if he wanted to meet her for lunch, she was willing to keep up the chase for as long as it took.

9

WASHINGTON, MAY 1990

Finding energy or landfill news that rose above the level of back-page filler was turning out to be harder than Vickie could have imagined. Despite spending hours talking to the aides and interns who seemed to run Congress and taking a mid-level Energy Department staffer to lunch, she hadn't broken a news story in three weeks. She was hoping her interview with a coal industry executive would yield a story on how "global warming hysteria"—his words—would jack up U.S. electricity prices.

"Shit," she said, listening to her messages.

"Good morning to you, too. What happened?" asked Jeff, grinning.

"The coal guy I was supposed to interview supposedly got called away—probably to the shore for the long weekend."

"Bummer. Have you noticed how the demise of the Cold War

is crowding out the rest of the news? I mean, what kind of travesty is this? Microsoft releases Windows three, and they bury my story on page twelve beside the jump from Ian's front-page story on a presidential election in Romania." Jeff put down the newspaper and gulped his coffee. "Nothing against Ian—he's flying in from Germany this afternoon for the Bush-Gorbachev Summit, by the way. But I guarantee you nine out of ten Americans could not locate Romania on a map to save their first-born child."

When Vickie told Thane that her interview with the coal executive had fallen through, he sent her to the EPA to cover a day-long meeting on disposable diapers. She returned to the newsroom in the afternoon to write her story, "Babies Produce a Ton of Poop." As an EPA staffer had told her, each baby using disposable diapers for two years generates 2,000 pounds of garbage. This plastic-wrapped poop will persist in landfills for hundreds, even thousands of years. Disposable diapers convert fecal matter from biodegradable waste into a toxic substance that will last essentially forever.

Vickie filed her poop story at five o'clock. It was not the most dignified of topics, but she had made it interesting and somewhat humorous. In any event, she was happy it gave her another byline.

Ian Hoffman made his entrance to the newsroom at half past five. Originally from Los Angeles, he had gone thoroughly expat. His tailored sports jacket, tasseled loafers, and leather shoulder bag gave him a decidedly European look. His hair was trimmed, in contrast to the shaggy look sported by most of the guys in the newsroom. He was tall with a freckled boyish face that pared a decade off his forty-three years. As he made the rounds, reporters stood to shake his hand, treating him like a demi-god, except for

Gabe. In a pointed snub, Gabe kept typing when Ian approached his desk.

Ian stopped by Jeff's desk, and Jeff introduced Vickie to him. She was surprised and flattered when Ian asked her to join a handful of friends at the Childe Harold for drinks after work. Since Molly was going to a sleep-over at her best friend's house, Vickie agreed at once.

At six, Vickie walked to the metro with Jeff. On their short ride to Dupont Circle, she asked him if he knew what was going on between Gabe and Ian.

"Gabe's pissed that Alan brought Ian over to cover the big summit," Jeff said. "He sees Europe as Ian's turf and the State Department as his. Gabe also would kill his own mother to be a foreign correspondent. He was furious when Alan gave Ian that spot in Germany. I'm pretty sure that's what's eating him."

The Childe Harold occupied the basement of a brick townhouse across from the Dupont Circle Station escalator. Vickie followed Jeff downstairs, where young professionals milled four-deep around the bar, smoking and laughing. Ian motioned to them from a table along an exposed brick wall.

"Terrific, you made it! You know Jeff Hodges, right? This is Victoria Evans," Ian said, introducing them to three people already seated at the table. "Steve Richards with UP, Frank Richter with *The Herald*, and Frank's wife Gretchen," Ian told Jeff and Vickie.

"How's Berlin treating you?" asked Jeff, settling into a chair beside Vickie.

"Incredible. It's supercharged. You can feel the energy walking around." Ian flagged the waiter. "We'll have another pitcher and glass here."

Jeff joined the beer drinkers, while Vickie ordered a gin and tonic. She listened to the five people around the table animatedly comparing Bonn and Berlin to other European cities where they'd lived. After finishing her drink in silence, she got up the nerve to enter the conversation.

"Were you there the night the Wall fell?" Vickie asked Ian. She'd been stunned when news broke that East Germans were ripping down the Berlin Wall, which had stood as an ominous symbol of the bipolar world. She had never expected to see it dismantled in her lifetime.

"He was," Jeff answered for Ian. "He convinced Alan to relocate our office from Bonn to West Berlin in October, a month before the Wall fell, if you can believe that."

"Tell us, Ian, is it true they opened the Wall by accident?" asked Gretchen.

Ian poured beer and launched into a description of the momentous event.

"Possibly. A bureaucrat at a press conference was describing new, liberalized travel regulations for East Germans wanting to visit West Germany. Someone asked when the new policy would enter into force. The bureaucrat looked confused, like he wasn't sure. After drawing a blank, he responded that it would take effect right away. One of the wire guys ran to the phone, and the report went out on the telly." Ian paused, chugging from his mug. "When hundreds of people converged on the gates, the police weren't sure what to do. One of them opened the gates—and there was no going back."

Frank motioned for the waiter to bring menus. After they ordered sandwiches and another round of drinks, Ian picked up where he'd left off.

"It was amazing to see Ossies walking and driving freely into West Berlin. Wessies were giving Ossies cigarettes and bottles of champagne. Everyone was swigging the bubbly. One man I saw was wearing his night robe and bed slippers. I saw people reunited after twenty-eight years throw their arms around each other with tears running down their cheeks. People sang and danced, and in the background, all night you could hear hammers clanging away, tapping at the Wall. Every fifth person was carrying a hammer and chisel."

"Instead of a hammer and sickle," Jeff interjected, to groans around the table.

"Did you grab a chunk of the Wall?" asked Frank.

"I pocketed a piece." Ian chuckled. "Everyone did."

"They're more valuable than moon rocks now," Jeff cracked.

"Yeah, Berliners are ripping up their walks and selling pieces to tourists," Ian said.

After the waiter brought their sandwiches, Ian jumped up and motioned to a tall man with dark, wavy hair and an inquisitive face, heading toward their table. He was carrying a seasoned saddlebag briefcase, which he dropped on the floor to embrace Ian.

"Glad you could make it, my man." Ian clapped his back. "I was telling these folks about the night the Wall fell. Sit down and let me pour you a beer."

"I can only stay ten minutes," the newcomer said. Even over the din, Vickie recognized his voice, though she couldn't place him. He had a high forehead and brooding brown eyes she felt certain she would have remembered.

"Let me introduce you to everyone. You know Steve, Frank, and Gretchen. Victoria Evans and Jeff Hodges are with Newhart News." Ian pointed around the table. "I assume you all know Darren Cunningham with the State Department."

Darren's eyes locked on Vickie's. She held his gaze until his entire face erupted in a smile.

"Finally, in the flesh!" Darren reached across the table to squeeze Vickie's hand.

"We've been missing each other on the phone almost since the fall of the Berlin Wall," Vickie joked, returning Darren's smile. Everyone laughed.

"Darren has Wall stories of his own." Ian cast an admiring glance at his source.

"Actually, I was late to the party." Darren said. "I spent eight hours driving across Germany and didn't get to Berlin till morning."

"What did you find most memorable about being there?" Vickie asked him.

After a moment's reflection, Darren answered, "Watching Rostropovich play his cello in front of Checkpoint Charlie."

"Rostropovich was there? I saw him play the Dvorak cello concerto recently." Vickie was having a hard time seeing Darren Cunningham as a buttoned-down State Department negotiator. A concert pianist, maybe, but he seemed too soulful for government work.

"Yes, he was in Paris when the Wall fell, and he persuaded a friend to fly him to Berlin. I happened to be near Checkpoint Charlie when Slava and his friend arrived. Someone found him a chair, and he played Bach's Second Suite for Cello," Darren recalled. "When he finished, he told the circle of us gathered around him that he wanted to honor the lives of East Berliners who had died attempting to reach freedom."

The waiter brought another pitcher of beer, and Ian asked for a mug for Darren. Looking at his watch, Darren begged off, insisting he had to pick up his daughter.

"Sorry to run." Darren waved and got up to leave. Walking behind Vickie, he tapped her shoulder and asked for a word. She followed him to an empty space near the door.

"I didn't want to leave without talking about that lunch I promised you," Darren said.

Tipsy from too much gin, Vickie tried to project a professional image. She had wanted to make a good impression during their first meeting, as a serious journalist, like Ian.

"How about Monday?" she asked, stifling a hiccup.

"It's Memorial Day weekend, and I have my daughter, so that's out," he apologized. "On Tuesday, there's a ninety-nine percent chance I'll be pulled into the negotiations in the morning and won't emerge until June first. I'm afraid we'll have to do it after the Summit ends."

"Perfect. Good luck with the negotiations," she said, hiccupping.

Darren lifted his beat-up briefcase in Vickie's direction and rushed out the door.

"What say we wander over to the Bayou?" Frank asked when Vickie returned to the table. "There's a group playing there Gretchen and I want to hear."

Vickie took the opportunity to wish the gang a good night. She was flying high from meeting Ian Hoffman, hearing stories about the fall of the Wall, and her fortuitous encounter with Darren Cunningham. She wanted time to savor the experience and plan something special to do with Molly over the long weekend.

⤲

Molly had spent three hours squinting through the viewfinder of her prized Kodak Retina. A serious child, she tended to be single-minded in pursuit of her interests, which currently included photography and baseball. In the morning, Vickie had hiked with Molly to the embassies of Switzerland, Lebanon, Syria, and China, where she took pictures for her scrapbook. For the past hour, Molly had been stalking animals at the zoo, trying to get frontal shots of cheetahs, elephants, and gorillas.

The day had grown warm, and they were deciding whether to get in line at the ice cream concession when a man called, "Victoria?"

Vickie spun around, shocked to hear a familiar voice calling her. "Darren Cunningham?"

"I can't believe this!" they both said together, laughing.

"This is my daughter, Madeleine." Darren extended his arm toward a tall, slim girl who had his high forehead and dark, wavy hair.

"Lovely to meet you, Madeleine. This is my daughter, Molly. Small world," Vickie babbled, agog at seeing the State Department official here.

Vickie wondered how she would be able to establish herself as a professional, wearing blue jeans, a cream tee-shirt, and sandals. She was relieved that at least she had put on mascara before leaving the house. As they began talking, she relaxed. After all, it was Sunday. She was on her own time—and he was wearing a yellow polo shirt, jeans, and running shoes.

"I bump into everyone here sooner or later." Darren grinned.

"Do you live nearby?"

"On S Street, near Nineteenth, a bit of a hike, not too far."

"Don't forget it's uphill the whole way, Daddy." Madeleine gave her father a world-weary look and shifted her weight from one hip to the other.

"We walked here too," Molly told him.

"You did? Hey, that's a neat camera." Darren crouched in front of Molly. "Did you get any good pictures today?"

"It's my Dad's. He gave it to me." Molly gave Darren a run-down of the embassies and animals on the roll of film inside.

"You're interested in embassies?" Darren asked.

"I'm making a scrapbook of world embassies and their flags. I have twenty-eight so far. I want to get them all." Turning to her mother, Molly asked, "Can I get an ice cream?" Vickie nodded.

"Me too?" Madeleine asked her father.

"Sure," Darren answered, claiming an empty park bench.

Vickie sat down primly, leaving a two-foot gap between her and Darren. He leaned back, stretching out his legs. She was tempted to ask him about radiation from Chernobyl and the atom bomb tests of the 1950s but decided this was the wrong time and place.

"This is our first visit to the zoo," she said.

"Really? How is that possible?" Darren sounded incredulous.

"We moved here from Indiana during the winter. I've been promising to bring Molly since the weather got warm. We live right up Connecticut Avenue, but I've been so busy on the week-ends, we haven't made it till today."

"Ah, that explains it. Where in Indiana?"

"Bloomington. Do you come here often?"

"Oh, yeah, this is our place. We've watched some of these animals grow up." He looked adoringly in Madeleine's direction.

Darren's attentiveness touched Vickie. She remembered how Jake used to look at Molly that way—before his college teaching career cratered and he withdrew from the material world.

"See, I was embroiled in an endless custody dispute with my ex-wife." Darren turned his attention to Vickie. "She's a super high-powered attorney from a family of lawyers. It's only been in the past couple years that the court granted me joint custody. Initially, I was restricted to six-hour visits on Sundays. This is where we came. Here and the Air and Space Museum in the winter. But I must be depressing you or sounding bitter."

Darren turned from Vickie to watch the girls chatting. "Look at them giggling, like they've been best friends forever."

Darren's openness surprised Vickie. They had only just met, and he was sharing painful details of his personal life. Yet he talked so freely it seemed perfectly natural to her. His candor made her feel comfortable sharing her own feelings.

"That must have been hard for you, wanting to be a larger part of her life and being shut out. Your daughter's lucky. Molly's father visits one Sunday a month and takes her for holiday vacations. Don't get me wrong. He's up in New Jersey. I know he loves her, and she adores him. I'm not complaining, but sometimes I wish he'd get more involved."

"I don't understand fathers who don't want an equal share in raising their kids, though I guess they're common." He crooked his arm over the back of the bench and leaned toward Vickie. "Have you been on your own long?"

"Three years. How about you?"

"Double that. I've been divorced since Maddie turned seven, and she's thirteen now."

"So much has happened since I moved to DC, it feels like a lifetime." Unexpected relief washed over Vickie as they talked about their daughters. Sharing mundane details with Darren about juggling work schedules and dealing with exes made her feel lighter.

The girls returned licking fudge bars.

"We're stopping by the cheetahs on our way out." Darren gestured toward Connecticut Avenue.

"We're heading to see the seals." Vickie pointed to the path behind them.

"It was great seeing you, Victoria. I'll call you after the Summit to set up that lunch," Darren promised.

"Did you like Maddie?" Vickie asked Molly, as they followed the path to the marine mammals.

"Yeah, she's nice. Her father seems really nice. I want to come to the zoo with Dad next time he visits." Molly looked up at Vickie.

"That's a fabulous idea, Sweetie. He's coming in two weeks. You can take him all around the zoo then." Vickie felt a pang of sorrow for her daughter. It pained her that Molly seemed fated to have the same solitary childhood she'd had. Vickie had been determined to make sure that would not happen. She'd dreamed of having a house noisy with children, but for whatever reason, she had not been blessed with another child. The one thing Vickie could control, she thought, was how she handled the curve balls life lobbed at them. She renewed her vow to be an emotional rock for Molly and to make her childhood a happy one.

The seals and sea lions scudded along the rocky ledge of their pool on flipper feet with their noses poking straight up, then plunged into the deep, turquoise water, showing off their acrobatics. Vickie and Molly marveled at their shiny coats and laughed at their croaky barks.

"I only have one picture left." Molly backed up, squinting through the viewfinder, then inched forward slowly before snapping a shot of an adorable seal with large, liquid brown eyes.

"Dad will love the seals, don't you think?" Molly asked as they started their climb home.

"Yes, I think you two will have a great time here." Drawing her close, Vickie draped both arms around Molly's shoulders, wrapping her in enough love, she hoped, for two parents.

10

WASHINGTON, JUNE 1990

Vickie was writing about a technology agreement Bush and Gorbachev had reached during the Summit when Gareth Will called. She kept her contact with Gareth quiet because Thane had dismissed him as a kook. But she found him to be a credible source of information. He had connections in the international anti-nuclear community, and he had tipped her off to her first byline story. She wasn't about to brush him off.

"I've got something huge. The Irish energy board is coming out with a report saying sheep are still contaminated with radioactive cesium from Chernobyl," Gareth boomed. "And get this. The radioactivity is higher now than it was in 1988. You know what that means? They can't slaughter their sheep for market."

"That does sound interesting. Do you have something you can fax me?" Ireland was far afield, but Vickie had learned that

Chernobyl stories could transcended national borders.

"Not yet. I can give you the number of a guy at the Irish energy board willing to talk."

"First hot snow, now hot sheep," Vickie joked, prompting a guffaw from Gareth.

Thane was at a press conference, so Vickie told Jeff about the radioactive sheep.

"I'm not sure this is a story for us, but why don't you look into it," Jeff said. Fallout had her name on it now, apparently.

She called Gareth's contact in Ireland, where it was late afternoon. While he sounded squirrely about divulging information, the official did confirm that the sheep surveyed were more radioactive in 1989 than in 1988. He promised to fax Vickie a copy of the final report when it became available.

Vickie called Darren Cunningham, hoping he could give her some background. When he asked if she could meet him at the Tabard Inn on N Street in an hour, she was thrilled. She finished her Summit story and hailed a cab.

Entering the Tabard Inn, Vickie walked past an old-fashioned check-in counter and through a narrow corridor that opened to a dimly lit lounge. Her eyes adjusted slowly as she took in an eclectic assortment of overstuffed sofas and armchairs.

"Over here!" Darren waved from a sofa in front of a fireplace. When she made it to the couch, he got up and began giving her a European greeting. He leaned forward to kiss her cheek, but she extended her hand, American business style. He pulled back to shake her hand as she leaned forward to kiss his cheek. They ended up doing neither and broke into laughter at the clumsiness of it all. Vickie followed him past the bar, where he asked the hostess for a table outdoors. They walked through the dining room, which led to a secluded garden with wrought iron tables. It was an archetypal June day, warm with a brilliant azure sky. A mild breeze rippled through the red flowers growing along the enclosure's brick walls.

"This is lovely, a secret hideaway." Vickie felt like she'd left the city and dropped into a village in Tuscany or Provence.

"Isn't it? Don't tell anyone about it. This is my favorite restaurant. They serve only a few items each day, and they're always superlative."

They ordered curried carrot soup, crab cakes, and pickled zucchini. Darren asked for a glass of white wine. Vickie didn't usually drink at lunch, but she followed suit and joined him.

In her limited experience, lunches with potential new sources generally started with small talk about the weather, the traffic, and where each person lived. Next, backgrounds were swapped, brief descriptions of how they came to their current occupations and where they grew up—the usual cocktail banter aimed at discovering common interests. By this point, each person had sized the other up and sensed whether the potential existed for a mutually rewarding relationship. Trust and credibility had to be established. It also helped if there was a semblance, if not a genuine spark, of enjoyment in each other's company. She and Darren had already met each other's daughters and shared personal details that ordinarily didn't come up with a would-be source until much later—if ever. What Vickie wanted to do now was establish a solid work relationship, but she wasn't sure how to start.

Darren eliminated her confusion by jumping right into the subject of hot sheep. "So Irish officials are finding sheep still too contaminated to eat?"

"I think so. The final report isn't out yet." Vickie told him that the Irish had surveyed 25,000 sheep in 1989 and found them more radioactive than in 1988. "The official I talked to promised to fax me the report when it's finalized."

"I'll be interested to see that. Could you fax me a copy when you get it?"

Vickie agreed, delighted to be able to pass this on to Darren. Now he might give her a heads up on something important.

"Why do you suppose the sheep contain more radioactive cesium than they did the previous year? How did radiation from Chernobyl get into Irish sheep, and why has it persisted this long?" she asked, reaching into her bag for her tape recorder. "What levels of cesium are dangerous? And what happens if people eat meat from the sheep? As you can see, I know almost nothing about radiation in the environment."

"Lots of questions. It would take hours to do justice to them. Let's start with how the radiocesium from Chernobyl got into Irish sheep and go from there."

"Is it all right if I tape?"

"Of course," Darren answered. Vickie hit the record button.

When the Chernobyl reactor exploded on April 26, 1986, Darren explained, millions of curies of radioactive particles and aerosols shot into the atmosphere. The reactor continued to burn, releasing massive levels of radiation for ten days. Winds carried debris from Chernobyl great distances.

"There have been several studies on the spread of fallout from Chernobyl around the globe—and as many different findings. I place most credence in a study done by the Energy Department.

DOE estimated that one million curies of cesium-137 fell on the Soviet Union, one million fell on Europe, and another million spread across the rest of the Northern Hemisphere. Countries that received high levels have tried to limit people's exposure to radioactive cesium in food," he explained. "Now, you need to understand that radioactive particles don't settle evenly across the landscape. There are hot spots where radiation is high enough that vegetables and meat could be harmful for people to eat, yet nearby, the soil may be only lightly contaminated."

"Where were hot spots found?"

"The region around Gavle, Sweden, was contaminated when rainstorms on April 28th and 29th brought fallout down on the land. Areas around Munich in Germany saw heavy depositions following severe rainstorms from April 29th through May 2nd. Strong rains also pounded Ireland, Scotland, and Northern Ireland on May 2nd and 3rd as the Chernobyl cloud passed over the UK."

"So, areas in Sweden, Germany, and the UK where it didn't rain while the Chernobyl fallout was passing overhead were never badly contaminated?" Vickie asked.

"Exactly! That's what researchers found when they measured cesium on the ground. That's also the pattern for fallout from atom bombs detonated by the U.S. government in the Fifties and Sixties, which we'll get into—after I finish my soup."

Darren leaned over and slurped his soup until his bowl was empty. Watching him eat, a picture she once saw of Glenn Gould hunched over the keyboard popped into Vickie's head.

"Has anyone ever mentioned you look a bit like Glenn Gould?" she asked him.

"Sure, people tell me that all the time," he deadpanned. "No, no one's ever compared me to the great Glenn Gould, so I'll take it as a compliment. I used to play the piano, but I realized my freshman year of college that I lacked talent, which is how I ended up in government work. You're interested in classical music?"

"I love it. I bought a season ticket to the National Symphony for next year," Vickie answered, pleased to have her intuition about Darren playing the piano proven correct.

The waitress cleared their bowls and brought the main course.

"You mentioned that studies showed different measurements. Why is that? I mean, shouldn't scientists all come up with the same measurements?" Vickie asked.

"You would think so, but there's very little straightforward about radiation studies. In the case of fallout from U.S. above-ground testing, for instance, Atomic Energy Commission scientists had a lock on information and kept most of what they knew secret from doctors and scientists who worked outside the AEC. In the 1950s the AEC published pamphlets insisting that fallout from atom bomb blasts would not harm Americans. Doctors who dared to challenge that assertion were painted as unpatriotic."

Darren held up his empty glass when the waitress passed by and looked at Vickie. She nodded.

"The Soviets have kept information about the effects of fallout secret from their people, too," Darren added. "Basically, you've had the world's two nuclear powers downplaying health effects of low levels of radiation so they could keep testing nuclear weapons and building nuclear power plants."

"But aren't there some objective studies?" Vickie pressed.

"Sure, acute radiation is well understood from studying

Hiroshima and Nagasaki bombing victims, who received massive external doses of radiation all at once. What we don't know much about are non-lethal doses. Is a tiny bit of radiation harmless? What level is safe? How many x-rays are safe? How much radiation will lead to cancer in adults? What about in infants or in the fetus? Is a full-body exposure more, or less, harmful than a concentrated exposure to one organ? These are the kinds of questions scientists have spent decades studying—and you'll find a range of conclusions."

Vickie was beginning to see how complicated and controversial this issue was, and why Darren said it would take hours to answer her questions.

"You mentioned you're from Indiana?" Darren asked, shifting gears.

"I spent most of my childhood in Indiana." Ordinarily, Vickie would have left it there, but she felt moved to share more with him. "I was actually born in Troy, New York," she added, entering territory she generally skirted.

"Troy?" Darren bounced forward, as if she had named an exotic city like Kathmandu. "I never run into anyone from Troy. Perhaps you know about the fallout, then."

"No, what fallout?"

"You're probably too young. There was an infamous incident after a bomb test in April 1953."

"I was born in 1952, but my memories of Troy are pretty sketchy. I moved to Santa Claus, Indiana, when I was eight."

"Santa Claus, for real?"

"Oh yes. Hoosiers are hokey but also honest and Midwest nice."

"Nothing to apologize for there. Are you an only child?"

"No, I had a younger brother who died when I was seven." Vickie paused to take a sip of wine, which was helping dissolve her usual reserve. "I know him mostly from pictures, though I have a few hazy memories. Same with my Dad. He died a year after Paul."

"My God, that must have been unbelievably hard for you and your mom. How in the world did your mother cope?"

"Oh, she found her own way to muddle through. Doctors prescribed uppers and downers and gave her electroshock therapy. She was transferred from one hospital to another," Vickie answered, offering details about her family she never divulged. "She bowed out of the picture not long after my aunt took me to live with her in Indiana. Six years later, when I was fourteen, she took up with a guy she met during her last hospital stay. By then she'd been zapped with so many electroshock treatments, any memory she had of her old self was long gone. That's what my aunt believed. She even changed her name—from Margaret to Susan."

Vickie paused. She absently traced circles on the table with the base of her wine glass. Darren watched her, waiting for more. "She traveled out West with him in his camper. For a while, my mother sent us postcards, signed Susan. The last one came from Yellowstone. Old Faithful, ironic, huh? After that, she disappeared."

"My God!" Darren leaned forward. "Tell me, were you and your aunt ever able to find her?"

Vickie shook her head. "We tried, but there were few leads. The wild West was wilder then. My aunt dipped into her savings and hired a detective. Even he came up empty. We didn't know her last name, or if she was still going by Susan. We had no idea where she had settled. At some point, we realized that if she ever wanted to get in touch with us, she would. Then in my senior year of high school we received a box in the mail postmarked from Reno, Nevada. It contained some old photos, costume jewelry, and a death certificate." Vickie paused, searching Darren's face.

"Go on, please," he urged.

"A note in the box from her husband, Clyde, explained that she had died of sepsis a few weeks earlier in a Reno hospital. That was when her life ended technically, but she may as well have died in that car crash with my father, a year after Paul died. My aunt always said her soul took flight at that moment, with her husband, if you believe in that sort of thing."

"Yes, I believe your aunt had it right," Darren murmured, nodding slowly.

"It was Aunt Lydia who raised me. She was my rock—my guardian angel, really." Emotionally spent, Vickie wanted to hear Darren talk. "Do you have any brothers or sisters?"

"A half-brother, Lance. He's in San Francisco. There's thirteen years between us, so I was pretty much alone as a child. My childhood was devoid of drama, boringly ordinary."

"Ordinary is fine. Did you grow up in California?"

"I moved there during junior high." Darren squirmed in his chair. "As a young kid I lived in the other Washington, in a town with one stop light called Waitsburg."

"Waitsburg? And you think Santa Claus is funny?" Vickie teased him.

"Yeah, I spent my first twelve years waiting to get out of

there. I felt like the whole world opened up when I set foot in California."

"I'll bet," Vickie replied, her mind on Troy. That was where the indelible events that shattered her childhood had taken place, yet she couldn't remember it clearly—and her brother scarcely at all. She had a few distinct memories of her father. Standing beside him at a pedestal sink, gazing up in awe as he spread a thick white lather over his face with a brush. Then he pulled a razor up his neck in long, even strokes, uncovering stripes of ruddy skin. Sitting at the kitchen table, watching his wild, glassy eyes as he stared at something beyond the room, something she couldn't see. She also remembered the sound of his voice. And his laughter on one cold afternoon as they pushed an enormous snowball across their backyard. Sometimes, when she was very still and shut her eyes, she could summon that wintry scene and hear his melodic voice and unbridled laugh. Each time she was graced with the sound of his voice, relief washed over her. She would stretch the moment for as long as she could. One of her greatest fears in life was that his voice would grow fainter with each passing year and finally disappear altogether.

Vickie was about to ask Darren to tell her more about the fallout in Troy when the waitress offered them dessert. She shook her head. Darren looked at his watch and jerked to attention.

"Holy cow! I hate to run, especially now, but I'm late for a meeting. God, I've barely started to answer your questions," he lamented, picking up his well-worn briefcase. "I'd love to do this again next week, Victoria, if you would. And call me in the meantime if you need to about the Irish sheep story."

"That would be great." She smiled faintly. "I'm not planning to write anything until I get that report from the Irish energy board."

Vickie lingered at the table after Darren left. Most of her memories from Troy were once removed, assembled from looking at photographs. She had spent hours studying the faces of the handsome, rugged man and adorable little boy in one picture in particular. It was her favorite because she and her brother were sitting together on their father's lap. Paul was pale and thin but smiling proudly under a cowboy hat cinched beneath his chin. She was wearing a lilac organza dress. Her hair was piled on her head in a ribbon. She looked like a princess wedged between her Daddy's muscular arm on one side and her brother's skinny frame on the other. The photo was taken in November 1958, not long after Paul turned five. Within a year he would be dead from a disease people only whispered about back then, as if to say *leukemia* out loud would heap more bad luck on their cursed family.

Returning to the newsroom, Vickie was already looking forward to her next lunch with Darren. There was so much she wanted to learn from this State Department official, who was rekindling memories she feared had vanished forever. She also felt heartened that he was shaping up to be a valuable source.

11

KIEV, MAY 1986

Polina Moroz was tidying her desk when her boss came into view in the corridor. Comrade Kulyk's jacket hung slack off his frame. His eyes appeared listless. It was no wonder, she thought, gathering a pile of message slips. He had been coming in before dawn to study pages of numbers, leaving for meetings that lasted until dusk, only to return to more numbers.

"You may go home." Anatoly glanced at Polina distractedly. She handed him a wad of messages, which he stuffed into his jacket pocket.

"Eat a hearty meal when you get home." Polina's voice cracked with emotion. Everything about the reactor demanded discretion. Based on messages flying back and forth, she knew that families of high Ukrainian officials had started fleeing the city before May

Day. She wondered if she should arrange for her parents and their Springer Spaniel to leave.

Anatoly shut the office door and dropped into his desk chair. He set two sheets of paper side-by-side and squinted at the rows of numbers, trying to make sense of the massive spike in radiation. After four days of relative stability, on May Day the temperature in the core had shot up above 5,000 degrees Fahrenheit—hotter than anyone had thought possible. The reactor then began spewing a cloud packed with dangerous levels of hot particles and radioactive gases. Why? No accident scenario had predicted such an increase in temperature. He couldn't explain this—neither could any of his peers who were privy to the problem. Nor could he say how long the reactor would continue to release high levels of radioiodine and cesium—although the bureaucrats were pressing him for a definitive answer.

The numbers blurred. His head throbbed. He massaged his temples, but his eyes refused to focus. Perhaps his secretary was right, he thought. Hunger may have degraded his ability to think clearly. He decided to go home, eat, and then reconstruct temperature and emissions data he had been collecting since April 26.

⁓

Returning to his flat, Anatoly draped his jacket over the wingback chair in the living room and put a pot of leftovers on the stove to heat. He went to his bedroom and pulled his leather-bound diary from the trunk. He had been so consumed by the reactor's temperature spike that he'd neglected to keep up with his journal, an oversight he planned to rectify. For the first three nights after the accident, he had recorded measurements of radiation collected in various locations surrounding the reactor. He had agreed with most of Moscow's actions and decisions until April 29th. But on that evening, everything changed. The winds shifted and began blowing radioactive particles and gases directly toward Kiev.

Anatoly winced, recalling the blistering words spoken during a meeting called on the morning of April 30th. He'd tried to expunge that day from his memory, but every detail remained seared in his brain. When the First Secretary of the Ukrainian Communist Party learned that the winds had shifted, he proposed canceling the May Day parade in Kiev.

"No, that is not possible," the Moscow representative at the meeting had stated. "Canceling the parade would give the impression that Chernobyl is not under control."

Next, two Ukrainian physicians risked their necks by openly opposing Moscow's position.

"Radioactive aerosol is blowing over Kiev, endangering millions. We must not allow children to march outside, given the gravity of this threat," a doctor from the Ukrainian Ministry of Health warned. The Moscow official answered the doctor with a withering gaze.

"We must give residents advice on precautions they can take to limit their exposure," a second doctor from the Ministry of Health added.

"Canceling tomorrow's May Day exercises could cause panic in Kiev, and panic must be avoided," the Moscow official hissed. There would be no further discussion. Parades in Kiev and other cities blanketed by Chernobyl's fallout would go forward as in any other year.

Sitting in the back of the meeting room with a dozen mute

experts, Anatoly had felt his throat tighten. Moscow's decision to send Kiev's children into a radioactive cauldron had roiled his gut. *These fools can no more hide radiation than blot out the sun or stop the wind,* he thought. Dosimeters across Kiev already had started clicking wildly. As Anatoly got up to leave the meeting, Pavlo Popovych had cornered him.

"Moscow has directed us to seal all dosimeters at laboratories throughout the city. I'm putting you in charge, Comrade Kulyk. Have laboratory heads lock them in closets or do whatever is needed," Pavlo had told him.

Anatoly stared at him in disbelief. In addition to massive amounts of cesium-134, cesium-137, and iodine-131, the reactor was belching krypton-85, xenon-133, curium-242, ruthenium-103, barium-140, strontium-90, neptunium-239, and plutonium isotopes into a plume spreading over not just Ukraine and Belarus but much of Europe. He could lock up every dosimeter in Kiev, but how did Pavlo expect him to hide these radionuclides from the rest of the world's scientists and their instruments?

"Don't gape like an idiot. Get to work," Pavlo had barked. "In addition, we will need to make sure the libraries remove reference books about radiation from the shelves. Our rich city has many libraries, does it not?"

Even now, remembering Pavlo's sickening orders, Anatoly felt his chest constrict. His fingers twitched. An urge overwhelmed him, as it had at that moment, to grab Pavlo's flabby, white neck in his hands and strangle him. Never before had he felt such a murderous impulse. But Anatoly had been impotent to act then, just as he knew he would be now. Reflexively, he had jammed his hands into his pockets and arranged his face in a neutral mask.

So it was that Anatoly Kulyk, scientist and seeker of truth, had become State keeper of lies. He recalled with shame the ensuing six hours. Fingers shaking so violently he had trouble dialing telephone numbers, he had carried out the order, directing laboratory chiefs to seal up their dosimeters. What else could he have done? He was not one of those saints like his brother Alexei—mortals with outsized souls, who dared to shout truth to the heavens and spit in the eyes of their executioners. No, Anatoly had always lacked courage. As a child, he had craved praise and suffered a paralyzing dread of being ridiculed or rebuked. Above all, he feared imprisonment. What choice did he have, a man with an exceptional mind but a stunted soul?

To save his position, perhaps his life, Anatoly had forfeited his scientific integrity. He had dragged himself home at dusk on April 30 emptied of dignity—a husk devoid of life force. The streets that evening were quiet, and the air was clear, with a strong wind from the north. He could picture how the streets would look the following morning as a million people came out for the May Day parade. Suddenly, he pictured Dmitry marching with his Young Pioneer contingent and Katya riding on her father's shoulders. He felt an impulse to call Larysa and tell her to close the windows and stay inside with the children.

Climbing the stairs to his flat, Anatoly had been poised to call her, but when he picked up the phone his determination had dissolved into a puddle of uncertainty. What if Larysa asked why the children should stay inside? Surely Dmitry would balk at missing his chance to march in the parade. What reason could he fabricate? He was sworn to secrecy. If he were caught revealing the true radiation danger, he could be stripped of everything or sent to prison. No, he couldn't risk telling Larysa the truth.

He had put down the phone. He realized that he would need to devise a clever stratagem to get Larysa to leave Kiev. He had brought a bottle of vodka to his armchair, thinking a glass would steady his nerves. A long night of scheming had followed. Anatoly possessed a scientist's habit of focusing on facts and was unpracticed at the art of fiction. Halfway through the bottle, however, he had hatched an idea he felt certain would work. He would send Larysa's family to his dacha on the Black Sea. As a pretext, he would tell her the journey was required to secure a space for Dmitry at Artek. He would say a camp leader wanted to meet Dmitry. The children would no doubt be thrilled to spend the holiday at his cottage, a short walk from the beach. He would call Larysa at daybreak to tell her the plan, then send a driver to collect them and deliver them to the airport. He would meet them there for the flight from Kiev to Odessa. They could return the next morning or stay longer if they wished.

Satisfied with his scheme, Anatoly had passed out in the chair. He was awakened by sunlight streaming through his living room window. Alarmed, he roused himself and telephoned his niece—though he had no idea what he would say. The plan that had seemed brilliant in the dead of night looked lame in the light of day, and it was too late to pull it off in any event. The phone rang and rang, but no one answered. Anatoly realized that the Marchenko family no doubt had already left for the parade. Feeling miserable, he had stumbled into bed to nurse a raging headache. An hour later, a phone call from the commission summoned him to deal with an urgent problem. He had dashed to a meeting dominated by physicists. That is when he had learned of the reactor core heating up.

Anatoly removed the pot from the stove and returned it to his refrigerator untouched. Reliving for the hundredth time the events of that horrible day and night left his stomach in knots. He retreated to his armchair with his journal. Staring in the direction of the stereo, he considered listening to an opera, but like his appetite for food, his hunger for music had vanished.

His mind focused again on the reactor's temperature spike. He stood up to retrieve the sheets of emissions data from his briefcase in the foyer but sank back onto the cushion, feeling lightheaded. It didn't matter. He knew the numbers by heart. He closed his eyes, and a hallucinatory image of clouds emanating from the inferno took shape in his mind. He watched the scintillating eruptions, fluid as a scarf dance. Following the initial reactor blast, he envisioned a magenta plume of radioactive particles shooting a kilometer into the sky. For three days, winds carried this plume to the north. Radionuclides bound with moisture in the clouds had rained down on Sweden. Soviet military pilots flew continuous helicopter missions over the reactor, dropping 5,000 tons of sand, dolomite, and lead into its core. The sand had smothered the graphite fire and stabilized the temperature for a few days.

He opened his eyes and skimmed through his journal entries. *"On 28 April, the shoes of Swedish workers reporting for their shift at the Forsmark nuclear plant set off radiation monitors… 29 April, the wind shifted and began blowing to the south… 30 April, temperature shot up above 5,000 degrees Fahrenheit, melting uranium fuel in the reactor core… millions of curies of radionuclides blew south over Kiev…"* He'd left off there.

Shutting his eyes again, he envisioned the second plume

as a crimson scarf advancing over Kiev like a tide of blood. It extended southwest toward Moldavia and Greece. As the winds shifted again, Anatoly pictured an orange scarf emanating from the reactor core and drifting to the east, toward Russia. Moscow ordered the Air Force to seed the clouds, and rain brought down much of the radiation on Belarus.

This morning's readings had shown a steep drop in emissions, which made Anatoly think that the reactor might be stabilizing. As the colorful plumes of shimmering isotopes settled over his mental map, he decided to sketch out their movements in his journal. The vibrant image would show the path of contamination in a way that rows of numbers could not. He reached into his suit jacket pocket for his fountain pen and brought out a handful of phone messages. He flipped through them quickly, casting each slip aside, until he came to three that were starred in the upper right corner as urgent. The first, from Pavlo, he tossed on the floor. The other two were from his niece. Larysa had called twice to ask if he could obtain two train tickets to Saratov for her children.

Reading Larysa's messages, he was overcome with self-loathing. He had tried endlessly to push his niece and her children out of his mind. They were hideous reminders of his shrunken soul. He should have warned them to shelter inside on May Day. They were his only family. What is more, he had taken a shining to Dmitry and Katya, who were bright, determined children, much as he and his brother Alexei had been. He should have taken the risk of warning Larysa to leave Kiev with her family—or at least to close their windows and stay indoors. He should have called her that fateful evening without trying to dream up excuses. He reread the second message, again berating himself. He wondered why Larysa wanted to send the children to Saratov. Then he remembered that her husband had family there.

Such a simple request, he mused. For him, getting two train tickets was child's play. But what would Larysa do? And why send the children by themselves to Saratov? He could secure train tickets for the whole family to any location in the Soviet Union openly now. There was scarcely a need for subterfuge any longer. This morning, the Minister of Health had announced plans to close Kiev's schools early and open summer camps ahead of schedule. Soon, authorities would warn people not to eat leafy vegetables and to keep their windows shut. In a few days, plans called for radiation checks to be conducted on people remaining in the city. There was talk of preparing sanatoria to receive mothers with young children. He shuddered, picturing Larysa and Katya shipped off to a tubercular-infested sanatorium. The thought repulsed him.

Suddenly he was struck by a brilliant idea. Of course! Why not put the whole Marchenko family on an overnight train to his dacha in Odessa? Larysa and the children would be able to breathe clean air by the sea. His cottage could use a woman's touch, and May was the perfect time. Already, the little cherry orchard would be in bloom and the strawberries would be ripening. A decade ago, while advising construction of the Southern nuclear plants, he had spent every weekend there from April to November. The dacha, which was awarded to him for his outstanding contribution to the Soviet Union's nuclear energy enterprise, was modest. While his cottage was nothing like the estates of Moscow's elite along the Crimean Riviera, he found it a pleasant garden retreat.

The structure, which had seen little use the past three years, had a small kitchen, a comfortable sitting room, two bedrooms, and a mansard roof with a loft. It had water, electricity, and a fireplace to take the chill off cool nights. Thickets of raspberry bushes surrounded a glazed veranda that hugged the dacha's west side. A vegetable plot lay on the south. Larysa's husband could put in a garden, Anatoly mused, already imagining the family installed for the summer. He would join them to enjoy the fruits of the garden and restorative walks on the beach. Picturing the tranquil scene had a tonic effect on his nerves, quieting his stomach and buoying his spirits. It was settled. All that remained was to call Larysa. The Marchenkos had preparations to make if they were to be ready to board tomorrow evening's train for a months-long stay in Odessa.

He walked to his phone and dialed his niece. Larysa immediately picked up her phone—the very phone, Anatoly proudly reminded himself, that he had procured for her. Feeling relief at the chance to redeem himself, he launched into a recitation of why her family would find it beneficial to spend the summer in Odessa. Perhaps he'd provided too much detail, he thought, when he stopped talking and gave Larysa a chance to respond. For a long moment, there was no sound from her end of the line.

When Larysa choked out the words, "Thank you from my heart," he could hear that she was weeping.

12

ODESSA, MAY 1986

Vasyl and Dmitry hauled a trunk and two suitcases along the Odessa Railway Station's gleaming floor. Katya, still sleepy from the train ride, held her mother's hand. Outside, the scent of spring blossoms infused the moist air. A milky blue mist enveloped the city. They lugged their bags down the stairs of the main entrance and waited for Anatoly's friend Sasha, who was supposed to meet them. Anatoly had assured them that Sasha, who served as caretaker of his dacha, had a thick mane of snowy hair that could not be missed. However, it was hard to make out anyone through the dense fog.

They needn't have worried, for within minutes a white-haired man in a tan shirt and work pants approached them and introduced himself. He motioned for the family to follow him, then strode ahead at a rapid pace. They struggled to keep up with Sasha, who finally stopped in front of an old red Lada on Pushkinskaya Street. Without speaking, Sasha helped Vasyl stuff the luggage into the boot and back seat.

Sasha's silence did little to quiet the nervous anticipation of his four passengers. For ten minutes he coaxed the car past faded storefronts and apartment buildings along city streets obscured by fog. Vasyl held Katya on his lap in the front. Dmitry, who was straining to pick out every detail of the new city, sat in the back beside his mother. When Sasha turned onto a broad, divided avenue lined with tall poplars, the sun broke spectacularly through the mist. Farmhouses and estates with orange-tiled roofs flanked the wide road, giving the scene a Mediterranean look. After a few miles, Sasha turned onto Derzhavina Street. Finding his voice, he announced that this gravel road ended at the Black Sea. He pointed to a brick house surrounded by well-tended gardens, where he and his wife lived and had raised their six children. The car crawled past three houses with fenced yards, then stopped in front of a small cottage set back from the road. A glassed-in veranda stretching the length of the cottage glinted through cherry blossoms. Berry bushes clung to the fence, and tall poplars edged the verdant grounds.

Katya, who had come alive during the ride, held Vasyl's hand as she skipped to the front wrought iron gate. Dmitry and Sasha trailed behind them, carrying the luggage.

"Here it is—and you have your very own cherry orchard!" Grinning broadly, Sasha opened the gate, and Larysa followed the procession up the stone pathway to the turquoise door.

Larysa glided over the threshold feeling like a damsel in a fairytale. All she needed to live happily ever after was for Vasyl to slash through the gnarled garden vines and slay a dragon, she thought, smiling at the image of her husband girded in metal armor.

Sasha told them he had met Anatoly ten years earlier while watching chess players in the square. They struck up a conversation that had turned into a lasting friendship, he reminisced, pointing to hand-carved ivory and ebony chess pieces on a table at the far end of the room.

"I miss playing with Anatoly. He tells me you will stay the summer?" Sasha asked, not waiting for an answer. "A bus into the city stops at the corner, where we turned off. The market has everything you could want. Our beach is at the end of this road. You will find it less crowded than Arcadia, especially in mornings. You won't find a sliver of sand on Arcadia beach."

Katya and Dmitry craned their necks, trying to sneak a peek at the bedrooms and the stairs leading to a loft while Sasha explained the idiosyncrasies of the stove and plumbing and instructed Vasyl on how to prime the pump.

"You must come for lunch after you get settled. My wife will have treats for the children." Sasha handed Larysa the key.

"Thank you. I look forward to meeting your wife—" Larysa paused.

"Alina Davidovna." Sasha stepped out the door. "I'll tell her you're coming then."

Once Sasha departed, Dmitry and Katya dashed from room to room, examining the objects in each. The main room was about twenty-five feet long, with rough wood beams running across the ceiling. At one end was a corner kitchen with pots, pans, spatulas, and ladles hanging from a metal rack. A large samovar sat on the counter under a window. A table with six chairs occupied the center of the room. From the beam above the table hung a brass light fixture. The back half of the room was furnished with a brocade sofa facing a fireplace with a stone hearth. A chess table and two chairs were pushed under a window on the wall perpendicular to the fireplace.

Two doors off the main room led to small bedrooms. The one beside the kitchen had a desk and chair, a bookcase, and a narrow iron bed. The room was a naturalist's dream. Dozens of dazzling butterflies floated on a black velvet box high on one wall. Dmitry admired a periodic table pinned to another wall while Katya spun a globe resting in a wooden stand beside the desk.

The second room contained a brass bed and oak wardrobe with mirrored doors. The children found little to attract their interest, but Larysa admired the carpet, embroidered bed linens, and cross-stitch hangings that adorned the walls. Larysa chose this as the room where she and Vasyl would sleep for the next few nights, until his return to Kiev. She began unpacking their trunk and hanging sundresses in the wardrobe. She heard the children race upstairs to explore the garret. Looking out the window, she saw Vasyl pacing the overgrown vegetable bed.

Katya picked the sunny loft, which had a bed and sofa, as her room. Dmitry asked if he could camp on the sofa on the veranda. Larysa approved her children's wishes. The arrangement would leave the study bed free for Anatoly whenever he was able to fly from Kiev to join them.

⁓

Walking back to the dacha after lunch, Katya swung a pail and shovel that Alina had found amongst her grown children's cast-off toys. Larysa clutched a tin of honey cake, Vasyl pushed a wheel barrel full of potatoes, and Dmitry carried bags of seeds Sasha had left over from his planting. They also had come away with a list of historic landmarks Sasha and his wife insisted they must see in their beloved Odessa.

"I'll have to start digging right away. You can help, Mitya. We've got three days to prepare the soil and plant the garden before I go back," Vasyl said.

"Can't we go to the beach now, Papa?" Katya pleaded.

Like his sister, Dmitry was itching to see the beach, but he didn't say anything for fear his father would judge him unwilling to work. It was Larysa who stepped in on Katya's behalf.

"Yes, why don't we make today a holiday, Vasya? I want to go to the beach too," Larysa said. "After we swim, we can go to the market and see the sights. We spent the whole night getting here, and I'm anxious to learn for myself why they call this the 'Pearl of the Black Sea.'"

"Did you not notice the garden bed? It's strangled by years of thistles and vines. It will take us a full day of pulling and chopping."

"Then you can start tomorrow morning and give the garden a full day. Today's half spent. Besides, we need food. I can't carry everything from the market myself," Larysa insisted.

Realizing he was outnumbered, Vasyl relented. "Change into your swimsuits then," he told Dmitry and Katya as they entered the cottage. He followed the path around the backyard with the wheel barrel and seeds.

"I put your swimming trunks on the bed," Larysa told Vasyl

when he entered their room. She was standing in front of the mirror in a bright blue bikini, tilting her head to adjust a floppy, yellow sunhat over her long blonde hair.

"You don't know how beautiful you look." Vasyl swooped behind her and kissed her neck. He couldn't remember when she had looked this carefree.

"It must be the magic of this place, Vasya," she laughed. "Every mile we put between us and Kiev on the train lifted a stone from my shoulders. I wish you didn't have to go back. I want you to stay the rest of the summer with us."

"Mikhail did his best letting me take a few days to get you settled. I'll be back for a proper vacation in June. It's only a few weeks away. What's important is Dmitry and Katya will have clean milk and food here. I'll rest easy knowing that." Vasyl turned in profile beside her and slapped his hard abdomen. "Not bad for an old man."

"You're almost as vain as my uncle," Larysa joked. "But I shouldn't talk that way after everything he's doing for us. He's changed, don't you think? What do you suppose has gotten into him?"

"I don't know, but his generosity is making me revise my opinion of him. He's flying down in a few days, isn't he?" Vasyl asked.

"He may drive. He wants to take Dmitry to Artek in person." Larysa ran her fingers down Vasyl's chest and stomach. "Not bad at all, Vasya."

The sun bleached the sky and baked their backs as the Marchenkos walked to the beach.

"The water's blue, not black!" Katya shouted, as an endless

expanse of turquoise shimmered into view. "Lift me up, Papa. I can't see the other side."

Laughing, Vasyl hoisted her onto his shoulders. Dmitry and Katya were used to a very different kind of beach. The Dnieper River flowing through Kiev was flanked by miles of white, sandy beaches. There was a thimble-sized one within walking distance of their apartment where Vasyl often took them to fish and swim. Still, nothing had prepared them for the vastness of the Black Sea—or the crush of humanity huddled on the beach. Scores of people of every imaginable shape crowded at the edge of the sand. Dozens more stood waist deep in the water, surrounded by splashing children.

"That's the difference between the sea and a river, Katyenka. We can see the banks on the other side of the Dnieper River, but you could board a boat here and sail a long time before you would come to Turkey, on the other side," Vasyl explained.

Katya squirmed to get down, then took Dmitry's arm. The two waded together into the gentle waves.

"Just imagine, we're standing at the edge of Ukraine," Larysa whispered, as she and Vasyl followed the children into the water. She felt intoxicated by the motion and sound of the waves and the idea that they were looking straight into the world beyond the Soviet Union. The dizzying sensation intensified later in the afternoon, when she wandered with Vasyl and the children through market stalls filled with pastries, birds, paintings, music tapes, and books in foreign languages. Looking through one bookseller's French and English titles, she was swept by the same giddy excitement she had felt as a teenager in the 1960s, when she and her friends used to listen to underground tape recordings of the Beatles and pass around forbidden novels. Those were brighter days, before the clampdown that had ensnared her father.

"Isn't it exotic? Like Naples or Marseilles must look," Larysa whispered to Vasyl as they squeezed past vendors selling perfume, blue jeans, and watches. "And listen to the languages. I've heard French, Italian, and Greek!" With a million people, Odessa was the largest city on the Black Sea. The Italian classical architecture of the Opera and other grand buildings coupled with the Mediterranean climate gave it a southern European flavor.

Wandering through Shevchenko Park, the four came upon a red granite obelisk reaching to the sky. An eternal flame flickered at the monument's base honoring unknown sailors who had died defending Odessa. Dmitry and Katya grew silent as six Young Navy Pioneers performed a drill. The boys wore dark blue pants and white shirts with wide, square collars. The girls, dressed in blue skirts and white blouses, wore frilly white bows in their hair. Their faces reflected the solemnity of the Navy War Memorial, which was erected in 1960 to commemorate the fifteenth anniversary of the defeat of Hitler. Katya watched mesmerized as the girls and boys marched in formation, kicking their stiff legs high into the air.

"I want to do that someday," Katya said when the group of six was replaced by a second contingent of Pioneers.

The family stopped at a machine for cups of seltzer water with strawberry syrup. Vasyl bought four meat pies from a woman at a cart, and they settled on a park bench to eat scrumptious fried dough filled with cabbage, beef, and potatoes. After eating, they headed in the direction of the Potemkin Steps. A massive bronze statue of the Duke of Richelieu stood in an open square at the top of the dramatic staircase. Odessa was founded in 1794 at the behest of the Russian Empress, Catherine the Great. She had named Richelieu as governor of the city, which he ruled from 1803 until 1814.

In front of the statue, Vasyl draped his arm around Larysa's warm shoulders, bared by her sundress. They lingered, watching silver sunlight dance on the amethyst sea. Katya and Dmitry ran ahead and waited for them at the top of the 192 stone stairs leading down to the water.

"What was it Sasha told us? Pushkin said in Odessa you can smell Europe?" Vasyl asked, lacing his fingers through Larysa's. She leaned into him, her body radiating the contentment he felt.

"I think I'm getting a strong whiff." Vasyl soaked in the smell of the sea, the warmth of the sun, the nearness of his family.

Three days later, the afternoon sun again warmed Vasyl's shoulders as he leaned over the garden bed to put in the last row of beets. Katya and Dmitry, who had helped him plant potatoes, cabbage, and tomatoes, had gone inside to wash their hands for supper. He rose slowly and stood back to admire the garden, which he had reclaimed from weeds. His gaze swept the horizon where songbirds flitted through cedars and poplars ringing the yard. Slipping through the front door of the cottage, he heard Katya singing a ditty Larysa had taught her: "*Sur le Pont d'Avignon, L'on y danse, L'on y danse.*" These were the sights and sounds he wanted to carry in his heart on the grim train ride back to Kiev.

13

KIEV, MAY 1986

A few days after returning home, Vasyl received a call from Larysa. She was at a phone booth, and he was at the print shop with Mikhail sitting six feet away. Although he didn't feel free to say much, he was happy hearing the excitement in his wife's voice. She assured him the cottage was a slice of paradise. She'd been making strawberry jam. Dmitry and Katya looked healthier than ever, tanned by the sun. They walked to the beach every morning to scour the sand for shells. Sasha and his wife, meanwhile, had adopted them like grandchildren. On Friday Anatoly planned to drive down from Kiev to enroll Dmitry in the Artek camp. Anatoly wanted her and Katya to come along so he could show them the spectacular scenery on the Crimean coast.

Larysa signed off with a promise to call him the following

Monday. Not long after Vasyl hung up, an officer from his Army Reserve brigade entered the shop. Mikhail spoke to the officer and pointed in Vasyl's direction.

"Vasyl Marchenko, did you not get a telegram sent last week?" the officer asked.

Vasyl shook his head, confused. "I wasn't home."

"We contacted you because we need volunteers. I'm looking for men of your caliber, with your skills and dedication to the motherland," the officer said. "We'll need you for this maneuver about a month, maybe a little longer."

Vasyl couldn't imagine why the Army needed a letterpress operator. His first impulse was to send this officer packing, but he checked himself, considering the possible dire repercussions. Would he lose his job, he wondered? He looked over at Mikhail, who was bent over a table, pretending to study a stack of proofs.

"My wife and children are in Odessa. I promised to meet them there in three weeks," Vasyl told the officer.

"That will be perfect, then. Your family's away. You can camp out with the guys for a month. How many children?"

"Two, a son and daughter."

"Good, I'll sign you up, then? Volunteers get a bottle of vodka in addition to triple pay. The motherland thanks you."

Vasyl didn't know how to react to this unwelcome proposal. A month wasn't such a long time, and he could use the extra money, he thought, trying to make peace with the heinous bargain on offer. The promise of additional money was not a real incentive, of course, as he never seriously considered saying no. Who knew what might befall him were he to decline? Also, there was the matter of defending the country. If his country needed men for an important cause, should he not do his part?

"When do I report?" Vasyl asked.

"Tomorrow morning, eight o'clock," the officer answered.

Everything was moving with uncharacteristic speed. Vasyl shot a desperate look at Mikhail, who continued to study the proofs as if someone had slipped a lost Rembrandt portrait into the pile of square-fisted workers. His boss might have been able to get him out of this, Vasyl thought. When the officer left, Mikhail tried to buck him up. He assured Vasyl that his job would be waiting for him at the end of the month.

That evening, Vasyl sat at the kitchen table alone to eat a cold sausage and bread. Figuring he should tidy the flat, he cleared food from the fridge. After cleaning, he sat on the sofa for an instant then jumped up, agitated. He paced, then returned to the sofa. He stared through the open French doors at his tomato plants, which had seemed so important two weeks ago. Looking at the limp plants, it dawned on him that they could not produce edible food. They were radioactive poison. The rage that had been building in his chest for weeks erupted. He rushed to the balcony, knelt, and ripped the plants from their pots. Clods of dirt scattered as he flung the plants on the concrete floor. His eyes glistened with despair. The sharp scent of tomato clung to his fingers as he brought the leaf of one plant close to his face. It looked like a normal leaf. Dropping it, he stood up and leaned against the balcony wall. Staring out, he saw stars sparkling in the heavens, as always. The constancy of the night sky steadied him. He took comfort in the thought that his wife and children were breathing pure air and eating clean food, safe from the noxious radioactive cloud. His jagged breathing slowed as his anger gradually subsided. In a few hours he would report for duty with the Army unit. He would do honorable work for his country, wherever he was needed.

At the kitchen sink, he scrubbed his hands with soap. Then he packed a toothbrush and change of clothing in a rucksack. He ached to talk to Larysa, but since the dacha had no phone, he wrote her a letter. He tucked a blank notebook in with his clothes. With nothing left to do, he climbed into the bed where he had always lain with Larysa and tried to sleep.

In the morning Vasyl posted the letter to Odessa and reported to the recruiting center. There he lined up with thirty other men, signed his name on a form, and boarded a bus, taking a seat beside a volunteer who looked only a few years older than Dmitry. The young recruit introduced himself as Artem and fell silent. The bus pushed north for over an hour and came to a halt at a police blockade.

14

WASHINGTON, JUNE 1990

Vickie took a cab to the Tabard Inn as soon as the House hearing on sludge disposal ended. When the hostess showed her to the sun-drenched courtyard, she saw Darren sitting at their table. He had shed his sports jacket and appeared to be lost in a daydream. He had ordered them each a glass of white wine. As she approached, his brooding face broke into a full smile.

"This spot is so beautiful!" Vickie felt her tension melt.

"You haven't told anyone about it, have you? Remember, we need to keep this secret." He glanced from side to side.

"What looks good to you?" she asked, scrunching behind the menu, playing along.

He suggested the calamari and savory tarts, and she nodded in agreement.

"To our hideaway," Darren toasted, lifting his glass.

Vickie repeated his toast as they clinked their glasses.

"I was glad the House passed the Downwinders' bill last week," Darren began after ordering.

"Oh? I'm not familiar with that bill." Vickie dug out her cassette recorder.

"This is something I think you might want to write about, the Radiation Exposure Compensation Act, or Downwinders' bill. I take it nuclear matters have not consumed every minute of your time since last week?"

Vickie shook her head. "In the past week I've written about hazardous waste Superfund sites, coal plant emissions, and a follow-up on disposable diapers clogging landfills. I came here from a House hearing on the appetizing subject of sewage sludge. In the newsroom they now call me the sludge queen."

"I'm always astounded at how quickly reporters digest new subjects. And this business of producing an article a day is beyond the pale! I've been known to spend three months tweaking seven words in a verification clause."

Vickie found Darren's unpretentiousness refreshing and rarer in Washington than a skyscraper. He had earned a reputation as a crack negotiator in 1982 during President Reagan's Strategic Arms Reduction Talks. He was fluent in Russian, played the piano, and had a degree in international relations, yet he seemed unaware of his brilliance.

"I dash off my stories in English. You have to worry about the subtleties of Russian, not to speak of being diplomatic. Now, what's this bill about?" She pressed the record button on her machine.

"Ted Kennedy and Orrin Hatch introduced it in the Senate in May of 1989."

"Over a year ago? It must be controversial."

"That's an understatement. It's been a long time coming. The bill will compensate people downwind of the Nevada Test Site who got cancers caused by radiation. They're entitled to fifty thousand dollars each. It's restricted to people in a few counties in Nevada and Utah. I don't think the bill goes far enough, but for those families that suffered cancer, it's a big victory. The real vindication comes in the government's tacit admission that their cancers were caused by fallout from the bomb tests."

"Hmm. This does sound important. Do you know any of the affected people who might be willing to talk to a reporter?"

"I can put you in touch with a mortician in St. George, Utah, who had never seen cancer in a child until 1956. By 1960, he told me he had seen more than a dozen children who died of leukemia. Plenty of people there would be grateful to talk to a journalist. Aside from local papers, they've been ignored."

Vickie listened attentively, the outlines of a story taking shape in her mind. To give this subject its due, she would have to be ready with the historical background and human-interest angle when the Senate passed the bill. She decided to ask Thane to send her to St. George, where she could learn first-hand from residents what it was like to live in the shadow of the bomb.

"For thirty-five years, they've been fighting to get the government to admit that fallout from the bombs was harmful. I suspect that justice is more important to these families than the fifty thousand dollars in damages," Darren said as the waitress brought a platter of calamari.

"I've never had calamari," Vickie admitted, eyeing the white, rubbery rings with suspicion. She dipped a piece into lemon sauce, took a tentative taste, and declared it delicious.

"You know what calamari is?" Darren grinned. "Squid tarted up with an Italian name."

"Segueing from spicy squid to hot sheep, the Irish energy board still hasn't released that report," Vickie said. "I was hoping you could give me some background on cesium-137 and other isotopes that get into food. Also—I should know this, but I don't—is fallout from an atom bomb the same as the fallout from Chernobyl?"

"The same radionuclides are produced in a nuclear reaction whether an atom bomb is detonated, or a reactor explodes," Darren began. He explained that iodine-131, cesium-137, and strontium-90 are the main isotopes that transfer to people through food. Iodine-131 settles on grass, cows graze on the grass, and the radiation transfers to the cows' milk. When people drink the milk, their thyroid glands absorb the radioiodine. Darren stabbed a piece of calamari with his fork, then continued. "Iodine-131 has a half-life of eight days. This means that half of it decays within eight days and most of it will be gone in eighty days. But in the case of U.S. weapons tests, there were times when the government detonated several bombs a month."

Vickie frowned. Darren was sounding so much like Gareth Will she was starting to wonder if he was an anti-nuclear activist who had managed to infiltrate the State Department.

"The spring of 1953 was notorious," Darren continued. He ticked off a string of atom bomb test code names: *Annie* on March 17, *Nancy* on March 24, and *Ruth* on March 31, *Dixie* on April

6, followed by *Ray* on April 11, *Badger* on April 18, and *Simon* on April 25, with *Encore* on May 8, *Harry* on May 19, *Grable* on May 25, and *Climax* on June 4.

"These names sound so innocuous."

"Don't they? And with each explosion, more fallout was deposited across the country."

"How many atom bombs did the government detonate in Nevada?"

"In round numbers, one hundred between 1951 and 1963," he responded.

Vickie's fork stopped midway to her mouth. "What? That's crazy! I had no idea our government set off that many nuclear bombs in this country."

"You aren't alone, Victoria. The press doesn't write about it, and this part of our history sure as heck isn't taught in school. Imagine the uproar if Russia had dropped one or two nuclear bombs on us, never mind one hundred."

The waitress brought their entrée and asked if they wanted more wine. They both nodded.

"One hundred—that's a mind blower." Vickie took a swallow of wine. "Well, getting back to Irish sheep—"

"Right, so sheep grazing on grass and mushrooms growing in soil contaminated by cesium-137 keep ingesting radioactivity for years. I don't know why the contamination is higher in Ireland now than a year ago." He squinted, puzzled. "As to health effects, cesium-137 is taken up by the heart and bone marrow. Strontium-90, which is similar to calcium, gets incorporated into our bone tissue and teeth. Once strontium-90 lodges in bone marrow, it can lead to leukemia."

"You don't know how helpful this is." Vickie turned off the tape recorder. Satisfied that she had enough background for her story on radiation from Chernobyl in Irish sheep, she was ready to ask him about the subject that had been playing on her mind. "Last week, you mentioned a fallout incident in Troy. I was wondering if you could tell me about it."

Darren relaxed against the back of his chair. "Ah, yes, Simon, infamous in the annals of atomic blasts. Here's how it went down. One morning in April, Herbert Clark, a professor at Rensselaer Polytech, noticed the Geiger counters in his lab showing radiation above background level. He had his students go outside and take readings. What they found was radioactivity five hundred times above normal background. There had been a huge storm the night before. Water pooling under the downspout of his lab building had the highest readings, one thousand times above normal! Clark was certain readings as high as these must have come from fallout from a nuclear bomb." Darren paused as the waitress stopped by their table.

"Can I interest you in dessert?" he asked Vickie.

She was about to decline out of habit, but she wanted to learn more about the fallout over the city where she was born. She was also enjoying the sun, the wine, and Darren's company. She felt drawn to his intensity and the way he slipped from serious to playful and back. "Why not?"

"Will you split a piece of double-fudge cake with me?"

Sharing a piece of cake struck Vickie as intimate, certainly not something she'd done during a work lunch. Then again, nothing about Darren seemed to fit into a conventional pattern.

"Who can turn down chocolate?" She grinned. "I can't believe I never heard of this fallout in Troy."

"The government kept it under wraps. Professor Clark knew about the bomb testing in Nevada, so he called a friend of his at the Atomic Energy Commission, and sure enough. His hunch was right. They had detonated a bomb the morning of April 25th. The mushroom cloud had risen more than forty thousand feet."

Vickie could picture a purple cloud shooting like a geyser from the desert floor to the sky, then spreading and flattening. As a child, she'd spent hours staring with morbid fascination at photographs in magazines of atom and hydrogen bomb explosions.

The waitress set a piece of cake and two forks on the table, but neither of them noticed.

"The fallout from Simon zipped across the country on the prevailing winds, west to east. The next night all hell broke loose when the fallout plume collided with a violent thunderstorm. Torrents of rain dumped radioactive fallout on Albany, Troy, and other pockets of upstate New York and western Massachusetts."

As he spoke, Vickie suddenly recalled rain clattering like reindeer across the roof of her grandfather's farmhouse and caught a whiff of the wood scent under the rafters. Her family had lived in his attic until the end of 1953, when they moved into a rental house nearby. She visited her grandfather often as a young child and enjoyed climbing to the attic to play with dolls in the crib. For a moment, she wondered if she might be remembering the storm Darren was describing. No, that was impossible, she thought. She would have been too young then to have a memory of that night. Still, the vivid memory lingered, palpable.

"You promised to help me with this." Darren slid the cake between them.

Shaking off her reverie, Vickie shaved a sliver off the wedge.

Flashing a fiendish grin, Darren scooped up a huge hunk. Vickie laughed, following suit, and the slice disappeared. Their forks clashed, as they scraped gobs of icing off the plate.

"Don't leave me hanging. Was the radiation dangerous for people in Troy?" Vickie asked, her mind returning to the sound of rain pummeling her grandfather's roof.

"Depends on who you believe. AEC scientists insisted it would not be hazardous for people's health. But some non-AEC scientists doing research on radiation from medical x-rays thought otherwise. Dr. Alice Stewart in the UK had been studying the effect of radiation from x-rays on the unborn child. A couple years later she was able to show that children born to women who received two or more x-rays during pregnancy were more likely to get leukemia."

Darren leaned forward. "And the plot thickens. It turns out the AEC's Health and Safety Laboratory in New York contracted with Professor Clark to keep monitoring radioactivity in area reservoirs. The AEC also surveyed the area from an airplane using radiation detection equipment."

"What did they discover?"

"We don't know. The New York lab wrote reports, but they were classified."

"Why? How could they keep that secret?"

"Perhaps the radiation was high enough that it might have worried people in the area. In 1953 the AEC wasn't going to let anything stand in the way of its bomb mission. One newspaper in the Troy area ran an angry editorial, but the episode was soon forgotten by everyone—except nerds like me—and now maybe you."

Vickie glanced at her watch. She wanted to hear everything Darren knew about the fallout in Troy and why the government kept it secret, but they'd already been talking for two hours. She needed to write her story on the House sludge hearing.

"I hate to cut this off, but I have to get back," she apologized.

"Holy Mackerel! It got late on us." Darren slung his jacket over his shoulder and grabbed his briefcase. "I'm going to messenger you a report on another radiation incident you might find interesting. Let's do this again soon."

"Definitely," Vickie responded, wishing they could talk for hours. Darren's revelations about the Simon fallout were upending her perceptions of her childhood and raising questions that left her feeling unsettled.

≈

Returning to the newsroom, Vickie banged out a story on EPA's proposed sewage sludge disposal rules. She expected Thane to condense it to a paragraph for the Federal News Briefs, but he felt the editors would want to run the piece in its entirety.

Thane's prediction proved true. Every municipality in America contends with forty-five pounds of sewage sludge a year for every man, woman, and child, and her story got big play in all eight Newhart newspapers. He asked her to write a series of follow-ups and put together a report for the "Earth Matters" section. This would give her a steady stream of bylines, but unfortunately, writing sludge stories also would eat into the time she had hoped to devote to researching the Downwinders' bill. Pursuing the radiation story felt urgent to Vickie, much more important than her story count, so she pitched it to Thane. She made a case for flying out to interview doctors and residents in Utah who lived close to the Nevada Test Site.

"When is the Senate taking up the bill? Do they have the votes to pass it?" Thane asked.

"The staffer I talked to predicts it will pass by the end of summer."

"It's not a story that warrants sending you to Nevada. We don't have any papers there. Write up a brief when they pass the bill." Thane turned to face his computer, dismissing her.

Vickie felt her temples pounding. "This isn't just a story about Nevada and Utah. It's a national story. Our government detonated one hundred atom bombs, and the fallout spread across the country for years. Fallout from one of the bomb tests affected people in upstate New York," she blurted out, speaking fast.

"New York?" Thane spun around to face Vickie. "You said this bill compensates people in Nevada and Utah."

"That's right, but fallout—" Vickie was about to explain that she planned to use the experience of people living downwind of the Nevada Test Site as a springboard to write about the fallout event in upstate New York. She stopped, aware that she was jumping ahead of herself. She needed to focus on the plight of people in Utah and Nevada. The Troy incident was a separate story, the dimensions of which she had barely glimpsed.

"This bill is not important for us," Thane snapped.

"The government assured people living near the Nevada Test Site that fallout wouldn't harm them. The government lied."

"Take off the rose-colored glasses. Those were the early days of the Cold War," Thane retorted.

Vickie didn't realize how hard she was clenching her fists until she felt her fingernails digging into her palms. She wanted to meet fallout victims face-to-face and have someone take her close to the spot where the government detonated a hundred bombs. Instead, she would have to get by with phone interviews—if Thane allowed her to do the story at all.

"By the way, I'll need you to cover my press conferences the next couple of days," Thane added. "I'm flying to Galveston tomorrow to check out the Mega Borg spill in the Gulf."

Vickie pursed her lips. Newhart News didn't have any newspapers in Texas, but Thane viewed a drop of oil spilled anywhere on the planet as a national story. That was his prerogative as editor, of course. The Mega Borg story would be the fourth in his series entitled, "Spilling Oil's Dirty Secrets." She gave him an icy look but held her tongue. She needed this job, so she would have to live with his capricious decisions.

As Vickie was leaving work, a messenger delivered an envelope from D. Cunningham. Dropping it into her bag, she thought about Darren's frustration with the media's failure to write about America's atomic secrets. She vowed to find a way to reveal what fallout had done to trusting citizens in Nevada and Utah and to learn what had befallen her family in Troy.

15

THE ZONE, MAY 1986

Vasyl disembarked from the bus of fresh recruits. Guards hustled them onto a second, older bus. The boy, Artem, stuck close to Vasyl and sat beside him again. They bumped over a gravel road through the forest past a rough military encampment surrounded by bulldozers, backhoes, and trucks. The bus made a sharp turn onto a narrower road that took them deeper into the woods. On either side of the road, tread marks scarred the ground. They stopped at a second camp littered with tents and tree stumps.

As soon as they got off the bus, the captain directed the soldiers to line up and count off by tens. Vasyl looked over the nine men he would be sharing a tent with for the coming month. Artem and another wide-eyed recruit in their group looked too young to shave. A short man with grizzled white stubble looked fifty. The rest, like Vasyl, appeared to be between twenty-five and thirty-nine, in the prime of their manhood.

"You have been called upon to provide the first line of defense in our war against the atom. The duty falls to us to decontaminate the land and save our people, and indeed the entire world, from the spread of radiation," the captain told the men.

Vasyl and his fellow recruits learned that they were now "liquidators," brought in to clean up radiation from the Chernobyl explosion. Their camp sat deep within the exclusion zone, a 30-kilometer radius around the smoldering nuclear plant. The entire Zone was under evacuation orders. Most people in large towns within the Zone had been removed, but many of the smaller villages had yet to be evacuated. Some residents who'd been ordered to evacuate refused to leave. Elderly people hid in the woods to escape capture by day and snuck back to their homes at night.

The soldiers glanced around warily.

"You've brought us on a suicide mission, is that it?" a wiry man who looked about thirty-five muttered. Artem turned toward Vasyl, panic painted on his smooth face.

The captain answered the challenger's question by extolling the courage and patriotism of the "volunteers," as he called them. Next, he mentioned the triple pay they would earn by working within 20 kilometers of the reactor. Finally, he talked about other rewards—medals, certificates, bonuses, and vodka.

"In three or four months here, you'll triple an entire year's earnings," he added. At this, the men exchanged alarmed glances. Like Vasyl, most had been asked to volunteer for a month. Now they realized they could be here beyond the end of summer.

Vasyl swore under his breath. He was boiling mad and wanted to turn and leave but knew he could not. He was trapped here. His thoughts turned to Larysa. He pictured her and the children tucked away in her uncle's cottage three hundred miles south of Kiev. That image calmed him. Having grown up in a village near Zhitomir, he felt at home in the woods, hunting, fishing, and sleeping under the stars. Radiation did not frighten him. He would return home later than he had expected, but as a hero with a fat wallet. He could think of worse fates. And what choice did he have?

Vasyl followed the others to a supply tent where each man collected a mattress and pillow, two pairs of pants, shirts, socks, boots, and a face mask. The sense of belonging that came from working together for the good of their country began to wash over them, or maybe it was the fatalism that had been ground into their psyches since birth. Curses gave way to gallows humor as the men carried their bedding, clothes, and protective gear into the tent.

At lunchtime Vasyl joined more than sixty soldiers passing through the chow line in a makeshift, open-air cafeteria. He brought his food to a table slapped together from hewn logs. Parched, he chugged a cup of water. He glanced around the camp perimeter, which was bordered on the north and east by a mixed forest, on the west by a meadow, and on the south by an old apple orchard. Sunlight illuminated gossamer apple blossoms, and a steady breeze rippled through the trees. The sylvan scene was beautiful. Yet something was missing. He began to sense something terribly wrong with the woods. He scanned the treetops and looked up at the perfect blue sky and puffy white clouds. Then in a flash, it hit him. There was no birdsong.

Vasyl looked carefully, watching for birds to flit between tree branches or swoop above the camp site, but he saw none. The smell was wrong too. He had always taken for granted the sharp scent of pine pitch and pungent aroma of moss and ferns. Bringing a forkful of food to his mouth, he became aware of a metallic smell, like a burning iron. The smell coated his tongue and throat, killing his taste. He wondered where the birds had gone and what had invaded the forest in their place. How was it that birds knew to take flight and he was here? His throat tightened as he began to absorb the reality of this mission.

After lunch, Vasyl waited in line near the command post. He couldn't take his mind off the eerie silence. He saw the dazzling sunshine as a mockery. Finally, he and a dozen others were given shovels, axes, and machetes. They walked to the camp perimeter, following heavy earth-moving equipment that began knocking down trees to expand the campsite. After the machines knocked over the trees, the men set to work cutting saplings, clearing brush, and chopping logs. Their leader directed them to wear their face masks as protection against radioactive dust and debris kicked up from the dirt and leaves. Within fifteen minutes, the men were sweating in the heat. Like most of the others, Vasyl pulled the mask down to his neck to ease his breathing. His arms began to ache from swinging the axe, but the rhythm of the work took his mind off the unreality of this place.

Time passed quickly, and the men were given a rest break. They sat cross-legged on the forest floor and guzzled water. A few flopped on their backs, stretching their legs in leaves thick as a featherbed. The single worker who had kept his mask on slid it down over his nose. Vasyl saw that it was Artem. The boy leaned over and gasped for air like a sprinter who had just broken an Olympic record. He knelt in the leaves and pulled the mask back up over his nose. Above the mask, Artem's black eyes darted from tree to tree like a scout searching for a camouflaged enemy.

After their break, the men traded tools. Vasyl took a shovel. Two hours of pounding the blade into gnarled roots left him too tired and thirsty to worry about radiation. Like many of his comrades, he was unaccustomed to continuous physical exertion. Aching, he straggled back to the outdoor mess hall and ate food tinged with a metallic taste.

At dusk, men returned to the tents alone or in twos and threes to face their first night in the Zone. Theirs was an unprecedented theater of war in which military training would prove useless. They were battling an invisible enemy that could not be defeated or subdued by conventional weapons. Like the others, Vasyl wondered how much radiation was seeping into his body, but he tried to push the calculation from his mind. To dwell on that question was to court madness.

"They say vodka kills radiation, so I say we take a healthy dose," said Ivan, a muscular man with shrewd eyes and a persuasive manner. He opened a bottle.

Yaroslav, a quiet man with an angular face, cleared his throat and interrupted Ivan. "Wait. It works better with Moldavian red." He pulled a bottle of wine from a bundle near his bedding.

"Where'd you get that?" someone asked. Gorbachev had instituted an alcohol prohibition the previous year in a futile attempt to increase productivity in the Soviet Union, and spirits had been hard to come by.

"Moscow had crates of Moldavian red shipped to Kiev after

Chernobyl caught fire. Mixing red wine with vodka washes radiation from your blood," Yaroslav explained, opening the bottle.

The scruffy crew gathered around Ivan and Yaroslav, offering toasts and chasing swigs of wine with shots of vodka. Artem, who had been curled up on his mattress, joined them for medicinal shots.

"That's it, boy! Drink up." Ivan clapped Artem's back.

Vasyl had no idea whether vodka and red wine could flush radiation from his system, but he figured it couldn't hurt.

When the wine bottle went dry, the men shifted to straight vodka, which worked as an antidote to rumination, if not radiation. Artem retreated to his corner where he rocked back and forth, clasping his knees against his chest.

Most of the men drank themselves into oblivion, laughing and telling jokes. A slim man with rheumy eyes and a misshapen nose that must have been broken more than once took out his Russian guitar. The men fell silent as he picked out the notes of a beloved folk song, "A Duckling Swims." His voice was soft and tentative at first. Soon others joined in the melancholy verses about a soldier going to war, a lament each man knew by heart. As Vasyl sang, he heard in his mind the round, perfect voice of his little Katya.

After breakfast, a line formed by the command post. Vasyl was standing beside Danil, a husky man in his mid-thirties, who had spent the previous night in the tent writing in a diary. When an officer asked for two marksmen for a hunting squad, Vasyl and Danil exchanged a glance and stepped forward. They followed the commander to the camp entrance, where he gave them each a rifle and ammunition. He handed Danil the keys to a flatbed truck.

"We've got a problem with dogs. Between here and Burakiva, the place is overrun with wild dogs. The first week after Pripyat's evacuation, dogs were friendly. They'd run up to you looking for a handout, but their fur was collecting radiation, so we had to shoo them away. Two, three weeks without food turned them vicious," the officer explained. "Before we can decontaminate the villages, these wild dogs have to be killed."

He directed Danil and Vasyl to crisscross the web of dirt roads and get out every few kilometers to patrol on foot. When they spotted dogs, they were to shoot them from a safe distance. Then they were to throw them in the back of the truck and take them to a ditch designated for burying radioactive debris.

"Be sure to wear your gloves and mask before you touch these animals. Their fur has been soaking up radiation," the officer warned them.

Vasyl had doubts about the ferocity of these dogs and the danger their fur posed to people, but he set off with Danil to follow orders. The first dog they spotted was long-haired and disconcertingly sweet looking. A cocker spaniel mix, he had the coloring of a fox, with white front paws that looked like socks. Danil stopped the truck, and Vasyl got out with the intention of tracking the animal. Instead of snarling and running away when he approached, however, the dog stopped and turned to face him. He gazed at Vasyl with round, moist eyes. Under his fur, Vasyl could see this pooch was a bag of bones. He seemed to want food and affection. Vasyl stood still as the dog cocked his head and whined. The dog's tail began to wag as it approached him.

"Shoot!" Danil shouted from the cab of the truck.

The spaniel stopped a few yards from Vasyl as man and beast took the measure of each other. Seeing the dog posed no threat, Vasyl lowered his rifle. The dog responded by bounding at him with a burst of puppy zeal. As the dog leapt toward Vasyl a shot rang out. He jerked backward, letting out a sharp yelp as his body thudded to the ground.

Vasyl reached down and was about to cradle the dog when Danil appeared at his side.

"Don't touch it." Danil tossed Vasyl a pair of gloves.

Vasyl and Danil glared at each other with mutual contempt. Vasyl put on the gloves and grabbed the dog's front legs. Danil lifted the animal's hind quarters, and they carried him to the truck.

Danil started the truck. "It had to be done." He glanced over at Vasyl, who looked straight ahead, saying nothing.

Three dogs they came upon two hours later growled when Danil and Vasyl approached. They tracked the dogs into the woods. The canines paused in a grassy clearing, and Danil took down two in rapid succession. Vasyl shot the third. One by one, they dragged the dead animals back to the road and hoisted them onto the truck. They passed the rest of the afternoon without seeing another dog. Their gunshots had scared them off, Vasyl thought. Before returning to camp, they dumped the four dead dogs into a clay ditch heaped with carcasses.

Lying awake in the tent that night, Vasyl pictured the soulful brown eyes of the dog he could not shoot, the innocent dog that had trusted him. He imagined coming upon the cocker spaniel on the gravel road in Odessa, where birds chirped, and fruit trees smelled sweet. The long-haired, reddish dog approached him cautiously. Vasyl extended his hand for the dog to sniff, coaxing him to come. The dog nudged a wet muzzle under his hand. He followed Vasyl back to the dacha, where his wife was preparing dinner and his daughter was playing with her dolls. Larysa cut a scrap of meat for the dog. Katya encircled his skinny body in her arms. "Good boy," she cooed, running her hand along his soft coat.

Vasyl wiped his wet cheeks with his hand. "They are safe," he whispered.

Milling about on his third day in the Zone, Vasyl feared he would be detailed to the hunting squad. He had never considered himself a coward. He took pride in working hard and fulfilling his duty. Nor had he ever been insubordinate, but he did not think he could kill another dog. Hanging back, he was relieved to see Danil head for the truck with another man.

An hour later, Vasyl was one of a dozen men selected for decontamination work. The men climbed into the back of a truck and rode ten kilometers along a narrow road with orchards on one side and a swamp on the other. They stopped in a village consisting of a school, an onion-domed church, and fifteen cottages, each surrounded by flowers and vegetable plots. Officially, the region had been evacuated. However, a few elderly people who hid in the woods to avoid capture had returned to tend their gardens and sleep in their own beds. The soldiers walked from house to house, peeking through lace-curtained windows and knocking on doors.

Radiation had spattered the landscape like paint flung on a

canvas with a loaded brush, saturating some places with dangerous levels of fallout while lightly stippling nearby patches. The squad leader carried a Geiger counter that clattered in front of some cottages and barely pinged near others. He broke the men into groups of four to begin decontaminating the most radioactive cottage. One team hosed the wood structure with water from a tank in the back of the truck. This water contained *bourda*, a substance that helped to dissolve and wash off radioactive dust. The water splashed off the roof and ran down the dwelling's sides. Another team dismantled the fence around the yard. Vasyl, Ivan, and two other soldiers dug up the vegetable garden, then shoveled the dirt and plants onto trucks. It was backbreaking labor, and they soon found it necessary to remove their face masks. Over the coming week, the men repeated this task, hosing down cottages with *bourda*, digging up a layer of soil rich with worms and vegetable matter, and chopping down fences.

"We're on a fool's errand, digging from the fence post to lunchtime," Ivan told Vasyl during one of their breaks.

Two weeks later, in early June, readings in the village registered almost as high as they had when decontamination efforts began. The houses and soil were again covered with radioactive particles, and the entire village was deemed too hot to save.

"Knock it down, everything," the squad leader commanded.

Vasyl's team began checking houses to make sure they were empty. When he and Ivan knocked on the door of a cottage with green shutters across from the church, they heard noises inside. After a few minutes a babushka wearing a baggy blue dress opened the door a crack. She squinted at them warily.

"What do you want, boys?" she asked. "Can I get you some

tea and cake?"

They declined, though the temptation of real food made Vasyl salivate. He had to remind himself that her cakes were radioactive waste.

"You have to leave, grandma. The radiation in this house will kill you," Ivan told her.

"Then I'll die here, son, won't I? Why don't you leave me be?" The babushka had no intention of vacating the home where she had lived her entire life. Her grandfather had carved the front door and built their furniture. Her ancestors were buried in a cemetery on a hillock behind the church.

As Ivan and Vasyl tried to talk her into leaving, a dirty white cat scurried out between her feet, prompting her to open the door wide.

"Where's my cat going? He's all I've got. Help me find my cat, will you, boys?" She started looking for the cat, tears filling the grooved landscape of worry beneath her eyes.

Ivan hoped to draw her away from the house. "Let's go find your cat." Confused, she followed him. The ruse worked, and Ivan led her to a truck. She turned around weeping.

"What about her clothes and the rugs? Shouldn't we save a few for her?" Vasyl asked another soldier when they stepped inside the cottage for a final look. An embroidered tapestry spanned the stucco wall behind the couch, no doubt, a cherished family heirloom.

"Everything in here is hot." The soldier scowled.

Vasyl knew he was right. They left the old woman's abode and checked the remaining cottages. They were empty, as were the church and schoolhouse. A unit rolled in with lead-plated tanks and bulldozers to knock over the structures. Backhoes followed, scooping splintered wood, stoves, blankets, sofas, icons, photographs, and dishes into dump trucks. Earth movers scraped a layer of soil from the yards and kitchen gardens. The soldiers dumped contaminated soil with the material remains of an entire village into unlined ditches a few kilometers away.

The night after they destroyed the village, Vasyl noticed Artem had not returned to the tent.

"Where do you suppose Artem is?" he asked Ivan, who seemed to know everything that happened in the camp.

"You didn't hear?"

Vasyl shook his head.

"They found him in the supply tent curled up between crates of canned goods. He thought the tins would protect him from radiation!" Ivan hooted. "I could see he was spooked from the start. They put him on a bus home. What he needed was more vodka, make a man of him."

As always, the soldiers drank late into the night. Vasyl wrote a letter to Larysa—a letter he would never send. How could he ever explain to his wife the futility of this decontamination work? How could he tell her that he killed a dog that had once been a family pet? That he spent his days digging up dirt and burying it in ditches? That he shoveled tapestries and icons into dump trucks to save the world from radiation? He planned to destroy these letters when he left the shadow of Chernobyl and returned to the light of the natural world. He only shared details of this grotesque place with his beloved wife each night as a hedge against insanity. He would need to have his wits about him and be strong as oak for the final assignment that would test his courage. This was the moment when he would go up on the reactor roof, the most radioactive spot in the Zone and on the planet. He feared this final charge, yet he also welcomed his moment, when he would prove his courage and return in glory to Larysa.

16

WASHINGTON, JULY 1990

Ten minutes before the Press Club Library's closing time, Vickie stumbled on a report about hot sheep on a ranch in southwest Utah. In the spring of 1953, according to a field report from Congress, 12,000 sheep were grazing in the path of fallout from two atom bomb blasts in Nevada. Sheepmen testified that more than 1,400 of their lambing ewes and 3,000 new lambs died during the spring and summer. A government scientist who examined several of the dead sheep had declared them "hotter than a $2 pistol." However, Atomic Energy Commission scientists brought in later contradicted the first scientist and insisted there was no evidence that radioactive fallout had caused the sheep to die.

Before discovering the report on hot sheep in Utah, Vickie had uncovered a 1984 court decision finding the government negligent for not warning residents downwind of the Nevada Test Site about the dangers posed by fallout. The 490-page decision by Judge Bruce Jenkins ruled that radioactive fallout from bomb tests had caused some plaintiffs to die of cancer. Their legal victory was short-lived. In 1987 an appeals court overturned Jenkins, ruling that the government had sovereign immunity and could not be sued. This meant that Congress would have to decide whether people living downwind of the Nevada proving grounds should be compensated.

Excited by finding the documents, Vickie thanked the librarian for staying late. She was heading to the elevator when she bumped into Gabe Green leaving the Press Club bar.

"Yo, Cinderella! What are you doing out past six?" Gabe asked.

"My daughter has an overnight at her best friend's house. Julia's mom and I trade off Friday nights, so I had a chance to do some research."

"Have you eaten?"

Vickie shook her head.

"I'm going to the Palm. Why don't you come?"

"I'm pretty sure that would break my budget." Vickie had heard of the swank restaurant.

Gabe rubbed his fingers together. "My treat, Victoria. I'm buying us a steak dinner we'll never forget."

Vickie could see Gabe was jubilant about something and agreed to join him. They took a cab to Nineteenth Street and managed to snag a table without a reservation.

"All right, Gabe. What are we celebrating?" Vickie asked him after they were seated.

Gabe cast a suspicious glance around the tony dining room. "This is totally off the record until next week," he whispered.

"Okay." She waited while Gabe ordered a bottle of Bordeaux.

"Alan's sending me to Riyadh, assuming Iraq invades Kuwait, which my sources say is one hundred percent a sure thing."

"That's amazing. Congratulations!" Vickie knew how much Gabe wanted a foreign posting, but she felt a twinge of loss. She couldn't imagine the newsroom without him. She would miss his jokes and his sympathetic ear when she needed to vent about Thane.

"Here's to your assignment, assuming it comes through," Vickie toasted.

They clinked glasses and drank.

"What were you doing at the library at this hour?"

Vickie told him about her research into the above-ground atomic blasts in Nevada.

"I thought they banned above-ground testing," Gabe interrupted.

"They did, but not until 1963. Did you know our government exploded one hundred atom bombs over Nevada between 1951 and 1963?"

"Nope. I was eleven in 1963 and into Spiderman comics," Gabe answered.

"I didn't know either. One bomb sent fallout all the way to upstate New York."

"Sounds like a subject for a history term paper," Gabe deadpanned.

"Between March and June of 1953, the government exploded eleven atomic bombs," Vickie continued, ignoring his jab. "I found some amazing testimony of shepherds who were herding their flocks in Utah during the spring of 1953."

"Who knew there were shepherds in modern-day America?" Gabe joked.

"They called themselves sheepmen, and they probably rode horses."

"And carried a rifle, not a staff."

Vickie nodded. "It turns out thousands of sheep in Utah died after the bomb blasts. Here's the kicker, though. Government scientists who examined the dead sheep said they died from radiation exposure. But later, their higher ups made them backtrack and say radiation was not to blame—"

"Hey, I get you're really into this, but it's 1990. Those tests stopped three decades ago. Where's the news?"

"Congress is about to pass a bill compensating people in some Nevada and Utah counties who got cancer. That will allow me to get into the nuclear testing program, which our government hushed up and classified as national security. Well, I suppose it was national security back then—"

"Bingo. Our military did what they needed to do then to defend against the Russians. That's history. When people open their paper, they want to find out what's happening now."

"Sure, but if something big happened in the 1950s, a secret program that affected the whole country, and no one knows about it, isn't it our job as journalists to find a way to make it relevant and inform the public?" Vickie leaned her chin on her clasped hands, her eyes locked on Gabe's. "Suppose a construction crew is excavating in Maryland. They come upon a mass grave with hundreds of bodies. You'd agree that's news, right?"

Gabe nodded. "Front page, no question."

"What if we have the bodies, but they're spread across the country. What if the perpetrators covered their trail and kept the circumstances surrounding these deaths secret for thirty years so their crime was never discovered?"

The waiter brought their steaks, and Gabe ordered another bottle of wine.

"How do I know all those people buried across the country didn't die of diseases and normal stuff?" Gabe shook his head.

"Because the reporter will prove there was a crime, a perpetrator, and a coverup. Anyways, I've just started digging. I don't know where it will go yet." Vickie picked up her silverware and started eating.

"Don't hate me, Victoria, but I love seeing you riled up." Gabe winked and cut into his steak. "Is this great or what?"

"Mm, I don't hate you, Gabe. I'm going to miss you."

"Here's what I want to know. What's a guy like me gotta do to get the elusive Victoria Evans in the sack?"

"Ha! That's never going to happen." Vickie eyed him playfully.

"Okay, you're screwing Ian's State Department buddy, right?"

"Darren Cunningham?" she asked.

Gabe nodded, eyeing her levelly.

"Good grief, Gabe, your brain's in the gutter. I've never slept with him. What gave you that idea?"

Gabe shrugged. "You're smart, you're put together, but you must know that. Who's the lucky guy? Someone back in Iowa?"

"Iowa? I'm from Indiana."

"Right, whatever. One of those vowel states in the Corn Belt."

"I'm not seeing anyone. I hit the pause button a couple years ago." Vickie felt flattered by Gabe's attention and enjoyed his sexual repartee.

"Hey, I wasn't proposing," Gabe protested.

Vickie regarded him thoughtfully. She was attracted to Gabe, but she couldn't see herself dating him. He was hip and flippant and breezy in ways she was not. Too much joking and fooling around wore her down. She was the type whose spirits were buoyed by achingly beautiful music. Discussions about heavy subjects energized her. She also felt certain that a fling with a colleague would end in disaster—even if he was about to fly halfway around the world.

"Are you nervous about going to Riyadh?" she asked, changing the subject.

Gabe shook his head. "I've never wanted anything so much."

"Even when the fighting breaks out?"

"Damn straight. I need to be in the middle of the action shaping history. I need to see it myself and be part of it, not read about it later. I've always wanted to be posted to a foreign country. I wanted Ian's job, but my German's minimal, and he's bilingual. I've wanted this for so long you have no idea." Gabe spoke from his heart, without a trace of cynicism.

"To doing what you've always wanted," Vickie toasted, moved by his sincerity.

"To finding what you want." Gabe clinked her glass. They drained the last of their wine and left the restaurant slowly, without talking. They lingered on the sidewalk. He suggested they make a pub stop, but Vickie was ready to head home.

Gabe hailed her a cab, but Vickie hesitated at the car door, reluctant to get in. He threw his arms around her and pulled her to him. She let her body sink against his, and he leaned over and kissed her. For a suspended moment, she was lost in their kiss and the immediacy of their bodies pressed against each other. She didn't want this sensation to end. She was on the verge of inviting Gabe to her place when a sober pang of clarity stopped her. A list of complications and ways things could go south popped into her mind. Knowing she would regret it later—either way—she jerked her head back and gave him a quick peck on the cheek. Taking his cue from her, Gabe let her go. He patted her back as she climbed into the cab.

"You better stay safe over there," Vickie whispered.

Gabe touched his hand to his forehead in a salute as the cab pulled away.

On Tuesday of the following week, one of Vickie's Hill contacts called to tell her the Radiation Exposure Compensation Act was slated to come up for a vote. The first call she made was to Dr. Dallin Farnsworth, one of several names Darren had provided her. He had opened his medical practice in the idyllic town of St. George, Utah, in 1934. The soft-spoken doctor told her that he saw only one case of childhood cancer in his first twenty years of practicing medicine. Then within the space of two years, between 1958 and 1960, he saw a sudden rise in children with leukemia, brain cancer, and thyroid cancer.

"You know something has changed when you see so many kids coming in with cancer. Other doctors and morticians were seeing the same thing. We alerted federal officials. When we suggested the cancers might be caused by those atom bomb tests, AEC folks assured us there had been no studies linking fallout to leukemia or other cancers," Dr. Farnsworth said. "Well, you have to understand there were some cancers in southwest Utah before the 1950s, but not as many as in other parts of the country."

"Why is that?" Vickie asked.

"Being Mormons, most of us don't smoke or touch alcohol."

"Ah, yes. What do you think about the Radiation Exposure Compensation Act, which President Bush is expected to sign into law soon?"

"Justice is finally being served. It's not about the money, you know. It's about hearing the truth spoken by our government. You can't put a price on that."

Dr. Farnsworth gave Vickie the names and phone numbers of women in Cedar City and Freedonia who had spent decades assembling cancer registries.

"You'll want to talk to Rose Spendlove. She's been keeping a tally of cancer cases. There was one neighborhood where nine out of ten children died of cancer before they reached the age of twenty."

Vickie thanked Dr. Farnsworth. It had been an adequate interview, but she wished she could have been in Utah. Face-to-face, she could often pick up as much from expressions, posture, gestures, clothes, and surroundings as from the verbal exchange itself. There are times, though, when a telephone conversation can be more intimate than talking in person. Many long-distance lovers have experienced this at one time or another. Without visual distractions, naked words have the capacity to deliver undiluted emotion. Her interview with Rose Spendlove in Cedar City turned out to be that kind of conversation.

The moment Rose answered the phone, Vickie could sense her physical presence. She told Vickie that in 1959 both her daughter and her husband died of leukemia. During the thirty years since their deaths, Rose had devoted all her energy, when she wasn't working to support her son, to cataloging cancer cases. She went from house to house, recording details of members of the household who'd had cancer. As her efforts became known, the boundaries of her neighborhood expanded, and she found herself tracking cancer cases for much of the city.

"I wrote letters to state and federal agencies demanding epidemiological studies. I petitioned our representatives to hold hearings and investigations," Rose said.

"It must have been hard for your son, losing his father and sister," Vickie said, returning Rose to her poignant story.

"It was devastating for Briggs. He was nine, you know. My husband's cancer was far advanced when the doctors found it. He died three weeks after his diagnosis. But my daughter, Sariah, she suffered terribly—the bruises and painful treatments, the nosebleeds—"

As Rose spoke, Vickie suddenly recalled her brother's last birthday. Blue balloons floated behind his chair. She could see the image vividly. Their mother was holding a cake with candles in front of Paul. He tried to blow them out, but he didn't have enough wind. Her parents urged her to help. "You blow, too, Vickie!" What did she know of Paul's illness? She leaned over the cake and blew hard until the tiny flames flickered out like shooting stars disintegrating in the atmosphere. When she glanced at Paul, he looked sad. She worried that he was mad at her for doing what he had wanted to do by himself. Then blood spurted from his nose. Their mother jerked the cake away and ran for a towel.

"I wanted to take Sariah home to die in my arms beside our collie. How Sariah loved that dog. But they didn't want her to leave the hospital. I should never have listened to them." Rose's voice hung in the air like a melody missing its final note.

"I'm so sorry. When did you lose Sariah?"

"November 1959." Rose's voice sounded close enough for Vickie to touch her cheek.

"That's when my brother died—of leukemia. I was picturing him while you talked about your daughter," Vickie confided.

"I knew right off there was a special connection between us. What was your brother's name?"

"Paul." Vickie's eyes watered. "It's been a long time since they died, hasn't it?" She wanted to linger in the moment with Rose.

"Yes, dear. I want to thank you for getting the truth about fallout from those atom bombs into the newspaper. Most people don't know what was done to us," Rose replied.

A silence ensued during which Vickie struggled for her footing.

"How do you feel about Congress passing the Downwinders' bill?" she asked, the encounter with Paul slipping away as she found her way back to her role as interviewer.

"No one can ever pay for the heartbreak of losing a child and husband. But it will ease the injustice that's been eating away at us. Knowing we were right, that it was the radiation caused those cancers. I believe that will help some."

⁓

On Wednesday the Senate passed the Downwinders' bill, and Vickie sent her story to Thane. She felt it was the best piece she'd ever written. Less than an hour later, Gabe's contact called to assure him that Saddam Hussein was about to invade Kuwait. Hussein had amassed troops along the Kuwait border, and diplomatic talks had broken down. Jeff called his trusted source in the Pentagon and got confirmation. Gabe and Jeff pulled together everything they could get from their sources. Alan announced that he would be sending Gabe to Riyadh. The following morning, on August 2nd, the front page of every Newhart newspaper carried news of the imminent invasion of Kuwait, with sidebars speculating on how President Bush might respond. Only two editors had opted to run the Downwinders' story, which Thane had cut down to five graphs.

Vickie's heart sank. She hadn't realized how much this story meant to her until she saw it essentially ignored. Nothing beyond the bare facts about the Downwinders' bill had made it into print. Rose had asked Vickie to send her a copy when the article was published, but she was embarrassed to send this short clip, especially since none of Rose's quotes had survived the cuts.

Unwilling to let the fallout story rest, Vickie decided to find another way to approach it. She called Gilmore Harris, the doctor she'd interviewed for her hot snow story, to see if he knew of any new studies on radiation. Somehow, she had to find a way to make Thane and the Newhart News editors see that this was an important national story.

Dr. Harris didn't have any news for her. However, he told her that the Association of Radiation Health Scientists planned to hold a conference the following week on the effects of low-dose radiation. He offered to register her as a member of the press. Vickie agreed at once, although she doubted Thane would approve of her spending a whole day covering the meeting. When Gilmore's fax arrived, she skimmed the agenda. An NRC official was slated to kick off the meeting with a talk on nuclear waste at landfills. That was perfect. Given that trash was Vickie's main beat, Thane would have no problem with her covering the meeting.

Reading through the agenda, Vickie spotted a session entitled: "Fallout from Atomic Weapons Testing and Cancer Risk." She felt like she might be holding a winning lottery ticket.

17

THE ZONE, SEPTEMBER 1986

"Forty seconds," the general told the men facing the Chernobyl inferno. "You will have forty seconds to climb the ladder, scoop a chunk of graphite into your shovel, dump it over the railing, and run back like a hare. Do you understand?"

"Understood," Vasyl answered. He had known every detail of this drill for weeks. Climbing to the roof of Reactor 3 and removing a piece of radioactive rubble was the final challenge each man had to face before being discharged. Some areas of the rooftop were so radioactive that in forty seconds a person would be exposed to twenty-five roentgens of radiation. Officially, this was the maximum the military allowed for a lifetime—although many liquidators had exceeded that level before their final task on the roof.

When Reactor 4 exploded, the blast spread more than one hundred tons of twisted metal components and graphite across the rooftop of the adjacent reactor building. Scientists wanted to entomb the uranium fuel remaining in Reactor 4 under a thick concrete-and-steel sarcophagus. Before such a shroud could be built, however, radioactive debris on the Reactor 3 rooftop had to be removed and dumped into the hole where hot remains of the crippled plant continued to smolder.

Initially, West Germany had sent state-of-the-art robots to clean off the rooftop, as the job was considered too dangerous for humans. Unfortunately, the intense radiation had destroyed the robots' electronic workings in short order, and they ground to a halt. Japanese and Soviet robots dispatched to the roof encountered the same problem. Ultimately, Moscow bureaucrats replaced the robots with men, each one carrying out a small bit of the cleanup. The time each group of men would spend on the roof — forty, sixty, ninety seconds — depended on the level of radioactivity mapped in the area.

The group leader was a liquidator who had been on the roof twice. He helped the men fashion strips of lead into two-sided aprons to sling over their shoulders. The men hoped that these lead coverings, which weighed more than twenty-five pounds each, would protect their spines from radiation.

"Be sure to line your boots," he directed the men. "And tuck a piece of lead in your underwear." Vasyl knew about this shielding from Ivan, who had told him to prepare by wearing two pairs. He cut a piece of lead and whisked it between the layers, praying it would preserve his manhood. He put on his gloves, pulled a mask over his face, and waited. There was nothing he could do now but keep his mind clear for the moment when he would charge into the valley of death. Despite his fear, a strange calmness filled his mind. Someone had to stop the radiation. This is my duty, he told himself.

"Now!" the leader shouted.

Vasyl was second in line. Heart racing, he sprinted to a ladder attached to the reactor's concrete wall. He ascended quickly as a siren shrieked. He picked up a shovel and ran toward a chunk of debris. He tried to slide the shovel under the piece of metal, but it was stuck. He chopped hard with the shovel blade, trying to free it. He worried he was taking too long. Finally, with a desperate twist of the blade he dislodged the chunk of graphite. He looked around and saw another man running to a railing and slinging a shovelful of rubble over the edge. Spinning, he hurried toward the rail, terrified he would trip and fall. He reached the roof's edge and hurled his heavy piece of metal over the rail. With a siren screaming in his ears, he raced back to the other side. He laid the shovel down where he had found it and backed down the ladder to solid ground.

Heart hammering his ribcage, Vasyl returned to the staging area. Relief washed over him. He had passed the final test. He slipped off his lead cape and removed the shielding strips from his boots and crotch. The pieces of lead, which had absorbed too much radiation to be used again, would have to be discarded.

Vasyl lined up with the soldiers in his team, waiting for their discharge papers. He thought back over his four months in the Zone. He had missed the summer in Odessa. He also had missed opening day ceremony, when his kids returned to school on the first of September.

"Count twenty years from today. My doctor friend says that's our lifespan," a soldier whispered, wiping sweat from his forehead.

"He can go to hell," a young man countered. "I'm going home to my girlfriend."

Living to fifty-four would not be so bad, Vasyl thought, before shaking off the soldier's words as nonsense. This afternoon he would board a bus that would take him to the edge of the Zone. He would disembark from the dirty bus and board a clean bus that would return him to Kiev, to his beloved wife and children.

The general entered the room and thanked the men for their service to their country and to the world. One by one the soldiers approached him.

"You are a true hero," the general told Vasyl, handing him an honor certificate. "May you enjoy long life and prosper."

18
WASHINGTON, AUGUST 1990

A doorman greeted Vickie as she stepped into the Grant Hotel lobby. After registering for the radiation health conference, she pinned a badge with a yellow ribbon labeled "Press" to her lapel. Then she made her way to a plush ballroom and sought an aisle seat close to the front. She needed to sit close enough to the podium for her tape recorder to pick up speakers' voices. She also needed to be positioned to hop up quickly and chase speakers to the lobby for impromptu interviews. Settling into the second row, she pored over a list of three hundred attendees from around the world. There were no attendees from Troy, New York, but she was excited to see two names from Albany and two from Rochester. She marked them with stars.

A government official opened the meeting by defending the Nuclear Regulatory Council's ill-considered proposal to allow radioactive trash in regular city dumps. An activist from Sacred Earth Defenders condemned the recently announced proposal as a "reckless endangerment of the public." Two physicians on stage piled on with warnings about risks to human health. When the panel ended, Vickie chased the beleaguered official to the lobby. During an on-the-fly interview, the official admitted that two senators had asked the agency to scrap the unpopular plan. Vickie got him to name the senators then hurried to the door. She hailed a cab to the Press Building and dashed into the Newhart newsroom, where she wrote an exclusive story based on the official's candid remarks.

After filing her story, Vickie rushed back to the hotel and eased into the darkened ballroom, where a slide show was in progress. She had barely settled into her seat when the lights came up and the moderator announced a coffee break. Hundreds of people streamed to the lobby and congregated around coffee urns, munching pastries. Vickie sidled through the crowd, scanning badges for people from New York. She circled twice without finding anyone.

Chimes sounded, calling people back to the ballroom for the session she'd been looking forward to on fallout from atomic weapons testing. Dr. Olsen, a white-haired researcher from Taarbaek Medical College in Denmark, kicked off the panel with a brief history of atomic testing. She was familiar with much of his presentation from her lunches with Darren Cunningham. Vickie's mind was drifting back to those sunny afternoons in their garden hideaway when Dr. Olsen made a statement that grabbed her attention.

"One study suggests that fallout in the Troy and Albany

area from a test in April 1953 caused an increase in childhood leukemia," Dr. Olsen stated.

Vickie realized that he had to be talking about the Simon test. She glanced at her tape recorder and noticed with alarm that the reel was close to the end. She scribbled fiercely, trying to get down his words in case her tape stopped.

Crediting the work of an American researcher, Dr. Olsen projected a slide showing five cases of leukemia among children born in 1949 and 1950, and six cases among children born in 1951 and 1952. The number of cases in the Troy region more than doubled, jumping to thirteen among children born in 1953 and 1954. Those dates took Vickie's breath away. She was born in March 1952, and her brother a year-and-a-half later, in October of 1953. This researcher was talking about her family.

The second panelist, a researcher from Albuquerque, New Mexico, rejected the idea that fallout from one bomb detonated thousands of miles away from Troy and Albany had caused the increase in leukemia cases. "Cause and effect cannot be proved here," he argued. "More likely, this is an example of a random cancer cluster."

However, a third panelist, a researcher from Chicago, seemed to back up Dr. Olsen. "Radiation is more damaging to the fetus than to the mother," the Chicago researcher contended. "Dr. Alice Stewart showed in 1958 that x-rays to a fetus in the first three months of a pregnancy increase the risk of childhood cancer tenfold."

Vickie couldn't believe what these doctors were saying. Working the dates in her head, she realized that her mother would have been three months pregnant with Paul in April 1953, when fallout from Simon rained down on Troy. Paul was diagnosed with leukemia in 1957, when he was four years old, making him one of these statistics.

She had never heard about this purported link between leukemia cases in upstate New York and fallout from an atom bomb test. She was bursting with questions for Dr. Olsen. How long had this link been suspected? Were there any papers on this?

When the session ended, she took a moment to eject her cassette, which had stopped recording. After unwrapping a fresh cassette and popping it into her tape recorder, she tried to catch up with Dr. Olsen. The aisle was choked with participants inching their way out of the ballroom to the luncheon room. When she finally managed to break free of the crowd, Vickie ran the length of the lobby only to see the Danish researcher climbing into a cab as she approached the hotel door. She stepped outside and waved at the back of the cab snaking up Connecticut Avenue. She was unable to gain the driver's attention.

Disappointed, she returned to the lobby and followed the crowd into a large room set with two dozen round tables. She searched the badges of people seated around the tables looking for attendees from upstate New York. She was about to give up when she noticed an elderly man with a badge identifying him as Doyle Chandler, PhD, from Rochester, NY. She took the vacant chair to his right. His head was tilted away from her as he listened to the man seated to his left.

Still warm from sprinting, Vickie peeled off her jacket and draped it over the back of her chair. A young man from Denver seated to her right was conversing with the man beside him. She strained to overhear them, but the clatter of plates and cutlery intermingling with dozens of conversations drowned out their words. She was beginning to think she'd picked the wrong place to sit when Dr. Chandler passed her a basket of rolls.

"I see you're from Rochester," Vickie shouted in his ear. He nodded. His eyes watered as he buttered his roll with trembling fingers. She estimated his age at upwards of eighty-five, making him one of the oldest men in a room dominated by graybeards. Rochester is more than 200 miles west of Troy, but Vickie was hoping he might have some recollections of the atomic testing era that he could share with her.

"I found that last talk fascinating. I was born in Troy," she told Dr. Chandler. This brought a bright flicker of recognition to his face. In a roomful of strangers, Vickie had created an instant bond with this old man.

"Troy, did you say? I'm Doyle Chandler, pleasure to meet you."

"I'm Victoria Evans," she shouted. "I was amazed at how much scientists have learned about the rainout in Troy from the Simon test. I guess it must have been the first time fallout came down so far from the Nevada test site."

"Not true," Dr. Chandler retorted, shaking his head vigorously. "That's not true."

"What's not true?"

"We had radioactive snow come down in Rochester two years before you had that rainout in Troy," he boasted, as if it were a matter of pride. Vickie frowned.

"It's true. It was in January of 1951," he insisted. "We measured radiation in the snow falling in Rochester at twenty-five times background level."

"Why were you looking for radiation in the snow?" Vickie continued to eye him with a show of skepticism.

"Radioactivity exposes film, ruins it."

"Ah, you're from Rochester, so you must work for Kodak!" Vickie said as the pieces of his background clicked into place.

"Did. I was a physicist at Eastman Kodak. I'm retired now."

A server removed their salad bowls, replacing them with plates of chicken and potatoes covered with a white sauce. Vickie's mind raced. She wondered why Kodak had employed physicists—and why they were looking for radioactivity in snow around their Rochester plant in 1951. She realized she hadn't introduced herself as a reporter—and her press badge was pinned to her lapel, hidden from view on the back of her chair. She knew she should say something, but what if Dr. Chandler clammed up? She wanted to keep him talking.

"Did you contact the AEC like Dr. Clark did when he discovered the radioactive rain? Dr. Clark knew that the level of radioactivity he measured in Troy had to have come from an atom bomb," she asked, playing on Dr. Chandler's pride at discovering hot snow in Rochester before Troy's rainout.

"Sure, we knew that. We threatened to sue the AEC for costing us money, spoiling our film." He chuckled. "You know, film is sensitive to radiation, fogs it up."

This was news to Vickie, but she nodded, taking in every detail. "What did the AEC say when you threatened to sue them?"

"They agreed to send us information about upcoming tests so we could see when and where the fallout would be likely to come down." Dr. Chandler stopped talking, brought a quivering forkful of chicken to his mouth, and concentrated on chewing.

Vickie found his story riveting, like something out of a spy novel. If she could find out why Kodak had been looking for hot snow in Rochester in 1951, she might have a hook for the story she wanted to write on the Simon rainout. She needed to pry more details out of Dr. Chandler but realized that she was going to have to identify herself as a reporter. She was wondering how to disclose this ticklish detail when his congenial expression abruptly hardened. He looked up from his plate suspiciously, as if he'd been reading her mind. The camaraderie drained from his voice.

"Who was it you said you're here with?" He probably assumed that she was the wife of an attendee.

"I work for Newhart News. I'm a reporter," Vickie answered. "I'd like to ask you—"

"A reporter? What the hell are you doing here? Where's your badge?" he demanded.

"Right here." She turned to pull her suit jacket off the chair and show him.

"You never told me you're a goddam reporter," he snarled, jowls florid. "You breathe a word of this I'll sue your goddam ass. You hear? I'll deny every word."

A hush fell over the table. Everyone stared at Vickie, assuming, no doubt, that whatever had caused this elderly man to become angry must be her fault. She didn't know how to respond. He looked so distraught she feared he would have a stroke. Dr. Chandler tossed his napkin on his plate of half-eaten chicken and grasped the edge of the table. His veiny hands shook as he struggled to rise from his chair. She extended a hand to steady him, but he yanked his arm away from her. She decided she'd better exit before the situation grew even more embarrassing.

Her face crimson, she folded her suit jacket over her arm, picked up her bag, and left the room. She felt a prick of conscience. It had been wrong not to tell him right away that she was a reporter. Still, once she reached the empty lobby, Vickie felt exultant. She searched for a quiet spot where she could write down everything Dr. Chandler had said. She couldn't be sure that what he told her was true. He might have been embellishing—or even inventing a grandiose tale—but her instincts told her otherwise. She suspected he got caught up in boasting about his professional prowess and comparing his exploits to those of Troy's famous Dr. Clark. Given that many conference goers bring their spouses, his assumption that she was the wife of an attendee had been reasonable. He no doubt had believed he was sharing an old war story with a young woman from Troy, who was lapping up his words with rapt attention. Slipping back into her jacket, she hurried to the empty ballroom, took a seat in the second row, and wrote furiously, reproducing their conversation as close to verbatim as she could.

After lunch, participants trickled back into the ballroom for a session on leukemia in survivors of Hiroshima and Nagasaki. Vickie was too wound up about Dr. Chandler's account to concentrate on what the Japanese researchers had to say. Questions flooded her mind. Why did Kodak have a physicist on staff in 1951? When did the company first learn that fallout from atomic explosions ruined film? Was it true that the Atomic Energy Commission had given Kodak advance information on when to expect fallout, so the company could protect its film? She wondered if the government had warned anyone else about where fallout might come down in rain or snow. Certainly, the people of Troy never got a warning. No one had warned her parents. She felt sure that Darren would have mentioned this.

If what Dr. Chandler had told her was true, this was an important story—and one that had never been revealed to the American public. Yet everything turned on Chandler's credibility. He might have been exaggerating or spinning a yarn—but she doubted it. After all, he'd been furious to learn she was a reporter. He felt that she'd tricked him into spilling a terrible secret. Vickie considered how to go about verifying his story. If Kodak had sued the AEC, perhaps she would be able to find court records. However, if Kodak had simply threatened to sue, there might not be a paper trail. Or everything about the episode might have been classified. Maybe she would be able to pursue the foggy film angle by searching scientific journals for information on the fogging of film by radiation.

Vickie decided to track down Gilmore Harris to see if he could give her any leads. Despite having to cover an EPA press conference on landfills at three o'clock, she lingered for the coffee break at half past two. As she was about to leave, she spotted Dr. Harris.

"Victoria, glad you could make it! Getting any news?" he asked her.

"I'm getting lots of background. I found the session on fall-out in New York fascinating."

"Great. We're doing a program on Chernobyl health effects in December. I hope you will join us for that."

"Definitely. I was wondering if you know how I might find documents from the early AEC days. Correspondence with companies, that sort of thing, in the 1951 to 1953 timeframe."

"Hmm. I doubt you'll get anyone to talk on the record. People were sworn to secrecy back then, and most things having to do with the AEC were classified," Harris responded. "But recently, the government has been declassifying vast amounts of stuff. The Energy Department has been releasing millions of documents," he added, brightening.

Chimes tinkled, signaling the start of the next session.

"I've got to get back inside." Harris turned toward the ballroom. "Why don't you try the DOE reading room? Look into those declassified files."

≈

The next morning, Vickie pitched a story to Thane on the Simon bomb test and the possible link to leukemia cases in Troy and Albany, based on experts who spoke at the meeting.

"Another old fallout story?" Thane challenged her. "You're beating a dead horse."

"This is something no one's heard about. It happened in upstate New York, and our *Syracuse Post-Dispatch* is in that region." Vickie pressed her case. "Fallout that rained down in New York blew all the way from Nevada. That's news people across the entire country would be interested—"

Thane cut her off. "The news is what we say the news is." He picked a copy of the *Newark Post* off his desk. I want you to follow this." He jabbed his index finger at her headline, "Senators Rip Radioactive Trash Plan."

"I will. I'm working on a follow-up. In my spare time, I also thought I'd go to the DOE reading room and look through declassified documents the public has never seen—"

"Documents from forty years ago?"

She nodded.

"Maybe you're not hearing me, Victoria. You're walking on thin ice." Thane's voice rose. "You want to write about nuclear energy? Find out what officials who run things today have to say instead of the quacks you've been glomming on to."

19

WASHINGTON, AUGUST 1990

The staccato ring from Vickie's heels bounced off the marble floor of the American Nuclear Power Association's foyer. She gazed out a wall of windows offering a million-dollar view over the Mall and across the Potomac River to Virginia. She passed a pair of sleek white leather sofas—the only furnishings in a space large enough to house two Newhart newsrooms—and checked in with the receptionist. Theodore Flint, president of the lobby group, kept her waiting fifteen minutes for their fifteen-minute interview. When he appeared in the lobby, Tedd—with two Ds—gripped her hand so hard she winced.

With his crisp shirt, pressed poplin suit, and perfectly coiffed hair, Flint could have posed for an *Esquire* cover. Like most of the men running the nuclear power enterprise in America, he had cut his teeth on a nuclear submarine under Admiral Hyman Rickover.

Before taking over the helm of the lobby group, he had spent a decade as CEO of a large Southern nuclear utility. He walked Vickie back to his suite and directed her to a leather couch in front of a glass coffee table. As he settled into a leather loveseat across from her, a young man in a rumpled olive suit rushed in and sat in a hard chair beside him. It was not uncommon for executives to bring PR staffers to meetings or to patch them in during phone calls, but Vickie preferred interviews without a flack running interference. She was able to develop a better rapport with people one-on-one.

"Pete here will keep track of things we might want to follow up on. So, what can we do for you today, Victoria?" Tedd asked, flashing his impressive white teeth.

"Two things. First, I'm wondering what your perspective is on the health effects of exposure to low levels of radiation from Chernobyl. I'm also interested in what issues you see on the horizon of importance to the industry." She set her tape recorder on the table. Pete produced an identical model and placed it beside hers.

"Well, on your question about Chernobyl, it's important to underscore that an accident like that could never happen here in the United States because our nuclear plants all have containments. The Chernobyl reactor is a Soviet RBMK model with no containment, which is why you saw radiation released to the environment. Folks at the International Atomic Energy Administration are working on a major health effects study taking into account socioeconomic conditions near Chernobyl. You hear all kinds of inaccurate reports blaming radiation for every imaginable physical and mental affliction. The IAEA is delving into facts.

They're finding less cancer than has been rumored and a lot of radiophobia." Tedd tilted his head sympathetically.

"Radiophobia? You mean fear of radiation?" Vickie had never heard this term before, but it was easy enough to guess its meaning. She considered asking Tedd if sheep can come down with radiophobia but held back.

"Precisely. Fear of radiation causes stress, which can lead to all manner of ailments—but again, I would refer you to researchers working on that comprehensive IAEA study."

Tedd turned to Pete, who amplified his statements about radiophobia. Pete also noted that the official IAEA count of fatalities from Chernobyl stood at thirty-one. It was a number Vickie had read in numerous articles.

"As to low radiation exposures, the fear is greatly overblown. We get a small dose of radiation every time we fly or get a dental x-ray. I do know that some scientists have even found low levels of radiation to be harmless. And, as you might know, the serious threat of global warming is causing a sea change in how environmentalists view nuclear energy."

"Really?" asked Vickie, curious.

"That's right. Some of the big environmental groups are starting to realize that nuclear energy may be humanity's best hope for solving the global warming crisis, which is caused by burning fossil fuels. Oil, coal, and gas emit millions of tons of carbon dioxide, which is heating up the atmosphere dangerously. Nuclear power is a safe, carbon-free source of electricity. In fact, nuclear energy might end up saving our planet," Tedd finished. He extended his arm and looked at his watch, signaling the interview was drawing to a close.

"What groups in particular?" she asked.

"EcoHarmony is coming out in favor of nuclear power, if I'm not mistaken, along with some smaller national groups."

"That's interesting." Vickie mulled over this piece of information. Tedd Flint had provided only stock industry responses to her questions on Chernobyl and radiation health effects, but this was something she hadn't heard before. If environmentalists were ready to endorse nuclear power, that would make a great story, she thought. Tedd had even planted the seeds for a sexy headline.

Back at work, Vickie pitched Thane a story on environmentalists dropping their opposition to nuclear power. She knew he would gobble it up.

"Can nuclear power save our planet from global warming? Love it!" Thane smacked his lips with relish. "It will work with the special I'm putting together on global warming. Get me something within a week. We want to run this while the weather is still hot."

A charismatic figure with salt-and-pepper curls and roving amber eyes, Miles Peters was known as the man who lived with wolves. In the early 1970s, he had spent three years with a wolf pack in Michigan's Upper Peninsula. When he returned to the society of humans, he had launched EcoHarmony, which he shepherded from a band of a dozen tree huggers in 1975 to a slick global empire with over a million members.

Peters welcomed Vickie to a dark room with forest green walls on the first floor of a townhouse on P Street. He pointed to a chair behind a bench covered with bleached bones. Gingerly, she placed her tape recorder down between two small mammal skulls and took a seat.

"Tedd Flint told me you're coming out in support of nuclear power. Is this true?" she asked Miles, coming right to the point.

"Yes, it is," Miles replied, slipping off his moccasins and assuming a Yoga posture on a tattered hassock across from her.

"EcoHarmony has always depicted nuclear power as dangerous to people and the environment. What has changed?"

"Two words: global warming. Scientists have learned that carbon dioxide from burning coal and gas and oil is heating up our atmosphere. Computer models can predict with precision how hot the Earth will become as CO_2 levels rise. And the predictions are terrifying, Victoria. Global warming threatens to wipe out civilization within our lifetimes if we don't stop burning coal and oil." Miles clutched the canine tooth hanging from a rawhide strip around his neck.

"What specific predictions frighten you?"

"First, if we don't cut emissions from cars and coal plants by half worldwide, the Earth's temperature will be two degrees hotter in 2010—"

"How can scientists predict the planet's temperature twenty years from now when weathermen have trouble getting tomorrow's forecast right?" Vickie asked.

"Computer climate models. They show that in twenty years much of New York City and Florida will be under water due to rising sea levels. By 2010, the models show that snow will be rare in the U.S. And the North Pole will melt permanently by 2013."

Vickie scribbled in her notebook and glanced at her tape player's cassette reels to make sure they were turning.

"By 2005, the canals in Holland will stop freezing over in the winter. Forever."

"How can scientists predict that in fifteen years there will be no ice in Holland?" Vickie asked, horrified. One of her favorite childhood storybooks, *Hans Brinker and the Silver Skates*, was set in Holland. She couldn't imagine a world without snow and ice. She hoped these computer programs were wrong.

"Disturbing, isn't it? And believe me, this isn't some theory like Big Oil wants you to believe, Victoria. It's proven science. We must cut emissions now. Nothing could be more urgent. That's where nuclear power comes in." He bounded off the hassock and began pacing.

"What about wind and solar power?" Vickie asked, wondering if she should douse Miles with a glass of water before he spontaneously combusted.

"Wind turbines spin only twenty percent of the time, when the wind is blowing, and solar is too expensive." He shook his head. "No, we must drop our prejudice against nuclear energy. Chernobyl was tragic, but only thirty-one people died. Nuclear plants crank out electricity round the clock with zero emissions. That's what we need to save the Earth's creatures."

Following her interview with Miles Peters, Vickie talked to the heads of several environmental groups. Sacred Earth Defenders and Planet Defense League still believed that nuclear plants pose a threat to people. However, Mother Earth Rights, which had always painted nukes as satanic, now believed they would save creation. Vanessa Lane, director of the Coalition against Nuclear Weapons and Power, the group Gareth Will worked for, told her that CANWAP planned to drop its opposition to nuclear power.

Vickie was shocked. When she called Gareth to get his response to Vanessa's reversal on nuclear power, he didn't want to talk on the phone. She invited him to the Ebbitt Grill for a more upscale lunch than their usual sandwich fare.

"This will be our farewell lunch," Gareth told Vickie after they were seated at the iconic restaurant. "I'm quitting CANWAP. Vanessa tried to get me to betray the cause. I told her where to shove it."

"Are other staffers leaving?" Vickie asked.

"No. Most everyone's drunk the Kool-Aid. They're willing to erect millions of wind towers across America with gigantic blades. The more bird blenderizers in the sky the merrier, right?"

"Don't you believe burning fossil fuel will heat the atmosphere?"

"You wanna know the truth? The Earth's been warming and cooling for millennia, as any geology major knows." He thumped his chest. Vickie had forgotten Gareth got his undergraduate degree in geology. "There was a warming period from about 800 A.D. to 1300. Vikings built settlements in Greenland, which may have been forested at that time. The Little Ice Age from 1300 to 1900 brought cooling, and those settlements were abandoned. That's a reminder, if these fools need one, that warming is actually good for agriculture. Beginning in around 1900, the Earth started warming again—and here we are. The climate will keep going through warming and cooling cycles. Count on it."

"What about the computer predictions?" Vickie asked as the waiter brought their food.

"Computer models are as good as the data you input. Current models are based on the premise that increasing carbon dioxide will force a rise in temperature, but what if other factors, like solar cycles, exert more impact on the climate? Garbage in, garbage out," Gareth finished.

They ate in silence, savoring their crab cakes. When the waiter cleared their plates, Gareth ordered apple pie a la mode.

"Make that two," Vickie told the waiter.

"All right! When did you stop boycotting desserts?" Gareth laughed.

"I've been known to indulge on special occasions. This qualifies, don't you think?"

"Absolutely! Hey, listen. Here's two respected scientists you can interview who think the global warming models are getting it wrong." Gareth scribbled on a sheet of paper.

"Be sure to take a look at the *Time Magazine* cover in 1974 warning of a coming Ice Age. Then tell me how in fourteen years scientists flip-flopped from predicting an Ice Age to catastrophic warming. What a crock!"

"But what if the global warming theory is right?" she persisted.

"Don't sweat it. Fifty bucks says we'll still have snow in 2010." Gareth reached into his backpack and pulled out a Baltimore Orioles cap. "I was cleaning out my cubicle, and I thought your daughter might like this. She's into baseball, right?"

"Thank you, Gareth. That's so sweet. Molly will be thrilled. What will you do next?" Vickie put the cap in her bag.

"What I've always done. Fight nukes." He flipped his braid over his shoulder. "I'm getting with a few guys in Germany who are into actions. That's more my scene. They're furious about radiation from Chernobyl contaminating their country. Unlike the sellouts in this country, they're serious about shutting nukes down. When they want to stop rail shipments of nuclear fuel rods, you know what they do? They tie themselves down on the tracks."

"When are you going to Germany?"

"I've got a ticket out of Dulles next weekend."

"One way?"

Gareth nodded.

Outside on the sidewalk Gareth leaned over and gave Vickie a bear hug, and they headed off in opposite directions.

When she returned to the newsroom, Vickie interviewed the two scientists on Gareth's list. Both doubted that manmade CO_2 emissions would cause dangerous warming.

"In 1972 the National Science Board found that the record of past interglacial ages suggests the present time of high temperatures should be ending soon," the first scientist, a researcher in Denver, told Vickie. "That will lead us into the next glacial age."

The second scientist, from a prestigious New England university, shot holes in the climate models. "Rising carbon dioxide levels follow warming, not the other way around," the professor argued. "And warming isn't necessarily bad. Warming expands agricultural zones. Our planet has been heating and cooling for millennia."

Vickie wondered how researchers studying the same temperature records and other indications of climate could come up with opposite conclusions. She decided to put together two articles. The first explored whether nuclear power could save the Earth from global warming. The second discussed how the pendulum of scientific thought had swung in fourteen years from warnings of an Ice Age to dire predictions of global warming.

"What's this bullshit? Global warming isn't a theory. It's proven science," Thane sputtered when he finished reading her second story. "Are you shilling for Big Oil?"

Vickie was stunned by Thane's accusation that she was in the pocket of the oil lobby. But in thinking about it, she realized that Thane's hatred of the oil industry was as visceral as Gareth's hatred of nuclear power.

"I'm not shilling for any industry. I'm trying to do even-handed reporting and lay out the opposing views held by scientists. I thought that's what we're supposed to do," she retorted.

When Vickie read her story in the *Newark Post*, she was not surprised to see that Thane had cut the quotes from scientists criticizing the climate models. She felt uneasy about giving readers only one side of the global warming debate, but she also realized that the idea of humans heating up the planet by burning fossil fuel touched a deep emotional chord in people. What if the dire computer predictions turned out to be right? She worried that Molly and her grandchildren would grow up in a world without snow. Humanity couldn't afford to get this wrong.

Global warming proved a boon to Vickie's story count. Apocalyptic headlines generated by scientists predicting that melting icebergs and rising seas would flood major cities in two decades found their way to the front pages. Protests against the NRC's proposal to permit radioactive trash in municipal dumps generated big headlines, as did the EPA's new sludge rules. In fact, her stories were vying with the military buildup in the Gulf for top billing. They were also elevating her stature in the newsroom. Guys who used to look through her now made eye contact or cracked a grin when they passed, acknowledging her ascension to their lofty ranks.

While seeing her stories on the front page gave her satisfaction, Vickie's joy was dampened by the pull of the story she wasn't covering, the one that Thane forbade her to pursue. Tracking down news on global warming and city dumps kept her busy during daylight hours, but at night, after Molly was asleep, Vickie's mind kept traveling back to Troy. The radioactive rains of Simon haunted her, as insistent as the ghost of Hamlet's father, demanding that she probe the truth of what happened to her family. Lying in her bedroom at night, she could hear the hot rains pelting her grandfather's farmhouse that stormy April night in 1953. Rationally, she knew she couldn't be recalling that momentous thunderstorm. She'd been only a year old. She must be remembering a different storm. Yet even as Vickie tried to shake free of the memory—or auditory hallucination, as she came to think of it—she found herself transported repeatedly to that fateful night under the rafters.

Time became unhinged, flinging her back to her parents' house in Troy. It was as if the winds of Simon had blown open a door in her mind that slammed shut when she moved to Aunt Lydia's house in Indiana. The miasma of confusion and grief she had escaped when she was eight years old engulfed her now. Lying in bed, she shivered in the late summer heat, shot through with the fear and helplessness she'd felt during her little brother's illness. Over and over, she saw the despair in her brother's eyes on his birthday when her parents cajoled her to blow out the candles on his cake. Her eyes welled as she realized that Paul had been too weak to blow out six tiny flames on his own. Paul hadn't wanted her to help. Reliving the moment, she remembered blowing hard and watching smoke trails squiggle from the black candle wicks. She flinched as their mother jerked the cake away from the blood spurting from Paul's nose.

As sleepless hours wore on, at times she was graced by her father's laughter. The sound of his laugh took her outdoors to a blinding world of white under a brilliant blue sky. Hip-to-hip, she and her Daddy leaned into a snowball that grew gigantic as they pushed it across the backyard and around the side of their house. They stopped in the front yard, unable to budge it further. Snow blew off her mittens, sparkling like diamonds against the sapphire sky. They pushed a second snowball till it grew almost as big as the first. She watched in awe as her father hoisted it up and sat it on the bigger ball, creating a belly for their snowman. But before they could make the snowman's head, her mind snuffed out her father's laughter. Her momentary respite was replaced by silence as she watched her father at the supper table staring into space after Paul's death stole the light from his eyes.

She tried to push away these memories, but they refused to be ignored. She had learned things about leukemia from scientists and Utah downwinders that she could never unlearn. Her aunt had seldom talked about Paul's illness. On those occasions when Vickie had pressed Aunt Lydia for an explanation, she answered that no one knew what caused leukemia. Vickie had spent her life believing leukemia arbitrarily struck an unlucky few—something awry in a victim's genes, perhaps. No one was to blame. Nothing could have been done. But now, she couldn't let go of Dr. Olsen's assertion that the spike in leukemia cases in Troy might have been due to pregnant women and infants being exposed to radiation. Maybe Dr. Olsen was wrong, she told herself. Certainly, other doctors disputed his ideas. She was a baby then and had also been exposed to radiation from Simon, yet nothing bad had happened to her. Why not? Why Paul and not her?

What if Dr. Olsen was right? This was the question that tormented her. Paul needn't have died. If radiation from the Simon blast and that hot rainstorm had caused Paul's leukemia, it would mean that her brother's death had not been a random, unavoidable act. Something could have been done to prevent it. Her mind replayed the conversation with Dr. Chandler at the Grant Hotel. If Dr. Chandler was telling the truth, the government had warned Kodak of when radiation from atom bomb tests might rain down. The warnings were intended to allow Kodak to protect its film. Why hadn't the government warned ordinary citizens in the fallout's path? How could it be that no one told the people of Troy that an invisible plume of radiation from a nuclear explosion over the Nevada desert was whipping across America, headed their way? Weren't pregnant women, infants, and children as valuable as film?

She imagined how different her life would have been if authorities had been required to give her parents and other families in the area a warning. They could have taken steps to avoid exposure to radiation. The thought that her brother's leukemia might have been avoided pressed on her chest like a granite headstone. Could they have been given those KI pills Gareth Will was so keen on dispensing to residents near nuclear power plants? Why hadn't radio and TV stations advised people not to drink milk from local dairies—a common practice in the 1950s—until iodine-131 levels dissipated? If the government had not insisted on keeping everything secret, maybe people would have pressured

Congress to halt above-ground nuclear weapons testing sooner. Maybe the Nevada Test Site never would have been built. Maybe a location would have been chosen on the East Coast, allowing plumes of radiation to blow out to sea, rather than across the entire continental United States.

Questions about the atomic winds of Simon swirled endlessly through Vickie's mind every night until she realized that she would have to find answers. She slept soundly that night, knowing what she would do.

20

KIEV, DECEMBER 1986

Snow crunched under Larysa's boots as she paced in front of Katya's school, waiting for her uncle. She was about to give up and go inside when Anatoly hurried up the sidewalk.

"I had a meeting," he fretted. "Do you think the good seats will be gone?"

"Are these good enough? It's not the Bolshoi Ballet, you know." Larysa joked as they grabbed two empty chairs a few rows back from the tall New Year's tree decorated with glass balls and silver snowflakes. Watching him fidget like a stage mother brought a smile to her face. For years, her uncle had struck Larysa as an aloof, self-centered man too caught up in his career to take an interest in her children. Since their summer in Odessa, however, Anatoly had become devoted to them. While Dmitry was at camp, he had stayed on at the dacha with her and Katya. Her uncle formed a close bond with Katya, who never passed up the chance to join him on his morning constitutionals. Larysa remembered fondly how Katya would take his hand as they headed down the dirt road to the beach.

"Is Vasyl not coming? Shouldn't we save him a seat?" Anatoly craned his neck to watch for the children's procession to begin.

Larysa shook her head. Katya had been disappointed that her father would not be here, but she had cheered on learning that her granduncle, her biggest fan, would be in the audience.

Parents hushed, straining to pick out their child, as the procession of second and third graders dressed as animals and fairies, ballerinas and jesters, filed in. Holding hands, the children encircled the decorated tree, singing, "*A little fir was born in the forest.*"

"There she is!" Anatoly pointed to Katya, who was dressed as the Sugar Plum Fairy from the *Nutcracker* in a pink tutu with gossamer sleeves and a rhinestone-studded crown.

"*It grew up in the forest. It was slim and green, in winter as well as in summer,*" the children sang, skipping around the tree.

"Do you hear her? With sixty children singing, it's easy to pick out her voice," Anatoly whispered to Larysa.

The children had been singing for several minutes when a teacher asked, "Is someone missing? Who is not here?"

On cue, the children shouted, "Father Frost! He is late!"

"Maybe if you sing nice and loud, he will come," the teacher prodded.

Larysa found herself drawn into the magic of the familiar scene. A tall, bearded Father Frost in a blue robe and cap trimmed with white fur appeared in the auditorium carrying a bag over his shoulder. The children dropped hands and cheered. Next, Father Frost's granddaughter, *Snegurochka*, a beautiful Snow Maiden, appeared. Her ice blue gown glittered as she floated across the floor. The robed figures entered the circle and guided the children in games. After twenty minutes of entertaining the children, Father Frost announced that he was tired and needed to sit. He sank into a chair and asked if anyone had anything to share with him.

A boy in a fox suit stepped forward and recited a poem about forest animals. Father Frost thanked the boy for the gift of poetry, reached into his bag, and handed him a book. A girl dressed as a princess inched forward and began singing. Her voice vanished after a few measures. She brought her fist to her mouth in distress. Father Frost thanked her for the gift of music and handed her a ball from his bag. Katya stepped forward next.

"*Oh, Frost, Frost, do not freeze me,*" she began, singing a song she had rehearsed for weeks. Katya stood with poise, her face radiant as she looked from Father Frost and the Snow Maiden to the audience. "*Do not freeze me and my horse, my white horse,*" she sang. Her composure and the expression conveyed in her voice made her appear older than eight. When she finished, several people burst into applause, Anatoly loudest among them. Father Frost thanked Katya for the gift of song and pulled a pen from his bag for her.

When there were no more songs or recitations, Father Frost asked the Snow Maiden to help him distribute presents. She pulled chocolate bars and red apples from Father Frost's bag and passed them out, giving the children one of each.

The next day Katya had a chance to sing her song to Father Frost again, this time at the Polytechnic Institute's party. The auditorium was packed with staffers' children, ranging in age from five to fourteen. The recitations wore on for longer, although Katya's song was still the biggest hit. Watching her stage presence, Larysa thought that her uncle might be right. Her daughter had a special gift. It should not have come as a surprise, given that Larysa's mother was a singer. She wondered where Katya's voice might take her in life.

Larysa found herself humming Katya's song throughout the last day of 1986 as she cooked a feast. After setting holiday dishes and bottles of champagne and wine on the kitchen table, she helped Katya get into her Sugar Plum Fairy costume for the family's celebration. Two hours before midnight, a bearded Father Frost arrived at their door in a blue robe, with a sack slung over his back. It was the first New Year Anatoly had celebrated with the Marchenko family.

Larysa couldn't stop laughing at her proper, fastidious uncle in this costume. Vasyl uncorked a bottle of champagne and poured glasses for the three adults and Dmitry—and a splash for Katya.

"This has been a hard year, but I am grateful for you, Anatoly. I give thanks for everything you've done for us." Vasyl toasted, raising his glass. Anatoly's eyes glistened as each member of the Marchenko family honored him in turn.

"No, I'm grateful to you. Larysa and you have become the daughter and son-in-law I never had. Dimochka, Katyenka, you breathe meaning into my life." Anatoly choked with emotion. "I was alone and now my life is full."

"I wish to bring the happy times from Odessa into the coming year and leave the memory of Chernobyl behind forever," Larysa said.

At midnight, fireworks and cheers erupted throughout the block. Anatoly jumped up, embracing Larysa, Katya, Dmitry, and Vasyl. They all kissed and hugged. Anatoly rushed to his bag and retrieved a bottle of fine champagne, which Vasyl uncorked to cheers. They ate and drank until they were stuffed, then began singing folk songs.

"Sing the song for us, '*Oh Frost, Frost*,' Katyenka," Anatoly urged.

"I will, but first I have surprises for everyone." Katya disappeared into her room. She returned carrying four tiny baskets she'd woven from strips of colored paper. Each contained a shell and two smooth stones that she'd collected at the Black Sea shore and brought home from Odessa. After she'd passed out the gifts to her parents, brother, and granduncle, whose eyes filled with tears, she began singing.

Not long after Katya finished her song, there was a knock on the door. Larysa welcomed Maria Rohan and Ilya with kisses and hugs. Anatoly picked up his sack again.

"Father Frost has oranges and tangerines for the children," he shouted, handing mesh bags of the citrus fruits to Katya, Dmitry, and Ilya.

"I haven't seen these for two years," Maria marveled.

There was another knock. Larysa opened the door to Nina, her husband, and their three children. The kisses and hugs began again. Like a magician, Anatoly pulled yet another bag of oranges from his sack for Nina's children to share. Soon the guests joined in the singing, and time slipped away.

It was half past two when Maria looked at her watch. Nina's family had already left. "Ilya, we should leave," she said. Their apartment block was a fifteen-minute walk away, and the wind was howling outside over the popping of firecrackers.

"Don't worry about it, Maria. I'll drive you home," Vasyl offered.

"You didn't get a car, did you?" Maria's jaw dropped.

"A blue Lada," Larysa answered, beaming at her husband. Vasyl's service in the Zone apparently had advanced his name up the list.

When Vasyl and Dmitry brought Maria and her son back to their flat, Anatoly retrieved two gifts from his bag and slipped them under the tree—a camera for Dmitry and white leather figure skates for Katya. When they returned, Anatoly urged Katya to search under the tree. Discovering the presents, she hugged her granduncle and thanked him for the skates. Anatoly reached into his robe pocket and retrieved a roll of film for Dmitry's camera. Everyone gathered around as Dmitry threaded the edge of the film into the take-up sprocket and snapped the camera case door shut.

Anatoly motioned for Katya, who leaned against his blue robe, smiling and displaying her skates. Dmitry wound the roll and snapped them. Next, he photographed his parents, sister, and granduncle in front of the tree. Anatoly took the camera, capturing the four Marchenkos on the sofa. Everyone was seeing spots from the camera flash by the time Dmitry finished off the roll and said goodnight. Vasyl brought Katya to her bed.

Before leaving, Anatoly opened a bottle of Moldavian red and filled three wine glasses.

As Anatoly toasted to a prosperous and healthy coming year, Vasyl saw a vivid image of the dead dog in the Zone he had tried to forget. Overcome by a powerful sense of foreboding, he clutched Larysa's hand and squeezed tight.

21

WASHINGTON, AUGUST 1990

Entering the lobby of the Forrestal Building, a concrete fortress in the brutalist style, Vickie passed an armed guard and a German Shepherd tethered by his post. The fortifications reminded her that the Energy Department controls America's nuclear weapons stockpile. She gave the dog wide berth as she walked to the reception desk to sign in and leave her license. Clipping a guest badge to her jacket, she descended to the bowels of the building and waited outside the reading room. By coming here at eight sharp, Vickie figured she could spend half an hour on her own time doing research and make it to the newsroom before nine. She knew she was defying Thane and might be fired if he found out, but it was a risk she had to take.

Within minutes, a thirtyish man with an alabaster face and a nimbus of blonde curls unlocked the door. Vickie entered a cavernous room that gave off the musty smell of a used book-store. Hundreds of metal bookshelves rose from floor to ceiling, crammed with flaking black binders and liver-colored accordion files. Given her time constraints, she didn't poke around. Heading straight to the counter, she asked Charles, as the nameplate iden-tified the flaxen-haired librarian, where she could find declassified Atomic Energy Commission documents from the late 1940s and early 1950s. Pointing to a clipboard at the end of the counter, he asked her to sign a log labeled "AEC-Declassified."

As she was studying the top log sheet, Charles went to his desk to answer the telephone. Embroiled in what sounded like a lovers' quarrel, he turned his back to the counter for privacy. That gave Vickie time to flip through the log sheets to see who had been perusing the files. Two names cropped up repeatedly: Denise Miller of Georgetown University and Gary Sloan from Citizens United Against Nuclear Weapons. While Charles shifted from foot to foot, pleading into the phone, she jotted down their names and phone numbers. Since she was doing this research without the approval of her news organization and against her editor's wishes, Vickie decided to enter her home phone number beside her name on the sign-in sheet. Under affiliation, she wrote "self." There was also a column in which visitors had entered alphanumeric codes. She recorded several of those.

"What can I get you?" Charles asked after extricating himself from the aggrieved party.

"I'm looking for AEC correspondence with the Eastman Kodak Company in the early 1950s."

"Sure," said Charles, a devilish grin creeping across his angelic countenance. "See, how this works is you give me a code, then I bring you the corresponding box."

"How do I find out which box code applies to the topic I'm looking for?" she asked.

"Well, uh, they've declassified millions of documents from the late 1940s to the mid-1970s. I'm not sure how they're organized exactly, other than by box number. I imagine someone will index them by topic eventually. You'll see each folder has a number, too."

Having no idea what box to request, she glanced down at the log sheet and read off the number of a box requested recently by Denise Miller. Charles disappeared through a metal door behind the desk. While he was retrieving the box, Vickie flipped through the log pages and copied random codes of boxes the repeat visitors had requested. She managed to jot down several dozen before Charles returned and handed her a cardboard box full of folders.

"Can I copy documents?"

"Sure, dime a page." Charles pointed to a coin-operated machine along the wall. "Just don't remove anything from this room."

"I won't." Vickie pictured the alert German Shepherd guarding the exit.

The first page she took out of a folder looked like a world traveler's passport, stamped with multiple boxes containing dates, times, signatures, and initials of various officials. A notice from the AEC's Division of Biology and Medicine announcing the appointment of two professors to the biophysics branch, it seemed of little importance. Moving to the next file folder, she pulled out a meaty report on the amount of iodine-131 released into the atmosphere during a 1957 test series code-named "Plumbbob."

Each page was stamped with block letters: "SECRET SECURI-TY INFORMATION." Skimming the report, she learned that the atom bombs detonated from May through October during the Plumbbob tests released more than twice as much radioiodine into the atmosphere as any other above-ground series.

Handling these pages stamped "SECRET" gave her a rush. Half an hour later—and a fraction of the way through the box—she wished she could spend weeks here reading the secret letters and meeting notes of scientists who went toe-to-toe with their Russian counterparts to build America's formidable nuclear arsenal.

The next morning, Vickie rolled out of bed at six o'clock and stopped for coffee and donuts on her way to the reading room.

"I've got jelly and chocolate covered. Take your pick," she told Charles, as he unlocked the door for her at eight o'clock. He chose jelly, downing the powdery donut in three bites as they walked back to the counter.

"I'll have the same box as yesterday." Vickie gave him the number and signed in.

By the time she finished plowing through the forty folders in the first box, her thrill at seeing documents stamped "SECRET" was fading. On Wednesday, after again sharing donuts with Charles, she dove into her second box. Like the first, this one contained letters to and from researchers, requests to contrac-tors, reports on nuclear tests, and notes from AEC committee meetings. She had an early press conference to cover on Thursday morning, so skipped the reading room. On Friday, when she finished skimming the contents of the second box, she started to realize that she was in for a long, possibly fruitless slog. Still, she felt optimistic that with persistence she would uncover answers to her questions about Simon's deadly winds.

"Going anywhere this weekend?" Charles asked Vickie as she was leaving.

"No, I'm sticking around. I promised my daughter I'd take her paddle-boating on the Tidal Basin Sunday. Then we're going to a barbecue at a friend's house on Labor Day. Do you have plans?"

"I'm driving to Rehoboth as soon as I get off work," he answered, a smile dimpling his smooth cheeks. "It's the last weekend of our beach rental."

Vickie's second week of visits to the reading room went much like the first. She brought donuts to share with Charles, and he told her about his beach weekend. She asked for a third box from the long list she had compiled. She had to skip her Wednesday visit to cover a press breakfast and Thursday for an early meeting at the EPA. She finished combing through the third box on Friday without finding anything of interest and asked for her fourth. Twenty minutes before she was about to call it a week, she pulled out a file containing a letter typed on a manual typewriter. She almost let out a whoop when she spotted the word Kodak.

The letter, written in 1947 to Dr. Julian Webb at Eastman Kodak, was from J.O. Hirschfelder, a chemistry professor at the University of Wisconsin. Hirschfelder noted that he also consulted for Los Alamos Laboratory, a key nuclear weapons research lab.

"I have been advised that you have the first hard information and data with regard to the films which were destroyed by radioactive particles falling down in the state of Illinois after the Alamogordo bomb test," Hirschfelder's short letter to Dr. Webb began. "I should like particularly to know whether you have enough information to determine the amount of radioactivity per square mile, the size of the particles which fell, and the half life of the activity."

Handling the letter with the care she would give to a newly unearthed Shakespeare folio, she brought it to the photocopy machine. Vickie left the reading room with a copy of the letter and a bounce in her step, anxious to see where this gem would lead her.

During her lunch hour, she took the elevator to the Press Club Library. When she ran a computer search on Julian Webb, she found he had published several articles in scientific journals. A triumphant smile spread over her face when she came to the title of his article in the August 1949 issue of *Physical Review*: "The Fogging of Photographic Film by Radioactive Contaminants in Cardboard Packaging Materials." She could scarcely contain her excitement.

On Monday morning she skipped her visit to the reading room and took a cab to the American Physical Society headquarters. She asked the public affairs official, an older gentleman with thick bifocals, if she could see a copy of the August 1949 issue of their journal, *Physical Review*. He disappeared for fifteen minutes and returned with a limp copy of the magazine preserved in a plastic sleeve. He agreed to make a copy of the Webb article for her.

During her cab ride to work, Vickie raced through Dr. Webb's theory of how Kodak's film came to be contaminated. For her, the dry, scientific article read like a thriller.

As Dr. Webb recounted, after the U.S detonated the world's first atom bomb, the "Trinity" test in Alamogordo, New Mexico, on July 16, 1945, a radioactive contaminant made its way into packaging material that Kodak used for sensitive films. Kodak was able to trace the radioactive strawboard packaging to a mill in Vincennes, Indiana. The mill on the Wabash River, which bordered Illinois, was located more than 1,200 miles from Alamogordo. A particular run of strawboard produced on August 6, 1945, about three weeks after the Trinity test, showed what Dr. Webb called a "new and unusual type of radioactive contaminant."

According to Kodak's studies, x-ray film began to fog after two weeks of exposure to the strawboard packaging. The contaminated spots showed no alpha-activity, but they did show strong beta-activity. "Absence of alpha-activity ruled out naturally radioactive materials," Dr. Webb wrote. This meant the contaminant was an artificial radioactive material, which had found its way into the mill through the river water.

"The most likely explanation," concluded Dr. Webb, "seems to be that it was a wind-borne fission product derived from the atom-bomb detonation in New Mexico on July 16, 1945."

Vickie closed the magazine and stared out the cab window, blown away by the revelations in this article. Fallout from mankind's first atom bomb explosion had drifted across the Midwest and contaminated river water in Indiana, a little over an hour west of her house in Santa Claus. This meant Kodak had known as early as 1945 that radiation from atomic bomb explosions fogs film. It explained why a physicist was monitoring snowfall at Kodak's Rochester facility for fallout in January 1951. Only a select group of people knew this covert activity was taking place.

Most Americans had no idea that radioactive particles were falling around them, on rivers, forests, and fields.

Julian Webb's article backed up Dr. Chandler's claim that he had been looking for radioactive snow because it fogged film. However, one crucial piece of Dr. Chandler's story was missing. She needed to confirm his assertion that the government had agreed to give Kodak a warning about upcoming bomb tests and locations where fallout was expected to come down.

22

KIEV, JUNE 1989

A faint pink glow smudged the horizon as Larysa dragged herself out of bed. Putting on a flannel robe, she shuffled to the kitchen to make tea. She found Dmitry slumped over the table, his cheek resting on an open book. The whistling kettle roused him.

"Didn't you go to bed last night? You should rest more." She poured two glasses of tea.

"If I don't pass the exams next week, I won't be accepted to the Medical Institute and my life will be ruined." Dmitry's bloodshot eyes pierced Larysa with a wild, disoriented look.

"You'll pass the exams, Mitya. I wouldn't be surprised if you score the highest in all of Kiev," she teased, setting slices of bread and a bowl of jam on the table. "And Anatoly will offer a recommendation on your behalf."

She mussed his hair on the way to her chair. He jerked away from her hand, bringing a wistful smile to her lips. She still saw Dmitry as her boy, even though he was intent on showing her he was a man.

"I thought he'd be furious with me when I decided against going to university in physics. For a long time, I idolized him and wanted to work in a lab like him, but not now."

"There was a time it would have broken his heart, but have you noticed? He's soured on physics. I believe it's since Valeri Legasov killed himself." Larysa had felt relieved when Dmitry decided against following in his granduncle's footsteps and had chosen instead to go into medicine. She found physics cold and a specialization in nuclear matters treacherous. Dmitry also was showing signs of disaffection with the Party as well, which pleased her.

"My uncle and Legasov were classmates, you know. He took the suicide hard," she said.

Legasov had hanged himself in April 1988, right after the second anniversary of the Chernobyl explosion. The Kremlin had been suggesting that he mishandled the response to the accident. In hindsight, bureaucrats felt that sending pilots to dump sand and lead into the burning reactor had been a mistake. Pilots who died from radiation had been needlessly sacrificed, authorities whispered. His suicide had shaken Soviet scientists. Rumors proliferated. Some insisted that Moscow had been putting the screws to Legasov in retaliation for his exposing flaws in the RBMK reactor design. Others believed he had ended his life because he was dying of cancer after spending too much time at Chernobyl.

"I know. He told me." Dmitry sipped his tea.

"When did he tell you this?" Larysa was curious what Anatoly had told her son.

"At Katya's performance—the big one when her chorus sang at the Pioneers Palace. I was wandering the halls and came upon him near a side door. His eyes were red, as if he'd been crying. It was strange seeing him that way. First, I thought the music made him emotional. You know how he gets whenever Katya's on stage. It wasn't that, though. He told me he had studied alongside Legasov. That one of the finest Soviet scientists was dead by his own hand."

"Legasov was carrying the weight of Chernobyl secrets on his shoulders. Of course, he suffered guilt," Larysa retorted. "The whole lot of them should feel guilty. Eat some bread with your tea."

"Why are you up early?" Dmitry asked his mother.

"An article I'm translating is giving me grief. I'll be glad when you're studying medicine. You can help me get through medical journals faster. Then I will be able to spend more time on my puppet group's scripts. Already your English is as good as mine."

"My English will never surpass yours. I want to be able to diagnose what's wrong with Papa, which is more than his doctors can do. After I diagnose him properly, I want to heal him."

"I believe you will. The doctor we saw yesterday put a stethoscope to your father's chest and listened, then he listened on his back. Finally, he looked straight at me and announced he's suffering from Chernobyl syndrome, same as the other liquidators—"

"How is that a proper diagnosis?" Dmitry interrupted, unable to contain his frustration. "That tells us where Papa contracted his illness but explains nothing of what's happening in his body."

"What about Ilya? Has he decided where to study?" Larysa asked, shifting the subject away from Vasyl's health. She didn't tell Dmitry that Vasyl had been having trouble standing at the press all day—or that he feared Mikhail would soon let him go. Dmitry already worried too much about his father. "The last time I talked to Maria, Ilya still hadn't decided."

"He's taking the Medical Institute exam too. We're planning to study together tonight," Dmitry answered. What he didn't tell his mother was that Ilya's passions did not lie with academics. For the past six months, Ilya had babbled nonstop about how Ukrainians must live as free people. At first Dmitry had been surprised by Ilya's total repudiation of the Party. Ilya had been a zealous Young Pioneer and a devoted Komsomol member. Gradually, however, he had come to agree with Ilya's views on the Soviet system's shortcomings.

Even without Ilya's influence, Dmitry had been waking up to Party failings that he had been unable to see as a youngster. Like many of his classmates, Dmitry had grown skeptical of the Soviet regime's rosy promises. He could see the empty store shelves. He also was witnessing firsthand the deteriorating health of his father and others who had served as Chernobyl liquidators. Yet Soviet authorities refused to acknowledge that their exposure to radiation in the Zone could be causing their health problems.

Tonight, after they finished studying for the exam, Dmitry had agreed to accompany Ilya to a meeting at the National Writers Union—just to listen.

Dmitry ate his bread, swallowed half his tea, and went to his room for a quick nap.

Larysa reached for *The New England Journal of Medicine.*

She and Vasyl were blessed to have such wonderful children, she thought, opening to an article in English on non-Hodgkin's lymphoma.

❦

"You won't be sorry you came," Ilya told Dmitry as they squeezed into the packed union hall. They found two empty seats midway back as a speaker in the front of the room was addressing the crowd. A short man in a brown fisherman's cap and threadbare jacket, he was slamming Volodymyr Shcherbytsky, the leader of the Communist Party of Ukraine.

"Last week Shcherbytsky targeted the Popular Movement of Ukraine for Perestroika as overtly destructive and anti-socialist. He assailed our brothers in Lviv for voicing nationalist slogans and carrying our flag at demonstrations. But I tell you, Shcherbytsky is out of step with the tide of history. Rukh, the Popular Movement, is the future. We have the right to reclaim our mother tongue and our culture," the man in the brown cap shouted.

"Not so fast," someone in a baggy jacket interrupted. "If there is to be change, it must come through reform of the Soviet system, not social upheaval. It's all well and good that a contingent in Lviv supports nationalism, but we must think also of our countrymen in the East. Change must be incremental, or we risk chaos, economic collapse, and a backlash. History is full of failed revolts. Acting without caution, without consensus, without a clear roadmap will only serve to invite a crackdown from Moscow."

"The East is filled with little Russians," the man in the fisherman's cap countered. "They don't know what it means to be

Ukrainian. They don't know what freedom feels like. None of us do. For generations, we have not tasted freedom. The Russians yoked us to their will. Now the iron curtain is tearing. This is our moment. The people will rise up. Shcherbytsky is on the wrong side of history—and no number of Russians can change that fact."

Ilya elbowed Dmitry. "He's right. Thousands across Kiev support Rukh. I've been to meetings."

Arguments flew between radicals, who stopped just short of demanding an independent Ukraine, and moderates, who supported Gorbachev's gradual approach to reforming Soviet society. Listening to the passionate proponents of a free Ukraine, Dmitry felt like he had been slapped awake from a long sleep. He leaned forward, electrified by the bold vision of the man in the fisherman's cap. In his arguments, Dmitry heard echoes of his father's voice. In his own quiet way, his father had always bristled at the Soviets for imposing their language on Ukraine and for trying to wash religion from the Ukrainian soul. Dmitry's heart pounded. He felt foolish to have blindly supported the Soviet system for so long while disregarding his father's wisdom.

"We don't know how to be free men. We are learning our heritage. We are just awakening," someone shouted.

A middle-aged man with a balding head and trim white beard stood to speak.

"Listen to this one. He's with the Green World Association," Ilya whispered to Dmitry.

"We may not agree on the pace or face of political change, but there is one thing common to us all, and that is the earth upon which we stand. We can all agree our precious land must be protected," the Green World proponent said. "Radiation from

Chernobyl continues to sicken our land and harm our people. Who here does not know a friend or family member sick or already dead from radiation? Let me see one hand," he cried out. A silence fell over the room.

"Not one of you raises a hand. We can all agree our ecology must be healed, as our people must be healed. We have been told nothing but lies," he continued, his voice rising. "We must insist the truth be told about exposures from Chernobyl. We must hold those responsible for Chernobyl lies accountable!"

The speaker had struck a chord. The audience was on its feet, cheering. Tears brimmed in Dmitry's eyes as he pictured his father resting on each landing while climbing the stairs to their flat. Dmitry trembled as the realization dawned on him that the government had willfully withheld critical information about Chernobyl's radiation from the people.

Ilya, whose uncle and cousin Natasha both were sick, cheered loudly.

"People in the East and West of Ukraine differ over language. Believers make different religious demands. The young and old have generational differences over the pace of change, but everyone agrees on the evil wrought by bureaucrats who withheld the truth about Chernobyl from us," the bearded man finished.

"Hold those bureaucrats who lied accountable," screamed someone a row behind Dmitry and Ilya.

"A Nuremberg trial for Chernobyl!" a man cried from the back. A second man picked up the chant, then another.

Dmitry was shaking. All around him voices were shouting, "A Nuremberg trial for Chernobyl!" Fireworks exploded in his brain.

When the meeting broke up, the crowd swept Dmitry and Ilya into the street. They tripped home intoxicated by the promise of independence, pledging to sacrifice whatever was needed to achieve it.

23

WASHINGTON, SEPTEMBER 1990

Vickie had been looking forward to the start of the National Symphony's season for weeks. She slipped into a black sleeveless dress, put on the aquamarine necklace her aunt gave her, and hailed a cab to the Kennedy Center. When she stepped from the cab into the red-carpeted lobby, she felt like someone had snipped the guy wire anchoring her to the ordinary world. Crystal chandeliers dangled from a five-story ceiling, lighting the way to the concert hall. She stopped for a moment of silence before a massive bronze bust of John F. Kennedy, which was flanked by floor-to-ceiling windows. Entering the concert hall, she found her seat in the orchestra section, fifteen rows back from the stage to the right of the conductor's podium. Further back than her ideal, but not bad for a first-time season subscriber, she thought. Soon the lights dimmed, the crowd hushed, and

Mstislav Rostropovich raised his baton.

Watching the orchestra, her mind wandered to an image of Rostropovich plucked from the concert hall and seated in a lone chair, cradling his cello at the Berlin Wall. During intermission, the Kennedy Center director took the stage to invite the audience to celebrate the National Symphony Orchestra's sixtieth season opening after the concert with free wine on the River Terrace.

For the second half of the program, Rostropovich conducted *Pictures at an Exhibition*, the piece Vickie had been waiting to hear. The majestic music flooded the concert hall, pulling her under its spell. The "Great Gate of Kiev" built to a powerful climax, and she jumped up with the rest of the audience, giving Rostropovich a standing ovation.

Vickie floated to the lobby high on the music. As she was inching toward the terrace, she spotted Darren Cunningham heading toward her.

"What a rush!" Darren said when he reached her.

Vickie nodded, still exhilarated.

"I was hoping I'd see you here tonight."

"What made you think I'd be here?" she asked.

"You mentioned buying a season ticket to the symphony, and I've had one for years, so I figured there was a fair chance I'd see you."

Darren guided Vickie through the crowd spilling onto the terrace. She felt his hand grazing the small of her back, a male gesture she found intimate.

They made their way to a table spread with glasses of white wine, then ambled to the edge of the terrace. Finding a private spot, they leaned against the rail. They stood quietly, sipping their wine under the starry sky, watching the city lights shimmer on the black Potomac. The tranquility was interrupted by the unexpected roar of a jet swooping over the river on a straight path for its landing at National Airport.

"When did you become interested in classical music?" Darren turned to face Vickie. "Do you remember?"

"When I was in the sixth grade, my aunt took me to Evansville to see the *Nutcracker*," Vickie recalled. "The ballerinas and the Christmas tree rising to the ceiling were enchanting, and the music was so beautiful, it transported me to a place I'd never been. I must have talked about it all the way home in the car because for Christmas, Aunt Lydia bought me the *Nutcracker* and Beethoven's Fifth. Every evening, I would go into our living room and play them. Nothing had ever affected me like this music. My aunt was so good to me. Records kept appearing—Schubert's Unfinished Symphony, Beethoven's Seventh, Mozart's Jupiter Symphony. Each one opened a new universe to me—" Vickie paused, searching for a way to describe the powerful feelings and thoughts that listening to these orchestral pieces unleashed in her. "It was as if the composers who created those symphonies knew the longings locked in my heart—and gave them wings to fly."

Darren nodded, waiting for her to continue.

"Words don't do justice to the experience. It was like a glimpse of Heaven, I guess," she finished, surprised at being comfortable talking about her love of classical music, something she usually guarded as a private refuge.

"You're describing exactly how I feel! Classical music is my religion. I worshipped Beethoven all through high school. Then came Mozart, and we mustn't forget Mussorgsky—"

"Or Mahler," Vickie interjected. "His Second Sym—"

"Darren Cunningham! You never know who you'll see here." A stocky man with a thin goatee appeared in front of them and thrust his hand out for Darren to shake. "I didn't mean to interrupt." The interloper turned to Vickie.

"Not at all. We were raving about the concert. Victoria, this is Gordon Dickson. He heads up the Nuclear Nonproliferation Institute, and his wife Betsy. She's an attorney with Price and Pearse." Darren introduced the power couple. "Victoria Evans is a journalist."

"Really! Who do you write for?" Betsy asked breathlessly. A platinum blonde, she was wearing a mauve suit and a strand of pearls that made the most of her tanned, leathery face.

"Newhart News—"

"Never heard of it." Betsy frowned, dialing down the voltage.

"It's a small newspaper chain. We have eight newspapers in California, New Jer—"

"Our oldest is interning with the *San Francisco Times*," Gordon interrupted.

"Our youngest rides at the same stable as Maddie," added Betsy, giving Darren a solicitous smile. "Do you have any children, Victoria?"

"A daughter. She's eleven." As Vickie answered Betsy, Gordon took the opportunity to pull Darren into a private conversation about nuclear weapons in Ukraine.

Vickie strained to hear what Gordon was telling Darren, but she could catch only every third word. Security... nuclear ... materials ... weapons ... Ukraine ... Soviet ... breaking up.

"Our oldest, Elinor, is twenty. She's the one doing the internship at the *San Francisco Times*." Betsy jabbered about her daughters loud enough to block out the conversation taking place between Darren and Gordon. "Does your daughter ride?" Betsy trained her eyes on Vickie, who shook her head. "If you'd like to get her started, I can give you a referral to Rosalind's instructor. He's got a waiting list as long as your arm."

Vickie tried to lean in closer to the whispered conversation on nuclear weapons, but Betsy was running superb interference for her husband.

"You were raving about the concert? I found Rostropovich's interpretation far too romantic. His true calling is as a cellist," Betsy pontificated, switching from equestrian judge to music critic.

Vickie looked to Darren for relief, but he was engrossed in an intense exchange and didn't notice her. Not wanting to lose the magic of the evening, she decided to extricate herself from the scene and bid Betsy goodbye.

The big news at work in the morning was that Alan had named Cynthia Ames as the new business reporter, replacing Robbie Clapp, who'd landed a job with *The Herald*. The buzz about promotions reminded Vickie that she was still on probation. She had generated so many stories over the past few months she'd been hoping that Alan would make her a full-fledged reporter on staff. That day had yet to come, however, leaving Vickie feeling nervous about her job security. After congratulating Cynthia, Vickie got a call from Darren. He asked if she could meet him.

"Sure. I have a press conference at eleven, but I should be

finished before lunch time." Vickie was looking forward to filling Darren in on her lunch with Dr. Chandler and what she had discovered about Kodak's fogged film.

"I don't want to wait that long. Can you get away for a few minutes now? I'm near the Press Building, at the coffee shop on Thirteenth and G, if you want to meet me," he suggested.

"Sure, I'll be there in five."

Vickie hurried to the elevator, wondering what juicy tip he had for her. It must be a huge story if it couldn't wait until lunch, she thought. She dashed up 13th Street, her mind racing with possibilities. Perhaps Darren would offer her information on nuclear materials in Ukraine. Or maybe he knew of something important about to break. She entered the coffee shop and spotted Darren at a café table wedged in a window alcove.

"First, I want to apologize for getting caught up with Gordon last night and sticking you with his wife. She can be insufferable." Darren pulled out a chair for Vickie.

Vickie rolled her eyes knowingly. "That's all right. I had to get home to Molly." Vickie sat on the edge of her seat waiting for Darren to tell her what Gordon had found so urgent. She didn't want to admit she'd been straining to eavesdrop on their conversation about nuclear weapons in Ukraine, so she waited for Darren to broach the subject.

"Do you want a coffee?" he asked, stirring cream into his cup.

"No, I just had a cup." She studied his face, waiting.

Darren leaned forward on his elbows and cleared his throat. "What I really wanted to say, what I want to ask you, is would like to have dinner with me on Saturday night? Afterwards, we could go hear the Juilliard String Quartet at the Library of Congress, if you'd like."

Vickie's heart galloped. She wasn't expecting this. The thought of going out with Darren sent a surge of excitement through her body. But her joy was chased by alarm as she realized that she would have to turn him down. She enjoyed his company tremendously, they had daughters close in age, and they both loved classical music. It would be a match made in heaven except for one fatal flaw: she didn't think it would be ethical to date a source.

She recalled the warning of her journalism professor: "Don't get too close to your sources. Always keep them at arm's length. Remember, the perception of a conflict of interest can be damaging to your credibility and that of your news organization." He had illustrated his point with a story about a young reporter who'd been fired from a Pennsylvania newspaper after the editor discovered she had dated the police commissioner while reporting on a crime case in the city.

Vickie tried to think of a way to turn Darren down without hurting his feelings.

"I can't, Darren. I can't date a source," she said, hoping he would understand.

"A source? Is that all I am?" He looked like a puppy that had been kicked.

"No, not at all. If circumstances were different, I would love to go out with you. I don't think we should get involved in that way when I'm a reporter covering energy, and you are a government official who gives me information—"

Darren stiffened. "Information about bomb tests decades ago? Everything I've talked about with you is publicly available in declassified reports. I've never told you anything that could be construed as confidential."

"It's not just me. What about my colleague, Ian? Imagine if it got around that you and I were dating. It could jeopardize our credibility as a news organization," Vickie protested. No one at work had ever talked to her about this kind of scenario, but she didn't want to risk wandering into a situation that might compromise Newhart News—or threaten her job.

"Jeopardize your credibility? I thought we were—" Darren's voice cracked and trailed off.

"You've known from the start that this is a work relationship. Granted, we've shared personal things, and we get along great, but dating is a whole other level," Vickie explained, desperate to make him understand her perspective.

"I guess I was out of line, then," Darren responded quietly, drawing into himself. "If you'll excuse me, please—" He stood abruptly and without looking back rushed out the door.

Vickie wanted to call after him, but what would she say? For a split second she burned with self-righteous anger. Why couldn't he try to understand her dilemma as a reporter? He should have known better than to try to mix pleasure and work, she thought. It always blows up. But her anger dissipated instantly, and her eyes filled with tears as she realized what she'd done. She liked Darren a lot. She felt natural talking with him in a way she didn't with anyone else, and now she would probably never hear from him again. The terrible irony was that she'd also no doubt lost him as a potential source.

KIEV, SEPTEMBER 1990

"The thyroid gland is shaped like a butterfly spreading its wings over the front of the throat," Dr. Rudenko explained in a mild voice. Larysa's hand flew to her own throat as he spoke. She pictured a sharp proboscis needling Katya's windpipe, as the lepidopteran's black, powdery wings choked off her little girl's breath. Desperate to push the image from her mind, Larysa turned to Dmitry, who was sitting beside her. They were facing the surgeon who would cut the malignant tumor from Katya's thyroid.

Dr. Rudenko had meant for the naturalistic metaphor to comfort Larysa, but he could see that in her extreme state of fatigue it had caused her distress. She'd been watching over her daughter since her admission to the clinic five days ago.

"We will remove the tumor tomorrow morning. Chances for

a complete recovery are quite good," he told Larysa, sensing she did not want to hear details of the surgery.

"Will you do a total thyroidectomy? Will it be necessary to remove both lobes?" asked Dmitry.

"My son's in his second year at the Medical Institute." Larysa touched Dmitry's arm.

"I wish to know every step of the procedure," Dmitry said.

"After she's prepped, I will make an incision and cut through the soft tissue until I locate the tumor on the right side of her thyroid gland. We don't know the full extent of the cancer. That determination will come during surgery. A total thyroidectomy is a possibility."

"How long will the operation take?" Dmitry asked.

"I have performed more than fifteen thyroidectomies on children this year. The time has varied from two hours to four hours, depending on what I encounter," Dr. Rudenko answered.

"I'm going to return to Katya's room, now," Larysa said.

"I'll join you after we finish," Dmitry told his mother. He had done a unit on endocrinology in the spring and wanted to learn everything he could from the surgeon. Dr. Rudenko remained at his desk, answering Dmitry's questions.

Larysa tiptoed down the cancer ward's narrow corridor to Katya's room. A gossamer curtain rippled in the breeze coming through an open window at the far end of the room. Yellow leaves papered the trees, giving off the bittersweet scent of autumn. Inside, a strong bleach odor overpowered the fall fragrance. There were four beds, one in each corner. Katya lay on the bed against the far wall, to the right of the window. She was the oldest child in the room. A girl no more than five lay on the bed across from

Katya. A fringe of short, dark hair framed the young child's frightened face. The girl's hand curled around the fingers of her mother, who sat on the edge of the bed reading a storybook. The bed three feet from the foot of Katya's had an empty mattress, its occupant having been transferred to Kiev's Clinic 14, the leukemia ward. The small child sleeping in the fourth bed had arrived yesterday afternoon.

The contours of Katya's body barely showed beneath the bedding. Her translucent skin and round eyes gave her the look of a much younger child. Gone were the poise and vibrancy she had radiated on stage at the Pioneers Palace. Since her diagnosis, she'd been clinging to her parents and Dmitry. Though she seldom complained, Katya's face wore the distant, wary look common to children on the ward old enough to understand the gravity of their illness.

Katya's ensemble leader had been the first to notice a problem. In May, she had mentioned that Katya's voice sounded hoarse. Everyone assumed it was a summer cold. By July, she was having trouble swallowing and singing. A doctor at the clinic had given her cough syrup and prescribed a week of rest. Rather than getting better, however, her health had taken a nosedive. She had to stop going to rehearsals. Katya had managed to get to the first day of school in September, but exhaustion had prevented her from returning the next day. On a return trip to the clinic, one of the doctors had palpated her neck and discovered the nodules, a telltale sign of the thyroid cancer cropping up in many Ukrainian and Byelorussian children. Further testing confirmed the grim diagnosis.

"Are you thirsty, Katyenka?" Larysa asked, lifting the back of her head to plump the pillow. She shook her head.

When Dmitry entered the room, Katya's face brightened.

"Great news! The doctor said I can do your surgery tomorrow, Katya," he boomed.

"What?" Larysa gasped, taken in by his joke. They all laughed.

"I'm going to get Papa now," Larysa said, relieved to have Dmitry keeping his sister company while she fetched Vasyl. She knew that Dmitry's presence was magic for Katya, lifting her spirits.

When Larysa returned with Vasyl, the family passed two hours sipping tea and talking to Katya. Her voice had all but disappeared. She simply listened and tried to smile now and then. Katya didn't ask her parents if her voice would return strong after the surgery, or if she would be able to sing again. She didn't dare to ask. She drifted into sleep sitting upright with her head against Vasyl's chest. He kissed the top of her head and eased her back against the pillow.

Dmitry urged his parents to go home and rest. They were reluctant to leave Katya's bedside, but Larysa was bordering on delirium from lack of sleep, and Vasyl's heart pills were at their flat. They finally agreed to leave, promising to return early in the morning. They wanted to be there after Katya came out of anesthesia.

Throughout the night, Dmitry paced the ward talking to the nurses, who soaked in his youthful energy and thirst for knowledge. At dawn, two nurses woke Katya and lifted her slender frame onto a gurney. Dmitry took her hand. As the nurses rolled her down the corridor, Katya's trusting eyes fixed on Dmitry's.

There was no one on this planet Dmitry loved more than his

little sister, his lighter half. He had felt lonely as a young child and had wished for a brother or sister. Katya had fulfilled his dreams. He walked beside her now, forcing a smile for her. He gave her hand a gentle squeeze then reluctantly let go as the nurses whisked her through the door to the surgical theater.

When the door closed, Dmitry felt a gust of helplessness blow through his body. Knees trembling, he returned to Katya's room and stood staring out the window. It was approaching sunrise, that time of day when so many souls slip into and out of this world. As he peered through the glass into the darkness, tears drenched his cheeks. He was an atheist lacking even the rudiments of religious belief. Still, an impulse moved him to pray.

"Please God, don't take her from me," he pleaded aloud, hoping someone was listening.

25

WASHINGTON, NOVEMBER 1990

I cy rain pelted Vickie's face as she trudged from the Forrestal Building to the Smithsonian Metro stop. Squeezing into a train bound for Metro Center, she found a sliver of standing room between passengers whose gloomy expressions reflected her mood. In close to three months of sifting through boxes in the reading room, she had yet to unearth anything about Kodak beyond the single letter to Dr. Webb. At her current pace, it would take her years to skim even a portion of the declassified documents. Worse still, she worried that she may have overlooked something important in the documents that she had perused.

Vickie wasn't ready to admit defeat, but she realized this job was too big for one person. She decided to try to enlist the help of Gary Sloan from Citizens United Against Nuclear Weapons or Denise Miller of Georgetown University, whose names she continued to see on the reading room logs. She waited until lunchtime to call them. Using a pay phone upstairs at the Press Club, she first called Gary Sloan. He explained that he was copying declassified documents for his organization's library. While Gary hadn't been reading the pages, he promised to tell her if he happened to notice any mention of Kodak. When she called Denise Miller, Vickie learned that the Georgetown University intern was copying pages for Christian Connor, a historian and scholar. Minutes later, Vickie was on the phone with Professor Connor. He suggested they meet after work for cocktail hour at the end of the week.

On Friday at six o'clock, Vickie took a cab to Martin's Tavern, Professor Connor's choice. Nestled in a quintessential Georgetown neighborhood, the restaurant's wood-paneled interior exuded warmth. Vickie was wearing a blue silk blouse under a gray suit and looking for a man with a crimson handkerchief in his suit pocket. She was scanning patrons at the bar when a portly man in his sixties with a silver mustache stood and gestured to her from a booth.

Christian, as the professor preferred, shook her hand, offering a stream of welcomes. He struck Vickie as the kind of teacher who would command the full attention of a packed lecture hall. Voicing astonishment that she'd never been to the Washington landmark, he regaled her with tales about presidents and socialites who had dined at the tavern since its opening in 1933.

"I'm a Scotch man. Your poison, or should I say pleasure?" he asked, waiving down a waiter.

"Gin and tonic," Vickie answered.

"So, you're a journalist?" he continued, getting down to

business.

"Yes, I'm a reporter for Newhart News, but my interest in these Atomic Energy Commission documents is personal. I'm not writing an article for our newspapers on this."

"We're off the record, then? To be clear—not that I mind either way."

"That's right. I'm researching this on my own time. If I decide at some point in the future to write about any of this on a freelance basis, I will set up a proper interview."

"Fair enough." Christian took a swallow of Scotch and peered across the table at Vickie. "What are you hoping to find in those dusty boxes?"

Vickie told him about her search for evidence that the government had struck a deal with Kodak to give the company advance warning about atom bomb tests and information about when to expect fallout to come down. "In addition to files about Kodak, I'm interested in evidence that fallout from the Simon blast in April 1953 rained down on cities in upstate New York."

"I haven't come upon either of those topics, but I'll be sure to let you know if I do," Christian promised.

"What are you researching?" Vickie asked, squeezing a lime slice into her drink.

"I'm having my intern, Denise, copy as much as she's able every week for my collection. It's such a treasure," Christian began. "My current research interest is Project Gabriel. I don't suppose you've come upon mention of this?"

"Project Gabriel? What a name! No, I haven't. I've only been spending half an hour at the reading room a few mornings a week. What's Project Gabriel? Can you tell me about it?"

"What comes to mind? Gabriel blowing his horn on judgment day. Apocalypse. Doomsday. The return of the Lord!" Christian's voice rose like a sounding trumpet as he raked his fingers through his thick silver hair. "As it turns out, one of the more accurate code-names military strategists came up with. Project Gabriel was hatched in 1949 to determine how many atom bombs could be exploded in the atmosphere before Earth became uninhabitable for humanity. I heard about this undertaking a few years ago from a scientist who had worked on the Manhattan Project."

"That's unbelievable!" Vickie leaned forward. "It means that in 1949 government scientists were worried about fallout from bomb tests—"

"That's right, and it didn't deter them from going forward with massive nuclear blasts in the Pacific Ocean and above-ground detonations in Nevada," Christian interjected. "Scientists knew that handling radium posed dangers. It wasn't only cancer they were concerned about, though. They also were worried about genetic effects. Radiation was known to cause genetic mutations, which led the government to wonder how many bomb detonations it would take to overexpose the world's population."

"And turn human beings into mutants. Did they come up with a number?"

"All this was top secret. I haven't been able to nail down a definitive answer. Chiefs of the AEC's Division of Biology and Medicine initially thought it would take about three thousand one-kiloton bombs to reach doomsday level. They kept revising that number upward as time went on, however. By 1951, AEC radiobiologists were estimating that one hundred thousand Naga-saki-sized atom bombs would have to be exploded to render the

Earth uninhabitable. They hiked their estimate again in 1953."

Over a second Scotch, Christian described how Project Gabriel had paved the way for Project Sunshine. During Project Gabriel, scientists decided that strontium-90, which is incorporated into bones like calcium, posed the greatest threat to humanity from fallout. Project Sunshine was christened to measure strontium-90 in bones of people born after the start of nuclear testing, compared with bones of people born before 1950.

"The secrecy surrounding Project Sunshine made it hard for scientists to obtain bones for studies. Researchers went about finding them—leg bones were prized—in scurrilous ways. Bones of dead infants and children were especially sought after. One researcher told me they used to chop legs off bodies in morgues—all in secret."

Vickie shuddered. "I can't believe they called it Project Sunshine! Whatever possessed the government to approve that kind of gruesome activity?"

"Grotesque as it sounds today, you must understand the times, Victoria. World War Two was brutal, and Americans were terrified of Russia after the war. I was fifteen when the war ended—old enough to remember. More than sixty million people died during the second World War, but in many ways the Cold War was even more frightening because people understood the atom bomb's power. Everything having to do with the nuclear enterprise was cloaked in secrecy. At first, we tried to keep the Russians from getting the bomb. When that failed, both sides set about building ever bigger bombs in what escalated into an unwinnable arms race."

Vickie was trying to wrap her head around the idea of stealing dead children's bones for research. "Were scientists able to determine how much strontium was getting into kids' bones and whether it caused more cancer?"

"I don't know. I'm hoping the answers lie buried in one of those boxes." Christian tipped his head back to swallow the last golden drops from his glass. "Researchers have answered some questions by studying teeth," he added. "Teeth are easier to obtain because baby teeth fall out. If I recall correctly, one study found that teeth of children born in 1963 contained fifty times more radioactive strontium than teeth of children born before 1950."

"Fifty times as much? That's huge."

Christian nodded. He glanced at his watch, prompting Vickie to do the same. They'd talked longer than they had expected.

Outside, the sun's rays painted a salmon stripe along the horizon. They stood for a moment in the golden light, waiting for a cab. Before parting company, Vickie promised to keep her eye out for papers on Project Gabriel and its ghoulish successor. Christian assured her that he would watch for documents on Kodak and the Simon test.

26

KIEV, OCTOBER 1990

Dmitry hurried to finish translating an article on thyroid cancer from English into Russian. He was proud to be earning money doing translations for doctors at the Medical Institute, which helped put food on his family's table. Even more exciting, he had been chosen to travel to Washington, D.C., as part of an official Ukrainian medical delegation. When he finished his translation, he joined a group of students heading to the demonstration on October Revolution Square.

"Are you sure you should do this, Mitya? We could be arrested," warned his friend, Yan. On October 2nd, more than 150 students had started a hunger strike in front of the monument to Lenin. Today, thousands of students were planning to march in support of the hunger strike. Tents were pitched around the square, and an orange banner displayed the students' demands.

They were calling for the prime minister's resignation and abolition of the Communist Party. They also demanded a shutdown of the reactors that were still operating at Chernobyl.

"Ilya's been striking from the first day. I need to support him," Dmitry told Yan.

"But if they arrest you, you'll miss your chance to go to America. We're counting on you to tell journalists there about the coverup of radiation from Chernobyl," Yan said.

"I have to march," Dmitry insisted.

As Dmitry and Yan approached the square, one of their classmates called to them. He was waving a blue-and-yellow flag.

"Have you heard? Gorbachev won the Nobel Peace Prize," he panted. "*Glasnost.*" Dmitry and Yan shook their heads.

Dmitry grew agitated. He held Gorbachev and his cronies responsible for perpetuating lies about Chernobyl.

"Gorbachev needed an army of Russians to suppress the truth, but free Ukrainians will release it," Dmitry said.

As the young men reached the square, they pressed close to their comrades, numbering 50,000 altogether. Thousands of blue-and-yellow flags rippled in the wind. Some students wore gas masks. Others carried radiation hazard signs and banners demanding the truth about Chernobyl. They marched with determination, shouting for an end to the Communist Party. Their words, amplified ten thousand-fold, rang like church bells in Dmitry's ears.

❧

Looking out over the throngs of students converging on Khreshchatyk, Anatoly feared for his life. Angry chants reverberated through the windows of his office. One particular chant made his blood run cold: "A Nuremberg trial for Chernobyl." He remembered hearing about the Nuremberg trials for the top echelon of Nazis. Leaders were hanged for their crimes against humanity. Scores of functionaries, who pleaded that they were "just following orders," had been sentenced to life in prison.

Anatoly thought back to the orders he had followed to help the faltering regime cover up the deadly radiation for ten days. "Was I immoral?" he wondered. He told himself that he was timid, but no more than most. Soviet citizens followed orders and drank vodka to numb their conscience and wash away memory. They were all in this together, he thought, and vodka was the balm that made their lives of obedience bearable. But the youth marching outside were a different breed.

Everything was changing. Anatoly could see unmistakable signs of the Soviet Union's impending downfall. He sensed that the days of this regime were numbered. What would become of him after it collapsed and these angry men in the street took over?

Pavlo Popyvich entered the office and came to stand beside Anatoly at the window. Like all Party bureaucrats, Popyvich was scrambling to paper over past misdeeds and position himself for future gains.

"We need to destroy files and documents pertaining to radiation exposures," Pavlo murmured, without turning to face Anatoly. "Thousands of medical records are being shredded as we speak, but there are thousands more, and they are scattered. It looks like we don't have much time."

Listening to Pavlo, Anatoly thought about his journal, where he had recorded numbers that revealed the unadulterated truth.

Once revisionists were able to doctor the history of Chernobyl, he realized, his journal might become the world's last repository of accurate radiation figures. For a moment he wondered if he could parlay his diary into some sort of amnesty. He dismissed this fantasy, however. History was a powerful force rushing forward like a swollen river, and he had already staked his life to low ground on the wrong bank. His journal would not save him from the retribution of the masses poisoned by Chernobyl and angered by the deceit.

Anatoly decided he would make no more deals with the devil. One day, the coverup would be exposed, of that he was certain. All the machinations of Pavlo and his ilk could not stop the truth from coming out. Even more haunting than his fear of being lynched by angry mobs or an international tribunal was the anguish he carried in his heart. He could not escape the consequences of his cowardice on that fateful day when he might have saved his beloved little Katya from cancer. He excused himself from Pavlo and walked downstairs to the lobby.

How many times had his mind dragged him through the night before that infamous May Day parade—a "March of Death," as one poet now called it? When the wind changed direction, he could have called Larysa and told her to shut the windows. He could have warned her to keep the children inside. He could have flown Katya and Dmitry out of Kiev. That's what most top Ukrainian Party officials had done—something Anatoly only learned a year after the fact. Had he known that others were taking chances and breaking their silence to save their loved ones, would he have been emboldened to call Larysa? He wondered— and this speculation about what might have been tormented him.

In an ultimate stroke of cruelty, which he mistook initially for kindness, Fate had given Anatoly a glorious reprieve from his guilt. He remembered every moment of that magnificent summer in Odessa, combing the beach with Katya for smooth stones and shells, singing songs with her on the veranda in the evening. Such a giving nature the child possessed! He enjoyed her pure voice and sweet disposition as freely as peaches and pears picked ripe from the garden.

Throughout the summer, while Dmitry was at camp, Anatoly had watched Katya for signs of illness, but she glowed with good health. Time had tricked him into forgetting. When 1986 slipped into 1987, during the New Year celebration with the Marchenko family, he let himself believe the children had skated through the catastrophe unharmed. Fate had bestowed on him more than three years of unearned joy. Vasyl's illness had come as the first warning of trouble, but that was not unexpected. Anatoly had been watching the government's secret figures on Chernobyl liquidator casualties. More than 3,000 liquidators had died already. Thousands more were developing cancers. Others, like Vasyl, had rotting bones and failing hearts.

But Katya? No, Fate had allowed Anatoly to believe the radiation had passed over her and Dmitry—his brother Alexei's two precious grandchildren, who had become like his own.

Anatoly could still hear the panic in Larysa's voice when she'd called six weeks ago to tell him about Katya's cancer diagnosis. Katya had been tired, she'd had sore throats, but she had been working hard with the youth ensemble. What she needed was rest, he had told himself.

If only he had found the courage to call Larysa and warn her to take the children away before the May Day parade, he could have saved Katya's health. He could have saved her innocence, he thought, choking back dry tears. He could have saved her voice.

Anatoly pushed against the heavy door, and the roar of the mob struck him like a boxer's blow to his jaw. Thousands of students streamed through the street demanding "a Nuremberg trial for Chernobyl." His breath came in shallow, jagged pants as he felt the noose tightening around his neck.

27

WASHINGTON, NOVEMBER 1990

With Congress out for Thanksgiving and most of the bureau's reporters away visiting their families, news stories trickled in from foreign capitals. Ian Hoffman reported from Paris on European and North American leaders declaring a formal end to the Cold War. Gabe Green filed a feature from Riyadh on U.S. troops hunkered down for a lonely holiday far from home. Vickie was one of three reporters who were staffing the office with Sean in case something unexpected happened in Washington. The morning crawled by uneventful. Even the teletype machines went silent for long stretches. Then at noon, Sean called Vickie over to his desk.

"Didn't you tell me a while back you were doing something on cracks in nuclear plants?" Sean asked her. A husky redhead with penetrating eyes the color of sherry, Sean was a constant presence, opening the newsroom before seven in the morning and closing shop after midnight. Without ever losing his cool, he kept track of the Washington bureau's sixteen reporters, deadlines for eight newspapers in three time zones, and correspondents in London and Berlin.

"Yes, I wrote a story on that at the end of April, but Thane didn't think it rated as national news," Vickie answered.

"Well, it does now. United Press has a story here saying the NRC issued a notice to utilities about cracks in nuclear plants in Illinois and New Jersey." Sean handed Vickie the wire copy. "Our Rockford and Jersey editors will want something on this."

Vickie suppressed the urge to say, "I knew it was an important story. I had a scoop." She wished Thane were here so she could see his expression, but he'd flown to Boston for the holiday.

"I'll call the NRC and get a copy of the notice," she told Sean. "I can pull in background from my old story and get reactions from the utilities."

"Sounds good," Sean said. "A few graphs will be enough on Thanksgiving Eve."

Vickie filed her story at five o'clock. By six, the newsroom had cleared out except for her and Sean.

"Got any plans for Thanksgiving, Sean?" Vickie took a seat beside his desk. Jake had taken Molly to his parents' house in New Jersey for the four-day weekend, so Vickie was in no hurry to get home. From newsroom scuttlebutt, she knew Sean had divorced fifteen years ago and never remarried. His ex-wife and estranged children lived in Seattle.

"I'm doing my usual—Sholl's cafeteria. Best mashed potatoes and gravy in the District." He leaned back in his chair, locking his fingers behind his head. "How about yourself?"

"I'm thinking Yenching Palace. If you change your mind about Sholl's, you can join me in my neighborhood for Chinese," Vickie offered.

"Yenching Palace, huh? A lot of history to that place," Sean mused, stretching out his legs and resting his shoes on the edge of his gunmetal desk.

Sensing he was getting ready to spin a yarn, Vickie joined him, extending her legs. She rested her high heels perpendicular to his scuffed loafers and scooted her skirt toward her knees.

"How so?" She wriggled back in the chair to get more comfortable.

"There was a time when everyone who was anyone stopped by there—I'm talking about rock stars, writers, politicians. What it's best known for, though, is the place where envoys for John F. Kennedy and Nikita Khrushchev held secret meetings during the Cuban Missile Crisis in 1962. They worked out a deal that ended that terrifying standoff between the globe's two nuclear powers." Sean's eyes twinkled. "To think they saved the world from a nuclear holocaust, right there in a booth at the Yenching Palace!"

"That's amazing. Anything else?"

"Kissinger reportedly dined there frequently with Chinese diplomats."

"I guess instead of getting takeout I should sit in a booth and eavesdrop."

"So, Victoria, I'm thinking cafeterias are fair game for a toothless old man like me, but aren't you too young to be eating solo on Thanksgiving?" Sean asked gently.

"What are you, forty-five?" Vickie asked, deflecting his concern over her spending the holiday alone.

"Try fifty-nine, sweetheart." Sean reached over his knees for the bottle of Maalox on the edge of his desk. He swigged a gulp and wiped his upper lip with his sleeve.

"I'm looking forward to sleeping in and catching up on reading while my ex has my daughter," Vickie responded, perhaps believing it herself.

Vickie awoke to a call from Molly. She jabbered excitedly about her cousins, who had flown to New Jersey from Hawaii. They were all getting ready to go to a high school football game before sitting down to a feast with ten people. Jake came on the phone, and they wished each other a happy Thanksgiving. When Vickie hung up the phone, a wave of sadness hit her. She wished she could be with Molly right now. It hadn't occurred to her that she might feel lonely today, as people alone on Thanksgiving were supposed to feel.

Telling herself this was just another day, she went to the kitchen to make coffee. She sliced a banana into a bowl of Cheerios and brought it to the table. The kitchen smelled empty. She missed the homey warmth of turkey and pies baking in the oven. Sean was right. It had been a mistake not to plan something for the one day of the year dedicated to sharing a meal with family and friends. She considered trying to find a shelter where she could volunteer to serve turkey and pie to the homeless. That would take some research, however—and homeless shelters generally overflowed with volunteers on Thanksgiving and Christmas.

Finishing her cereal, she decided to take a walk. She slipped into jeans and a pullover and stepped outside. The weather was mild, with a balmy breeze evoking Florida. Misty fog muted the white sun. She walked briskly, for the sake of moving her limbs, breathing in moist air and enjoying the whooshing of leaves under her feet. When she got to the zoo, she turned in on a whim and wandered past the cheetahs. She hadn't been here since the day she and Molly ran into Darren and his daughter—six months ago. She imagined Darren appearing around the corner. She pictured him as he spotted her, his earnest face bursting into that contagious smile of his. They would remark about how astonishing it was, such serendipity, happening upon each other in the same spot as before! Her rational mind knew the odds of bumping into him today were zero. Still, she couldn't stop thinking she would see him right around the next bend. She wondered if she subconsciously had walked here hoping to see him. Trying to shake off her magical thinking, she retraced her steps to Macomb Street.

Back at home, Vickie paced from the kitchen to the living room, too restless to sit. She decided to walk to the Yenching Palace and get an early meal. Remembering Sean's stories, she asked to be seated in a booth. A cheerful current of chatter and laughter flowed through the restaurant. She followed a waiter past families in holiday outfits seated around tables to her right and pairs of love birds nestled in booths to her left. She sensed their eyes on her and felt too self-conscious to eat alone.

"I changed my mind. I want takeout," she told the waiter. Cheeks burning, she followed him back across the dining room to the cash register. The kitchen took forever filling her order.

When she got home, she set the boxes of shrimp with snow peas and pork fried rice on the coffee table. She fetched the stack of magazines and papers that had been piling up for ages on the radiator by the front door and brought them to the couch to sort through. Midway down the pile she found a manila envelope that Darren had messengered to her several months ago. She was trying to get him out of her mind and considered tossing the envelope aside, but she couldn't resist opening it.

What she found inside were pages of documents like those she'd been combing through in the DOE reading room. On the first page of each file was a large square stamped "DECLASSI-FIED." The files, which had been declassified between 1986 and 1989, focused on a report with the dry title, "Dissolving of Twenty Day Metal at Hanford." A note in the margin written in Darren's hand read: "The Green Run." The report described an experiment in Hanford, Washington, that had gone wrong. Hanford was a secret facility built in the 1940s to produce plutonium for atom bombs. During the experiment, dubbed the Green Run, officials had planned to release 4,000 curies of iodine-131 into the atmosphere. Somehow, they ended up releasing 7,780 curies. Darren had written in the margin that the Three Mile Island accident in 1979 released less than 24 curies of radioactive iodine.

The massive release, which began on the night of December 2, 1949, lasted for seven hours. Hanford officials were counting on the wind to disperse the radioactive iodine, but the weather grew calm. A radioactive plume measuring 40 miles by 200 miles spread out from Hanford and stalled. Radiation settled on small towns and pastures under the plume, posing a threat to children drinking milk from local dairies, but the government didn't warn anyone. They kept the entire incident secret.

The purpose of the Green Run wasn't explained. The document suggested it may have been part of a scheme to help the Air Force locate Soviet plutonium facilities. If the Russians had been racing to build atomic weapons, the thinking went, they might have used "green" uranium. This green uranium was reprocessed for only sixteen days, instead of the usual one hundred days. Green uranium gave off more radionuclides.

Continuing through the files, she found a detailed map showing towns that were contaminated by the Green Run's radioactive plume. She felt a pang of recognition when she saw the town of Waitsburg on the map. She remembered Darren telling her that he spent the first twelve years of his life in Waitsburg. She realized that his family must have been among those who were irradiated while sleeping in their beds that December night in 1949. This explained Darren's passionate interest in nuclear testing.

Right now, more than anything, Vickie wished she could talk to Darren, but she had blown that relationship. She thought back to their lunches. Darren had given thoughtful answers to her questions about radiation, speaking on the record—nothing more. Why had she thought it would be unethical to date him? She could see now that she'd been caught up in her ambition to rope him in as a source who would leak secrets to her leading to front-page stories. Even harder to understand now was why she had been so worried that dating Darren would present a conflict of interest. After all, he was an arms control negotiator, and she reported on energy and the environment. She doubted anyone at Newhart News would have cared if she had dated him. Ironically, Gabe Green had assumed she was sleeping with Darren—and his only reaction was mild jealousy.

Her mind wandered back to the Kennedy Center, to the

excitement on Darren's face when he approached her in the foyer. Her eyes watered as she recalled talking about her love of classical music with him. She remembered the surge of excitement that ran through her body when his fingertips brushed her back as he guided her to the terrace. As she pictured the city lights shimmering on the Potomac, she blinked back tears. How she longed to experience another night like that one, with Darren the man, not Darren the source.

Setting aside the Green Run files she stared out the window. Smokey clouds streaked a dusty rose sky. The black silhouette of a lone bird skimmed the treetops and landed on a bare branch at the back of the yard. Watching the light gradually seep away, she realized that she had been putting everything into her job. She thought for a moment about calling Gabe Green, but he was probably turning in after a night spent at a hotel bar trading stories with famous war correspondents. Who else could she call? Gareth Will was following his passion, plotting anti-nuclear actions somewhere in Germany. She thought briefly of dialing Sean—and quickly dismissed the urge. Confiding in a superior was a cardinal sin in any workplace. Newsrooms were no exception. She pictured Sean hunched in front of his computer screen at this very moment, chugging Maalox. He would have marched boldly into the Yenching Palace and occupied a booth by himself like a king surveying his fiefdom. He had a sharp mind and never got ruffled, but he hadn't seen his children in years—a loss she couldn't imagine enduring. When she moved here with Molly, she had wanted more than anything to succeed as a journalist—yet she was still on probation, on shaky ground. After her marriage failed, she'd sworn off dating—a vow she had kept. Now there was only Molly in her life, she thought, getting up to make a cup of tea. Much as she had always dreamed of having a big family generating rooms full of raucous laughter, maybe it was her destiny to be alone with her daughter here in Washington. She would be enough for Molly. Just as she had been alone with Aunt Lydia, and it had been enough.

28

WASHINGTON, DECEMBER 1990

Two weeks after Thanksgiving, Vickie came upon a letter in the Atomic Energy Commission files she suspected would be of interest to Professor Connor. The letter, written in February 1952, was from W.D. Glass, chief of the biophysics branch of the AEC's Division of Biology and Medicine, to the Rand Corporation.

"We are interested in a broad study that would be the basis for replying to the following general question: What number of A-bombs detonated under random conditions and over what period of time might create a world-wide hazard in terms of radiological contamination? This is a question that continually arises, and our General Advisory Committee has recommended that further studies be undertaken," Glass wrote.

The letter, stamped "SECRET SECURITY INFORMATION,"

did not mention Project Gabriel by name. However, it showed that the AEC was contracting for studies aimed at calculating how many atomic bombs could be exploded before the Earth became fatally contaminated. Had it not been for her conversation with the professor, she realized, the significance of this communication might have escaped her.

At lunchtime, she called Professor Connor, who was ecstatic to hear about her discovery. He sent a messenger to pick up a copy of the letter. Three hours later, a florist delivered an extravagant arrangement of white lilies and red roses to her at Newhart News. Vickie smiled at the note card, which read, "Yours, with thanks, Christian."

The following Monday morning, Vickie discovered an astonishing document in the same box where she'd found the letter she'd copied for Christian Connor. The document was entitled, "Progress Report to the Joint Committee on Atomic Energy from December 1952 through May 1953." The dates piqued her interest. She flipped through the pages, which described fallout depositions in Nevada and Utah from bombs detonated in the spring of 1953. Fifty pages into the report, the word "Simon" jumped off the page. Then her eyes zeroed in on the name of her hometown.

"The only anomalous fall-out recorded in distant parts of the nation occurred on the second day after the seventh detonation in the Troy-Albany, N.Y. area during a heavy rain," she read.

Vickie reread the words twice. Hidden by the government for more than 35 years, this single sentence contained proof that radiation had rained down on Troy—just as Darren Cunningham and Dr. Olsen described. The "SECRET" report in her hands felt like a long-lost family heirloom. She skimmed through dozens of pages preceding and following the sentence, searching for additional details about the event in upstate New York. She didn't see anything else. When she realized there was no further mention of the Troy-Albany fall-out, she became incensed. Was a single sentence all the government could spare for an entire community? What about people like her brother for whom this "anomalous fall-out" had meant death? The bloodless tone of the sentence seemed aimed at minimizing the possibility of serious harm to anyone. She felt cheated. What if Professor Clark had not happened to see his Geiger counters going crazy on that April morning? No one would have learned about the radiation that fell on Troy and Albany. Thanks to Dr. Clark, the government couldn't pretend nothing had happened. They'd been forced to acknowledge the fallout event in an official report, in writing.

As she read the sentence again, she began to feel calmer. Vindicated. The atomic secret that destroyed her family had merited only one sentence in an obscure government archive, but she had found it. She knew the truth now. She could see it and touch it. She brought the report to the copier with a handful of change and copied the title page and the page with her sentence, the one that mattered to her family. Deciding one copy was not enough, she put six more dimes in the slot. She lifted the warm pages and pressed them against her chest, sure her parents and brother would be proud of her for discovering the truth.

Vickie tucked the pages into her bag and slipped the leather strap over her shoulder. She left the reading room and climbed the stairs to the lobby. Walking boldly past the German Shepherd on guard, she exited the concrete building. Clutching the strap close to her chest, for the first time in her life, she felt firmly tied to the family she had lost as an eight-year-old girl.

~

The next morning Vickie covered a Senate hearing on hazardous waste. After filing her story, she headed to the Grant Hotel for a panel on Chernobyl health effects. It was the final session of an international conference organized by the Radiation Health Physicians. The lead-off speaker, Dr. Hungerford, was working on the International Atomic Energy Administration's health study. He painted a rosy picture of life in the Soviet Union after Chernobyl.

"The biggest problem facing people in Ukraine and Byelorussia is not cancer, but depression, poor nutrition, and radiophobia," Dr. Hungerford stated. Vickie recalled her interview with Tedd Flint, where she had first encountered this term.

"It's possible that in the future we may see an uptick in cases of thyroid cancer, but fortunately it is what doctors call the good cancer. With proper treatment," he added, "ninety-six percent of thyroid cancer patients will survive."

Vickie found Dr. Hungerford's cavalier dismissal of health effects from the Chernobyl explosion shocking. She glanced behind her, trying to gauge the audience's reaction, but the impassive faces watching the speaker betrayed nothing. After trivializing thyroid cancer, the IAEA mouthpiece stated that although the accident was tragic, only thirty-one people had died. "This tells us serious nuclear plant accidents can be managed," he concluded.

Dr. Gilmore Harris, who had invited Vickie to the meeting, spoke next.

"I get uncomfortable when I hear people like our previous speaker call thyroid cancer the good cancer. That attitude discounts the trauma to children whose surgery and medical treatment prove successful as well as the incalculable suffering of families whose children don't survive," Dr. Harris began.

"We must never forget the words of President John F. Kennedy in 1963 when he pushed Congress to pass the test ban treaty. Kennedy said, 'The number of children and grandchildren with cancer in their bones, with leukemia in their blood, or with poison in their lungs might seem statistically small to some, in comparison with natural health hazards, but this is not a natural health hazard—and it is not a statistical issue. The loss of even one human life, or the malformation of even one baby—who may be born long after we are gone—should be of concern to us all. Our children and grandchildren are not merely statistics toward which we can be indifferent.'"

In a direct challenge to the IAEA representative, Harris argued that "humanity cannot tolerate many more nuclear plant accidents on the scale of Chernobyl."

Dr. Ivanov, an endocrinologist from Kiev, was the final speaker. While he arranged his papers, Vickie scanned the audience for reporters. She didn't see anyone else with a press badge. This didn't surprise her. It was late in the day, and "low-level effects of radiation" lacked the ring of a headline that would entice many Washington editors.

"Already there are dozens of excess thyroid cancers among children in Byelorussia and Ukraine, and thousands more cases can be expected in coming years," Dr. Ivanov stated. The doctor's accent was thick, but his message was clear. He talked about ten-year-old children who had cataracts and high or low blood pressure. "These illnesses can only be explained by exposure to radiation. Yet Soviet authorities deny radiation is the cause."

When Dr. Ivanov finished speaking, the moderator invited questions for the panelists. A slim man who looked no more than nineteen years old rushed to the microphone. He wore a brown wool jacket over a white shirt and paisley tie. Dark, wavy hair fell on his forehead as he leaned over the microphone.

"I have a question about conclusions—" he began.

"Your name and affiliation," the moderator interrupted.

"I am a Kiev Medical Institute student. I come here with the Ukrainian Medical Delegation. My name is Dmitry Marchenko."

"Proceed with your question," the moderator said.

"I have questions about the truthfulness of conclusions presented by Dr. Hungerford. My sister suffers from thyroid cancer. She is one of dozens of thyroid cancer cases in my home of Kiev. Doctors in Byelorussia document even more children with thyroid cancer. Many of these are aggressive cancers, not good cancer." Dmitry's eyes flashed with rage.

"Your question?" the moderator interrupted. "I must ask for your question."

"I have many questions. Why does this propagandist insult my people by suggesting we suffer from a phobia of radiation? Where is the science to support such a conclusion? Does a ten-year-old child get cataracts in his eyes from fear of radiation?"

"This panel already has exceeded its time limit, and your monologue is pushing us over. These topics have been covered." The moderator cut Dmitry off. "You are all welcome to make your way to a reception across the hall for wine and cheese."

Vickie hurried to the spot where Dmitry remained planted at the dead microphone. She introduced herself and asked to interview him. He agreed at once. While she put on her coat, Dmitry asked his professor if he could join them. Dr. Ivanov had plans to meet with a colleague, but he encouraged Dmitry to participate in the interview. Vickie wanted to find a place where they could talk in private. She recalled a coffee house a few blocks north of the hotel that didn't seem to get busy until later in the evening.

As she and Dmitry stepped outside the hotel, they were hit with a frigid gust of wind. The sun broke through a bank of indigo clouds to the west, spreading ethereal rays over the city's rooftops.

Vickie clutched the lapels of her coat against her chest. "I hope you don't mind the cold. The place I have in mind is a few blocks."

Dmitry shook his head. "I'm happy to leave that stuffy room."

"No kidding!" Vickie tucked her chin into her collar. "That's an American idiom," she added.

Dmitry loped beside Vickie without a trace of the anger he'd shown in the ballroom. Entering the coffee house, the two edged past a young man with matted blonde dreadlocks puffing a hand-rolled cigarette and blowing smoke rings. At a table near the bar, an aging couple in tie dyed dashikis nibbled veggie burgers. Portraits of jazz musicians and a poster of Earth from the moon papered over cracks running down the walls. Despite its shabbiness, the room radiated warmth. Dozens of lights twinkled from a high ceiling, illuminating a second-floor balcony. A warped floor rippled under their feet as Vickie and Dmitry walked to a table along the side wall. They ordered coffee and a plate of hummus.

"Thank you for the honor of allowing me to present Ukrainian Medical Delegation views to a member of the American press," Dmitry began, as Vickie set her tape recorder on the table.

"The honor is mine. I should explain that I write for a chain that owns eight medium-sized newspapers in five states around the country—not the major papers you might be familiar with. Your English is excellent, by the way." Vickie asked for Dmitry's permission to tape their interview, and he consented.

Dmitry recounted that his delegation had met with Ukrainian-Americans in New York, visited the Statue of Liberty, and talked to a handful of lawmakers on Capitol Hill. While he had enjoyed his tour, Dmitry voiced frustration that he had not spent time informing journalists about the coverup of Chernobyl's health effects.

"Tell me what you wanted to say about Dr. Hungerford when the moderator cut you off," Vickie began. At the mention of that name, Dmitry's nostrils flared.

"He lies. Scientists in Kiev calculate Chernobyl released radiation equivalent to more than three hundred fifty Hiroshima bombs. Yet it is forbidden for Soviet doctors to name an illness from radiation as an official cause of death. I know a journalist who wrote an article telling these things. Her manuscript sits in the drawer of a cowardly editor in Kiev." Dmitry paused to pour three packets of sugar into his coffee. "Hundreds of liquidators have died, and many more are ill with disorders doctors do not understand. They diagnose these medical problems as 'Chernobyl disease,' but people suspect they result from radiation."

"What is a liquidator?" asked Vickie.

"Liquidators are men—my father, Vasyl Marchenko, is one—the authorities sent to the radioactive Zone surrounding Chernobyl to clean up the mess." Dmitry leaned forward, speaking softly. "They were mostly soldiers. Some volunteered, but many were pressed into service under false pretenses. Men sent soon after the explosion received massive doses of radiation, like my father. They had to run across the reactor roof carrying shovels full of radioactive rubble." He stopped talking and looked down at his coffee.

"Your father is sick?"

Dmitry tried to answer, but a lump formed in his throat. "My father was strong as a bear when he was sent on that mission," he managed, his voice thick. "Now he is weak, short of breath. He suffers cardiovascular problems. Some men he served with are sicker. Three of his comrades have died."

"Do you know how many men served in this capacity, as liquidators?"

Dmitry shook his head. "Their exact number is not known. Some estimate as many as 600,000. Others say as few as 300,000—men from across the Soviet Union."

Dmitry told her about the anger growing in the hearts of Kiev's students. When he described the protest marches and hunger strike, his words flowed easily again.

The waitress refilled their coffee mugs and lit a candle at their table.

"Can you tell me about your sister, her thyroid cancer?" Vickie asked Dmitry tentatively. She remembered how his voice had trembled at the microphone when he spoke of her.

"Yes, Katya—" Dmitry began, the rock returning to his throat, squeezing off his words.

"What a pretty name. I'll understand if you can't talk about it." Dmitry looked so young and vulnerable Vickie wanted to put her arms around him and comfort him.

"My sister, Katya, is eleven. She is the most beautiful girl you can imagine, full of joy and light. She brings happiness to everyone who knows her. And her voice was that of an angel—before. Everyone who heard her sing agreed." Eyes glistening, Dmitry described his sister's surgery and her current precarious condition.

"Three months ago, she was diagnosed with papillary thyroid cancer. This is not the good cancer, as that monster Hungerford says." Dmitry's index finger traced a half-moon under his Adam's apple. "There were lymph node metastases and neck involvement. The surgeon performed a total thyroidectomy. He had to sever Katya's right laryngeal nerve because it was encased by the cancer. There are recurrent laryngeal nerves on both sides of the thyroid gland." His voice gained authority as he described medical details. "If one is severed, the vocal cord on that side becomes paralyzed. Since the surgery, Katya's voice is reduced to a hiss, and she grows short of breath quickly. My mother's heart aches. She nurses my sister and father and invests faith in me—that I will become a doctor and heal them." Dmitry stopped speaking.

Outside the window, the sun had set. Candlelight illuminated Dmitry's face, spreading a golden glow over the sharp planes of his cheeks and the soft roundness of his lips. His deep-set eyes shone. Sitting in the gathering darkness, surrounded by disaffected souls, Vickie felt an intense spiritual bond with this Ukrainian medical student. Dmitry was many years her junior and came from the nation her country had waged a Cold War with for both of their lifetimes. Yet she felt certain they were destined to meet each other here, in this exact place, at this precise moment in time.

Staring into the candle flame, her mind's eye pictured a fiery mushroom cloud rising like a bright sun over the Nevada desert followed by an iridescent blue light illuminating the Ukrainian night sky. She perceived in a flash how two blinding explosions thirty-three years apart had inexorably altered the course of their lives. Her parents, given no warning of the fallout plume racing toward a collision with storm clouds over Troy, had watched their son die of leukemia at the tender age of six. Dmitry's parents, given no warning of the radiation in winds from Chernobyl blanketing Kiev, watched their daughter suffer from thyroid cancer.

For the first time, Vickie understood that her parents never recovered from the agonizing death of their son. Her father died one year after Paul when the car he was driving skidded off the road and slammed into a tree, but the inner light had faded from his eyes when his little boy passed away. No one had ever explained to her satisfaction how his car spun out of control. Black ice, Aunt Lydia believed, but her father had been a steady driver. She wondered now if he had rammed the tree on purpose in a moment of despair. Her mother had carried on after her son's death but lost her will to live after her husband died. Multiple hospital stays later, after electric shocks had obliterated her identity, she abandoned her remaining child and traveled West in search of a new life. Fortunately, Aunt Lydia had come like an angel into Vickie's life, giving her enough love for two parents. These thoughts swirled through her mind, demanding expression.

"My brother Paul died of leukemia when he was six," she told Dmitry, unable to hold back. "I was seven-and-a-half."

Dmitry leaned his elbows on the table and watched Vickie, his body coiled tight.

"I attended a conference recently where a researcher talked about leukemia cases from fallout in Troy, New York. That was the town where we lived. The researcher said that radiation from an atom bomb detonated in Nevada in April 1953 blew more than two thousand miles across America, to the area around Troy. A fierce thunderstorm brought the radioactive particles down on reservoirs and farmland. He believes that radiation exposures to fetuses growing in their mothers' wombs led to excess cases of leukemia in those children. My mother was three months pregnant in April 1953. Another researcher at the same meeting stated that effects of radiation on the fetus are ten times stronger than on the mother, so my brother could have absorbed radiation in the womb. Paul was born in October 1953."

Dmitry was leaning so far over the small bistro table Vickie could feel the warmth of his breath on her face.

"You're the first person I've talked to about this," Vickie finished.

"We come from opposite worlds, but we share so much." Dmitry touched Vickie's arm.

They sat in silence, suspended in time, until a young woman bumped against their table. The woman shrieked and threw her arms around a long-haired guitar player. The guitarist joined a bass player by the microphone.

"Forgive me," Vickie said, jolted back to reality. "Here, I'm supposed to be interviewing you for a story, Dmitry."

"Call me Mitya, please. You are my sister now. Don't apologize. I know you will write a good article because more than anyone, you understand the truth. In your heart."

Thanking Dmitry for the interview, Vickie told him she had to get home to make dinner for her daughter.

"You have a daughter? What is her name? How old is she?"

"Molly is eleven." Vickie put on her coat.

"No kidding!" Dmitry grinned. "You look too young to have a child my sister's age."

As they prepared to leave, Vickie asked Dmitry for his card and contact information for Dr. Ivanov.

"Articles about Chernobyl radiation are not allowed in my country." Dmitry gave her a card. "You will write the truth, no?"

"I'll write the truth, Mitya, but I can't promise you that my editor will be willing to print it. Articles about radiation can be hard to publish in my country, too." Vickie thought about Gorbachev's popularity at the moment, and the high hurdle a Chernobyl coverup story would have to clear, assuming she could persuade Thane to let her write such a story.

When they stepped outside, snowflakes were swarming under a streetlamp like lightning bugs.

"I'm happy to see the snow." Vickie tilted her head back and smiled.

"You will like my country." Dmitry laughed. "You must come visit my parents and my sister."

They lingered on the sidewalk, snowflakes frosting their hair, then kissed each other's cheeks before parting.

∞

The next morning, Vickie got up the courage to pitch a story to Thane on the health effects of Chernobyl.

"There's a massive human tragedy unfolding in Ukraine and Byelorussia. Apparently, dozens of children and hundreds of clean-up workers have cancer. Scientists at a conference I popped into yesterday and a medical student I interviewed claimed the Soviets are hiding the extent of Chernobyl's health impacts just as they downplayed radiation releases immediately after the accident," she told Thane. "The IAEA also seems intent on whitewashing radiation health effects."

"Chernobyl medical coverup, huh?" Thane mulled it over aloud. "Alan wants us to put together a special in April for the fifth anniversary of the accident. Ian's planning to cover it for us in Kiev. Send Ian your contacts. Maybe he'll be able to work something in on this." With that, Thane picked up his phone, dismissing her.

Vickie stood in front of Thane's desk lost for words. She wanted to protest that this was her story. She'd spent hours re-searching it. She'd written two Chernobyl radiation stories. She'd sought out these scientists to interview. Ian wouldn't feel deeply about Dmitry and his little sister's thyroid cancer. He wouldn't care about the fate of Vasyl Marchenko and his fellow liquidators. Not in the way she cared. She wanted to report on this story and write it for the world to read. She wouldn't simply regurgitate official IAEA talking points, like most reporters seemed content to do. But this decision was not hers to make. She understood too well the newsroom's pecking order.

Returning to her computer, Vickie thought about quitting her job and trying to pitch the article to another publication. But who would buy this piece from her? She was an unknown. Even if she did sell this piece, what would she do next for income? It took months, sometimes years, for stringers to piece together a steady income. She was responsible for Molly, and Molly was thriving and happy here. She couldn't afford to walk away from this job. No, she would have to swallow this injustice. As she was getting ready to telephone Ian in Berlin, the Bureau Chief stopped by her desk.

"Got a minute?" Alan asked her.

She followed him to his office. He closed his door and asked her to take a seat. He smiled warmly.

"I've been meaning to talk to you for a while now. I wanted to let you know that you're no longer on probation. Your work has really come along, Victoria. Keep it up."

Vickie was relieved to learn her job was safe and glad she wouldn't have to uproot Molly. She thanked Alan and managed an anemic smile. Six months ago, she would have savored this moment as a blazing triumph. Now, it felt more like a loss.

29

WASHINGTON, DECEMBER 1990

The curtain rose on a Viennese Christmas Eve party, transporting the audience to a magical place and time. Vickie watched the wonder play over Molly's face as mysterious Herr Drosselmeyer appeared on stage carrying a Nutcracker doll to the party. He gave the doll to ten-year-old Clara, who was wearing a pink nightgown and ballet slippers. In a fit of jealousy, Clara's little brother, Fritz, grabbed the doll from her and broke it. Herr Drosselmeyer mended the Nutcracker with a red kerchief, and Clara fell asleep cradling it under the family's Christmas tree. She dreamed of enormous mice who threatened her, and the Christmas tree grew to a gigantic size. Clara threw her slipper at the bellicose Mouse King, knocking him out, and the Nutcracker turned into a prince.

Vickie had seen this ballet at least twenty times, but it never failed to pull her under its spell. A smile formed on her face as the curtain fell over a glittering land of snow, ending the first act. During intermission, she and Molly were sharing a cookie in the lobby when a tall girl with long, dark hair shouted hello. Molly approached Maddie Cunningham, and the girls began chatting.

Vickie spotted Darren a fraction of a second before he saw her. His face looked more handsome and his eyes more soulful than she remembered. Still under the thrall of the ballet, Vickie was bursting with romantic feelings. She wanted to tell Darren how she had been longing to see him.

"How have you been?" she asked instead, hoping that he could read her feelings.

"Not bad. Yourself?"

Miserable, she wanted to say.

"Truthfully?" she asked, studying his face.

Darren nodded, his eyes narrowing.

"I've missed our lunches."

Darren watched her, waiting for more. Vickie sensed that if she didn't tell him right now how much she regretted turning him down for that date, she would forfeit any chance for happiness in her life. The urge to tell him was so strong she had to speak.

"If we could rewind time to September fourteenth, that morning in the coffee shop when you asked me out, I would say yes." Her words came in a rush. "I guess I wonder if that's possible."

"But I still work at the State Department, and you're still a reporter," he retorted.

Vickie had put everything out there, hoping Darren would give her another chance. Her eyes brimmed, and she turned away.

At that moment, the house lights flashed.

"Time to get back to our seats," Vickie called to Molly, fighting to find her voice. Blinking back tears, she glanced in Darren's direction. He looked distressed. His mouth parted like he was about to say something, but his daughter asked him a question, diverting his attention.

At the start of the second act, Vickie daubed her eyes inconspicuously, determined not to cry. She didn't want Molly to see her upset. Fortunately, Molly was taken with the pageantry on stage. Gradually, Tchaikovsky worked his magic, washing away some of her sorrow. By the final pas de deux, Vickie watched mesmerized, her spirit soaring with each of the Sugar Plum Fairy's breathtaking leaps.

When Vickie and Molly got home, they brought bowls of ice cream into the living room. Vickie plugged in the lights of their Christmas tree. Molly loved the tree, which was so tall the star on top touched their nine-foot ceiling. They talked about all the places where they had seen the *Nutcracker*, beginning with Molly's first performance in St. Louis when she was six. Then Molly asked to hear about the first time Aunt Lydia took her to see the *Nutcracker* in Evansville, Indiana.

"I wish she was still alive," Molly said, after Vickie finished telling her the familiar family story.

"Me too, Pumpkin. She was one of the kindest, bravest people in the world." After Vickie left Santa Claus for college, her stalwart aunt had lived alone in her cottage in the woods with two sweet Golden Retrievers for companionship, until almost four years ago. She was seventy-three and in robust health when a stealth brain aneurysm took her life.

"We had fun making cookies. Remember all those pretty tins she had?" Molly asked.

Vickie nodded. She was glad Molly had fond memories of her aunt. She, Jake, and Molly used to spend a week with Aunt Lydia in Santa Claus every year over Christmas break.

"We made stars and angels and bells," Molly continued. "And gingerbread men. Those were her favorite."

"And Christmas trees and snowmen," Vickie added, smiling.

"Don't forget candy canes." Molly giggled.

"You want to make Christmas cookies tomorrow? It's Saturday."

"Yes! Can Julia come make them with us? And sleep over?" Molly asked, excitement mounting in her voice.

"Sure, that's a wonderful idea. I'll call Sandy."

After Vickie tucked Molly in, she closed the bedroom door so she could play Christmas music without disturbing her. At midnight, before going to bed, she decided to get out the box containing her aunt's cookie cutters and hand-made Christmas trinkets. Rummaging through the hall closet, Vickie thought back to the bleak December day when she learned of her aunt's death. Aunt Lydia had been her everything—mother, father, guardian angel. Her passing had left Vickie hopelessly unmoored. She hadn't realized how much her own stability and sense of belonging in the world had depended on her aunt. For months she'd ventured outside only to shop for food. Eventually she got a waitressing job and returned to school, doubtful she possessed the will or stamina to finish her degree. Yet somehow, writing for the college newspaper had worked magic on her soul, reawakening her curiosity and her senses.

Vickie retrieved the box and brought it to the couch. Opening the box, she spotted the Christmas stocking Aunt Lydia had knitted for her from green yarn, decorated with a soft reindeer. When she rubbed the angora reindeer on her nose, she was flooded with a memory of climbing into her aunt's car and breathing in its sweet, dusty smell. The first time Aunt Lydia arrived in Troy was in November 1959, for Paul's funeral. Picturing the red Woody wagon pulling up in their driveway, as real as if thirty years had not elapsed, dislodged an avalanche of buried memories. Standing outdoors in the cold, wedged between her father and her aunt, she watched a man with a shovel approaching the gravesite.

"What's he doing, Daddy?" she asked her father, though her heart knew. When the stout man thrust his spade into a pile of dirt, she flinched.

"He's burying your brother, Sweetie," her father replied, his voice hoarse.

"Make him stop," Vickie pleaded, but her father didn't hear her over the wind.

This was a part of dying no one, not even her sagacious aunt, had explained. Aunt Lydia had arrived at their house from Indiana two days after the ambulance took her brother to the hospital. She had proven herself an authority on death, answering Vickie's many questions.

"I won't be able to play with Paul or see him ever again, right?" Vickie had prodded Aunt Lydia for the second time that morning, before they drove to the cemetery. She knew the answer, but she had to be sure.

"That's right, dear. You won't be able to play with Paul again until you die and go to Heaven," her aunt answered. "But when you see him in Heaven, he'll be all well and happy, like he used to be, before he got sick."

Playing with Paul in Heaven had sounded fair enough to Vickie at home, in the warmth of their kitchen, but that was before she'd seen the deep hole and the box with her brother inside. A clot of dirt thudded against the coffin, causing her to flinch. She wanted to see her brother, but she did not want to be buried in a box in the ground. She worried this meant she wasn't a good sister. She reached up for her father's hand, but he was turned away from her, wrapping his arms around her mother, who seemed unable to stand upright on her own.

A strong gust off the Hudson River pricked her cheeks with needles of ice and whipped her hair across her face. Vickie reached up and patted the black ribbon pinned to her hair to make sure the wind hadn't blown it off. Shivering, she inched one shoe backward, away from the hole. She was about to turn and run when she felt Aunt Lydia's hand cup her shoulder. She looked up into her aunt's kind eyes, the same shade of green as her own, took her offered hand, and held on tight.

The second time Aunt Lydia came to their house was one year later, after her father died. Vickie remembered seeing the policeman at their door and her mother falling on the kitchen floor. The policeman took Vickie's mother to the hospital, and the next-door neighbor stayed at their house until Aunt Lydia arrived. This time Vickie didn't have to ask her aunt about dying. She knew exactly what death meant. She understood how it stole the sounds from a house and swept away the singing and laughing, leaving in its wake a dreaded silence.

This time at the gravesite, Vickie pressed close to Aunt Lydia.

She knew this plot well. She'd come here often with her mother to place flowers on Paul's grave. When she spotted the stout man with the shovel approaching, she covered her eyes. As a shovelful of gravel slammed her Daddy's coffin, she squeezed her eyes shut and clapped her hands over her ears. She tried to block out the sound as the man buried the person she loved most in the world. When Aunt Lydia gathered Vickie into the folds of her skirt, she buried her face in her hands and wept.

For the next several days, Aunt Lydia visited her mother while she colored and made puzzles in the hospital waiting room. One evening, after their hospital visit, Aunt Lydia helped Vickie pack her favorite books, clothes, and toys. As they sorted through Vickie's belongings, Aunt Lydia babbled about the white-tailed deer that lived in the woods near her lakeside house. She described her cottage as a special place, alive with the sounds of nature, and her pond as a sparkling jewel in the forest. When the trunk and suitcase were full, Aunt Lydia asked Vickie if she would like to see the animals and skate on Hidden Pond with her. Vickie nodded solemnly. At the age of eight, she understood her life here was over.

When Vickie slid into the front seat of the Woody wagon beside her aunt for the long drive to Indiana, she pulled the handle shut hard, thinking she had closed the door forever on Troy.

As the palpable image faded, Vickie looked around her living room, disoriented. Setting the reindeer Christmas stocking on the coffee table, she wondered how such vivid memories had remained hidden in her mind for so long, protected intact from the ravages of time. And why had they graced her tonight? Her aunt's ineffable scent had somehow carried her back to the Woody wagon, cracking open a window to devastating events she had buried. Much like the curtain rising on the *Nutcracker*, allowing the audience to accompany Clara on her journey through fantastic landscapes of snow and ice, then falling when it was time for everyone to return home to the real world.

Thinking of the *Nutcracker* performance, Vickie's mind wandered to Darren and that night at the Kennedy Center when they stood under the stars, his arm brushing against hers as they watched lights shimmer on the inky Potomac. She pictured laughing over lunch with him at the Tabard Inn. She burned to tell him about Dr. Chandler's dark Kodak secret and her amazing encounter with Dmitry Marchenko. Her eyes welled as she thought about all the things she would never be able to share with Darren because she had been so ambitious and bent on turning him into a source. Then she thought about the mother, father, brother, and aunt she would never see again, and a dam gave way inside her. All the sadness and fear she had been pushing away for as long as she could remember broke over her in waves of sobs. Tears streamed down her face. She didn't try to stop them or talk herself out of her sorrow. She simply cried until her heart was emptied of tears.

❧

Vickie woke up in a bright mood. Humming the "Waltz of the Flowers," she marveled at how morning had a magical way of breaking shiny and new each day, shooing away sorrows that had felt overwhelming the night before. Molly got up a few minutes after her, and they leaped around the living room together. Vickie felt liberated, twirling with her daughter like ballerinas. She made pancakes for breakfast and got out tubes of food coloring and baking sheets. After Julia arrived, they arranged Aunt Lydia's cookie cutters on the counter.

By noon, the aroma of sugar cookies filled the kitchen. Julia was spreading green frosting on Christmas tree cookies, and Molly was cutting angels from rolled dough. Two trays of snowmen and candy canes were baking in the oven when the phone rang.

Vickie wondered if Julia's mother might be calling about a change in plans. When she picked up the phone, she heard Darren's voice.

"I'm sorry to call you at home. I hope you don't mind, but this is not about work. I wanted to tell you I spent the whole night awake, thinking about what you said about wanting to go back to that morning in the coffee shop in September and say yes, if that's possible. And I don't see why it's not possible. I mean, I definitely think it is possible, if you still want to after I was such a jerk last night. You've been on my mind a lot, too, Victoria, and not only last night." When Darren stopped talking, Vickie realized she was holding her breath.

"Sure." She exhaled.

"Great! Do you want to grab lunch? If you haven't eaten."

"I can't. I'm in the middle of baking Christmas cookies."

"Ah, maybe later—whatever's good for you."

"Molly has a friend here. She's sleeping over," Vickie apologized.

"How about dinner Friday, then? I know this special restaurant with a fireplace."

"That sounds wonderful." Vickie recalled the Tabard Inn's cozy lounge.

"Oh, wait. Darn, there's a cocktail reception at the French Ambassador's residence I have to be at after work on Friday. No getting out of that one. Would you mind coming along as my guest? We could meet there and eat after."

"I'd love to. Can we talk later? I don't want the cookies in the oven—"

"To burn. No, that would be terrible. I'll make sure you get an invitation," Darren promised.

30

WASHINGTON, DECEMBER 1990

Walking through the doors of the Ambassador's residence on Kalorama Street, Vickie felt like she'd entered a French chateau. A gentleman whisked away her wool coat, and she entered the grand foyer wearing a sleeveless black silk sheath with a plunging neckline. Her long, chestnut brown hair, which she usually tied back, swept over her shoulders. Before she spotted him, Darren appeared at her side.

"You look beautiful," he whispered. His face broke into an appreciative smile that made Vickie's heart pound.

A waiter offered Vickie a glass of wine. Another brought a tray of duck and brie canapés, which she sampled. Darren introduced her to a clutch of well-preserved European diplomats, who squeezed her hand one-by-one, slathering her with a chorus of "*très belle*," "*quel plaisir*," "*enchanté*."

Darren pointed out a tall, silver-haired gentleman standing alone by the window and told Vickie he needed to talk with him in private for a few minutes.

She wandered alone through the opulent rooms trying to soak in every detail. She'd promised to give Sandy a full report on the prestigious venue. Vickie practiced her rusty French with a sullen woman standing in front of a Neoclassical painting and nodded politely to several guests. After circulating for twenty minutes, she didn't know what to do with herself. She found the elegant gathering much like any other cocktail party in Washington, where people discreetly searched the room for someone important, whose name they might drop later at another prestige venue. The most exciting thing about being at the French Ambassador's residence, she decided, was being able to say that you'd been there. At least she was off duty and didn't have to swap business cards or try to make any contacts. Tonight, she was content to be Darren's "enchanting" guest.

After he finished his *tête-à-tête* with the solitary figure, Darren sidled against Vickie in front of a contemporary painting. "I'm ready to blow this joint if you are," he whispered. Then he folded his arms across his chest and stood back, as if he were commenting on the artwork. "The other person I need to talk to hasn't shown up, and I don't feel like waiting around for him. His flight could be delayed until tomorrow, for all we know, and we've got a reservation."

A short cab ride brought Vickie and Darren to the Tabard Inn, where they made their way to a couch in front of the fireplace and sank into the velvet cushions. For an awkward moment, neither of them spoke. Vickie had been aching to talk to Darren for months, and now she was unsure where to start.

"It feels so right being here with you." Darren broke the silence. "I really want to thank you for baring your soul at the *Nutcracker*. It took courage, and then I was a total jerk. I wanted to take back what I said right away. We probably should clear the air on the source thing. Do you still have any reservations about dating me because of our jobs?"

Vickie shook her head. "When I told you I couldn't date a source, I was pretty new to all this, and my thinking about sources was pretty fuzzy," Vickie confessed. "My idea about the kinds of stories I would be writing was what you might call a little inflated then, too."

"You thought I would be Deep Throat, and you would topple the president?" he teased.

"Something like that," Vickie admitted, smiling sheepishly. "I've given a lot of thought to journalistic ethics in the past few months. It's not something anybody talks about where I work, but my beat is energy and environment, which generally doesn't involve the State Department. If I were assigned to cover an environmental treaty, and you were negotiating the treaty, I would tell my editor I was dating you. He might pull me off the story, but maybe not. Either way, I don't care."

"Believe me, that's not a scenario we have to worry about. My plate is full with nuclear issues. I want you to know I respect you, Victoria. Frankly, I figured you were seeing someone else," he added, lightening the tone.

"No, that wasn't it. I'd actually sworn off dating. I was totally focused on succeeding at my job. I had just moved here with Molly, and that's all I could think about then."

Over a candlelit dinner in the main dining room, their conversation glided from silly to heavy subjects in that effortless way it always had during their lunches. Darren talked about what his life had been like since his divorce half a dozen years ago, including a string of dating misadventures. His story about the woman who wouldn't go anywhere without her Great Dane Luigi—including restaurants and concerts—had Vickie in stitches. She talked about her ups and downs in the three years since Jake had renounced the material world for his stint in a monastery.

"I'm afraid your ex didn't know what he had." Darren reached across the table and put his hand over Vickie's. "Did I mention how gorgeous you look tonight?"

"It must be the dress." Vickie felt special and exhilarated, like the entire world was coming alive after a long, deep freeze.

When they finished eating, Darren suggested they go back to his place for dessert. She agreed, wanting the evening to go on forever.

Darren helped Vickie into her coat and put his arm around her shoulders as they left the restaurant. The night was clear and cold. They huddled close during the walk to DuPont Circle. They headed up Nineteenth to S Street and turned left. Midway down the block, Darren took Vickie's hand and led her up the stairs of a brick rowhouse. He unlocked the door, which opened into a foyer with a Tiffany light fixture hanging from the ceiling. The foyer led to a living room furnished with an oversized sofa and chair, a coffee table, and an ebony baby grand.

"Wow, your place is amazing." Vickie admired the polished floors and tall ceilings.

"You like it? I bought a fudge cake." Darren winked. "I

thought we could split a piece." He took her coat and draped it over a cane coat tree.

"If you want coffee with—" The phone rang, interrupting him. "I'd better get that. Might be Maddy."

Darren hurried to the kitchen and answered the phone. "Now? It's almost nine o'clock." Darren grimaced and pointed to the phone, giving Vickie a look that suggested this was an unpleasant but important call.

Vickie wandered around the living room, trying to give him privacy. She could tell by his tone and responses that the call had to do with a geopolitical, rather than a domestic, emergency.

"This is such an unbelievable drag." Darren returned to the living room. "You have no idea how much I want to stay here with you, Victoria, but I have to go back to the Ambassador's. That official I was supposed to meet with has arrived. His flight got in late, and this can't wait till morning," he apologized. "There's no way around it."

31
WASHINGTON, JANUARY 1991

Vickie buttered two English muffins, took a mug of coffee to the couch, and turned on the TV to watch Desert Storm news. A CNN anchor in Atlanta was on the phone with three correspondents, who were describing flashes of light and streams of tracer fire they could see outside their window at the Al-Rashid Hotel in Baghdad. In the background, she could hear the steady pounding of anti-aircraft guns. Molly plopped down beside her. They chewed crispy English muffins while listening to bombs exploding. It was the war, live from Baghdad, unedited and captivating.

The CNN anchor switched to a correspondent reporting live from Dhahran, Saudi Arabia. A siren blared behind the correspondent, who had to cut his report short, given the threat of an Iraqi Scud missile attack. The siren turned out to be a false alarm, but it made Vickie worry about Gabe Green. Yesterday, he had called in a story from Dhahran, the site from which the U.S. was flying bombing missions over Baghdad. She thought how strange it was that she could see the war unfolding live from her living room couch in DC before the stories filed by Gabe and other print journalists would appear in the papers.

While she was dressing for work, Darren called from Kiev to tell her how much he missed her. He had spent the previous week in Geneva and planned to fly to Moscow the following week. He was trying to forge a verification agreement for the Strategic Arms Reduction Treaty that Bush was negotiating with Gorbachev. The Senate wasn't willing to ratify START without a strong side agreement on verification, which made Darren's role critical to the success of the talks.

Vickie realized Darren acted so unassuming around her that she sometimes forgot how important his job was. She understood how passionate he was about cutting the number of nuclear warheads on the planet, but she also wished he could be in Washington. In long, earnest phone calls, Darren had been telling her he was sure they were meant for each other. He knew in his gut they would spend the rest of their lives together—once the START negotiations were over and he could return to the States. She wanted to believe him, but she wondered how they would ever get to finish a single date if he spent most of his time on the other side of the Atlantic. Not that she would ever ask him to give up what he did. She admired his idealism and dedication.

At work, Vickie learned that Gabe planned to make his way to Tel Aviv, which was under attack by Iraqi Scud missiles. During a hearing on Capitol Hill about hazardous waste, her mind wandered to the big news spots in Europe and the Middle East. Back at the office, she received a fax from Dmitry Marchenko about an important conference slated to take place in Kiev from April 21-25 on the health effects of Chernobyl. In a postscript, Dmitry wrote that his mother would be willing to provide translation services.

Vickie would give anything to be able to report from Kiev in April, but Ian had snagged that assignment. She faxed Dmitry a note promising to forward the conference agenda to her colleague, Ian Hoffman, who would be covering the fifth anniversary of Chernobyl for Newhart News.

~

On a dreary March morning, Cynthia Ames, who had grown chummy with Vickie since her soiree at the French Ambassador's residence, shared an intriguing rumor with her. "Scuttlebutt has it Alan's planning to send either you or Jeff to Kuwait to cover the oil fires. This could be the biggest environmental story of the century," Cynthia said, as they rode the elevator up to the office.

"I'm positive it will be Jeff, in that case," Vickie responded.

"Why? You're the one who's been working the story with Thane," Cynthia countered.

Vickie put little stock in the rumor, even though it was true she had spent hours on the phone helping Thane report on the horrific oil fires blotting out the sun over Kuwait. Iraqi forces had blown up more than 600 oil wells during their retreat from Kuwait in February. Black smoke from the fires had created an environmental catastrophe visible from space. Thane believed that without having someone on the ground, it was impossible to convey the scope of the damage. He was hounding Alan to send a reporter to Kuwait.

When Alan called the E-team into his office later that day, Vickie thought that maybe Cynthia had been right after all. She found the idea of traveling through war-torn Kuwait frightening—and she would miss Molly terribly—but she was ready to accept the assignment without hesitation if Alan offered it to her. She imagined riding around the desert in a jeep, if not on a camel, and interviewing Texas oilmen battling the inferno. She fantasized spending evenings at a hotel bar in Kuwait City where the network TV anchors congregated. Maybe she would even have a chance to spend some time with Gabe Green. She awakened from her reverie when Alan announced that he planned to send Thane to Kuwait. Jeff, who also had heard the rumor, looked as crestfallen as she felt.

A week after the disappointing meeting in Alan's office Vickie got an unexpected call from Ian Hoffman in Berlin.

"There's something I want to put by you, Victoria." Ian got right to the point. "You know I'm down to cover the fifth anniversary of Chernobyl in Kiev. Here's the thing. I've had something big come up, and I'm wondering if you could cover for me. The competition for a spot in the Ministry's tour of Chernobyl was too keen for me to bow out. And I would need to know that you could step in for me before telling Alan about this. You've written stories on nuclear stuff, and you've got contacts in Kiev you've been sharing with me. I can make the case to Alan that you'd be perfect for this assignment—if you want it, that is."

Vickie couldn't believe what he was telling her. "Ian, I'd love to go to Kiev and cover the events in your place, but will the

Ukrainian officials allow you to make a substitution?"

"Sure, there's enough time. I'll call the Ministry and let them know you'll be standing in for me. You'll have to get your visa on an expedited basis and fill out a mountain of forms. Soviet bureaucracy, you know. But those are technicalities. I've got an outstanding photographer lined up to work for us. My concern was making sure you could do it before I talk to Alan."

"I want to go to Kiev more than you can imagine, Ian."

"That's a relief. I'll call Alan."

"What's come up, if you don't mind my asking?"

"Well," Ian began. "Mum's the word. Through a source, I've gotten the go-ahead to accompany the United Nations team that will be searching for nuclear materials in Iraq."

"Seriously? That could be the story of the decade."

"Could be. Problem is, no one knows exactly when Iraq will allow the inspection team in to begin its work. I need to be ready to fly to Baghdad at a moment's notice. My source is guessing late April or early May. I don't want to be stuck in Kiev when the call comes."

"I, on the other hand, welcome the chance to be stuck there," Vickie interjected. They both laughed. "Seriously, I promise to do your good name credit."

Fifteen minutes later, Alan called Vickie into his office. "So, have you got a passport? Ian and I agree you're well suited to fill in for him in Kiev next month."

Vickie resisted the urge to pump both fists in the air. She floated out of Alan's office high on a mix of pride and nervous anticipation. She sent a fax to Dmitry telling him she would be coming to Kiev in April. He was thrilled. He promised to arrange interviews for her with doctors, political activists, and a top Ukrainian nuclear physicist.

She thought about calling Darren, who was in Vienna until mid-April, when he was slated to finally return home to the States. She decided to wait until her visa and permissions were approved by Ukraine's authorities before sharing the exciting news with him. Given that he would likely be back in the States for at least a day or two before she flew to Kiev, Vickie hoped she might be able to tell him in person.

When her permissions were granted and her flight was booked, Vickie realized that she would be taking off from Dulles fourteen hours before Darren's plane would be touching down at the same airport. That evening, when Darren called her from Vienna, she told him the news about her Kiev assignment.

"This is a bad time for you to travel to the Soviet Union," Darren said after a long silence.

"What? I can't believe you're saying this," Vickie shot back, stunned by his reaction. "You spend months at a time traveling around Europe and the Soviet Union. You're fine with spending weeks in Kiev yourself, but now you're against me going?"

"It's totally different. When I travel to Kiev or Moscow, I'm part of a delegation. The Secretary of State knows where I am. I have diplomatic protections—"

"Reporters go to Kiev and Moscow too," Vickie countered. She could hear genuine concern in Darren's voice and told herself he simply wanted to make sure she would be safe. "Look at Ian. He returned to Berlin from Moscow last week. He briefed me on everything. He said the Soviet system is on the verge of collapse. He wandered around wherever he wanted without a minder, as if he was in England or France. Things are much more open. I'll be fine."

"That's why I'm worried. The Soviet Union's about to fall."

"That's a good thing. Look at East Germany. The Cold War's last gasp," she argued.

"But the Soviet Union is the behemoth. We don't know how it will come apart. It could get ugly. There could be a coup. Generals and bureaucrats in Moscow are invested in retaining power."

"This is all hypothetical. There's always risk in life. I could be hit by a bus crossing the street in Cleveland Park tomorrow morning." Vickie was shaking with anger. "I thought you'd be excited I was chosen for this assignment."

"I'm sorry for sounding like a mother hen. I care about you, Victoria. I suspect I'm being overly protective."

"Do you support me in this?"

He relented. "Yes, of course. You know I admire you."

"Good, because this trip means the world to me, and I'm going no matter how you feel. I'd just feel a lot better about *us* if I believed you understood."

"I do understand. You have to promise to call me if you sense even a whiff of danger when you're there," he wheedled.

"I will." Vickie felt relieved that Darren understood how much she wanted this assignment—and relieved not to be fighting with him. "You have to promise to pick up the phone if I call." As they both knew, he was seldom in his DC house or office to take calls.

"Touché," he responded. "I'll be flying back to Washington

on the twenty-first of April and staying put. I will be at Dulles to meet you when you get back and at home or sitting in my office if you need to call me while you're in Kiev."

Two days after her phone call with Darren, Vickie was going over a checklist for her trip when Molly came into the living room and sat down beside her on the couch.

"Hey, Pumpkin, what's up?" Vickie asked. Molly bit her lower lip then burst into tears.

"What's wrong, honey?" She leaned toward Molly and kneaded her shoulders.

"Please don't go to Kiev, Mommy. I want you to stay here," Molly pleaded.

"Oh, honey. I have to go. It's my job." Vickie wiped the tears off her cheeks.

"No, you don't." Molly wriggled out of her mother's arms. "They can make someone else go," she screamed.

"This is my job, Molly. I have to make this trip." Vickie was caught off guard by her anger.

"You do not! Daddy said you're going because you want to be a famous reporter. He said people don't have to stay in a job they hate."

Molly stomped across the living room and hurled herself on a chair. Arms folded across her chest, she glared at her mother. "If you really, really don't want to go, you could quit your stupid job and get another one. And stay here with me."

Vickie couldn't believe that Jake had talked to Molly about her this way. She jumped off the couch to call him and tell him this was none of his business. Before she reached the kitchen to pick up the phone, however, she thought better of it. Cooling down, she decided that Jake had the right to give Molly his view of things. She felt it was important to be honest and explain herself to Molly.

"Maybe I could quit my job, Sweetie. I suppose your father is right." Vickie walked back to the couch and sat down. "That's an option for anyone, to quit when they get an assignment that's tough or makes them afraid. I suppose a pitcher could decide to walk off the mound halfway through the inning because the batter on deck is a slugger who's been getting hits off her. Who would want a pitcher like that on their team, though? I'm not going to be a quitter. I want to go to Kiev and do a great job and show everyone that I'm not afraid. I want to make everyone proud of me. And I hope to write true, powerful stories about something I think is important for people to read. Do you understand that?"

Molly leaned her chin on cupped hands and looked down at the floor.

For a long time neither of them spoke.

"Do you understand, Molly?" Vickie asked again, softly.

"I guess so," Molly answered, finally. "I wouldn't quit either."

"I know you wouldn't."

"Can I come with you then?" Molly returned to Vickie's side on the couch.

"No, Pumpkin, I can't bring you. I'll be going to places where only adults are allowed."

"I'll miss you so much, Mommy. What if something bad happens to you?" Molly hugged Vickie ferociously.

"I'll miss you too, honey. I don't think anything bad is going to happen to me. Sandy will take super-good care of you." Vickie turned and looked straight into Molly's eyes. "Plus, your dad will be coming down to be with you."

"Can I come with you when I'm older?" Molly asked.

"I would love to take you with me someday."

"Promise?" Molly asked. Vickie nodded, holding her tightly.

"I'm going to bring you back a special kind of doll that's popular there." Vickie smothered the top of her daughter's head with kisses.

Molly pulled free, giving her a tentative smile. "Maybe you could get one of those dolls for Julia, too."

"I'm glad you thought of that. I'll bring you both one."

32

WASHINGTON, APRIL 1991

The morning before she was set to leave for Kiev, Vickie got a call from Christian Connor. The professor had a letter for her and asked if she could join him for lunch. Curious about the mystery letter, she met him at an Italian bistro on H Street, a short walk from her office. They embraced and eased into a window booth. Prolonging the suspense, he ordered a carafe of wine and two plates of the house specialty, fettuccini Alfredo. After pouring them each a glass of wine, he produced the letter from his briefcase and handed it to Vickie.

The date of the letter, October 29, 1953, leapt off the page at Vickie. That was her brother's birthday. The two-page letter was from James Forrestal, chairman of the Joint Congressional Committee on Atomic Energy, to Representative Sterling Cole.

"Thank you for your visit of last week and your kind interest in the problems of the photographic industry brought about by the testing and use of nuclear weapons. Several years ago the National Association of Photographic Manufacturers established a Committee on Radioactivity," Forrestal wrote. "Dr. E. K. Carver of Eastman Kodak is chairman."

Vickie looked up at Professor Connor, then continued reading. The letter named other members of the radioactivity committee as Dr. F. G. Middleton of duPont; Dr. Julian Webb of Eastman Kodak; M. Insalco of Haloid; and H. W. Morreall of Ansco. "The AEC has worked cooperatively with this committee, particularly the Health and Safety Division, New York Operations Office," Forrestal continued. "The industry has consistently sought to avoid publicity because it is felt that no useful purpose would be served by it."

Vickie's eyes flew across the page. "As discussed with you last week, the photographic problem is primarily due to small air-borne and/or water-borne radioactive particles finding their way into close proximity to the sensitized product." One way the problem can be minimized, the letter stated, was by scheduling "critical raw material manufacture during periods of low radioactive contamination. This is being partially achieved at present by advance information from the AEC concerning United States' tests."

Vickie reached across the table to squeeze Christian's arm. "I can't believe you found this." At last, a document proving the Atomic Energy Commission had warned Kodak about upcoming atom bomb tests, just as Dr. Chandler had told her. But it wasn't only Kodak that received a warning. It was the entire U.S. photographic industry.

"Do you mind if I read it again?" she asked Christian.

"Go ahead, please."

The waiter set enormous plates of pasta on the table. While Christian ate, Vickie reread the letter, soaking in every detail. The letter noted that the photographic industry's Committee on Radioactivity had been established several years earlier, which comported with what Dr. Chandler had said. She attached almost cosmic significance to the fact that the letter was written on the day her brother was born. Her rational brain told her this was nothing more than a coincidence, but intuitively she felt something larger at work.

Vickie put the letter down and leaned across the table. Speaking rapidly, she told Christian about Dr. Olsen's theory that the fallout that rained on Troy and Albany after the Simon bomb test caused a spike in leukemia among children born the year her brother was born.

"It's as if everything in the universe and my life has aligned for me to see this letter. I feel like I'm supposed to know about this for a reason. How can I ever thank you, Christian?"

"You can start by taking a bite of your pasta." The wrinkles around Christian's eyes and mouth deepened with his smile. "Then you must write about this."

His demeanor turned serious. "I'm curious about something you said when we met at Martin's Tavern, Victoria. You told me you weren't doing a story on this, but if you ever decided to, you would set up a proper interview with me. You're obviously passionate about this subject, and, I have no doubt, better informed than any journalist in America. What's holding you back?"

"I have wanted to write about it, but my editor explicitly

forbade me to waste my time—his words—looking through declassified documents dating back forty years. I've been signing in at the docket using my home phone number and hoping he never gets wind of my research there. I'm pretty sure he would fire me. He's a proponent of nuclear power and dead set against me writing about fallout from U.S. nuclear testing." Vickie took a sip of water. "I need this job. Newhart News pays my bills, but I couldn't let this subject go. It was something I've had to pursue, for myself. I had to try to get to the bottom of what happened to my brother."

"In my opinion, your editor's a damn fool." Christian wiped his face and tossed his napkin on the table. "Why don't you write a freelance article? This is a subject of enormous importance and something I think Americans will want to know about."

Vickie nodded, giving the idea serious thought. Dr. Webb, in his article on fogged film, had discovered that particles of radiation were to blame for contaminating packaging materials made in Indiana. She wondered where else radioactive snow and rain might have fallen. With iodine-131 settling on the fields of dairy farmers across the Heartland—and with children drinking radioactive milk—she realized this could be a far-reaching story, affecting almost everyone east of the Nevada Test Site. She wondered how many cases of thyroid cancer might have been caused by radiation from America's one hundred atomic bomb tests, not only in Nevada, Utah, and upstate New York, but everywhere in between.

"I'm flying to Kiev tomorrow to cover the fifth anniversary of Chernobyl. When I get back from Ukraine?" Vickie paused, locking eyes with the professor. "Maybe you're right. Maybe I need to write about our country's nuclear secrets and stop clinging to this job."

"Revealing the truth or remaining employed—shouldn't have to be a choice. Whatever you decide, I don't know of anyone better prepared than you to do this issue justice. Be sure to call upon me if I can be of help. And best of luck in Kiev." Christian flagged the waiter.

Vickie slipped the priceless letter into her bag. As a journalist, interviews were her lifeblood, but it was documents she cherished above all else. During interviews, people could forget. They could embellish, invent, err, or exaggerate. The printed page did not lie.

33
KIEV, APRIL 1991

A tall man with flaxen hair and red cheeks flirted with Vickie as he lifted her heavy case from the overhead compartment. "*Spasibo,*" she said in butchered Russian, bringing a good-natured smile to his dimpled face. She followed him down the aisle, her hard case thumping against the seats. Inside the terminal of Boryspil Airport, she retrieved her other suitcase and made her way to the border check line. The long wait lulled her into a numbed state until she noticed the middle-aged man in front of her shrink under a beefy official's insistent questioning. She wondered what the man had done to provoke such a sharp inquisition. The sudden realization that she was alone behind the Iron Curtain sent a jolt of fear through her limbs. Thoughts of U-2 spy planes and Solzhenitsyn's *Gulag Archipelago* flooded her mind.

After dismissing his quaking victim, the official fixed Vickie with a hard gaze. He gestured to her with impatient fingers, causing her knees to go gelatinous. She reminded herself that she had sought this assignment, there was no going back now. Steeling her nerves, she took a deep breath and walked to his station. She handed him her passport. He studied her photo then peered into her eyes until she looked away. When he barked a command, she mangled a phonetic rendition from her phrasebook of "I don't understand Russian." He stared at her indignantly, color rising in his cheeks. Her heart leapt into her throat as it occurred to her that she might have inadvertently uttered something offensive, like, go to hell, you ugly bastard. She fished through her bag and pulled out documents from the Ministry that was supposed to shepherd her and eleven other journalists through the Chernobyl plant in the coming week. After glancing at the papers, he gestured to a man leaning against a wall smoking. Not much taller than Vickie's five feet, five inches, he had the physique of a body builder. His gold-flecked eyes studied her from beneath a prominent brow ridge. He crushed his cigarette under his shoe and motioned her to a table scarred with knicks and burns.

"Victoria Evans, journalist?" the muscle-bound man asked in heavily accented English.

Vickie nodded. He introduced himself as Bohdan Volkov, her guide. She wondered why he knew of her, and why she was being singled out. She immediately regretted her decision to come to Ukraine a day early, ahead of the other invited journalists.

"Open bag," Bohdan directed, pointing to her hard case. She unlatched it, revealing a portable typewriter, a tape recorder, cassettes, batteries, notepads, pens, paper, and a bottle of white-out.

The beefy official stepped away from his duties and joined them. She watched in horror as Bohdan manhandled her tape recorder, punching buttons and shaking it. The tape recorder was the one tool she could not do without. She was afraid he would confiscate it, but he set it down and told her to open the typewriter case. She released the hinges, and he yanked off the cover. A Care Bear sticker with an "I Love You" balloon was stuck under the lid. Vickie's eyes watered as she pictured Molly placing the teddy bear on her typewriter case, as a surprise.

Bohdan then directed her to open the other suitcase, which was neatly packed with skirts, blouses, toiletries, and shoes. The customs official pawed through her clothing, holding up a silky undergarment. Sizing him up as slimy but predictable, Vickie no longer found him threatening. Bohdan, on the other hand, showed no interest in her tape recorder or her underwear. Folding his arms across his chest, he regarded her belongings with disdain, as if he had yet to discover what it was he was looking for.

Bohdan unnerved her. She hadn't expected to be assigned a minder before the start of the official Ministry program. According to her colleague, Ian, the Soviet system of minders had pretty much broken down. Last month, Ian had zipped through customs in Moscow and had been able to travel solo wherever he wanted. He had led Vickie to believe that she would be free to roam at will, without an escort. What worried her now was how she would ditch Bohdan for the interviews she planned to conduct that were not sanctioned by the Ministry. Larysa Marchenko had arranged an interview with her uncle, who was a high-placed nuclear physicist. Dmitry had lined up interviews with doctors and activists whose words could land them in prison.

But it was these unofficial interviews that would shed light on the coverup she hoped to reveal. She would have to find ways to shake Bohdan, she told herself.

The customs officer returned to his post, leaving Vickie alone with Bohdan, who struck a match and lit another cigarette. He extinguished the flame with a violent snap of his hand inches from her face.

Vickie's fingers shook as she shoved her clothes and shoes back into her bag. She knew Bohdan was watching her hands, but she couldn't steady them.

"I drive you to hotel," he said, the cigarette clamped between yellow teeth.

"I can take a taxi." Vickie summoned her courage. She gave him a strained smile, her eyes meeting his. She was tempted to ask if he'd heard of *glasnost* or *perestroika*, but nothing about his expression invited irony.

"Too dangerous for attractive young lady." Bohdan's voice was more yielding than before.

"I read that this city is safe and friendly," she countered.

Bohdan knew as well as she did that the Soviet Union took pride in its low crime rate, especially compared to violent American cities like Washington, D.C., where Vickie lived. His metallic eyes traveled from the neckline of her V-neck sweater down her blue jeans and back up to her throat. She glanced around the concourse, looking for someone to hail for help. She considered sprinting back to the customs official, but before she had time do anything, Bohdan picked up her bags and headed for the exit.

Willing her watery legs to step forward, Vickie zipped her leather bomber jacket up over her sweater and followed him into the chilly Kiev night.

Bohdan stowed Vickie's luggage in the boot of a black sedan parked outside and opened the passenger door for her. A voice inside her was screaming to run, but she dutifully climbed into the car. During the ride into the city, he asked about her plans for the following day. His voice, less imperious than before, sounded almost welcoming. Vickie tried to convince herself that Bohdan was not threatening, that perhaps her panic in the airport had grown out of a lifetime of fearing the Soviet Union. She told him she intended to tour the city, hike, and shop for souvenirs.

"I'm a fan of puppets, and I'm looking forward to taking in shows at the Puppet Theatre. I've been told your puppeteers are the best in the world," she added. This is something that Dmitry had prompted her to mention if she was assigned a minder. Bohdan sneered and had little to say for the rest of the drive. He pulled up to the Dnipro Hotel, an imposing establishment in the heart of downtown Kiev. After carrying her bags to the reception desk, he announced that he would see her at breakfast.

Entering her hotel room, Vickie felt like she was stepping into a bordello. Heavy red draperies and a red bedspread overpowered the small space. Even the lampshades beside the bed were crimson, casting garish shadows on the room's dingy white walls. Overcome with exhaustion, she managed to unpack, spreading her typewriter and office supplies on the desk. She hung her suit jacket and blouses in the closet, lay back on the bed, and fell into a deep sleep.

Vickie woke up early and put on jeans, a sweater, and running shoes in a conscious effort to look touristy. On her way to the breakfast buffet, she noticed Bohdan in the lobby by the Intourist Office. She filled her plate with bread, jam, and sausage, then found a seat. After a waiter poured her a glass of tea, Bohdan sauntered to her table.

"Your program does not begin until tomorrow. I can assist you with transportation and translation today," he offered.

"I'm on vacation today. I don't plan to work. I want to walk around the city and see your cathedrals and shop for *Matryoshka* dolls. I'm also hoping to hike on the Dnieper and enjoy the beach. Can you recommend a nice hiking trail along the river?" Vickie doubted Bohdan did any hiking. His pasty complexion looked as if it hadn't seen sunlight in decades.

"Hundreds of miles of beaches." Bohdan took a drag on his cigarette. "Trukhaniv Island is popular with Europeans. On other side of Parkovy pedestrian bridge," he added without concealing his annoyance.

After Bohdan left, Vickie opened *The Joy Luck Club*, the novel she'd packed, and drank tea, trying to look leisurely, though her stomach was in knots. She ran her eyes over the pages without registering a word. As much as she wanted to meet Larysa, she decided to spend the entire day playing tourist—unless Bohdan grew bored with her and left her alone. Twenty minutes went by, and Bohdan did not reappear. She pretended to read for another five minutes before leaving the hotel.

Stepping outside, she was bowled over by the grandeur of the city. Gold onion domes and spires adorned the blue skyline, glinting in the sun. Everything was on an immense scale. She ambled around the square, passing massive granite buildings, marble arches, and a huge monument to Lenin.

The sky was clear and the temperature cool, ideal for walking. She tried to stop worrying about Bohdan and enjoy her free day in Kiev. She wandered down Sofiivska Street to St. Sophia Cathedral, which was built in 1017 to honor the city's founder, Prince Yaroslav the Wise. It was a magnificent church, with gleaming domes. Inside, she admired the lustrous frescoes and old mosaics. She saw no sign of Bohdan as she left the cathedral and strolled to the Golden Gate. After meandering back to the square, she walked to St. Michael's, a golden-domed cathedral she found even more beautiful than Saint Sophia.

Not far from St. Michael's she happened upon a street with several vendors selling carved eggs and *Matryoshka* dolls. Seeing the colorful nesting dolls in hundreds of patterns brought a smile to her face. She was thinking about Molly when she spotted Bohdan out of the corner of her eye. He was leaning against a stone wall, smoking. She shivered, realizing that he must have been following her without her noticing. She realized she would have to be far more observant. She lingered for close to an hour, combing through the dolls until she settled on two for Molly and Julia. Stopping at a table piled with the painted wooden Easter eggs, she bought one for herself and one for Sandy. She brought her purchases back to her room and found a restaurant near the hotel for lunch.

Seeing no sign of Bohdan at the restaurant, she decided to make her way toward the Marchenko apartment by way of the beach. If Bohdan followed her, she would abort the visit to Larysa and spend the afternoon reading on the beach. Comfortable with her decision, she walked to the metro station on the square to catch the northbound line. She had heard people rave about the Kiev metro system, but it was more spectacular than she could have imagined, with high ceilings, Gothic arches, and dramatic lighting. She didn't see Bohdan on the platform, but as she was boarding the train, she glimpsed a figure entering a rear car. Worried it might have been Bohdan, she decided to spend a good deal of time at the beach before risking a visit to Larysa's apartment.

She disembarked at Minska Station and crossed Marshal Tymoshenko. She cast a furtive look around for Bohdan but didn't see him. Following Dmitry's meticulous directions, she continued walking toward a traffic circle then bore right on Pryrichna Street. She glanced behind her shoulders now and then. There were only a few pedestrians around, mostly women and children, but out of caution, she continued walking past Larysa's apartment block, which was on her left. Not far beyond Larysa's building, the street ended at a sandy beach on the Dnieper.

Vickie was relieved to find a cozy spot where she could take in the view until she felt certain that Bohdan hadn't followed her. Sitting on the sand, she watched a young couple chase a toddler with a balloon along the water's edge. Two older women were engaged in an animated conversation in Russian or Ukrainian— she couldn't tell which. After forty-five minutes passed and she felt sure she had ditched Bohdan, Vickie doubled back to the building on Pryrichna Street. The ten-story concrete block was drab, but the apartments had large balconies. The door was ajar, so she climbed to the third-floor flat and knocked lightly.

Larysa greeted Vickie with a hug. Her round blue eyes gazed out from a broad face with translucent skin, giving her an otherworldly appearance. Thanking Vickie for coming, she urged her to sit at the kitchen table. She poured tea into glasses in ornate silver holders. Larysa had agreed to an interview, but neither she nor Vickie seemed in a mood to rush it.

"My son tells me wonderful things about you. You made a favorable impression on him during his trip to America. You are like family. I'm sorry Dmitry is not here. He is at class." Larysa went on to explain that Vasyl and Katya were not available either. They were staying at her uncle's cottage in Odessa.

"I had hoped to interview your husband." Vickie couldn't conceal her disappointment. She had been looking forward to meeting Vasyl and Katya.

"Everything is falling apart." Larysa apologized, gesturing around the apartment. "My uncle insisted that Vasyl will do better there, and he needs to plant the garden. We hope Katya's health will improve by the sea. My uncle has gotten Katya on a list to travel to Germany for special treatments." Larysa brought a tray of pastries, a bowl of jam, and plates to the table.

"My uncle is right, you know. My husband can't manage these stairs. He grows short of breath. Since he no longer can work, he feels useless here in the city. My husband and Katya took the train with many of our possessions to Odessa a little over a week ago. Vasyl is pruning berry bushes and fruit trees and planting the garden with vegetables. He has a way with plants—but I'm talking, and you haven't taken a bite. Please, eat!"

Vickie took a sip of tea and a bite of a cherry-filled pastry. She tried another pastry, this one with a dollop of strawberry jam. Both tasted delicious. After chatting about food for several minutes, Vickie melted into the comfort of Larysa's presence.

"I'm looking forward to seeing Dmitry again," Vickie said.

"He is eager to see you too—at six o'clock at the Puppet Theatre." Larysa grinned. Vickie looked puzzled at first, then a smile crept over her face. Larysa explained that either she or Dmitry would meet Vickie at the theater each evening. Larysa was an amateur puppeteer and knew everyone there. If Vickie wanted to interview someone, they would arrange a backstage room for her.

"There's not so much surveillance as before, but people do not want to be seen talking to an American. My uncle has agreed to an interview with you on Thursday evening. I have something to show you." Larysa jumped up and darted to the living room, returning with a framed photograph taken on the last night of 1986.

"What a wonderful family! Your daughter is beautiful, and Vasyl's so handsome." Vickie studied the picture. In this photo, taken before her cancer, Katya was smiling, her blue eyes joyful. Vickie pulled a school photo of Molly from her wallet, which Larysa admired. Molly had rosy cheeks, chestnut curls, and earnest green eyes. For several moments, the two women basked in the simple bond of motherhood. Looking at the photos, they grew quiet. Larysa's eyes brimmed with tears, which she wiped away with her shirt cuff.

Vickie sensed how hard this would be for Larysa, but she knew the time had come to begin. She put a cassette in her tape recorder and pressed record. When Larysa spoke this time, undiluted pain poured from her lips.

She described the innocent day before her world cracked apart. It was a holiday, warm and sunny. Balloons bobbed against a bright blue sky as on any other May Day. She recalled how handsome Vasyl had looked in his suit and how Katya laughed when he hoisted her on his shoulders. Dmitry had been bursting with pride, bearing the red banner of his Pioneer group.

"You must understand how hot May Day was. This is why I dressed Katya in a pinafore with short sleeves. The dress was her favorite, plaid with ruffles. We had no need for a sweater to cover her arms. May Day was so warm. Many girls wore short skirts, the sun soaking their bare legs." Larysa paused. Her pale eyes penetrated Vickie's with a plea for forgiveness. Her words described ruffles, but her voice quavered with the rumble of the apocalypse.

"How could I know I was bringing Katya outside to breathe radioactive dust? No one told us. They knew how dangerous the radiation was. Top officials already had sent their children to the airport to fly them to safety. But we didn't know this." Larysa's voice gathered a swell of anger.

"Do you have proof? I need to verify that," Vickie interrupted.

"Yes, we can prove that. Children of top Party officials were flown away. There are drivers who know. These secrets dribbled out with time. The rest of us only learned days after the parade that dangerous radiation engulfed Kiev. Authorities banned the sale of milk. Then they told us to wash our shoes. Radioactive dust covered the sidewalks. Panic set in. Vasyl tried to buy train tickets to send Dmitry and Katya to Saratov to stay with his sister, but there were no seats. On trains, all seats leaving Kiev were filled. Same with seats on every flight from Kiev—to anywhere. But this was later. On May Day we didn't know yet what was happening. How could Vasyl and I know that radiation was falling on our little girl's arms and covering her legs? Deadly particles were coating her neck and throat and settling in her hair? Did I tell you I combed her hair off her forehead in a ponytail and tied it in a ribbon?"

Vickie noticed that Larysa couldn't stop thinking about the amount of Katya's skin left uncovered and exposed to fallout that day.

"Last September the surgeon cut a tumor from her throat, but Katya has an aggressive cancer. I am not speaking only of my Katya. Dozens of children bear half-moon scars on their throat. You are a journalist in America. You must write about this. Party officials keep this all secret. They lie about the cause of illness and deaths in our country. Some doctors talk to our journalists, but newspapers refuse to print their stories." Larysa leaned forward, her eyes filling with tears.

"When I see the scar on Katya's throat, I am in agony. We would have wrapped her in blankets, closed the windows, and kept her safe inside if we had known radiation was falling."

In the coffee house in Washington, Vickie had felt like a sister to Dmitry. She shared with him the pain of an older child who escaped an illness that attacked a younger sister or brother. Here in the kitchen with Larysa, she understood the pain from a mother's perspective. All at once, Vickie fully grasped how terrible it must have been for her mother to lose Paul, and how the loss of her beloved husband a year later had crushed her. With this realization, something tight inside Vickie's chest gave way, and she felt sympathy for her mother.

"Vasyl is sick. Doctors say he has a neurological problem and trouble with his heart. He was a cleanup worker," Larysa continued, collecting herself. "Some people say radioactive cesium contaminates the food we eat, but authorities keep this secret. Our Dmitry was spared. He remains healthy—and I am healthy. For this I thank God—to give me strength to care for Vasyl and Katya. My uncle knows a book seller in Odessa who needs help. I will leave Kiev soon to work for this book seller and be with my husband and daughter." Larysa's voice brightened as she talked about joining them.

"Radiation attacks the innocent and guilty alike. You cannot see it or smell it. How do you escape an enemy you cannot perceive with your senses? You have to rely on leaders and scientists with instruments to tell the truth. Where is our protection when our leaders lie and our scientists remain silent?" Larysa's voice broke.

"Dmitry has the spirit of an avenger, but he has a hole in his heart, an ache that never goes away for his precious sister with her throat slashed, and for his father. Vasyl was a powerful man. He sprinted to the river in minutes, carrying a child on his shoulders. Now, he has trouble walking a block. Joy was stolen from us. There is much that must be written. Will you help?" Larysa pleaded, her visage shining with hope.

When Vickie entered the lobby of the Puppet Theater that evening, Dmitry approached her and squeezed her hand. She followed him to a small auditorium. They hugged and slid into middle seats in the back row.

"What a discreet meeting place—public yet completely private," Vickie marveled. She told him about Bohdan and the fear she had felt at the airport.

"I'm surprised. That's not so common lately as it was. Maybe because you're from America," Dmitry speculated.

"I'll be under the watchful eyes of the Foreign Ministry when the official program starts tomorrow. Maybe he wanted to keep an eye on me until then."

"It's wise to be careful. That is why my mother or I want to meet you here every night. You can tell us if you have any worries. If there are people you need to interview, we might be able to bring them here for you. My mother's a terrific puppeteer. Everyone here adores her."

Dmitry said he would attend the Euro-Chernobyl conference that Vickie planned to cover in the morning. He also told her he knew someone from the Chernobyl Union of Liquidators who would be able to talk to her in the evening.

"I'd like to interview a driver who brought children of Party officials to the airport before the May Day parade, if that's possible. It would show that top officials knew of the dangerous radiation blowing over Kiev from Chernobyl and withheld the information from the public. This is important in proving a coverup," Vickie told Dmitry.

The front section filled with children, and Vickie and Dmitry stopped talking to watch a charming production of Popelyushka, the Ukrainian version of Cinderella. Without comprehending a word of Russian, Vickie was able to understand the gist of the fairytale. When the show ended, she and Dmitry hugged good-night. She returned to the hotel feeling safe in the knowledge that Dmitry and Larysa were watching over her.

34
KIEV, APRIL 1991

Vickie put on a gray suit and high-collared white blouse, dropped a handful of blank cassette tapes into her bag, and hurried to the hotel buffet. She wolfed down a piece of bread with fruit preserves. She glanced around the lobby for Bohdan but didn't see him. In fact, she realized that she hadn't seen him since noon, at the Russian doll vendor's table. Leaving the hotel, she hurried up Khreshchatyk to the Ministry of Foreign Affairs Press Center. The guard at the entrance studied her credentials then gave her a badge showing her name, city, and country. He escorted her to a paneled room festooned with USSR flags and larger-than-life portraits of Lenin and Gorbachev. She took a seat beside a thirty-something woman whose badge identified her as Helen Black, London, UK. She was wearing a smart, double-breasted suit and gnawing the plastic cap of her ballpoint pen.

"My first time to the Soviet Union," the woman whispered. "How about you?"

"First time as well," Vickie replied. Much like trench mates in a theater of war, they bonded within minutes. Vickie scanned the badges of people around the table for Igor Pavlychko, the photographer Ian had told her to meet. She didn't see him, although she did note reporters from Poland, France, Denmark, Germany, Ireland, Canada, Australia, and Japan. When a lanky man with unruly black hair and a thick mustache entered the room hauling camera gear, Vickie motioned to him. Igor set his bags near a row of flag stands and took a chair beside her.

By eight o'clock sharp, twelve reporters and six photographers were assembled at the conference table. Olga, the assistant press secretary, made her entrance. Dressed in a calf-length brown skirt and chunky shoes, she circled the table with pomp, placing a stack of papers in front of each reporter. Except for the trip to Pripyat and Chernobyl, which would be tightly controlled, the program turned out to be loose. Everyone was expected to check in each morning to receive a daybook of activities in Kiev. Otherwise, reporters were free to set their own schedules and wander without supervision.

Most of the reporters, who had applied to the program primarily for the chance to tour the reactor, scattered after the briefing. Helen, like Vickie, was interested in covering the Euro-Chernobyl health conference. On their walk to the conference, Helen confessed that she was getting cold feet about going to the reactor.

"The prospect of seeing Chernobyl held a lot of cachet three months ago when I asked for this assignment, but don't be surprised if I have a dicky tummy tomorrow and bail." Helen's half laugh did not reach her eyes, which remained serious.

Vickie realized that she had been so invested in covering this story—and in convincing Molly and Darren of her right to come here—that she hadn't thought much about the danger of being close to the crippled reactor.

At the Euro-Chernobyl meeting, the buzz was about the draft IAEA health effects report, which found no excess cases of thyroid cancer or leukemia in Ukraine or Byelorussia. The final report wouldn't be released until May, but Byelorussian and Ukrainian doctors vehemently condemned the draft. IAEA researchers attributed illnesses suffered by tens of thousands of people in the Chernobyl region to poor diet, anxiety, and stress due to fear of radiation.

At noon Vickie accompanied Igor to a café. The eating place was accessible only from an alley, and there didn't seem to be any tourists at the tables. She and Igor enjoyed a lunch of borscht and bread. Vickie was relieved to see no sign of Bohdan. After lunch, Igor photographed the Ukrainian and Byelorussian doctors Vickie interviewed. The doctors provided her with case studies and tables showing evidence of a significant increase in thyroid cancer in children. Before parting company for the evening, Vickie asked Igor if he'd ever been near Chernobyl.

"No, this will be my first time."

"Are you nervous about it?" she asked.

"As long as that sarcophagus holds, we should be okay." Igor told her the European press had been reporting that the tomb built to contain radiation inside Reactor 4 was cracking.

"That doesn't sound good." Vickie grimaced, hoping he was exaggerating.

"Don't worry. We'll hop in and out like hares." Igor grinned. "My interest is in Pripyat. People have taken unbelievable photographs there."

An hour later, when Vickie entered puppet theater lobby, Dmitry was waiting for her with a member of the Chernobyl Union of Liquidators. He had agreed to speak on tape. They retired to a room backstage, and he detailed the frustrations of liquidators, who were trying to prove that their debilitating illnesses were from radiation. Next, Dmitry introduced Vickie to a man who had driven a bus of children of Party members from Kiev to the airport two days before May Day. She was thrilled to get that interview on tape—though the driver was not willing to give his name. After both men left, Dmitry told Vickie that his mother would be here on Thursday evening to take her to interview his granduncle, the physicist Anatoly Kulyk.

On her way back to the hotel, Vickie stopped at a market for bread and cheese. Once she settled in her room, she began writing a story based on the IAEA draft report and her interviews with doctors who disputed the IAEA's findings. She typed for three hours and turned into bed late.

⁓

On the bus, everyone was talking about cracks in the sarcophagus. The remains of Reactor 4 had been rumbling like a volcano, and people were warning the top would soon blow like Mount St. Helens. She was wondering how these foreign journalists knew so much about Mount St. Helens, when the Chernobyl plant rose in front of them. The group was approaching the pump room for all four reactors. Most of the reporters were ensconced in white hazmat suits fitted with bubble helmets, but she didn't get one. There weren't enough to go around. She was wearing a white jacket, with nothing to protect her face. Suddenly a sonic boom ripped the air. Hot raspberry dust engulfed them. Anyone without a helmet received an immediate lethal dose of radiation. The helmeted reporters regarded her with horror.

She felt nothing but fear. No pain, no lacerations, only sheer terror. She knew that she had been fatally contaminated. She would be carted off and placed in quarantine where she would go through the gruesome stages of acute radiation poisoning until she died within two months. She had read about the firefighters who died after putting out Chernobyl's flames. She knew the agony they had endured. Her body blew up, and she became aware of an unbearable burning from within. Hunks of flesh turned necrotic and sloughed off her arms and legs, leaving a nauseating stench. Her fingers fell off. One eye bulged, growing so large it burst.

She could see only through a slit in her left eye, and what she saw was attendants covered from head to toe in protective suits. They brought a tray with pudding and a glass of water, though she could not eat. Looking up she saw Molly's face at the window in the room's door.

"No, don't come in, Molly," she shrieked. "I want you to live."

Molly was not wearing protective clothing. She opened the door and was approaching when Vickie jerked awake from a nightmare so real she had to grasp one hand with the other to make certain her fingers were intact. She switched on the light and ran her fingers over her face. What joy—it was only a dream! Molly is safe, far away from the reactor. More than anything, she wanted to hold Molly in her arms and promise to keep her safe. She wished she could fly home to Cleveland Park right now, to be with her daughter.

Sitting up in bed, Vickie feared that coming here had been a terrible mistake. She questioned why she had wanted this assignment so badly. She had grown intensely competitive, a trait she saw as essential for success at this kind of work in DC. And she needed to keep her job to be able to support herself and Molly. But she had to admit that there was more driving her than ambition and the need to maintain her livelihood. She had come here to discover the truth about how fallout from Chernobyl was affecting people. In that regard her role as a journalist was above reproach. As the nightmare receded, Vickie tried to gin up her courage. She reminded herself that workers and scientists came and went regularly to and from the nuclear station. She would be with a gaggle of other journalists. They would spend only a few minutes near the infamous sarcophagus, just long enough for the cameramen to get their shots. She resolved to perform her role with dignity, to keep her eyes open and bear witness to the worst nuclear power plant accident in history.

❧

When Olga ushered the eighteen reporters and photographers onto a bus, Vickie was too sleepy to be nervous. Yawning, she took a seat near the front. Igor settled in beside her. Once outside Kiev, they headed north through a bucolic landscape bursting with pink and lavender flowering trees. Looking out the window Vickie couldn't help but think of springtime in southern Indiana. After several miles, Olga and her French-speaking assistant walked up the aisle handing out Geiger counters, one per pair. As Igor would be toting photographic equipment, Vickie held their Geiger counter. Olga explained in Russian how to interpret the readings. Vickie looked to Igor for a translation, but he threw up his hands, befuddled. It didn't matter. The clicks swelling to a fevered pitch and the numbers rising on the meter told her everything she needed to know.

The road narrowed and the bus stopped at a gate. After a brief conversation with their driver, a guard waved them through. Alert now, Vickie watched soldiers congregating by the sides of the road smoking. Yellow signs with red triangles nailed to fence posts and trees warned of radiation. Soon their bus pulled up to a makeshift station.

"Off the bus, everyone!" Olga commanded in Russian.

Moving quickly, the journalists crossed a parking lot and boarded a vile-smelling bus. This "dirty" bus was used to transport people within the exclusion zone. Vickie was wary of sitting on the seat for fear of contaminating her pants but figured she could throw them away when she got back to the hotel.

The road deteriorated as they traveled deeper into the Zone. Soon they passed through the town of Chernobyl. Vickie was so obsessed with the eerie clicking of her Geiger counter, she hardly noticed the town. Not long after they left Chernobyl, they saw two concrete structures rising from a large stand of bushes. These were the unfinished cooling towers for Reactors 5 and 6, which had been abandoned after the accident at Reactor 4.

Suddenly the Chernobyl station was upon them. They got off the bus in their regular street clothes. Vickie's Geiger counter screeched like cicadas on a hot August afternoon. In a few yards, the crackling abated—bringing to life for her the concept of hot spots that Darren had described. Following the lead of the other pairs, Vickie lowered her Geiger counter close to the ground. The clicks jumped faster and louder. Everyone was questioning whether it was safe to be here. They stepped up their pace as they crossed concrete paving stones leading to the entrance.

Inside the door, two engineers greeted them—one with a welcome "hello" in English. They handed out bulky white jackets and overalls, but no face masks. After donning their whites, the reporters followed the engineers down a long corridor. They stopped in front of the control room for Reactor 2. The English-speaking engineer explained to Vickie, Helen, and the Irish and Australian reporters that Reactor 2 had restarted operations in November of 1986.

Workers in the control room were wearing white jackets and pants but no face masks or other protective gear. Vickie asked the engineer about the radiation level where they were standing.

"The radiation level in this part of the station is 0.6 millirems per hour, which is sixty times higher than normal background," the engineer explained. "You will see it get much higher nearer to the sarcophagus. Follow me."

The group walked down a long corridor and stopped within view of the sarcophagus. Their Geiger counters clacked frenetically. Igor's shutter clicked several times.

"Here the reading is 1.6 millirems per hour," the engineer said. "If we stood right beside the structure, you would see readings above ten millirems per hour, which would be one thousand times above background."

Vickie's Geiger counter warned her to get out of this place.

She imagined a siren blaring. Where would she go? Ghastly images from last night's dream seeped over her surroundings like a palimpsest. She wanted to get far away from that sarcophagus before it blew.

"Are you finished?" Vickie asked Igor, her voice ragged. Every fiber of her being wanted to turn and run, but she resisted.

"Just about." Igor twisted a long lens, squinted through the viewfinder, and depressed the shutter-release button. "Done, let's go."

They quickly retraced their steps to the door. Joining the others, Vickie and Igor peeled off their white jackets, stepped out of the pants, and scurried to the bus. Within minutes, they crossed a bridge, and the city of Pripyat came into view. Olga announced something in Russian, then German. Her assistant followed in French. She and Igor checked with each other to make sure they had understood correctly. The radiation level on that bridge the day following the explosion had been 80 rems per hour. This was 800,000 times higher than normal background. It was a level that could give humans a fatal dose of radiation in three hours.

Glancing out the rear window, Vickie shuddered. She was grateful the driver had not lingered on that bridge. The bus crawled through a city honeycombed with flaking white apartment buildings, all of them vacant.

"You will have thirty minutes to walk around the city and take photographs," Olga and her assistant announced when the bus stopped. "We will depart promptly to return to Kiev."

The journalists filed off the bus like shell-shocked soldiers. Pripyat looked as if a neutron bomb had vaporized human life while sparing buildings. Igor, who had studied the city's layout in advance, made his way to a high-rise apartment building. Vickie hurried to keep up with him. They climbed the stairwell to an upper floor hallway. Apartment doors hung open. They encountered a profound quiet, interrupted only by their footsteps and the incessant clicking of their Geiger counter.

Peeking inside an apartment, Vickie saw moldy dishes in the sink—remains of a meal left unfinished five years ago. In a child's room a teddy bear languished on the floor, its face whitened with plaster dust from the crumbling ceiling. In another room, she saw a photo album open on the floor. Feeling like a voyeur, she squatted and peered at the photographs. She had the urge to take it with her and search for the family it belonged to—although removing anything was forbidden. In any case, the ticking Geiger counter reminded her the album was hot.

"Did you notice there's no stove or refrigerator in the kitchen?" she asked Igor. "Wait, there's no furniture in the living room, either."

"These places were ransacked by thieves. They no doubt got a good price for high quality appliances and furniture at the time. I'm sure they never told the buyers the goods came from Pripyat," Igor speculated.

They wandered through another apartment strewn with books and broken glass. Vickie didn't touch anything. She tiptoed to a window that looked out over an abandoned playground. Brown leaves coated a slide and a rusty roundabout. The bright blue sky and sunshine heightened the roundabout's glum emptiness.

"Let's go, Igor." Vickie left the window. She could see how absorbed he was in trying to capture the profound sense of loss in these rooms, but they'd used up twenty of their thirty minutes.

"It's time to head back to the bus."

Outside they walked toward a high Ferris wheel, a playful hoop mocking the motionless landscape. The city's population had been evacuated four days before the amusement ride was set to open for the May Day celebration in 1986. For Vickie, the Ferris wheel crystalized the Chernobyl tragedy. Frozen in time, it would never spin. The children who would have thrilled to its heights, scared out of their wits, now faced grim fears for their future that were all too real.

Heading back to the bus, they walked through knee-high weeds, their Geiger counter screeching like a swarm of alien bugs. They turned for a last look at the vacant white apartment buildings. Vickie was struck by how quickly Nature had reclaimed the city, covering every manmade object and structure with mold, rust, dirt, and weeds. No one talked on the bus. Vickie took out her notebook to write about the meaning of what she and Igor had seen, but she couldn't find words to convey the otherworldliness of this place. A city once humming with the sounds and sites of human life now stood empty, a monument to the hubris of scientists who unleashed the power of the atom.

§

In the morning, with Dmitry translating, Vickie interviewed activists demonstrating in October Revolution Square. At noon Dmitry brought her to his student hangout, which was down a flight of stairs in a shabby building off Artema Street. Entering a windowless space with a low ceiling, she felt like she had been transported back in time to an American college town in 1970. Young people with shaggy hair crowded around tables, talking and smoking. Absent were the portraits of Lenin and Gorbachev. A juggler wearing a black silk shirt and red vest kept three balls aloft in one corner of the room. "Every Rose Has Its Thorn," a popular ballad by an American band, played in the background. Dmitry had obligations the following day, and Vickie was to fly out Saturday morning, which meant this was where they would have to say goodbye. They lingered over soup, reminiscing about their evening in Washington at the coffee house.

"You still haven't met my father and sister, so you must come back soon and visit Odessa. You haven't seen Ukraine until you've seen the Black Sea," Dmitry said. "Did my mother tell you she's going to be working at a bookstall there?"

Vickie nodded, a lump forming in her throat. She wanted to meet Vasyl and Katya, but she couldn't foresee a time she would be able to return to Ukraine. When she and Dmitry could put off the moment no longer, they hugged and kissed each other's cheeks.

Vickie returned to the press center to meet Igor. The Dane and Aussie from their group were using the computers, but there was no sign of Igor. She waited for half an hour and was about to leave when he rushed in, black stubble smudging his face. He had spent the night developing film and making prints. When he showed her the contact sheets from their Chernobyl trip, she was blown away. She studied the shots of dilapidated rooms, crumbling buildings, and rusted amusement park rides through a magnifying glass. The images of Pripyat succeeded in capturing the eeriness of the city so perfectly that she decided they should make a photo essay.

"These are wonderful, Igor. You're unbelievable!" Vickie and

Igor worked for the next few hours choosing the progression of photos and composing descriptive captions to flesh out a visual story.

***

In the evening Vickie arrived at the Puppet Theater before Larysa and took a seat in the lobby, grateful for a chance to rest. Within minutes Larysa entered, greeting her with kisses. Noting that Anatoly wanted to conduct the interview at his flat, she led Vickie down a windowless corridor and through a backdoor. Outside, they made their way to a blue Lada parked nearby. On the drive to Chekhovsky Street, Larysa talked about her uncle.

"For fifteen years, I despised him," Larysa told Vickie. "In 1970, he spoke out against my father, who was persecuted for publishing translations of Western poets. My father was sentenced to seven years of hard labor and died of pneumonia. Anatoly shunned my father and our family, watching out for his career. Over the past few years, though, he's been different. I've watched him soften and change."

"What made him change?" Vickie asked.

"I'm not sure, but he adores my children—of that I am certain."

Larysa parked the car, and they climbed the stairs to Anatoly Kulyk's apartment building. He ushered them into his lush flat. Standing in front of Vickie, he searched her face with a look so penetrating she shivered involuntarily.

"I can see you are honest," Anatoly said in Russian. Larysa translated. "I have something for you. It's an accurate radiation record." Larysa translated as he disappeared into his bedroom. He returned with a journal.

"You must bring this with you to the West. Show it to a trust-worthy diplomat or physicist. They will understand its meaning," he said, with Larysa translating his words seconds after he spoke. He handed Vickie a leather-bound journal, which she stuffed into her bag.

Larysa appeared dumbstruck by this gesture. She gave her uncle a puzzled look. He offered no explanation about what the diary contained, and Larysa did not press him for one. This was part of their agreement. When he consented to an interview with an American journalist, Anatoly had insisted, initially, that some-one else should translate. He had finally agreed with Larysa that for the sake of discretion she would be the best choice. However, he had made his niece pledge to act as a professional translator—without a show of emotion or interruptions. She had agreed.

Vickie and Larysa sat on the couch facing Anatoly's armchair. Vickie opened a notepad and placed her tape recorder on the edge of the table closest to Anatoly. When she asked permission to tape, he leaned back in his armchair and stared into the distance for a moment. Clearing his throat, he trained his eyes on her and nodded. Vickie decided to pose a bold question that drove right to the heart of the matter.

"People here in Kiev talk about a government coverup of Chernobyl. They believe that Moscow knew dangerous levels of radiation were emanating from the reactor but suppressed the information—and that Moscow continues to downplay health effects. As a Ukrainian physicist, what did you know about the dangers from Chernobyl radiation, and when did you first know it?" she asked.

A dark shadow passed over Anatoly's countenance. His eyes flashed with an emotion so frightening Vickie felt her legs go hollow. She was afraid it had been a mistake to challenge him with such a direct question. She feared he would cut off the interview. An eternity passed before he spoke.

"We knew everything within hours of the explosion and kept it secret from everyone," he answered, finally. Larysa frowned, but she continued her simultaneous translation. Vickie started to ask him to explain, but he waved his hand, motioning her to be still.

"Listen to me. I will tell you." He sat tall, his shoulders square. His deep voice steadied, taking on authority even as his gaze grew more distant.

"Ukraine's officials called an emergency meeting at six in the morning, less than five hours after the explosion. By nine o'clock, we had readings—all the measurements of radiation are in the journal I gave you. They were dangerously high. The evacuation of Pripyat on Sunday should have been ordered sooner. Every decision from Moscow was taken with the intent of concealing the severity of the accident. But secrecy could only last until radiation crossed international borders. The winds were blowing to the north after the explosion. As I'm sure you know, the Swedes alerted the world. Our scientists knew long before then, of course. We had physicists in Minsk and Gomel who were measuring radiation off the scale.

"When Moscow was forced to acknowledge the accident, they portrayed it as a fire at Reactor Four that was under control. That was for the consumption of our people. The outside world already knew better. On the last day of April, some of us were called for another meeting—an emergency meeting. By then,

Moscow's committee was meeting around the clock in Pripyat, and our committees were meeting constantly. We learned the winds had changed direction and were blowing to the south. Our representatives at the meeting wanted to cancel the May Day parades in Kiev, Gomel, and Minsk, but Moscow authorities insisted that would be impossible. Two Ukrainian doctors at the meeting were courageous enough to dare to propose that we warn people to stay inside and close their windows."

Anatoly trained his dark eyes on Vickie. "Read my journal. Everything is written there. Moscow insisted cancelling the parade would cause panic. Going forward with the parade in Kiev would reassure the world at large—but especially people inside the Soviet Union—that everything was under control. That was a lie, of course. Nothing was controlled. In fact, on May first, the temperature in the Chernobyl reactor shot up to levels higher than anyone believed possible. It was a fiery cauldron spewing radiation—and the wind was blowing over Kiev, over children marching in the parade, over the million people celebrating Soviet labor."

Anatoly folded one leg over the other and braced his arms on the chair. He spoke for several seconds, but Larysa stopped translating. She let out a raw scream. Angry words poured from her throat in Russian. He snapped at her, and she shouted back.

"What? What did he say? What are you saying?" Vickie asked, watching Larysa's fingers tremble as she put her hands over her face. "What is it?" she persisted, desperate to learn what Anatoly had said to trigger this explosive exchange.

Larysa composed herself. Her fingers still trembling, she grasped one hand in the other on her lap. Tears streaked her face. Avoiding eye contact with her uncle, she tilted her body in Vickie's direction.

"He says that he wanted to warn me to keep my children inside on May Day, but he was sworn to secrecy. He devised a plan to fly my family to Odessa for the day—May Day—but he overslept in the morning." Her voice sounded thin and far away. "By the time he tried calling us, we had already left for the parade."

Anatoly resumed his narration, and Larysa continued to translate in a bloodless voice.

"Significant radiation releases continued unabated for ten days. On May fifth, releases spiked high, nearly matching the first day. None of us could understand why. And then it stopped." He paused, his face momentarily reflecting the relief he must have felt that day.

"On May fifth, when the reactor core was still burning, plans were made to evacuate Kiev's children. It was no doubt prudent. There was radioactive dust on the streets and buildings. But inside the reactor core, the worst was already over. The children had marched and played in the oven, and only when the temperature cooled were they shipped off to camps far from Kiev. Such was the response to Chernobyl." He stopped, his eyes clouding. For a long time, the room was silent, save for the sound of his breathing.

"I learned only later, much later, that my friend Vladimir had called his daughter when the plume began blowing south to warn her to leave Kiev with her husband and baby. I have asked myself thousands of times why did I not do the same for Larysa?" Looking into the distance, his eyes watered. "When I learned that the surgeon had to cut the nerves for Katya's vocal cords, I wept. Each day since then has been a living hell." He paused, collecting his voice.

"For the past five years, it has been what you would expect. Liquidators are dying by the hundreds. Too many children here in Ukraine and in Byelorussia—more in Byelorussia—are contracting cancer. Young children suffer cataracts. We have a whole population with unexplained immunological problems, but I am not a medical doctor. Health statistics you must obtain from others qualified in medical fields." Anatoly shook his head, looking down.

"You ask who knew of the coverup, as if the Chernobyl accident was unique in calling for a bureaucratic response of hiding facts." He turned a sharp gaze on Vickie. "But everything pertaining to nuclear weapons and nuclear energy was kept secret from the beginning—the same with your country, no? All those bombs detonated in the 1950s in the Southwestern desert of your country. Radiation drifting across America and around the globe. The steep rise in leukemia. Was there not a coverup in your country too?" He clenched his fists.

"Maybe this is the wrong word, coverup. Assuredly, there was a determined effort on the part of government officials not to tell people what they knew and not to know more. Not to study the negative effects of our clever nuclear projects. A lack of curiosity on the part of bureaucrats about whether fallout from those bombs was to blame for the unsettling rise in cancers—" Anatoly stopped, looking away.

"But my purpose here is to confess, not to philosophize or rationalize. I have done that now. The actions I took as State keeper of lies are documented. Any questions you have will be answered in my diary." He stood, folding his arms across his chest to signal that the interview was over.

Startled by the abruptness with which he ended the interview, Vickie picked up her cassette recorder and mumbled a thank you. Larysa got up from the couch and slipped past her uncle without making eye contact.

35

KIEV, APRIL 1991

Vickie showed the guard her badge and was escorted to the briefing room, where she took her usual seat beside Helen, whose hair was pulled back in a ponytail.

"Your last day here?" Helen asked, tugging at the wrinkled collar of her blouse. Dark pouches under her eyes gave her a sad, weary look.

Vickie nodded, taking a gulp of cold coffee. "I feel like I've been here for weeks."

"Months," Helen said. "Next time you pop across the pond, I'm expecting you to stop by my place."

"I'm afraid the bureau won't be sending me to London anytime soon. I'm standing in for Ian Hoffman for this assignment. That means you'll have to visit me when you come to Washington."

Olga brought a thick stack of papers into the room and distributed them to the disheveled band of reporters who'd stayed for the final day. With twenty events listed to commemorate the fifth anniversary of the Chernobyl catastrophe, Vickie realized she would have a hard time choosing venues.

She allotted her first hour to a group of students at the Zelenyi Svit, Green World, demonstration. Next, she and Igor attended a protest organized by Rukh, the Popular Movement of Ukraine. After they ate lunch, he went to his flat to develop film while Vickie made her way to St. George Cathedral for a requiem concert. An exhibition of children's drawings in the vestibule showed Chernobyl's emotional toll in heavy black and red crayon. Inside the sanctuary, Vickie listened to haunting music sung in a minor key. She returned to the press center late in the afternoon for a final meeting with Igor. He showed her his contact sheets, which were masterful, as always.

In the evening, her last in Ukraine, Vickie decided to take in a candlelight vigil outside St. Sophia Cathedral. She lingered on the periphery, scanning the multitude of faces. She wondered about their stories—aging women wearing floral scarves, children entranced by the tiny flames entrusted to their care, soldiers, whose candles cast deep shadows under wary eyes. Suddenly moved to join them, Vickie stepped into the crowd. A stooped woman offered her a taper, which she lit with the candle held by a spindly young man beside her. Standing so close to the epicenter of the Chernobyl disaster, cradling her candle in silence, she felt a deep bond with these people. She reflected on the hot snow in Antarctica that had set her journey here in motion and felt honored to be part of this sacred observance.

It was ten o'clock when Vickie returned to the Dnipro Hotel. The lobby that had seemed alien a week ago felt comfortable now. She was anxious to return home, yet sad to be leaving behind the amazing people she had met here. Igor, Helen, Larysa, and Dmitry—even Anatoly—had touched her deeply. Her biggest achievement had been personal, overcoming her terror of the crackling Geiger counter in Pripyat and completing the reactor tour, when her instincts had told her to run. She was proud of the stories she had written and the photo essay she had put together with Igor. What excited her most, however, was the interview with Larysa's uncle, whose account detailed his role in the Soviet cover-up. Anatoly's confession would feature in the story she planned to begin writing on the flight home. The thought of home brought with it an acute longing for Molly. It was three in the afternoon in Washington, which meant she would be getting out of school.

The line at the registration counter was longer than usual. Vickie waited with growing impatience as two Frenchmen argued with the clerk about a block of reserved rooms.

"Victoria Evans, room four sixteen, please." Vickie showed the clerk a card on which she had lettered her name and room number. She generally used French with the hotel staff, but she didn't want to be associated with the party that had left in a huff.

The clerk handed her the room key and an envelope.

Walking toward the elevator, she opened the envelope, which contained a brief note from Larysa scrawled in English. Vickie pressed the button for the elevator and read the short message: "*I am delivering this to you by hand. You should know that Anatoly is dead. He shot himself last night. Remember, we were seen leaving. Be careful, Larysa.*"

Vickie felt her throat tighten. Reflexively, she glanced up and down the lobby. Seeing no one, she stepped into the elevator and hit the button for the fourth floor. Her mind raced as she tried to understand the meaning of Dr. Kulyk's suicide. Picturing him in his armchair just twenty-four hours ago, it was impossible to imagine him dead—until she thought about the gravity of his confession. He no doubt had agonized for months before making the decision to acknowledge his role in the Chernobyl coverup.

She recalled the look of horror on Larysa's face as he described the emergency meeting on the last day of April, when he had learned of the radioactive cloud descending on Kiev. How Larysa had screamed at him, posing frantic questions. Vickie felt compassion for Anatoly. His moral dilemma had been one of historic proportions, yet he'd had little time to consider his decision. He had done the State's bidding, keeping the radiation secret even from his own niece, and had ended his life tormented by guilt.

Vickie had asked only a single question. She hadn't wanted to interrupt the riveting story that flowed from Anatoly's lips without prompting. She recalled the distant, stoical look in his eyes as he spoke. Still, never for a moment had she suspected he would commit suicide.

No doubt there would be an investigation into his death, she thought. "Be careful," Larysa had written. Fear squeezed Vickie's chest as she realized that she and Larysa must have been among the last—perhaps the very last—people to see Anatoly alive. She remembered the older gentleman who held the door open for them as they left his building. Larysa had said little in the car on the drive to the hotel, where she'd hugged Vickie goodbye.

Getting off the elevator, Vickie glanced up and down the

hallway. Seeing no one, she hurried the length of the corridor to her room. After two tries, she turned the key in the lock, and the door opened. Relief washed over her as she closed the door behind her. She turned on the light switch and saw Bohdan on the desk chair. She gasped. He leapt up and was beside her in an instant, his hand over her mouth. She struggled for air.

"We walk to lobby quietly," Bohdan hissed. She felt hard metal pressing against her side. "If you want to return home tomorrow, you will say nothing. Stay close beside me. Understand?"

Vickie nodded. Her legs trembled as she walked beside him to the elevator. Passing through the lobby, she tried to gain the attention of the clerk and telegraph to him with her eyes that her life was in danger. He was looking down at his paperwork and noticed nothing—not that Bohdan would have occasioned any suspicion. He was a familiar fixture in the hotel lobby.

Silently, Bohdan guided her out the door and down the block. Twisting her arm sharply, he veered into an alley. When they reached an area in deep shadow, he grabbed her wrist and pushed her against a stone wall. His bulging thighs pressed into her legs. She recoiled at the stench of his breath.

"You were seen leaving Comrade Kulyk's building last night before he was found with a bullet in his head. His death gives every appearance of suicide. Still, a nosy American reporter snooping around where she should not be could be detained for questioning."

Vickie could barely make out his words over the pounding in her ears.

"Detention in Soviet prison can be drawn out. A long time without seeing your daughter. What would become of your Molly?"

At his mention of Molly, Vickie's fear turned to rage. "What do you know about my daughter? Don't touch her." She felt sick recalling the pages of personal information she had provided in her application to come here. She imagined Soviet agents surrounding Molly as she walked home from school.

"What do we know? It is my job to know everything of diplomats and journalists." He sneered, his lip curling back. "But all this trouble of detention can be avoided. I could assure you safe passage. You could board jet tomorrow and fly home to your daughter. I can fix everything and promise her safety." His voice softened and he loosened his grip on her wrist. "Everything depends on you."

"What do you want? Money? Tell me, just don't hurt my daughter," Vickie pleaded.

"Money? No, what I want is free for you. I need you to procure a guarantee for me." Bohdan's gold eyes glinted as he pressed close to her again.

"Tell me. I will do it." This was a negotiation for Molly's life, Vickie told herself. There was something she could do to get home to her daughter, something Bohdan wanted in exchange for Molly's safety. She clung to this bargain.

"We will call a State Department official you know, Darren Cunningham." At the mention of Darren, Vickie's stomach clenched. This agent knew every detail of her life.

"He is good negotiator, no?" Bohdan let out a brutal laugh. "This is private call. He must tell no one. You must tell no one. This is private negotiation."

"What do you want from him?" Vickie didn't ask how he knew of Darren. All she could think was that she had put not only her own life in danger but also the lives of Molly and Darren.

Bohdan said he wanted assurance of travel documents to allow him safe transit out of Ukraine when the Soviet Union fell. If the revolution was bloody, he wanted a guarantee of legal entry into the United States.

Vickie was waiting for more, but that was the extent of his demand. Safe passage, false identity papers, an airline ticket. She agreed at once to talk to Darren.

Bohdan grabbed her elbow and guided her to his car. He drove to a building several blocks from the hotel. They walked up one flight and entered an apartment with a few sticks of furniture. She doubted anyone lived in the flat. Perhaps it was a KGB safe house, she thought. They walked to a table with a phone and sat in chairs Bohdan had placed inches apart.

"I make call, and you will tell Mr. Cunningham what is required," Bohdan instructed. He picked up the receiver and talked to an operator in Russian.

Vickie prayed that Darren would be at his desk. At least she knew he was in Washington. Bohdan held the phone in silence. After what felt to Vickie like an eternity, Bohdan shoved the phone against her ear.

"Hello, this is Darren Cunningham," he was saying as Vickie took the phone. Hearing his voice, she felt flooded with hope.

Vickie's voice quavered with urgency as she began speaking. She knew Darren sensed something was wrong. She explained what was happening and told him what Bohdan wanted. "I have to comply. He knows everything about Molly and us."

Bohdan yanked the phone from her and spit out rapid-fire Russian. After a minute, Bohdan went silent, listening to Darren.

Vickie tried to read Bohdan's face, but his expression revealed nothing. She held her breath, praying Darren could make this nightmare end. Bohdan shot off a second volley in Russian, followed by an impossibly long silence. She feared the line had gone dead.

Suddenly, Bohdan's lips formed a satisfied smile. He spoke Russian in a more congenial tone, then hung up the phone.

"Everything settled." Bohdan's voice sounded gentle, almost lilting, as if he had never threatened her or Molly. He led Vickie from the building to his car and drove in silence to the Dnipro Hotel. When he pulled up to the curb, he turned to face her.

"A driver will pick you up tomorrow morning at seven. If you remain quiet about tonight, you will be in Helsinki before noon. You will reunite with your daughter and Darren Cunningham tomorrow evening. The memory of this night will fade. Now, get out." He turned from her and peered straight out the windshield.

When she was sure he had nothing more to say, Vickie climbed out of the car.

Back in her hotel room, she dashed from the wardrobe to the edge of her bed, shoving clothes and toiletries into her suitcase. She packed her typewriter, tape recorder, and notepads into the valise. She had the presence of mind to split up the cassette tapes containing her interviews, stuffing some in the pockets of her jeans and others in the blazer inside her suitcase. When she stopped moving and sat on the bed, her whole body shook. She pulled her knees up to her chin. The worst is over, she told herself. She had to assume that whatever Darren told Bohdan had met his demands. Bohdan had what he wanted. Harming her now, after making a deal with a U.S. government official, would draw unwanted attention. The call to Darren had been the best protection she could have obtained.

Gradually it occurred to her that Bohdan's future depended on her safe passage out of Kiev and her reunion with Molly. Otherwise, Darren would pull the plug on Bohdan's escape plan—and worse, inform Soviet authorities. The realization that she and Molly were no longer in danger quieted her shaking. There was nothing she could do but wait for dawn.

She curled up on the bed. Sleep came and went, bringing terrifying nightmares from which she jerked awake. At dawn she dressed for what she prayed would be her promised trip home.

Vickie's one remaining worry was what to do with Anatoly Kulyk's journal. She considered throwing it away. She could look for a waste bin in the lobby and quickly drop it in. But the journalist in her could not do that. She knew its value. Giving her this diary to bring to the West had been Anatoly's final act before killing himself—and perhaps his most courageous moment. She tried to think of ways to conceal it. She could wrap it in a skirt in her suitcase, or stash it under her typewriter, but if the authorities searched her luggage carefully, they would find it. She finally decided to carry it in her shoulder bag, in plain view, as if it were her own journal or a gift—though the Cyrillic script inside would raise suspicions if authorities opened it. Still, if she made no attempt to conceal it, no one could accuse her of hiding anything.

She wrapped a velvet hair ribbon around the journal and placed it in her bag with a novel, a sweater, the carved Easter eggs, a small notepad, and the two *Matryoshka* dolls. It was in the hands of Fate now. If authorities confiscated Anatoly's journal, it wasn't meant to leave Kiev, she told herself. She had the facts she needed to write her article, with or without Anatoly's piece of history. She dragged her luggage to the lobby and waited for the ride that would take her to the airport.

The line at Boryspil Airport was long, as authorities sifted through everyone's luggage. When her turn came, a middle-aged official with a narrow face and dull eyes fingered through each item in her suitcases. Vickie held her breath as he emptied her shoulder bag on the counter. He passed over the journal, sweater, novel, notepad, and carved eggs, and picked up one of the Russian dolls. He uncapped the round-bellied smiling doll, finding nothing but a smaller doll inside. He uncapped the second doll, revealing a third. Stubbornly, he repeated this until he got to the seventh doll, the size of a peanut. Frustrated, he set upon the second Russian doll. Color rose to his cheeks as he uncapped the last tiny painted doll. He shoved the doll pieces into her bag and waved her through.

Vickie's legs almost buckled as she boarded the plane to Helsinki. Images of being nabbed in Finland and shipped back to the Soviet Union for questioning dogged her during the short flight. Finally, after an uneventful layover, she stepped onto a jet that would take her home to Washington. In the air over Scandinavia, she slipped Molly's picture from her wallet and gazed at it. Relief washed over her as she realized that in eight hours, she would be reunited with her. She returned the photo to her wallet and pulled Anatoly's diary from her bag. She ran her index finger over the leather cover, removed her black ribbon, and leafed through the pages. Admiring the fine script interspersed with rows of numerals, she wondered what mysteries the journal held.

Vickie thought of what Anatoly had said about the absolute

secrecy of the nuclear enterprise. In Washington as in Moscow, authorities had shown a notable lack of curiosity about the link between fallout and rising cancer rates. Her mind flashed on the single sentence locked away in Energy Department files that described "anomalous" fallout from the Simon atom bomb raining down on Troy and Albany in 1953. She took out her notepad, wondering how she could do justice to the two stories she wanted to write. The United States and the USSR were littered with victims sacrificed to the Cold War. As she began writing, she realized that what happened in Troy and Kiev were two parts of the same story. It was a tragic story of how America and the Soviet Union, in their quests to gain nuclear superiority, had irradiated their own people, then lied to cover up their malfeasance.

"When the deceit is monstrous, people of good will everywhere struggle to accept the truth," Vickie began. Ninety minutes out from Dulles International Airport she stopped writing. Weariness overtook her, and she fell asleep.

36

WASHINGTON, APRIL 1991

Vickie lugged her suitcases through the crowded international arrivals area at Dulles, awash in a mix of exhaustion, relief, and joy. When she spotted Darren rushing toward her, she dropped her bags on the floor. Her eyes filled with tears as he threw his arms around her.

"I thought he would kill me, Darren. He threatened Molly. If I had known, I never would have gone."

"You don't have to worry now. Nothing will happen to Molly or you." Darren held her tight. His steady voice carried authority. "You're both safe."

"Are you positive? I can't wait to see her."

"I promise you. A deal has been struck at the highest level, and Bohdan is more than satisfied. You won't hear from him again." Darren picked up Vickie's bags, and they headed to the parking lot.

"Sandy Carlson and her daughter are with Molly at your place. I think they're hatching a surprise welcome home party for you." He winked. "But I didn't breathe a word."

On the drive into the city, Darren talked about the offer to Bohdan.

"We've made him a happy man. He wants an escape hatch if things turn bloody when the Soviet Union falls, and he's been promised that, as well as the option of coming over now."

"Did I put you in a compromising position, in terms of your job?" Vickie asked, raising a question that had been troubling her.

"No, the administration is perhaps more pleased than Bohdan about this. Don't worry about my job." He reached over and squeezed Vickie's hand. "I'm going to tell you some things. I know you understand the importance of keeping this between us."

"Of course, Darren. You and I and Bohdan—none of this will ever be part of any story I write. Everything you tell me is between us only."

"Well, as you know, I spent a lot of time in Kiev over the past four months working on that verification agreement." He paused.

"I know." Vickie wondered where he was going with this.

"What this means is that Bohdan has a complete dossier on me. The KGB must have been watching my comings and goings a lot more closely than I imagined. Bohdan must have been listening in on my calls to you, which were frequent and personal. I should have been more discreet. I'm guessing that when you showed up on a list of journalists coming to Kiev, he saw it as an opportunity to get to me. From the moment you landed, he was probably looking for something on you to scare you into putting through that call to me. So, I'm the one who needs to apologize for compromising your safety."

They rode in silence, the significance of this surveillance sinking in for both of them.

"I hate being watched. I hate it that you're being watched. That our phone calls are being listened in on. How long do you think we'll have to live with this threat hanging over us?" Vickie asked, breaking the silence.

"Not long, I'd wager. The Soviet Union is on the brink of collapsing. Intelligence gives it six months. That's why we've been working overtime. We've got to lock down those nuclear weapons before the Soviet Union disintegrates and they get into the wrong hands. I guess I shouldn't go into details, but I want to be able to share everything with you," he blurted out, stopping at a light on Massachusetts Avenue.

"Given who we are, I don't think we can wall off parts of ourselves, Darren."

"No more wall?" He leaned over to kiss Vickie.

"The wall's history." She returned his kiss. The car behind them honked.

"Settled, then. I've got something remarkable to share with you. I was having lunch with a colleague three days ago, and he mentioned that the Cancer Institute just finished a draft study on excess thyroid cancers from the above-ground nuclear testing era."

"You're kidding!" Vickie grabbed Darren's arm. "They've decided to study that?"

"I knew you'd be excited. He didn't mention any names, but he told me they've finished a draft. Congress wanted a report on thyroid cancers expected from U.S. above-ground testing. But the lead researcher doesn't want it released yet."

"That's incredible. I have no idea how to confirm this, but I'll find a way."

"I have no doubt you will." Darren grinned.

They were stopped at a light three blocks from Vickie's house when she realized that she had neglected to bring a present back from Kiev for Darren.

"I bought Russian dolls for Molly and Julia, but I didn't get you anything," Vickie apologized.

"We're together now. That's the only present I want." He leaned over for another kiss.

"There's one more thing I wanted to tell you about." Vickie turned serious. "Anatoly, the scientist who committed suicide after I interviewed him, gave me a journal where he recorded radiation measurements from Chernobyl that were kept secret."

"Wow, that would have been something to see."

"I've got it right here." Vickie pointed to her shoulder bag.

"You have his journal? How in the world did you smuggle it out of the Soviet Union?"

"I wrapped a ribbon around it and put it in my carryon with the Russian dolls and trinkets I declared. No one even took the ribbon off."

"I'm blown away. Do you know how gutsy that was?"

"Anatoly told me to show the diary to a trustworthy diplomat or physicist in the West. I guess you qualify."

"You have no idea how much I want to pull over right here and ravish you, Victoria Evans. But there's a twelve-year-old girl around the corner dying to see her brave, beautiful mother, and I've got to take you home to her first."

Darren stole a long kiss and turned onto Macomb Street.

"Is that the Black Sea?" Molly peered out the window.

Craning her neck, Vickie glimpsed an expanse of water glittering like amethyst beyond the silver wing. "It must be. We should be landing soon."

"I can't believe we're going to Ukraine!" Molly sat back in her seat long enough to jot a few lines in the notebook on her lap, then returned her gaze out the window.

"Neither can I." When Vickie first received Dmitry's email, she had doubts about pulling this trip together in three days. She'd considered sending regrets at being unable to attend the funeral, but she couldn't let Dmitry down. He was like her brother. She replied that she would be there—with her family. Plying his charm and influence, Darren had been able to obtain their travel documents and plane tickets yesterday. Molly would miss a week of school, but she already planned to take a year off and travel in Europe.

Vickie looked across the aisle at Darren cradling Paul in his lap. He tooted, honked, and beeped as he tapped their three-year-old's nose, ears, and chin, in turn. Paul giggled hysterically. Darren paused. "Again, Daddy," he chortled. As she watched Darren's patience and easy rapport with Paul, a sublime contentment washed over her.

The plane began its descent, and Darren buckled Paul into his seat. Vickie retrieved a baggie of crackers from her pocket and handed it to Darren, who kept Paul busy chewing until they landed.

When they exited the border check, Vickie spotted Dmitry at once. His appearance hadn't changed since she kissed him goodbye in Kiev. His hazel eyes still burned with intensity. His slim body looked tightly coiled and his bearing strained.

"Thank you for coming." Dmitry hugged Vickie. "You give me strength."

"Mitya, I'm so sorry about your father. May his memory last forever. I want you to meet Darren and Molly and Paul."

Dmitry and Darren clapped each other's backs. Darren offered words in Russian that brought a smile to Dmitry's face. Molly hung back, clasping her hands in front of her. Dmitry reached his hand toward her, and she extended hers. They eyed each other shyly.

"Thank you for honoring my family with your presence." Dmitry shook Molly's hand gently. She blushed.

"My sister is at home with my mother. It was Katya who found Papa in the garden Tuesday. I took the first flight back from

Paris Wednesday," Dmitry told them as they piled into the car. "I'm doing my residency in endocrinology there."

They drove in silence. Vickie enjoyed watching the look of wonder on Molly's face as she took in the city's ambiance—the people going about their lives, the Cyrillic signs, the crumbling pastel building facades. Dmitry pointed out landmarks in English, then fell into a discussion with Darren about politics that slipped into Russian. Traffic thinned as Dmitry turned onto an avenue lined with poplars and country houses. A right turn put them on a narrow dirt road. They passed several farmhouses surrounded by lush gardens. He slowed down and pointed out the home of Sasha and Alina, close family friends.

"My grandmother, aunt and uncle, and cousins are staying there. They came in from Saratov yesterday afternoon. We had dinner with them last night. Sasha is devastated." Dmitry turned to face Vickie and Molly. "He and my father were close. They gardened together in summer. In winter months, they spent hours talking by the fire."

A few dozen yards beyond Sasha's house, Dmitry parked the Lada in front of a storybook cottage surrounded by berry bushes and cherry trees. Behind a glassed-in veranda, green shoots poked through the soil of a raised garden bed.

"He was putting in the tomato seedlings when his heart gave out," said Larysa, stepping onto the walk to greet them.

Vickie let go of Paul's hand and embraced Larysa.

"So, this is your new expanded family?" Larysa asked, a glimmer of joy creeping over her face.

"Everyone but Maddie, our oldest. She's finishing her first year of college and had to study for final exams," Vickie explained.

Darren added a few words in Russian.

After answering Darren, Larysa approached Molly, kissing one cheek, and then the other. "I saw a picture of you six years ago. You've grown, and no more glasses? But those green eyes of your mother's I would recognize anywhere!"

Dmitry and Darren brought the bags inside.

"Everyone will be here soon for dinner," Larysa said. She called upstairs to Katya.

When Katya came downstairs, she welcomed Vickie, Darren, and Molly in halting English, her voice a whisper. Although she was the same age as Molly, Katya's diminutive frame and pixie features gave her a childlike look. Her face lit up when she saw Paul, a sturdy boy who had his mother's eyes and his father's high forehead and wavy, brown hair. Katya held out her hand and guided him to the shelf where she kept her treasures from the sea.

In the evening, fifteen people crowded around the table sharing food, drink, and stories. Vasyl's mother, his sister Eva, and her husband and children had walked to the cottage with Alina and Sasha. They conversed in Russian, with Darren giving Vickie a summary and Dmitry translating for Molly. Larysa had told the others about her husband's death. Now she looked across the table at Vickie and Molly and related the story again, this time in English.

"Vasyl showed such courage. He refused to give in to the radiation ravaging his body. His breathing was labored, and his heartbeat was irregular. There were days when he couldn't feel his feet on the floor and had to crawl on his knees. But on Tuesday, he had a burst of energy. The sun was shining. I was leaving for my bookstall." Larysa looked down, fingering her wedding ring.

"He gazed at the trees full of birds flying back from all parts of the world. He motioned for me to come admire the rows of vegetables, almost fully planted. His eyes shone with a brightness I hadn't seen for weeks. Perhaps I should have known such a light came from his nearness to God. Maybe he knew how close he was to the end. I told him not to work too hard. He smiled that smile of his." Larysa halted, her eyes brimming with tears.

"He said to me, 'Listen, Larya, how the birds are singing their courtship arias! This isn't work. This is life.' He put his arm around me, and we kissed. I am so thankful to God for that chance to say goodbye. I started the car and looked in the mirror. He was kneeling to put in a tomato plant. That was the last time I saw my Vasyl alive." Larysa turned to hug her daughter. "Katya found him right there, in the garden."

After dinner, Molly joined Katya in her loft to make friendship bracelets. Paul was already asleep on a mattress in a corner of the garret. Larysa and Darren adjourned to the veranda to get acquainted, giving Vickie and Dmitry a chance to talk in the living room. They sat on the sofa facing the fireplace.

"How has it been for your family living here? Was it hard leaving Kiev after Anatoly's suicide?" Vickie asked, probing the subject Dmitry had never broached in their years of email correspondence.

"You can see for yourself the beauty of Odessa and how perfect this little place is. After the trauma of that night—the night you interviewed him—it was not hard leaving Kiev. Sasha had his body brought here for burial," Dmitry began. "At first my mother and father could not forgive him. I hated him. I held him responsible for Katya's cancer, as did my parents." Dmitry stopped talking. Vickie watched as fury clouded his eyes. When the storm passed, he continued.

"All that time, Katya never stopped loving her granduncle. I told you she is an angel. It was Katya who mourned his death, Katya who forgave him. It was through her example that my father and I came to forgive him. He was cowardly. He made a terrible mistake, but he tried to redeem himself by making sure this home would become ours. I was rooming with students in Kiev, and the vegetables and fruit my father raised in the garden helped get us through those hard times after the collapse. Here, my mother is surrounded by books and foreign languages. Katya teaches arts and crafts to children." Dmitry glanced toward the loft where Katya and Molly were talking softly.

"After a time, my father forgave him. He was grateful we could eat clean food, as he always called it. Seeing my father's big heart open to Anatoly, I also forgave him. Because of Anatoly, my father got to be outside in nature, not end his days an invalid, trapped in a city flat." Dmitry paused, his words strangled by emotion. "My mother does not speak Anatoly's name. I don't know if her heart will ever find forgiveness for him."

"It must have been hard for you to forgive Anatoly. Thank you for telling me this, Mitya." Vickie hadn't realized how much she'd longed to see Dmitry again and to meet his sister. "I'm so glad for the chance to meet Katya. She's as beautiful and kind as you described. I only wish I could have met your father."

This was the first time Vickie had returned to Ukraine since her flight from Kiev. She could have covered the tenth anniversary of Chernobyl last year. *The Global Environment Times* had wanted to send her. Instead, Vickie had proposed sending a young reporter on staff who was hungry for the assignment. Everyone had assumed that after winning an award in 1991 for her Chernobyl reporting Vickie found the idea of a second trip to Kiev anticlimactic. In truth, the idea of landing at Boryspil Airport had filled her with terror. Now, coming to Ukraine with her family, being here in Odessa with Dmitry's family, she no longer felt afraid.

Darren came inside with Larysa, who bade everyone goodnight.

"How far is the sea?" Darren asked, looking from Vickie to Dmitry.

"A short walk. This road ends at the shore," Dmitry said. "You might want to wear jackets."

The air was cool under a clear sky. Darren and Vickie walked in silence, holding hands, hearing only the sound of their shoes crunching the gravel. Cottages set back from the narrow road blended into the dark woods. A dog barked, disturbing the quiet momentarily. After a few minutes, they heard a hushed lapping of waves on a beach, and all at once it was upon them. The Black Sea. Their feet sank into the sand as they stopped at the water's edge. The endless sea met a sky drenched with stars, making the world swim. Vickie grabbed Darren's sleeve. He put his arms around her, and they kissed under the stars, on the other side of the world.

≈

Vickie stepped outside the church with Paul, who couldn't stand still through the funeral service. When the service ended, they joined the mourners walking in procession to a walled cemetery where Sasha's family members were buried. Pallbearers carried the open coffin, setting it down beside a hole a few yards from the grave where Sasha's dear friend, Anatoly Kulyk, had been interred six years earlier.

A priest cloaked in red vestments and an embroidered miter brandished a silver cross over the casket. His mournful chant rose and fell with the rhythm of the sea. Sasha, Larysa, and Eva were sobbing. Darren pressed against Vickie's left side, holding Paul, whose pensive eyes studied the man lying perfectly still in the box. Molly stood to Vickie's right, the wind ruffling her hair. Dmitry was wedged between Molly and Katya. Vickie noticed Molly ask Dmitry a question. He leaned over to whisper in her ear.

A brilliant pearlescent cloud passed over the sun, casting purple shadows on mounds of red and white flowers. Standing in this ancient Ukrainian cemetery surrounded by the people she loved, Vickie felt a reverence for life in all its anguish and majesty. She looked at her daughter, who was wearing a short black dress and high heels and seemed to have grown up since they landed. As if reading her thoughts, Molly turned to face her.

"Thank you for bringing me here," Molly whispered, her eyes sparkling.

Pallbearers covered the coffin and lowered it into the ground. Dirt flew from the priest's hand, landing on the wood with a clap of finality. The mourners picked up handfuls of earth to toss into the grave.

As the dirt left Vickie's hand, an image flashed through her mind of Vasyl in his moment of glory, sprinting across the reactor roof, trying to stop atoms with his shovel. Her mind wandered to Anatoly, who split atoms for peace, and the nameless scientists who smashed atoms to win the Cold War. They would all be gone soon, but their legacy would live on, scintillating in the frozen snows of Antarctica for generations to come.

Acknowledgments

I am deeply indebted to photojournalist Igor Kostin, who documented the Chernobyl disaster in *Chernobyl: Confessions of a Reporter*, Umbrage Editions, 2006.

I want to acknowledge Jack E. Dibb, Paul A. Mayewski, Christopher S. Buck, and Scott M. Drummey, Glacier Research Group, Institute for the Study of Earth, Oceans and Space, University of New Hampshire, Durham, "Beta-Radiation from Snow," *Nature*, 3 May 1990. I also wish to acknowledge Ernest Sternglass, *Secret Fallout: Low-Level Radiation from Hiroshima to Three Mile Island*, McGraw-Hill, 1981; Pat Ortmeyer and Arjun Makhijani, "Worse Than We Knew," *Bulletin of the Atomic Scientists*, November-December, 1997; Senate hearing on "Radioactive Fallout from Nuclear Testing at Nevada Test Site, 1950-60," October 1, 1997; "Fallout from Nuclear Weapons Tests and Cancer Risks," *American Scientist*, 2006; "The Forgotten Guinea Pigs," House Committee on Interstate and Foreign Commerce and Subcommittee on Oversight and Investigations, 1980; and Atomic Energy Commission documents in the Department of Energy archives.

Special thanks to Svetlana Hart for her valuable insights, and to Timur Tsutsuk, Nancy Hart, and Russell Stinson for their comments on the first draft of the manuscript. Heartfelt thanks also to Jeremy Berlin, Melissa Keller, Cynthia Port, Ana Weil, Janet Greenblatt, Amy Holmes, Margaret Londergan, Linda Pickle, Charlie Pickle, Angela Siffin, Anita Todd, Alexis Ovitt, Tony Hale, and Juneanne Kimbrough. My thanks also to "Ukrainian table" participants in Bloomington, Indiana. Finally, I want to thank Craig Stinson for his boundless encouragement, open heart, and keen eye.

About the Author

Kathleen Hart worked as a reporter in Washington, D.C., for 23 years, covering nuclear nonproliferation, energy, and environmental health. Born in Holden, Massachusetts, she received her B.A. from UMass, Amherst. She published a nonfiction book, *Eating in the Dark: America's Experiment with Genetically Engineered Food*, with Random House and has appeared on NPR and C-SPAN. *The Kiev Confession* is her debut novel.

www.ingramcontent.com/pod-product-compliance
Lightning Source LLC
Chambersburg PA
CBHW030919300726
48970CB00001B/231